RAVES FOR AMANDA SCOTT
AND HER SPECTACULAR NOVELS

LORD OF THE ISLES

"Ms. Scott's diverse, marvelous, unforgettable characters in this intricate plot provide hours of pure pleasure."

—Rendezvous

"Scott pits her strong characters against one another and fate. She delves into their motivations, bringing insight into them and the thrilling era in which they live, and proves herself a true mistress of the Scottish romance."

—Romantic Times BOOKclub Magazine

"Amanda Scott writes great tales during this turbulent time in Scotland's history."

—RomanceReviewsMag.com

"A fine fourteenth-century romance . . . Fans will appreciate this tale of marriage starring the wrong bride."

—TheBestReviews.com

"A good book . . . a readable story with a well-done plot."

—FreshFiction.com

more . . .

Prince of Danger

AMANDA SCOTT

Prince of Danger

WARNER FOREVER

NEW YORK   BOSTON

Cover design by Diane Luger
Cover illustration by Franco Accornero
Hand lettering by David Gatti
Book design and text composition by L&G McRee

Warner Books

Time Warner Book Group
1271 Avenue of the Americas
New York, NY 10020
Visit our Web site at www.twbookmark.com

Printed in the United States of America

First Paperback Printing: November 2005

10 9 8 7 6 5 4 3 2 1

In Memory of Carolyn Hardy Leach,

With love and gratitude for the many good memories she provided several generations of Scotts, Drennans, Leaches, Clevengers, and all the other families she touched with her kindness, generosity, patience, good humor, and positive outlook. Rest in peace, dear one, and tell Mom we love her and miss her, too.

Author's Note

St. Clair is pronounced "Sinclair." It is the way the clan originally spelled its name.

Daughters of Murdoch Macleod of Glenelg

Murdoch Macleod
1320–1400

Anna Nicolson
1336–1364

Cristina Macleod 1353–

Hector "the Ferocious" Maclean 1330–1400
m: May 1370 at Castle Chalamine

Mariota Macleod 1354–1371

Adela Macleod 1355–

Maura Macleod 1357–

Adam Frazier 1352–
m: 1371

Kate Macleod 1358–

Donal Sean Macrae 1350–
m: 1372

Isobel Macleod 1359–

Sir Michael St. Clair, Master of Roslin 1350–
m: August 1379 at Duart, Isle of Mull

Sorcha Macleod 1361–

Sidony Macleod 1362–

West Loch Tarbert, Scotland, October 1307

Fingers of thick night mist crept in from the sea, shrouding the dark forests and glens of Knapdale and Kintyre in ragged cloaks of gray and veiling the stars and the slender crescent moon overhead as four ships, barely visible, passed one by one into west Loch Tarbert. Although their sails were furled for lack of wind to fill them, the ships moved silently on the inflowing tide, like hulking black ghosts.

The small watcher on the hillside, having successfully escaped the confines of his bedchamber to breathe the damp air of freedom, began to fear that if the mist rose much higher off the loch, he would not find his bedchamber again that night. The consequences of that might be painfully severe, but freedom from authority, even for an hour, was worth the risk, especially with ghost ships for entertainment.

Curious to learn how such large galleys could move so

silently without wind to drive them or any splashing of oars, he moved quietly down the hill, nearer the shore. General visibility was even worse near the water, but he could still discern the ghostly black shapes through the mist.

Now, faintly, came the occasional splash of an oar, although not the heavy, rhythmic splat and splash one associated with galleys as their great banks of oars flashed in and out of the water to the beat of a helmsman's gong. Nor did the ghost ships' gliding progress resemble the speedy pace of those greyhounds of the sea.

A moment later, the curtain of mist parted enough to reveal that the ship directly in front of him followed a smaller towboat, the oars of which made little sound as they dipped gently in and out of the water. And if the mist was not distorting other sounds he heard, a second towboat moved between him and the bulk of the ship, telling him that smaller boats were towing the galleys into the loch.

The child frowned. Should he run and warn someone? Had the men-at-arms who usually guarded the loch entrance all fallen asleep? He could not imagine such a thing happening, not when the penalty for dereliction was a hangman's noose and a speedily dug grave. But perhaps the wee folk had cast a spell over the guards.

He would face punishment if he told anyone, because then his father would find out that he had disobeyed him. But it was curiosity, not fear of punishment, that made him decide to follow the boats farther up the loch. Galleys required at least twenty-six oarsmen, sometimes four times that number, and might carry men-at-arms, too. Before he told anyone, he should acquire more information if he could.

Moments later, as he paused after scrambling around a boulder in his path, a rattle of stones behind him nearly stopped his breathing. Standing perfectly still, he fought to calm his pounding heart as his ears strained to hear more.

Another rattle, a scraping sound as if someone had slipped, and a hastily-suppressed cry brought a sigh of irritation when he recognized the voice.

He waited grimly where he was, blocking the way, until his small follower scrambled around the boulder. The result was a startled, louder cry when they met.

"Shut your mug or by the Rood, I'll shut it for ye," he hissed.

"Aye, sure, but ye scairt me near t' death!"

"I'll do worse than that if ye dinna hush up. D'ye no see them ships?"

"O' course, I do. Whose are they?"

"I dinna ken," he muttered. "But if any man wi' them sees or hears us, he'll likely cut off our heads and fling 'em in the loch so we canna tell anyone else."

"Faith, why should anyone do that, when your own da's wi' them?"

The lad frowned. "He is?"

"Aye, for I near bumped into him when I ran through the hall t' catch up wi' ye. I had t' dive under the high table whilst he rousted out some o' his men sleeping on the lower-hall floor t' go wi' him and me own da' t' meet the strangers."

"We'll ha' to get back quick then," he decided, suppressing disappointment. "Sithee, someone will catch us if we don't, and that'll get us both skelped sure. I warrant we'll learn all about them ships anyhow, come morning."

But the next morning, when the sun shone brightly on the loch again, the ships were gone. Not a ripple remained to bear testimony to their passage.

Chapter 1 _____

Scottish Highlands near Glenelg, July 1379

Nineteen-year-old Lady Isobel Macleod, having escaped the confines of Castle Chalamine and her father's carping criticism, rode her pony bareback and with abandon along the tree-and-shrubbery-lined river path through Glen Mòr toward the steep track that led down into Glen Shiel. The day was glorious, and the cool salty breeze blowing from the sea caressed her face as she rode. Wildflowers bloomed in vast, colorful splashes, and not another human being was in sight.

She had not yet found the lone isle of her dreams, with the solitary tower to which she had often told her sisters she intended to remove as soon as she had means to do so, but her morning ride would provide solitude for an hour or two.

She had a sennight more to endure at Chalamine before she could return to Castle Lochbuie on the Isle of Mull, her home for the past seven years. She missed the Laird of

Lochbuie and his wife, her sister Cristina, and she missed their three bairns and her two favorite cats, Ashes and Soot, as well.

Although she had lived at Chalamine until she was twelve, it no longer felt homelike with only three of her six sisters remaining there. The eldest of the three, Adela, burdened at twenty with household responsibilities, was rapidly turning into a bitter woman, while Sidony and Sorcha, at sixteen and seventeen, were champing at the bit to find husbands and marry so they, too, could leave. Isobel, however, intended never to marry.

She could be grateful at least that her father, Murdoch Macleod of Glenelg, had given up making each sister wait until her elder ones had married. That superstition had died years before, along with her sister Mariota and Macleod's dreams of a grand future for them all.

Firmly banishing further thought of Mariota or Macleod, Isobel considered her options for the next few hours. She could continue to Glen Shiel and Loch Duich or she could stay off her usual tracks and seek someplace new.

As she pondered the possibilities, movement above on a hillside to the north caught her eye. Thanks to Glen Mòr's steep slopes and narrow floor—no wider in most places than the swift, tumbling river that flowed through its center and the narrow track beside it—the distance was not great, and she easily discerned two horsemen. When they disappeared into the dense shrubbery, she decided they might be following a track she had not known was there.

Curious to know if that was the case, she touched her pony with her whip, guiding it toward the nearest place where she could safely ford the river. Once across, she urged her horse up the hillside. Although she was no longer certain she would be able to find the exact place where the two had vanished, even a search for the track they followed gave more purpose to her outing than mere escape.

Ten minutes later, she entered a dense grove of aspens, oaks, and chestnuts that she believed was the one the men had entered, with a narrow burn wending its way downhill through the trees to the river. Riding into the shady woods, she drew rein and listened. She did not want to meet anyone, and it had occurred to her that the two men, having vanished nearby, might reappear at any moment.

Certain that anyone from a neighboring glen would know her, and that she need tell any stranger only that she was Macleod's daughter, she felt no fear. Her sisters or father would have mentioned any feud that had erupted in her absence.

Hearing no sound but gurgling water and normal forest chirps and chatters, she urged her pony on and soon found the track she sought. That she had not come upon it before was no wonder, because it began at a narrow cleft between two huge boulders on the far side of the burn, led up and away from the water, and dipped into a ravine where it looked as if it might end. Instead, the passage widened, and shortly afterward, she came to a grassy clearing surrounded by more woods. Just beyond, a high, sheer, solid backdrop of granite rose forbiddingly toward the sky.

Seeing no sign of the riders she had followed, she rode across the nearly dry streambed that divided the clearing to see if the path continued on the other side. Entering woodland again, she savored its silence until a man's scream shattered it.

The scream had come from a short distance ahead and did not repeat itself, so although she urged her pony forward, she did so with care, listening for any other sounds that might tell her more. The woodland darkness lessened, and hearing male voices, one speaking sternly, she drew rein. She could not make out his words.

"Doubtless we should leave," she murmured to her pony. "Whatever is going on here is probably no concern of ours, but curiosity has always been my besetting sin, and I suppose it always will be." With that, she slipped off, landed lightly on soft ground, and looped the reins over a nearby tree branch.

Patting the pony's nose, she said softly, "No noise now, if you please."

Knowing she could not depend on its silence, and recalling the many times her parents or foster parents had punished her for letting curiosity get the better of her, she sent a prayer aloft that this time no one would catch her. Then, carrying her riding whip, she gathered her long, dark-gray cloak closer around her so that it would not catch on any shrubbery and moved swiftly but quietly through the trees toward the voices.

Stopping behind a large chestnut tree near the edge of the woods, she peeked cautiously around it into the small clearing beyond and gaped at what she saw.

Six men had gathered around a seventh, who hung by tautly outstretched arms, roped to branches of two ancient, entangled oak trees. He was dark haired and wore only his breeks and boots. His muscular back and arms were bare, and blood oozed from four vicious stripes across his broad shoulders. As she realized what she was witnessing, one of the six raised a heavy whip and said grimly, "You'll tell us soon enough, you know. It might as well be now whilst you can still talk sensibly."

"Demons will roast you in hell first," his victim said in a deep, vibrant voice that easily carried to Isobel's ears. She did not recognize it or him, however, nor did she recognize any of the men watching. Under the circumstances, the hanging man's calm demeanor astonished her, as did his educated diction.

"You know my skill," the one with the whip said. "Faith, man, you screamed at only the fourth stripe. Do you dare to test me further?"

When his victim remained silent, he raised the whip again.

The victim's muscles clenched, and Isobel's did likewise as the lash descended. His scream of agony ripped through the air again.

"Well now, what ha' we here?"

Startled, she whirled, raising her riding whip, but a large hand clamped hard on her forearm, and the black-bearded man whose hand it was growled, "Nay, lassie. Drop it, and be glad ye didna strike me. Lads, hold your whisst now," he called out to the others. "We've an inquisitive lass here, come to amuse us all!"

Isobel sighed, but it certainly was not the first time God had failed to heed her prayers. Nor could she blame Him, since she was not always conscientious about honoring the promises she made when she hoped that one might sway Him.

She made no protest as her burly captor hustled her across the clearing to the others, but when he jerked her to a halt in front of the one with the whip, she said, "I don't know who you are, but I am Macleod of Glenelg's daughter, and you have no business here, certainly not to be doing what you are doing. If this man has broken a law, you should hail him before the laird's court for a fair trial."

"Aye, sure," the man with the whip said, "but that depends on whose laws he's broken, does it not?"

"The only ones that matter here are Macleod laws and

mayhap those of the Lord of the Isles," she said, but as she did, she realized she had misjudged the group. She had assumed that a band of local ruffians had attacked a gentleman, but hearing the chief tormentor speak as his victim did told her the assumption was wrong. Likewise, the tormentors' clothing and weapons were not those of common folk.

Two of the henchmen wore swords that any of her father's men-at-arms or those at Lochbuie or Ardtornish would have cherished, and the man with the whip wore a black velvet doublet and silk trunk hose of excellent cut and styling. A chill tickled her spine, but she ignored it, glared at him, and said, "Cut that poor man down at once."

"Faith, lass, but you're full of orders for one with no army behind her," he said, adding as an aside to the others, "I warrant she'll provide rare sport in bed."

"Let her go," his victim snapped. "She knows naught of what passes here, but she is clearly of noble birth, and if she goes missing, many will come searching for her. She may even have an escort nearby. Heaven knows, she ought to have one."

Isobel could see his face now and thought it handsome despite his scowl. But when his gaze met hers, a wary tingle shot up her spine. He was tied up, helpless, and in pain, but the look he gave her reminded her powerfully of those she received from the formidable Laird of Lochbuie when he was displeased with her.

The leader jerked his head toward the trees where Isobel had been standing, and said to the man who had captured her, "Have a look, Fin."

"But I saw no one with her," the other said. "She were alone."

"Look anyway, because he's right. A lass like this is bound to have keepers." Motioning to two of the others, he said, "Cut him down for now, and stow them both in the cave until we sort this out. I don't want any more surprises."

Despite her fierce struggles, the two men forced her toward the sheer granite wall and soon came to a high, narrow opening. Beyond lay the pitch blackness of an underground cavern. Isobel shut her eyes at the sight, gathering courage, telling herself that it merely led to another adventure and was not a gateway to Hell.

They paused long enough for one of the two to light a torch before entering. Fascinated despite her fear of such darkness, and wondering how such a cave could lie so near Chalamine without her ever hearing so much as a whisper about its presence, she soon saw that although the passage was narrow, the rough granite ceiling rose far above them. Clearly Nature, rather than man, had carved both.

Hearing footsteps behind them, she glanced back and saw by the light of a second torch that two others were dragging their bare-chested victim in her wake. Soon the two captives found themselves stretched out on the hard floor, securely bound hand and foot.

"I wish that horrid man had not pulled off my cloak to tie my hands behind me, because it's cold in here," she grumbled when the men had gone, taking the torches and thus all the light with them. "But I suppose I should be grateful that they did not gag us."

"No one would hear us from here even if we shouted," he said, his rich voice coming calmly to her through the dense blackness.

Although his voice was a comfort, she was testing her bonds and did not reply. She could not see a thing now that the light was gone, not even shadows.

"You're mighty cool for a lass in such a dire predicament," he said. "*Do* you have keepers nearby?"

She sighed. "Unfortunately, no. I came alone, and no one will look for me for hours. When they realize that I'm missing, however, many will search for me."

"Is your father so powerful then?"

"Powerful enough," she said, grimacing when the rope around her wrists pinched in protest of her squirming. "He is a member of the Council of the Isles. But my sister's husband is even more powerful, and I have fostered with them these past seven years. He'll soon join the search if my father's men don't find us straightaway, and he'll find us, too, if those evil men haven't murdered us first."

"How is it that your foster father is more powerful than a Councilor of the Isles?" he asked, and she thought she detected amusement in his voice.

"He is Hector the Ferocious," she said simply.

Silence greeted that information, and the amusement was gone when he said, "I think you will survive longer if you do not mention that detail to our hosts."

"But why not? Hector terrifies most men."

"Just so," he said.

She thought about that. "You fear they might kill me rather than let him discover that they have done this to me. But they'd have to kill you, too, would they not, lest you tell him."

He did not reply.

"Who are you that you've drawn their interest in such a way?" she demanded.

"You may call me Michael," he said.

"I'll call you anything you like, but your speech tells me you are educated and doubtless a man of more extensive identity than just Michael. Why have they done this to you?"

"Their reasons can be of no import to you," he said.

"If they mean to kill us, I certainly want to know why!"

"They will not kill me—not yet—not intentionally, at all events."

"It may surprise you to know that your fate interests me far less than my own," she said tartly. "Am I more dangerous to them than you are?"

"Only if they learn about Hector Reaganach," he said. "They do not fear me, you see, for I have taken care to give them little cause."

"That man wanted you to tell him something," she said, remembering.

He sighed. "You heard that, did you? If you are wise, you will not reveal that bit of information to them either."

Others had said of her that she was wise beyond her years, but somehow that did not seem to be what he meant. In any event, she rarely took those words as a compliment, for too often the same people questioned her judgment and scolded her for trusting it. "Why don't you just tell him what he wants to know?" she asked.

"Because I cannot."

"Then we had better find a way to escape."

Her companion's chuckle reverberated from the cavern walls.

"I do not know why you laugh," she said. "When one recognizes that a necessity has arisen, one should greet it with resolution and make a plan."

"You'd better plan quickly then, mistress, because they'll soon be back."

She was still testing her bindings, seeking loose ends, but her sharp ears had caught no sound of footsteps or voices yet, and she could discern no light, so she still had time if she could just untie herself.

Thoughts whirled and danced through her head as her

fertile imagination sought possible avenues of escape. Her wrists, tied behind her, felt raw from her struggles against the rough binding. If only she could reach . . .

Memory shifted to a time in her childhood when her sister Kate had tied her hands behind her and threatened to tickle her witless if she did not stop chattering and let Kate finish some chore or other. The minute Kate had turned her back, a younger, smaller, and doubtless much more agile Isobel had slipped her bound wrists beneath her bottom, up her legs, and over her feet. Then, loosening the binding with her teeth, she had run up behind her sister on silent, bare feet, poked her sides, and startled Kate nearly out of her skin.

Wondering if she could still do such a thing, she gave it a try. Her hips were broader now, but her arms were longer, too, and with only a slight hitch when a seam in her heavy skirt snagged against the rope, she managed by pulling, scooting, and at last rolling backward over her bound hands and lifting her backside as she forced them underneath her, wincing when they scraped rock.

She was glad now that the villain had taken off her cloak and cast it to the floor, because had it still covered her, it would have been very much in her way.

"What are you doing?" Michael asked.

Grateful that he could not see her, and knowing she would sound breathless if she tried to talk, she said nothing, hoping to show him her success instead.

"Answer me, lass. Are you all right?"

"Aye," she muttered. "Just listen hard for them, will you?"

Rolling to a sitting position, she tried to reach under her skirt, but the dirk Hector had given her when she turned thirteen sat in its snug leather sheath on the outside of her right leg above the knee, and she could not reach it. Nor, in that earlier incident, had Kate tied her ankles. No matter how she twisted, she could not seem to stretch far enough to force both feet at once through the small opening. She had to try harder. Their captors would not stay away much longer.

Rolling backward again, she exhaled as much air as she could and lifted her legs and backside as if she were attempting a backward somersault, using her bound hands to pull her hips and then her legs as close as possible to her torso. She was still flexible enough to bend double at the waist, but whether she would be able to slide her hands far enough to do the trick remained to be seen. In any case, she was glad her companion could not see her. Her position lacked dignity, to say the least.

Sir Michael St. Clair, having painfully exerted himself to test his bonds and found them tight enough that they would soon cut off his circulation, believed the lass was struggling as futilely against hers. But believing as well that she might hurt herself in such a struggle, his first inclination was to warn her to be still so he could at least hear as soon as possible when Waldron and the others returned for him.

Not that hearing them would make much difference to his fate at their hands, but at least he had seen enough of the cavern now to be fairly certain it was not the one he saw so frequently in his dreams.

Sounds of her movements continued. Mayhap the belief that she could do something was somehow aiding her, he mused. That she was not screaming in terror or berating him for getting them into such a fix was surely admirable behavior that he ought to encourage as long as possible. She was undeniably an unusual female. He had never known one before who, in distress, could manage to hold her tongue.

When she gave a barely audible cry of pain followed by a mutter of what he suspected was a most unladylike epithet, he said, "Are you sure you are all right?"

Silence greeted him for a long, uncomfortable moment, broken then only by another indecipherable grunt.

Stretching so much that she feared she might hurt herself, Isobel had at last reached her feet with her hands, but the rope binding her wrists had snagged on the ankle bindings. Gasping from frustration as much as from her exertions, she forced herself to exhale more, expelling so much air that she wondered if her stomach might scrape her backbone.

A dull, rhythmic thudding sounded distantly in the passageway, and with the impetus of near panic, she slipped her hands over her feet at last. Rolling upward again, still unable to reach the dagger through the slits in her skirt and underskirt, she yanked the skirts up instead and grasped its hilt.

Blessing Hector for insisting that she keep the weapon sharp, she drew it at once, sliced through the ropes around her ankles, and got awkwardly to her feet.

"Make a noise so I can find you," she whispered. "I cannot see a thing in this cursed blackness."

"I'm here," he said. "But you're standing. Did you manage to free yourself?"

"Aye, but only my feet, so beware, because if I trip and fall, I may stab you."

"You've a knife then! Mind your step," he added hastily. "That was my foot."

Already kneeling, she found the bindings at his feet, then the space between them, and sliced through the rope.

"Someone's coming, so don't talk anymore," she murmured.

"Aye. I heard them."

"If you will turn so that I can find your hands, I'll free them, too."

He obeyed, and although the sounds drew ever nearer, she discerned no light.

Feeling her way, she stiffened when her hand touched the bare flesh of his shoulder. Ignoring the impulse to snatch it away, she slid it further down his back, seeking the rope that bound his wrists.

When he gasped, she knew she had brushed across his injuries, and then she felt stickiness on her palm that was harder to ignore. Her stomach heaved at the thought of congealing blood and the knowledge that she had hurt him.

Moving as swiftly as she dared, she tried nonetheless to be careful, fearing to do him greater injury. She felt him trying to help, pulling his hands apart as the blade cut through his bindings. Then, in a twinkling, he was free.

"Give me the knife," he said, his voice sounding strained.

"Be careful," she said. "The blade is sharp enough to shave a man's face."

He chuckled again. "So I guessed, lass," he said, adding as he felt for her bindings with one hand and sliced with the other, "You are a most extraordinary female. I have no doubt that you know just how to get us out of here."

"Faith, I did not even know this cavern existed until they brought us here," she said. "You seem strong enough. Can you not overpower whoever is coming?"

"I doubt it. Heaven knows how many will come for us. Moreover, I've had naught to eat or drink since this morning, so I'm feeling a trifle unsteady on my feet. And even if only one comes and I could knock him down, what good would that do with the other five outside, just waiting to get on with my questioning?"

She had no answer and little time to think. The footsteps were so close that she could see a dim orange glow in the distance. Under ordinary circumstances, she would have been surprised that so little light could prove useful, but she could discern the near wall now and enough of the floor to see that no obstacle stood in her path.

She felt her way along the wall, certain that she had caught a glimpse earlier of some sort of side passage but having no idea how one might be useful, even if she could find it. Without light, they could not hope to escape down an unknown pathway, because their captors would find them in a trice. Still, she knew that only a witless fool would ignore any opportunity to find concealment or means of escape.

Her companion remained silent, and she was grateful, because his silence let her concentrate. Puzzles always had answers. One just had to find the right one.

"Give me back my dirk," she said, moving back to him.

"Faith, do you mean to murder him?"

"If I must," she said as she reclaimed the dagger, her mind already leaping ahead, seeking more possibilities.

He muttered something, but she ignored him. She could see a figure coming toward them now and felt a measure of relief that the waiting was nearly over.

"I think only one comes," she said. "Could you not *try* to knock him down?"

"Lass, much as I'd like to oblige you, I dare not promise anything. I'll do my best, but I should warn you that even if I do manage to knock him out, it will accomplish little more than to make him angry, and without any way out of here—"

"But how do you know that? Do *you* know this cavern?"

"No more than you do, but you must agree that it does not look promising."

"It would be less promising if the passage ended here," she pointed out. "But we know it does not, and I swear there is at least one side passage just yon—"

"Hush," he interjected. "He's close enough to hear us."

Although the orange glow had increased steadily, she could see little, for she had dropped to her knees to feel around on the hard-packed earth, and her body kept blocking the dim light. At first, she found only pebbles, two boulders near the wall, and her cloak, but at last she touched a good-sized stone that she thought she could heft. Quickly, using both hands, she picked it up and stood again.

Her companion was barely visible, no more than a thickening of the darkness near the opposite wall. She went to him as silently as she could.

"Here," she whispered, pushing the rock into his midsection. "Take this. I'll divert his attention before he realizes that we are both free, and you can bash him on the head."

"Faith, lass, I'm a man of peace."

"If that is true, you are the first such man I've ever met," she retorted. "Do try to resist predicting failure at every turn and summon up some resolution instead. You may recall that you said those louts are likely to murder me. I'd infinitely prefer to remain amongst the living, so—"

"Shhhh," he hissed.

Gripping her dagger tightly, Isobel flitted back to the wall across the passage.

Chapter 2 —————————

Here now, who untied ye?" the man asked as he loomed over Isobel, holding his torch high, its flaring brightness making her shield her eyes and hope he would not put it too near her.

"I untied myself," she said, lowering the hand shielding her eyes and smiling at him. He was the one who had caught her in the woods. "I don't like being tied up."

"Faith, but ye're a beauty," he said. "I'm partial to flaxen-haired wenches. Come here and see if ye can persuade me to speak to Waldron on your behalf."

"Would you do that for me, sir?" she said as she put her free hand to her breast and leaned slightly toward him, her years attending the Court of the Isles making it almost natural to let him see a flirtatious gleam in her eyes. "I surmise that Waldron is your leader's name?"

"Aye." The glint in his eyes was predatory as he reached for her.

She stepped back, still smiling, fluttering her lashes as she held his gaze with her own, the dagger clenched ready in her right hand behind her back.

He followed her, grinning in anticipation of what he meant to do, but what that was exactly, she would never know, because as she braced herself to raise the dagger and strike, a silent shadow loomed out of the blackness behind him, a dull thud sounded, and the man collapsed toward her without another word.

She jumped out of the way, and when he hit the ground, he lay still. She looked up again and saw to her amazement, as Michael stepped forward a pace, that he had somehow managed to grab the torch as the villain fell.

"Now what?" he asked, gazing down at his victim. His tone was as casual as if he had inquired about the weather.

Isobel grimaced. "The others will not be far behind him. We must hurry."

"I agree that haste is warranted, mistress, but as neither of us knows precisely where we are or, for that matter, where the others are—"

"Faith, sir, we know we are in a bad place and must remove ourselves from it forthwith. We must at least take advantage of his torch whilst we can, to see where that narrow passage yonder leads and how much farther the main route will take us."

"We cannot do both at once," he said. "May I suggest that you let me hold the torch aloft for you whilst you inspect that narrow passageway? I'm thinking it looks utterly impassable for a man of my size."

"What about him?" Isobel said. "Is he dead?"

"Would you mind if he were?"

"No. He is a vile creature."

"So I thought, but I own I'm relieved that he seems still to be breathing."

"That only means he may awaken at any moment. We should tie him up."

"An excellent notion," he said, handing her the torch. "I shall do so if I can find enough uncut rope."

"Tie some bits together if you must."

Nodding, he gathered the longest pieces and quickly trussed the other man up. Then, taking the torch again from Isobel, he gestured toward the narrower passage.

A brief glimpse inside revealed that it was no more than a shallow alcove.

"We could bundle him into it," her companion suggested diffidently. "They won't see him straightaway, and if they have to look for him, untie him, even revive him, the delay will occupy them for at least a few minutes. If we are lucky, they may miss him altogether and thus even mistake the exact spot where they left us."

"Can you lift him?" she asked. "I shan't be much help to you unless I put down this torch, and if it falls over, we may be plunged into darkness again. I'm not sure how much longer it will burn as it is. It's already dimming." She fought to speak calmly despite her fear that the pitch blackness would swallow them again, but she was not sure she had succeeded. Her voice had seemed to tremble a bit.

He had begun wrestling their captive into the opening, however, and if his method of shifting him about was rough and ready, it stirred no sympathy in Isobel. She hoped the villain sustained at least as many scrapes and scratches from banging into the rock walls as she had in her graceless contortions to free herself.

The task was soon finished, and Michael said, "If you will lend me your dagger again, mistress, I can cut away a strip of his shirt to gag him."

She gave it to him, straining her ears for any hint of the enemy's approach, fearful that she would not hear them in time to extinguish the light before they saw it.

Though he worked quickly and in relative silence, her impatience stirred. "Mayhap I should just go a little way on whilst you finish with—"

"Nay, lass, I'm done. I'll take that torch again, shall I? I can hold it up and light the way for us both if you lead the way—although I cannot help but believe they will simply follow us."

"Which is why we must hurry," she said, reaching down to snatch up her cloak. "The more distance we can put between us, the safer we will be."

"But I cannot think how we can escape them unless we do find a side tunnel. Even then, they have only to divide their party to search both routes."

"True," she said. "We would therefore be wiser to seek a hiding place."

"An excellent notion, if you can conjure up such a place."

She sighed, biting back a sharp comment, certain of its futility, as she donned her cloak. Grateful for its warmth, she led the way carefully along the passage. Aware that she was not going as fast as she had hoped, she said apologetically, "We must tread warily, sir. I know little of caverns, and the flickering light of that torch creates odd shadows that obscure the path. I've no desire to find myself suddenly plunging toward the center of the earth."

He made no comment, but a few moments later, he said quietly, "Look up to your left, mistress. Does it not appear there may be a ledge of some sort up there?"

He raised the torch higher, and she saw what might have been some such thing, but it was well above even his head and much too close to where their captors had left them to suit her notion of a refuge. "It is too high," she said. "We could not climb up there, and even if we could, they would surely see us."

"Not if that ledge is deep enough," he said. "If I can manage to lift you to my shoulders, I believe you can scramble up there. Are you stout-hearted enough to try?"

"I think we should move on as quickly as possible and put more distance between us and those dreadful men."

When he did not reply but only waited with a nearly tactile air of patience, she said, "Oh, very well, but I do not see what my getting up there will accomplish."

"You can at least judge for yourself whether we both can fit up there."

"But do you really think you can lift me? Only a few moments ago, you said that you could barely stand."

"Now who is the naysayer?"

"But you did say that!"

"Aye, sure, but I find myself astonished at how much strength fear can lend one at a time like this," he said. "Come now, and we'll see if we can do the thing."

With startling ease, he lifted her to sit on his right shoulder and then steadied her as she braced herself against the wall and stood up, moving her left foot to his left shoulder. Standing so, she experienced a dizzying sense of the immodesty of her position, but he seemed unaware of it as he took the torch from the crevice in which he had jammed it while he lifted her, and raised it higher. Her chin was even with the ledge, and she saw that it was much deeper than she had expected it to be.

"The space is large enough for both of us," she said. "Indeed, it is more crevice than shelf, for it slopes downward."

"It doesn't plunge to the center of the earth, does it?"

"No, for I can see its back wall, but I don't think I can pull myself up onto it."

"Hold onto the edge, and I'll lift you by your feet."

Almost before she realized what he meant to do, his

thumbs slid beneath her arches, he grasped both booted feet firmly, and then lifted her straight up so that she was able to pull herself over the ledge into the space beyond.

No sooner had she done so than blackness swallowed them again. Gasping, she fought new terror as she squeaked, "What have you done?"

"Hush," he muttered. "I've put out the torch because I hear them coming. "Move as far back from the edge as you can, and if you can manage to slip off your cloak, we'll use it to cover ourselves."

"But how will you—?"

"Shhh."

Hearing then the distant thudding footsteps and murmuring voices, she scooted back from the edge. With her apprehension increasing, she strove again to calm herself, but so little success did she have that when a large hand grasped her hip, she nearly screamed. All that prevented it was a surge of terror so overwhelming that it paralyzed her vocal cords long enough for her to realize that the hand was his.

"How did you get up here?" she muttered when at last she could speak.

"I had ample opportunity to study the face of the wall whilst I helped you up," he whispered back glibly.

"You *climbed* it?"

"Since I had no one to assist me, it seemed the only way. Doubtless the same fear that had lent me strength before lent wings to my feet then."

His bewildered tone made her smile, but she could still scarcely believe that he had climbed the sheer wall. She had not even heard him doing so.

Louder voices and footsteps, nearing quickly, banished levity, and she pressed hard against the back wall of the ledge.

"Lie flat and give me your cloak," he whispered. "Its dark fabric should help to conceal us, but it would do us no harm to pray that this tunnel draws them on for a mile or so before it ends."

"Don't be a noddy," she retorted. "I'm already praying that the earth will open up and swallow every one of them."

"The Fates won't be so kind. Now hush, mistress, and keep very still."

A heartbeat later, he had stretched out beside her, very close beside her, touching her, in fact, along her entire length—and he seemed suddenly much larger than she had thought him. He shifted, settling himself, then pulled her cloak over them both until she could barely breathe. She opened her mouth to tell him so but shut it when she heard a voice she recognized as the leader's shouting in outrage. The villains had reached the place where they'd left them tied up, and to have recognized it so surely, they must have found the man she and Michael had left in the alcove.

Michael shifted slightly, then went still as she mused that their captive might have regained consciousness in time to hear his friends and, although gagged, could have groaned loudly enough for them to hear. He might even have come to his senses in time to overhear some of what she and Michael had said to each other.

That last thought increased her terror, but she dared not speak. She wondered what he had done with the torch. What if he had left it in the crack or on the floor?

Scolding herself for indulging in the same useless worries she had disliked so much in him, she decided he would not have been so stupid. Then, normal thought ceased altogether when she heard the voices again, so near that she could make out their words.

"Ye're a fool, man!" one said. "How'd ye let one wee slip of a lass get the better o' ye?"

"I tell ye, she were free when I got there, and I never saw him. Doubtless, he'd already fled, leaving her behind a-purpose to divert me."

Another voice, the leader's, said harshly, "You're daft, Fin. Did her pretty face stun you so that you fell flat and hit your head? You've a lump on it as big as a pigeon's egg."

"I must ha' stumbled," Fin said. "I dinna recall exactly, but seems she did keep a hand behind her back. Mayhap she held a rock in it."

One of the others laughed, saying, "Hoots, man, mayhap she cast a spell on ye, too, making ye bend a knee t' her so she could reach that thick head o' yours."

"Be silent, the lot of you," the leader snapped. "If one was free, they both were, and you don't know our man, Fin, if you think he'd have left that lass to face us alone. He's the one who hit you, so you're damned lucky the blow didn't speed you to your Maker. Now, hush your gobs, lads, and set your ears aprick. They'll not be able to hurry along this passage without making some noise."

Michael felt Mistress Macleod stiffen. Although, now that he came to think about it, if her father was a Councilor of the Isles, she was doubtless Lady Something Macleod rather than Mistress Macleod. But the less said of names at this point in the game, the better.

The lass had no notion of what she had bumbled into, but whatever occurred, she had given him respite from the whip and for that alone he owed her aid and protection. He would have felt obliged to protect her in any event because she was female and he had had it drummed into him from birth that defense of the weaker vessel was one of a knight's primary duties. A lass as intrepid as this one, however, deserved safeguarding even when she naïvely courted trouble, even when she foolishly flirted, if only for a moment, with the likes of Fin Wylie.

He smiled at the memory of her fierceness but hoped she would have the good sense to ignore whatever Waldron and the others might say of her.

With the slightest movement, he touched the back of his near hand to her hip in warning. That she relaxed at once did not surprise him. Except for what one could only describe as her reckless behavior in being out without a proper escort, she seemed practical and sensible, and thus remarkably atypical of her sex.

He had taken the precaution as soon as he had stretched out beside her of using a finger to poke up a tiny portion at the edge of the cloak that concealed them, so that he could see down into the passageway. The cloak barely covered him from head to knees, but his breeks and boots were dark and well back from the edge. He was confident that if he and the lass could remain silent and motionless long enough, none of them would see him.

But Waldron had extraordinary instincts to match his extraordinary skills as a warrior. Where he was concerned, they could take nothing for granted.

Isobel scarcely dared to breathe. The men below had fallen silent at their leader's command, and nothing they had said before then indicated that they suspected aught except that their quarry had hurried on ahead. Still, with no idea how far the passage would take them before it ended, she had no confidence that she and Michael would remain undiscovered.

When the footsteps below passed and faded in the distance, and her companion moved, a temptation to grab him and order him to stay still nearly overwhelmed her. She was glad she had resisted when he turned and murmured in barely audible tones, "There were five of them."

Just as quietly, she said, "I heard only four."

"Aye, but I could see them, Waldron and four others."

"Then only one waits elsewhere."

"They must have left him to guard their horses."

"Whatever he is doing, we cannot get out of the cave the way we came in."

"We don't know that," he said. "We know only that he's not with the others."

"So you think we should go back through that passage."

"I would willingly consider any other suggestion, mistress, but surely leaving that way would be wiser than following them, or do you disagree?"

She could not argue that, but neither could she deny the instinct screaming at her that they were safe where they were. "We could just stay here until they leave," she said.

"Nay, mistress, for as safe as it feels now, I ken Waldron fine, and he'll not leave whilst he believes we are still inside this cavern. Once they reach the end of yon passage and return to wait outside, we're sped."

"But we've no light. And in any event, how can we get down again?"

"We'll get down the way we got up," he said.

And to her further astonishment, he shifted his weight as he spoke and moments later, she was alone on the ledge and could hear nothing to indicate that he had been anything more than a spirit beside her.

The blackness consumed her, weighing so heavily that she wanted to cry out to him to make certain he had not abandoned her. Her body felt as if it had turned to stone, so resistant that she feared she would be unable to move and wondered briefly if someone hundreds of years in the future would find her—or the mound of dust she had become by then—still lying on that ledge. When he hissed from below, he nearly startled her of her skin.

"I dare not show a **light,**" **he whispered,** "but if you slide to the edge and over, **I shall hear where you** are, and if you fall, I believe that I can keep you from suffering any injury. But try to find a foothold or two as you ease your way over the edge, until I can grasp your feet."

"But I cannot see a thing," she protested.

"The only other choice is for you to remain hidden here whilst I try to escape and summon aid for you," he said reasonably. "If that is what you'd prefer—"

"No! I'll do as you say." She did not even have to think about it, because the decision made itself. She ached for sunlight and freedom.

Second thoughts assailed her as she inched to the edge, but knowing that haste was essential, she forced herself to lie on her stomach and dangle her feet and legs over the precipice into space.

Her skirts caught on the rough rock face but she ignored that detail, focusing on finding blind footholds until she rested on her forearms and elbows with only her shoulders and head still above the ledge. The rest of her felt perilously heavy.

"Just a bit farther, lass, and I'll be able to reach you," he said.

Wondering how on earth he could know such a thing, and muttering a brief prayer that the Almighty would not let her fall on him, and either kill or injure him, she pressed her toes to the face of the wall and eased herself lower. When her foot slipped, she gasped, but a strong hand caught and steadied it, and moments later she stood beside him on good, solid earth.

"Where's the torch?" she whispered.

"Yonder, but 'tis useless to us, because we've no way to relight it. It would be too dangerous to do so in any event."

"But how can we see where we are going?"

"You may follow my lead, lass. The floor of this passage seems even enough if we just trust ourselves. I'll keep one hand on the wall to our right and hold your hand with the other if you like. Now, come."

She did as he suggested, knowing nothing better to suggest and certain that at any moment they would hear their pursuers returning. His hand was warm and strong as it enfolded hers, and she gripped it tight, putting her right hand on his right hip a moment later, taking care to avoid the bare skin of his waist. He was right, she decided, in believing that fear lent one powers that one did not ordinarily possess.

He moved as though he could see perfectly, and although at first she found herself stumbling in his wake, resisting both his speed and direction of movement, after bumping against one wall and then the other a couple of times, she discovered an awareness in herself of their proximity even though she could not see them. After that it became easier to trust both his movements and her own.

Only once did she hear voices behind them, but the sound came from a considerable distance. She refocused her attention on her own progress and, in less time than expected, saw the dim, distant glow of daylight ahead.

Automatically, now that she could see, she let go of his hand and moved to walk beside him.

"Stay back, lass," he said. "I doubt he's standing at the entrance, but if he is, he's more likely to see two of us moving toward him than one. And tread as lightly as you can. This passageway echoes noise, as you've heard for yourself."

She almost argued with him, because the daylight was enticing and she did not want to plunge herself again into the shadows behind him, but she guessed that his warning arose from some masculine notion of protecting her. Experience had taught her that if that were the case, he would resist any argument she made, so she stifled her protest, did as he bade her, and they soon reached the arched entrance.

Moving slowly, barely concealed behind jutting boulders, he peered outside.

"Well?" she muttered. "Do you see anyone?"

"Nay, but it will take an act of faith for us to walk across that clearing."

"Go," she urged him. "You said he'll be watching the horses."

"He'll be watching for approaching horsemen, too," he said. "I'll wager that he's positioned himself near the entrance to the glen so that he can spot riders, if there are any, in Glen Mòr."

Memory of the narrow entrance to the wee glen from the hillside above the river Mòr told her he was likely right. "How are we going to get out of the glen then?" she asked. "Can we overpower him, do you think?"

Amusement touched his voice as he said, "Do you mean to divert him the same way you diverted Fin Wylie, the lout who came to fetch us?"

"It might work," she said. "But I'm sure we can climb a

tree as easily as we climbed that cavern wall, and most trees hereabouts have summer foliage dense enough to hide us."

"If it is all the same to you, I'd prefer to leave these men far behind us."

"Aye, well, it will certainly be better if we can get to Chalamine," she agreed. "We'll both be safe there."

"Are you ready to cross the clearing?" he asked.

"Aye," she said, ignoring the shiver of fear that stirred at the thought. Then, as much to bolster her courage as for any other reason, she said, "Shall we run?"

"Better to walk briskly but quietly," he said. "I reserve running for when speed counts more than grace or silence. Presently, extreme silence seems best."

Again she knew he was right and followed willingly as he led the way across the clearing and into the thick growth of trees beyond.

"My horse is gone," she noted. "Yours, too, if you had one."

"I'm not surprised," he said. "They are both fine beasts, and they'd not want them to wander off or bolt for home without us."

"We should not talk anymore until we locate that watcher," she said.

"Aye."

Despite the danger, Isobel felt near euphoria at being in sunlight again. The woods offered concealment and thus safety, but it was not long before she recalled how narrow the passageway was that lay just beyond the second clearing. How they could safely pass the man who was likely watching there, she could not imagine.

As they crossed the second clearing, Michael bent his head close to hers and murmured, "If you'd like to take cover behind one of those trees, I'll see what I can see before we go farther. No sense risking both our lives until we know where he is."

"It might be wiser for me to go back and watch the entrance to the cavern for our pursuers," she said.

"Perhaps so," he said, looking at her directly for the first time since they had emerged from the cavern. "However, whilst I cannot deny that your reasoning has been perfectly sound from the outset, I'm thinking we may not have much time to make decisions. So putting more distance between us now than necessary . . ." His voice trailed to silence, but he held her gaze. She saw that his eyes were a clear cerulean blue, almost exactly the same color as the sky above them.

She said, "Go then, but hurry. We dare not hope that searching the passageway will occupy those horrid men much longer."

He disappeared as she was speaking, and she turned to keep her eyes on the direction from which they had come. Realizing that any tree she might choose to hide behind would serve to hide her from one direction but could do no more unless she climbed it, she looked for a better hiding place and decided on a willow thicket alongside the burn. Near the gently murmuring water, she would not hear them as easily, but they would likewise be much less apt to see her.

He was away only a few moments before he reappeared and looked anxiously for her. When she stood, he motioned for haste, and when she joined him, he said, "He is on a rock some distance below the passage into the glen, staring off across Glen Mòr. Occasionally he looks right or left but never behind, so I'm guessing he expects trouble to come only from the west or from Glen Shiel. If we hurry, I think we can make our way uphill and away to the east without attracting his attention. If we can get over the ridge before the others come, we should be safe enough."

"But what if they—?"

"They will waste a good bit of time searching that cave for us, I believe, because they will tell themselves that we had no chance of slipping past them and must be hiding behind a boulder or in some crevice. Eventually, though, they will sense the cave's emptiness and will come to confer with their sixth man. So I suggest that we waste no more time before putting this place well behind us."

Again, his logic left her with no argument to make, so she followed him warily through the narrow entryway until she could see the man on the boulder.

As Michael had said, the lout fixed his attention on the opposite hillside with only an occasional glance east or west. How she would have liked to see Hector Reaganach just then, leading an army of Lochbuie men!

As it was, she dared not say a word even to ask Michael what help he thought might come from Glen Shiel. They were too close to the watcher to talk, and had to move as silently as possible.

Michael moved like a cat, and a ghost cat at that, because his steps dislodged no stones and crackled no dry leaves or twigs. She exerted herself to move as silently, but her feet slipped from time to time on the steep slope, and she kept looking back over her shoulder, expecting the watcher to hear them.

He did not turn.

Michael moved with deceptive speed, too, angling higher on the hillside, away from the glen floor, and she wondered if he had any idea what sort of terrain lay beyond the ridge. Although not as imposing as the Cuillin of Skye or the Five Sisters of Kintail, jagged, craggy peaks that one could see easily from the ridge top, the landscape beyond was nonetheless forbidding, steep, and rocky. Surely, he did not think they'd be safe on a high crag, so where did he think they were going?

Following him easily enough, she held her tongue with uncommon patience until the uneven landscape hid them from the watcher below. But when she knew that her voice would not carry beyond the ravine they had entered, she said, "I thought we were going to make for Chalamine, sir. 'Tis only a few miles south of here, and we'll both be safe there, I promise you."

He stopped, looked beyond her, and then, clearly satisfied that the man below could neither see nor hear them, took a seat on a nearby boulder. Smiling ruefully, he said, "I will do what you think best, because this is country you know better than I do, but if you will recall, you did tell them where you live."

The memory of that declaration struck hard, but even so, Chalamine had always protected its occupants.

"'Tis a sturdy castle, sir, and my father is a powerful man."

"Where does Chalamine stand exactly?"

"On a promontory at the head of the loch in our glen."

"Then it lies lower than ridges surrounding it, does it not?"

"Aye," she admitted, her quick mind grasping the problem. "They'd simply make camp on one of those ridges and keep watch until you left, wouldn't they?"

"Or until they devised a plan to get inside."

She glanced at the sun, saw that it was past the meridian, and sighed. "They still have hours of daylight to search for us, too."

"Aye, so we need to move on, but do we continue east or go over the ridge?"

"That man is watching the west end of the glen for men from Glenelg, but do you know why he keeps glancing east toward the road down into Glen Shiel, sir?"

"I have been staying with a friend on Loch Duich," he said. "Mayhap the watcher fears my host will send men to search for me."

Her eyebrows shot upward. "Who is your host?"

"Mackenzie. He was a friend of my father's."

Mackenzie of Kintail was a friend of her father's, too, and of the Lord of the Isles and Hector Reaganach. His primary seat was Eilean Donan Castle, strategically located on an islet where Loch Duich met Loch Alsh and Loch Long.

"It may be even harder to reach Eilean Donan safely from here than to get to Chalamine," she said. "Those men were clearly up to mischief at the cave, so what demon possessed you to follow them there?"

"I'm afraid you have that backwards," he said.

"They followed you?"

"Apparently so."

"But what were you doing there? This is my father's land, and I have never heard about that cave, so how could a stranger learn of its existence?"

He shrugged. "Kintail mentioned it, and I have long had an abiding interest in caves, mistress. I've had recurring dreams about one in particular since childhood."

"But if Mackenzie knows you came here, surely he'll miss you and send . . ."

He was shaking his head.

She sighed. "You did not tell him you were coming here, did you?"

"No, and he mentioned the cave two days ago, so he may not recall that conversation. I awoke early and could not sleep, so I decided to see if I could find it. My . . . my man will eventually realize that I'm missing, but it may be a while before he does. Can you think of a good place hereabouts for us to hide until help comes?"

She narrowed her eyes. "I think you had better tell me just who you are, sir. Or should I be addressing you as 'my lord'?"

"My name is Michael, lass, and so you should call me. The less you know about me, about all of this, the safer you will be."

"Don't be daft," she said sharply. "I am anything but safe in your company, and as you say, you have small knowledge of this countryside, so you need my help. I suggest—nay, I demand—that you tell me the whole truth without further delay!"

Chapter 3

Only years of experience at concealing his emotions made it possible for Michael to keep from revealing his amusement. She was so fierce and even more beautiful than he remembered from his first impression of her, clouded as that had been by his pain and his deep gratitude for her intervention.

Her flaxen hair, loosely plaited and bereft of a proper headdress, shone brightly in the sunlight. His mother would disapprove of its informal style, but he liked it. Her beautifully shaped eyes with their unusual soft-gray irises outlined in black fascinated him. Her lashes were likewise unusual, astonishingly lush and dark for so fair a wench. But it was her animation, the way her expression altered so swiftly from curiosity to interest, then to suspicion and stern determination that most strongly attracted him. Doubtless, however, next would come fury.

That last thought stirred a hope that she was not one quick to slap men.

Her eyes flashed, and he knew his silence had increased

her displeasure with him, but any reply he could make to her demand was unlikely to please her.

"Well?" she said.

"I'm at a loss, mistress, and can only say, as I said before, that 'tis best you ken no more until you are safely out of this business. Indeed, I'll be unable to tell you much then, for as yet I ken little about it myself."

She met his gaze, her eyes narrow with skepticism.

He continued to gaze calmly back, and after a long moment, she nodded.

"Very well," she said. "I will trust you for a short time longer. I know a herdsman with a summer shieling not far from here. Once we're over the ridge, we'll come to a brook and can find his place easily if we follow it. He'll grant us shelter, and if those villains should chance upon him, his favorite doltish expression will persuade them that he speaks the truth when he declares he's seen naught of us."

"We will hope he never meets them," Michael said, knowing that few men could long withstand Waldron's methods.

They climbed out of the steep ravine quietly and with caution. However, noting no indication of pursuit, they increased their pace and ten minutes later crossed over the ridge. The high glen they entered boasted grassy, rock-strewn slopes, and Michael could hear the burn she had mentioned rushing downhill.

"That aspen thicket follows the course of the burn and will shield us from view if your friends look for us from the ridge top," she said.

He noted a pair of sheep grazing nearby but decided that even Waldron would recognize them for strays and pay them no heed.

"How far?" he asked.

"Perhaps a half mile," she said, giving him a searching look.

"Good," he said and headed doggedly toward the aspens.

Concealing his increasing fatigue required more exertion now, and despite exercise and sunlight he was growing chilly, so whatever miraculous power had kept him going was rapidly waning. The dizziness he had felt earlier had returned in full measure, and what he had dismissed as sweat running down his back, he realized, was more likely blood from the deep whip cuts Waldron had given him. He feared he was near collapse and did not want to disgrace himself before the lass.

She walked a step or two behind him, and he knew from the measuring look she cast now and again that she recognized his fatigue. But she had said nothing about his wounds, although she had been able to see them plainly since leaving the darkness of the cave.

He glanced at her and saw that she had fixed her attention firmly on the ground at her feet. Her movements remained confident and graceful, making it easy to imagine her in courtly dress, and stirring a strong desire in him to see her so.

She looked up and met his gaze, raising an eyebrow.

"My back is bleeding again, is it not?" he said quietly.

"Aye, your wounds have been oozing or dripping blood all along," she replied in the same tone. "I'll tend them when we reach MacCaig's shieling."

"So your herdsman is a MacCaig then, not a Macleod?"

"Aye, but the MacCaigs are close kinsmen of Mackenzie's, and I know Matthias well. We can trust him."

"Then we will," he agreed.

The aspens grew thicker, and he feared they had made a mistake in seeking their shelter until he noted a barely discernible track near the water. No more than an occasional deer trail, it followed the burn and would therefore serve their purpose well enough.

He had little energy and knew he needed food and rest. He wondered if Waldron had coated the lash with one of his devilish potions, then decided the man would take no chance of killing him until he was sure he could not provide the information he sought.

Michael's foot slipped off a wet rock, and although he caught himself easily enough by grabbing a stout aspen branch, he did not allow his thoughts to wander from the trail again until the lass said quietly, "There, sir, just ahead."

He saw the low roof of a hut then, no larger than one of his sheds at Roslin. It looked much like the crofts one saw throughout the Highlands but smaller, with a grassy-looking thatched roof that drooped so low that he would not have been surprised to see rabbits and deer, even sheep, contentedly grazing on it.

"Do not call out," he warned in an undertone.

"Nay, I know how far sound travels up here," she said. "It seems empty, though, and the animals are gone. Matthias may have taken them up the glen to fresh pasturing."

Just then, a lanky, red-haired lad of twelve or thirteen emerged from the hut and looked around. When his gaze discovered them, a wide, toothy grin split his face and he hurried forward.

"Lady Isobel, welcome!" he exclaimed. "If ye're looking for me dad, he's taken the beasts off t' the high pasture and willna be back till tomorrow."

Isobel glanced at Michael, but he remained silent, apparently content to let her take charge of the situation.

To give herself a moment to think, she smiled at Ian MacCaig, whom she had known since his birth, and said, "'Twill doubtless seem strange to you, but we have come to request your hospitality."

His eyes widened, and he glanced doubtfully at the hut behind him. Then, straightening, he nodded in a grown-up way and said, "Ye're welcome t' what we have, m'lady, but there be sma' space inside for the two o' ye."

Isobel looked again at Michael. His face was ashen, his eyes glassy, and she knew his strength was nearly gone. He had not said a word, and if Ian looked askance at him, she could not blame the lad. Doubtless he thought Michael a servant of some sort, garbed as he was in breeches, boots, and little else. Doubtless, too, Ian wondered why they sought shelter so near Chalamine on so sunny a day.

The air had grown chilly, though, and that became the deciding factor.

"I will trust you with the truth, Ian," she said, "but you must repeat it to no one. Outlanders are hunting us in Glen Mòr and elsewhere, so we need help from Chalamine, but the strangers know who I am and may seek us there. This gentleman is"—Michael made an almost inaudible sound of warning—"is ill and must have food and rest before we can go farther. So I want you to take a message to my father, telling him of our plight and requesting a sizeable escort of armed men to take us safely home. Will you do that for me?"

"Aye, m'lady, o' course," Ian said. "I could go t' me own laird, too, if ye'd rather. He has men aplenty and can raise them in a twink."

That was true, but she remembered that the men had

followed Michael from Eilean Donan, and this time when she looked at him, he gave a slight headshake. She recalled, too, that the track to Eilean Donan, hemmed by Loch Duich on one side and steep banks on the other, would be easier to block than the track to Chalamine. The latter route would be safer until they knew more.

To Ian, she said, "The men after us are less likely to seek us at Chalamine than at Eilean Donan, but since they do know of Chalamine, there is at least a chance that they may go there and may even reach the castle before you. If they do, you must not let them guess that you carry a message from me."

"I can say I'm looking for me cousin Angus from Skye," Ian said. "If I make me way round about and approach Glenelg from Kyle Rhea way, they'll no think aught o' my being there than that I followed him from the Isle."

"An excellent notion," Isobel said. "But before you go, have you food to spare? My friend needs to recover his strength as quickly as he can."

"Aye, we ha' cheese and bread inside—ale, too. Take what ye want. I'll be as quick as I can," the boy added, casting another curious look at Michael.

"Just be careful," Isobel warned him. "We know of six men looking for us, but there may be more and they may have separated into smaller groups. Trust no stranger, and keep clear of any you see. Your safety is more important than speed."

"Then they'll no see me at all, m'lady. Ye can depend on that. Will ye come inside now?" He gestured toward the entrance to the hut. "I should shut the door, lest the critters get in and eat our food."

She nodded, and as they went inside, he carefully shut the lower half of the door, leaving the upper half latched back against the wall to let in the light. The tiny hut boasted no windows.

He was off as soon as he had shown them the larder—little more than a large straw basket—and had cut bread and cheese for himself.

The rest of the hut's contents consisted of only a thin straw pallet, a rickety stool, and an equally rickety table, on which sat a tinderbox and several loose tallow candles. The pallet had a thick wool blanket folded on top, and a pile of wood lay nearby to provide a small fire when evening came, but Isobel saw nothing that she could use to tend Michael's wounds.

"How long will it take him to go and come back?" Michael asked.

Surprised by his grim tone, Isobel said, "Why, I do not know, sir. On horseback and without concern for who might see me, I could be home in an hour. Afoot as Ian is, and on the watch for strangers, I warrant it will take him a good bit longer. The track to Glenelg from Glen Mòr is narrow and steep, and there are many places where one can overlook much of it. Had the men I saw this morning chanced to look my way, they most likely would have seen me. Fortunately, though, I expect they had their attention fixed on following you, and I had paused to enjoy the sunshine, and thus was still for a time. I only caught sight of them because of their movement as they entered the wee glen."

"You saw just the tail of Waldron's party," he said. "I'm only guessing they followed me from Eilean Donan, because I don't think they can have known about the cave before they discovered me on the point of entering it. They seemed surprised to see it, and Waldron sent two men into it straightaway whilst the others strung me up and ripped my shirt from me."

"I should tend your wounds," she said. "Would you prefer to lie down on that pallet now whilst I do it, or do you want something to eat first?"

"I'd better eat something," he said. "I don't know what you can do for them anyway, so mayhap after I eat, I'll just sleep until the lad returns."

"You'll do no such thing unless you want your injuries to putrefy," she said as she sliced bread and cheese with her dirk. "After you eat, we'll go to the stream. I see no cloths here that I want to use, but my shift is clean enough. I can rip strips of it to tend the worst of them, and I saw herbs near the streambed from which I can make a plaster to ease your pain. Then you may sleep until Ian returns."

His wan smile revealed his exhaustion more than anything else had, making him look more like a weary child than a grown man. "I am yours to command, my lady," he said. "After a few bites of food, I'll be in fine fettle again."

"Sit on that pallet then, sir, and eat what I've cut for you," she said.

"You should not call me 'sir,' you know," he said as he lowered himself to the pallet. "I warrant that lad thought me your servant until you identified me as a gentleman and friend. That may prove a costly error if he is caught and questioned."

"They won't catch him," she said confidently.

"Still, it would be easier if you could bring yourself to call me Michael."

"I do not know you well enough for such familiarity, sir."

"Aye, well, at least now I ken you to be more properly called Lady Isobel."

"But so I told you from the outset," she said, watching as

he bit off a large chunk of the bread at last and chewed. "My name is no secret."

"At the cavern you identified yourself only as Macleod of Glenelg's daughter. If memory serves me, the man has many daughters."

"That is true," she admitted. "There were eight of us, but only Adela, Sorcha, and Sidony remain at home. The others are all married or dead."

"I see," he said, his tone harsh again. "Tell me something of your husband then, madam. Who is he and what manner of man is he that he allows his lady wife to ride about the countryside without anyone to guard her from evil assailants?"

"Sakes, sir, I don't have a husband!"

"You said that all but those three of your father's daughters were married or dead," he reminded her. "You are certainly not dead."

"No, but as I'm sure I told you earlier, I have lived with Hector Reaganach and my sister Cristina at Lochbuie since I turned thirteen. I was not counting myself as part of the group that remained at Chalamine but merely describing the others. I do see, though, that I did not make myself clear when I said that about my sisters."

"Your denial was most vehement, lass. Do you dislike men so much?"

"I don't dislike them at all, most of the time, for they can be quite useful creatures," she said, chuckling. "Indeed, they are indispensable at court if one wants to dance or to flirt. 'Tis not men I have no use for, sir, only husbands."

"I see."

That reply being more encouragement than usual to express her point of view on the subject, she said, "Marriage is forever and ever, sir, and in my experience, it is the nature of husbands to be tyrants." When he frowned, she added with a sigh, "Should I cut more bread and cheese for you, or may we go out to the burn now?"

"We'd better go now if we're going to go at all," he said.

He did not look much steadier as he got to his feet, but after she peeked outside and decided no one would see them if they took care to keep to the shelter of the shrubbery, he followed her meekly. When they neared the swiftly flowing burn, he sat on a boulder and rested while she ripped a generous portion of her shift away and soaked it in the chilly water.

He remained stoic while she tended the cuts across his back, but his skin rippled from time to time in shudders that told her more than words that her ministrations were hurting him.

"The plaster I'll make will help as you rest," she said, gently dabbing the deepest of the cuts. "Sicklewort will help protect against putrefaction, too, but you may have trouble sleeping, especially if you often turn over in your sleep."

"'Tis a pity I've no southernwood with me," he murmured. "It makes a fine brew that sends one straight off to sleep."

"I've chamomile at Chalamine," she said. "It would make you drowsy, but I doubt that it would ease your pain. I do not know southernwood. Is it an herb?"

"Aye, and useful for dyeing, too, but 'tis rare in Britain," he said. "One finds it more easily in Spain and . . . and elsewhere. I usually carry some with me."

"Have you been to Spain, then?"

"Aye, because my foster father believes travel is educational."

"I'm sure it is," she agreed. "What color dye does southernwood produce?"

"Deep yellow. In some areas, its plants bear large flowers in great profusion, and the ancient Greeks and Romans thought it magical, especially as an aphrodisiac when placed under a mattress. I cannot vouch for its worth in that way," he added with a smile. "But as a composer it is far more efficient than chamomile."

Feeling heat in her cheeks at his casual mention of aphrodisiacs, she applied her attention to rinsing out her cloth in the burn. Then, realizing that she would not get all the blood out of it, she bent to tear another piece of cambric from her shift.

As she turned back to face him after soaking the second piece, he said gently, "I should not have said that about southernwood's aphrodisiacal powers, lass, not to a maiden who clearly understands the meaning of such. Forgive me."

"I have naught to forgive, sir. You made a learned observation, nothing more."

"Faith, but you should not even be alone like this with me, and if that lad does not return before nightfall . . ." He left the rest unsaid.

She had not considered that detail while the necessity of escaping their captors and fears that her companion might expire had consumed her thoughts, and she dismissed it now. Michael's recovery was more important. She did not want anything to happen to him, certainly not before he had done much more to satisfy her curiosity about himself and the men who had captured them.

Until he mentioned aphrodisiacs, she had thought of him only as a fellow victim of mysterious assailants, albeit a distractingly handsome one.

That last thought startled her, and in order to divert her

imagination, she said abruptly, "We can go back inside now."

He nodded, and when he stood and turned toward her with a smile that reminded her of how warm and sensual his voice had been in the darkness, she added hastily, "I have been wondering about something else, sir. How is it that those men were able to follow you all the way from Eilean Donan to that cave without your seeing them? The distance must be at least five miles."

"Waldron is highly skilled at such things, and his men likewise," he said, gently touching her arm to nudge her toward the hut. "Moreover, I failed to realize they might predict my visit to Kintail and was not as wary as I should have been."

"But might they not simply have followed you to Eilean Donan? Indeed, if they did not, then how—?"

"Waldron would not have had to follow me. He knows of my friendship with Kintail and . . . and other details that might have led him to make the conjecture, but I do not think he has allies of his own in this area. As to whether he might have followed me, I am certain he did not, because I traveled by boat from Oban."

"Is your home near Oban then?" she asked. Oban was not far from Lochbuie.

He smiled. "Nay, lass, but I do know the countryside thereabouts better than here. 'Tis how I ken Hector the Ferocious. Is the man really such a tyrant?"

She blinked at the abrupt transition. "What makes you think he is one at all?"

"You said that all husbands are, so I supposed that your experience living with him and your sister had produced that opinion. And, too, men do call him Hector the Ferocious with good cause, I'm told."

That her words had stirred him to think such a thing of
Hector startled her, and she paused to think just how she
could most honestly reply.

Michael watched her as they strolled back to the hut,
wondering how strongly she would cling to her harsh
opinion of husbands—indeed, of men in general, if he was
not mistaken. He hoped she would not prove intractable on
the subject. So bonnie a lass should not go through life
alone, not when she would so clearly make any man an excellent and delightfully stimulating partner.

She paused twice to gather herbs on the way but still had
not replied to his question when they entered the hut, where
the only light came from a narrow golden path of sunlight
spilling through the open portion of the doorway.

"Why so quiet, lass?" he asked. "Is Hector Reaganach
not tyrannical?"

"He is always kind to me unless I do something to dis-
please him," she said.

"Ah, but then he becomes tyrannical."

"Nay. He knows how to make me sorry, to be sure, but
he is a fair man. Certainly he has been kinder than my father, but both are exceedingly domineering men, sir, as is
every other man I have met. That is simply the nature of
men."

"Is it? I expect you would know more than I about that,"
he said.

"Aye, for my sisters' husbands all expect the sun and
moon to rise by their wants and desires, and my sisters to
exert themselves at all times to please them, although those
same husbands show small consideration for their wives."

"Most vexatious, I agree."

"Well, it is," she said, giving him a look that told him she suspected him of mocking her. Instantly confirming his deduction, she said with a decisive nod, "You are teasing me, but do you not agree that life would be more pleasant and peaceful if men were not continually fighting each other as they do? Women's lives certainly would be if men were not always making demands upon them, or making war with their neighbors, or dashing off to Spain or other foreign places where they might get themselves killed even more easily than at home."

"And all the beasts should be at peace?"

Her eyes narrowed. "My aunt often quotes verses from the Bible, too, sir, when she wishes to make a point. 'Tis a most annoying habit."

"Aye, well, I was more likely misquoting from it," he said. "Do you compare our plight now to a war?"

"Is it not similar?" she asked, gesturing toward the door. "Those horrid men!"

Michael was adept at recognizing thin ice before he fell through it. If she linked Waldron's quest with war, her assessment of the danger in which they stood was accurate enough. He would do naught to make it more so. Instead, he said, "Life and the simple need to survive creates conflicts, lass, and survival requires the ability to make good decisions quickly. That need produces men who do not always seek counsel with those they must protect, but I do not agree that that simple fact of life provides you with sufficient cause to avoid all men or the married state. 'Tis possible that you have simply not met the right person yet."

"I do not intend to marry," she said flatly.

She had shaken out the blanket folded atop the pallet as

they talked, and now spread it wide so that half of it lay on the straw and the other half on the floor. She gestured for him to lie down on the portion that covered the pallet.

"Lie on your stomach," she said as she reached through the slit in her skirt to take her dirk from its sheath. "I'm going to chop these herbs and mash them with water to make a plaster."

"You don't mean to rub that mess into my wounds, I hope," he said as, with a sigh of relief, he lay facedown on the pallet.

She smiled. "You deserve that I should, mayhap even that I should add salt to the plaster, but I mean only to spread the mixture on the clean piece of cambric I ripped from my shift. With hot water I could make it into a true jelly that would spread more easily, but we don't want to risk smoke from a fire."

"No, we do not," he agreed, turning his head to watch her sleepily, and resting his cheek on his folded forearms.

Isobel expected him to fall asleep the moment he lay down, but he continued to watch her as she prepared her plaster, putting the minced sicklewort leaves into a wooden bowl that she found hanging on one wall and mashing them to pulp with the dirk's hilt. She had left the cleaner bit of cambric from her shift to drip dry over the lower half of the door, so she fetched it and wrung some of the remaining water into the cup, then continued to mash until the concoction resembled watery gruel.

"I'll be as gentle as I know how to be, but I fear it will feel cold at first," she said as she knelt to spread the damp cloth over his back. "Indeed, I do not know that it will do you the least bit of good, but I do not think it will do you any harm."

"Stop fretting, lass," he murmured drowsily. "Just be sure you wake me at once if you hear so much as a twig crack outside."

"I will," she promised. "It will get cold, though. Do you think it will be safe to build a fire in here later?"

"Nay," he said. "Even if they cannot see the smoke, they may smell it. 'Tis better if the glen looks deserted."

He fell silent then and did not stir as she carefully spread the cloth over his wounds, but when she moved to cover him with the second half of the blanket, he reached out and caught her hand.

"You need to rest, too," he said. "If you leave the blanket spread, I can move over onto the floor and let you have the pallet. I've slept on the ground often, and I vow, nothing can keep me awake tonight, as tired as I am."

"You'll need warmth, sir," she said, pulling her hand with reluctance from his. "Without good wool atop that cloth, you'll feel only the chill, and the herbs will do you no good. With the blanket on you, your body heat will stir their vapors."

Silence greeted her, and she said no more. When his breathing deepened to that of sleep, she covered him with the blanket and sat back on her heels. Wanting food more than sleep, she cut herself some cheese, glanced outside to find the glen gloomy with dusk and silent. Only the murmur of the burn and a distant night bird's cry broke the stillness.

Knowing that at that time of year, the sky was unlikely to grow darker before midnight, and fearing that a watcher on the ridge might detect movement if she went for a walk, she sat down near the hut's wall, ate her small meal, and leaned back to rest. She knew no more until she awoke with a start, shivering.

The temperature had dropped considerably, it was much darker than before, and a creeping dampness had settled around her.

Getting up carefully so as not to waken Michael, she tiptoed stiffly to the doorway and looked out into darkness nearly as dense as they had experienced in the cave. A deep breath and years of experience told her that a thick Highland mist had crept into the glen as they slept. Even if Ian MacCaig had reached Chalamine, he would bring no help tonight. By the same token, however, strangers to the area would not try to find them in such a mist. She could let herself relax and be fairly certain that, for a few hours at least, they were safe.

Making her way to the pallet, she felt for the blanket and made certain it covered him. Then, wrapping herself in her cloak, she lay down on the hard floor beside the pallet and fell asleep almost before she shut her eyes.

Reluctantly half-awake and vaguely aware of gentle warmth at his side, Michael gratefully moved closer to the source. When his movement stirred responsive movement beside him, his eyes snapped open.

The first thing he noticed was that the interior of the hut was lighter than it had been before he fell asleep. Mist seeped over the bottom half of the door, because apparently the lass had not thought to shut the top, and thus it was as chilly and damp inside as outside.

The warmth felt strongest along his right arm. Logic told him he had only to move his head to see the source, but something was in the way, something that tickled his chin. Realization came then to his brain and to his body, the latter reacting more swiftly than the former.

Shifting his right arm with care, he slipped it gently around her and drew her closer, hoping she would not waken and noting that although his back still felt stiff and sore, the previous day's pain had eased considerably.

The lass did not wake but snuggled closer with a contented sigh.

Knowing the damage had already been done and that they would both deal with the consequences better if they were rested, he let himself drift back to sleep.

Hours later, the mist silently lifted, letting sunlight back into the high glen, but it was not the sun's golden brilliance that awakened him. It was the sound of footsteps hurrying toward the hut.

Instantly alert, he moved to get up, easing his arm away from the still-sleeping lass. His ease of movement told him that he was in far better condition than the previous day. Even so, when he stood, he swayed with dizziness.

Ignoring the vertigo, he let the now-dry plaster slip from his back and stepped silently to the doorway, only to come face to face with an anxious-looking, slender woman in a hooded dark-green cloak.

"Who are you?" she demanded. "And where is my sister?"

Chapter 4 _____

Isobel heard the familiar voice distantly and rose reluctantly to consciousness, blinking against the brightness spilling through the upper half of the doorway. "Adela, is that you?" she murmured.

"Isobel, what are you doing here, and who is this man?"

"Man?" Rubbing eyes sticky with sleep, and wholly disoriented, Isobel wondered why she was apparently lying on a hard-packed dirt floor.

Memory flooded back on a wave of dismay.

Sitting up so quickly it made her woozy, and peering groggily toward the doorway, she could discern the outline of a hooded figure—then a second, taller one—against the brilliant sunlight.

She heard Michael's quiet voice saying, "Be at ease, my lady. No act worth your condemnation has occurred here. Lady Isobel took pity on an injured man and attempted to help him, little knowing that she risked danger to herself thereby."

"But if she has put herself in danger, how can you say that naught has occurred to cause alarm?" Adela asked.

Wondering what Michael would say to that, Isobel pushed hair out of her eyes, knowing she must look as if someone had held her by her feet and shaken her, and knowing, too, from experience, that Adela would condemn her appearance if she condemned nothing else. Surreptitiously, she tried to straighten her skirts, but they had twisted around her legs, and her movements drew her sister's attention.

"Bless me, Isobel, did you sleep with this man?" Adela demanded as she pushed open the lower half of the door and entered without further hesitation. "What Father will say to this start, I do not want to imagine!"

"Where is he?" Isobel asked. "And why are you here, Adela? You are the last person I expected to see this morning."

"Two strangers came to Chalamine," Adela said, her voice dripping disapproval. "They said they sought a man wanted for many crimes, and the man they described could easily be this fellow standing here," she added, gesturing at Michael. "They did not mention, however, that he lacked even a shirt to his name. They did say he had run off with a woman claiming to be our father's daughter."

"What did you tell them?"

"I told them nothing. I am not one to speak to strangers when Father is home. Had it occurred after his departure, I should not have known *what* to say to such men."

"Well, since you and the girls would have gone with him, you would not have had to say anything," Isobel said. "You *are* going to Orkney, are you not?"

"I've not decided," Adela said. "Sidony and Sorcha must go, of course, if Sorcha can manage *not* to infuriate Father before then, and I think that our aunt may go. If she does, then she can look after them. I thought I might visit you at

Lochbuie instead, since you have not said yet what you mean to do, but we need not discuss that now. Indeed, if this business redounds as badly to all of us as I expect it will, both Father and Hector Reaganach will doubtless forbid me to visit you."

Isobel's eyes had adjusted to the light, and she saw that Ian MacCaig had stepped into the doorway to stand by Michael. Adela, she decided, was right about one thing. It was no time to discuss future events that would have no relevance if the villains found and murdered them first.

For Michael's benefit, she said, "Many Islesmen are traveling to Kirkwall in the Orkney Islands next week to attend ceremonies at the great cathedral there for a Scotsman being installed to a Norse princedom. I believe that even the Lord of the Isles means to attend. But Adela is wise to remind us that we must deal with the present before we need worry about the future. What are we to do?"

Adela snapped, "Sakes, Isobel, would you ruin yourself? You will come home with me at once, of course!"

"I cannot," Isobel said. "Did Ian not explain how we came to be here?"

"He sputtered some nonsense or other about men hunting you, and said that you wanted Father to send an armed escort to protect you. But then he said that the two strangers were doubtless your hunters and that we must do naught to draw their attention. Not only did an army seem excessive to protect you against two men but so many men leaving Chalamine at once would certainly have drawn notice, and since Ian would not answer any question I put to him—not sensibly, at all events—I made him bring me here to you."

Deciding that her position on the floor put her at a distinct disadvantage, Isobel stood and shook out her skirts.

But although she felt less vulnerable to Adela's displeasure now that she was standing, she still had no idea what to do.

To Ian, she said, "Did the strangers take any interest in you?"

"Nay, m'lady. I wandered about looking like me dad does when he wants folks t' think he's daft, and they left me be. We—Lady Adela and me—slipped down t' the loch gey early this morning whilst the mist were still in, then walked over the ridge, past Glenelg village, and came here. Nae one caught sight of us."

Isobel looked at Michael, who had not said a word since telling Adela to rest easy, even to explain why she should.

He met her gaze silently.

"We certainly dare not go to Chalamine now," she said.

He nodded.

"What about Mackenzie?" she asked. "We could go to Eilean Donan."

"Aye, we'd be welcome, and my man is there," he said. "But 'tis a fair distance without ponies, and the difficulties we discussed yestereve remain. Waldron is certain to have left men to challenge anyone approaching Eilean Donan. Lady Adela, you said two strangers visited Chalamine. Are you sure 'twas only two?"

"Two who came to the castle," Adela said. "But one of our lads said two others had stayed behind to watch the track through Glen Mòr. That is why Ian and I slipped away as we did in the mist and chose the route we did."

"If they learn that you left in such a sly way," Isobel said, "they are bound to challenge you on your return and demand to know where you have been."

"I'd not tell them anything if they were so insolent!"

"Sakes, Adela, they would see in a trice that you were hiding something, and they'd soon have it out of you."

"They would not!"

Isobel shook her head, saying more gently, "You are wholly incapable of the simplest prevarication, my dear, let alone of uttering falsehoods."

"But my business is none of theirs, and so I would tell them."

Gesturing toward Michael, Isobel said, "When I first came upon them, they were beating him with a whip. What if they did that to you?"

Adela turned pale but muttered staunchly, "They wouldn't dare."

"You would do much better to avoid them, my lady," Michael said. "They have small respect for the fair sex. She accounts for only four of them," he reminded Isobel. "So of the ones we saw, two are missing. In truth, we don't even know how many there are altogether, only that we have seen six."

"If you think they might be waiting at Chalamine to challenge Adela, they'll certainly have set one man or more to guard against your return to Eilean Donan."

"Aye, and at least one to watch the . . . the place where they caught me."

"But who are they?" Adela asked with a sharp look at him. "They told us only that they hunted a dangerous criminal. How am I to know they spoke falsely?"

He met her gaze with his usual calm. "I can offer you only my word for that, my lady. I have no idea how I could prove such a thing to you when I do not even know what charges they might lay against me. I have done naught."

"But I do not even know your name! Why should I trust you?"

"Because he is a gentleman, a guest at Eilean Donan," Isobel said. She had been thinking as they debated, and an idea took form while her sister digested the information that Mackenzie would speak for Michael. Softly, barely realizing that she spoke her thought aloud, she said, "We'll go to Lochbuie."

"How could you get there?" Adela demanded. "And how would you dare?"

"I do wish you would stop asking how I can do this or dare that, and predicting my ruin," Isobel snapped. "Getting to safety is the only necessity now, and necessity acknowledges no law except to prevail."

"I doubt that Hector Reaganach or our father would agree," Adela said dryly. "But I know you, Isobel. You will do what you will."

"Lady Adela does pose a good question," Michael said. "How would we reach Lochbuie? The boat that carried me to Eilean Donan lies in harbor there, effectively unreachable, and I think the sooner we can elude them, the better."

"A boat is the least of our difficulties," Isobel said. "We have only to cross the Sound from Glenelg Bay to Kyle Rhea, where kinsmen of MacDonald's, who are also friends of my father, will see us safely to Lochbuie. Adela can tell Father where we've gone, and mayhap Ian can go to Eilean Donan for you and tell them."

"Aye, m'lady," Ian said eagerly. "I can do that. Likely, me dad willna be back wi' the beasts till this afternoon, though, and I shouldna leave here afore then."

"That will be soon enough," Michael said. "It would be as well, I think, if we create as little dust as possible, and Lady Adela must keep safe, too."

"I left word for my father that I'd be away most of the day, visiting tenants," Adela said. "I doubt that I would be in any real danger, in any event, since those men do not know me. When they arrived, they demanded to speak to

Father. And when he told them Isobel had gone riding early and had not yet returned, they said they'd wait. They spent the night, but they must have gone by now."

"I think we should leave at once," Isobel said. "It must be well past the hour of Terce, so the morning is departing, and we still have to find a way across the Sound."

"Beg pardon, m'lady," Ian said. "I ha' been thinking since ye said ye'd seek help from his grace's kinfolk on Skye. Me dad's got a wee fishing coble ye could use, wi' four oars and a lug sail. 'Tis beached betwixt the bay and Ardintoul."

"Do we not have to go through Glen Mòr to get there?" Michael asked.

"Nay, sir, for just north o' here a rough track leads right down t' the bay. 'Tis a bit steep but it be how me and me dad go, most times."

"But surely they'll be watching for us to cross the Kyle," Michael said.

"They're less likely to see us than if we traipse through Glen Mòr," Isobel said impatiently. "We won't be on the water long either, because we'll cross at the narrows north of the bay. The current is vicious enough there to sweep us right into Loch Alsh if we don't take care, but the wind is blowing as hard today as it did yesterday, and from the north, which will help."

"But won't they just follow us?" he asked.

"Matthias's boat is beached near the narrows, so we should be able to get on the water without anyone noticing. They might see us and give chase, but they won't have horses on Skye, and we will. We'll also have his grace's kinsmen to protect us."

"Aye, but . . ."

"Faith, sir, those men cannot expect to continue riding all

over the place unchallenged, particularly on Skye or on Macleod and Mackenzie lands. They'll draw more attention than they can possibly want as soon as they leave Chalamine, and if only two are lying in wait for us there, they'll not risk angering my father."

He frowned, then nodded. "We'll do as you suggest, lass. Ian, mayhap you can describe exactly where to find your coble. We don't want to leave Lady Adela alone here whilst you take us there."

Adela looked mutinous. "I'd be safe. No one would dare harm me."

Michael's frown deepened, making Isobel instantly recall the look that had reminded her so unnervingly of Hector Reaganach in a temper.

She gritted her teeth and strove to control her impatience as she said, "Adela, everything that we've said is true. We're all in danger. Those men think Mich—"

"It may be better if she goes with us," Michael interjected. "Or, perchance she'd not mind going with Ian to Eilean Donan. I'm thinking she looks a lot like you, Lady Isobel, and if the ones who've seen us should recognize her as your sister—"

"But, as you said, we've no horses here," Isobel pointed out. "Adela would have to walk all that way and back again to Chalamine."

"Now, lass, you cannot think Mackenzie would make her walk back," he said with a smile. "She'd be safe there and would be more likely to pass watchers there unchallenged than any she meets returning to Chalamine from here."

"It is still too far. Moreover, my father is going to think his daughters are all deserting him," Isobel added with a wry smile.

"She is right about that, sir," Adela said, clearly having

not considered Macleod. Isobel noted, too, that her sister had unconsciously addressed Michael more formally, just as she herself had instinctively done from the start.

"Father will be angry," Adela added unhappily.

"He'll be angrier if anyone harms you," Michael said.

A whistle sounded in the distance, and Ian turned alertly. "That be me dad wi' the beasts," he said, adding with a look at the sun, "He's come afore his time."

Isobel's gaze met Michael's.

"Matthias is trustworthy," she said. "I have known him all my life."

"I, too," Adela said, clearly relieved. "Matthias will know what to do, and I doubt that he will approve of your going off anywhere with this man, Isobel."

Isobel sighed, knowing that Adela was probably right.

A few minutes later, they saw the flock, two dogs dashing and wheeling along its flanks, and the wiry shepherd with them. He waved to Ian, who ran to meet him. Leaving the boy with sheep and dogs, Matthias strode toward them.

To Isobel's astonishment, he did not seem surprised to see his visitors. "Bless us, my lady, I'm that glad t' see ye safe," he said, casting a curious glance at Adela and a more searching one at Michael.

"Sakes, Matthias, how could you know I was in danger?"

His pale blue eyes twinkled under bushy, grizzled brows. "Ye've lived here and about all your life, so ye shouldna ha' to ask that question. I met a lad walking up from the glen as I were coming down from high pasture. He said he'd heard strangers be seeking Macleod's daughter and another stranger in the glens. The only one o' Macleod's daughters as goes about by herself these days be yourself, m'lady, and I thought ye might ha' come here t' me shieling, did ye ken they was seeking ye. I own, though, I were that surprised t' see Lady Adela. He didna speak o' her."

"She came to find me, Matthias," Isobel said. "We were hoping you would lend us the use of your coble to get us across the Kyle. We mean to ask his grace's kinsmen at Kyle Rhea to take us to the Isle of Mull, where we'll be safe."

"Aye, ye would be safe there," he agreed. "The wind be picking up, though, so I'm thinking ye'll do better wi' two strong oarsmen than one."

"Do you mean to send Ian with us then?" Isobel asked. "I own, I was wondering how we'd get the boat back to you."

"Och, lass, ye needna ha' fretted about that, because Gowrie o' Kyle Rhea would send it back t' me," Matthias said. "Still, I'm thinking I'll go m'self an ye'll allow it. I've another suggestion as well," he added, twinkling again. "We've extra clothes in yon kist. Ian should ha' given ye a shirt," he said to Michael, "but ye can take one o' mine. And if her ladyship willna be vexed, I'm thinking she'll draw less notice on the water an she covers that hair o' hers and dons a pair o' Ian's breeks."

"Isobel, you'll do no such scandalous thing!" Adela exclaimed.

Had Isobel required encouragement, those words provided it.

"Don't be a noddy," she said. "'Tis an excellent suggestion."

"Aye, sure, I ken fine it'll no be the first time," Matthias said, grinning.

She grinned back at him. "You ken too much, old man. That kist?" she added, pointing to a wicker chest against the wall opposite the doorway.

"Aye," he said, "and dinna forget t' take out a shirt for your friend."

Michael extended a hand to Matthias. "I'm Michael," he said, "and I am most grateful for your help."

The shepherd wiped his own hand on his thigh and gripped Michael's.

Smiling, Michael said, "I'll not forget this, Matthias MacCaig, nor what young Ian did for us, either."

"Lady Adela should bide here wi' the lad until we're well away," the older man said. "We'll see her home again safely, the two of us, when I return."

"My man, Hugo, is at Eilean Donan," Michael said. "I must get word to him that I'm safe, and let him know where to find me."

"First, we'll get the pair o' ye beyond the strangers' reach," Matthias said.

Michael nodded, took the shirt Isobel handed him from the kist, and put it on. Matthias found a leather jerkin for him, and the two of them went outside so that Isobel could have privacy to change her clothes.

Tight-lipped, Adela helped her. "I do not know what you deserve for this," she said. "You will never get a husband, Isobel, if you continue to behave so."

"I don't want a husband, as you know perfectly well," Isobel said. "I mean to play Aunt Euphemia to your children when you finally have some, Adela."

Adela had knelt to tie the breeks' lacings for her, but at these words she looked up, bit her lip, and then burst out laughing.

Pretending outrage, Isobel said, "What? You do not think I'll make them a good aunt? I'll have you know that my nieces and nephews think I'm splendid."

"I don't doubt it," Adela said, gasping. "But that you

could compare yourself to our meek, even scholarly aunt in such an absurd way . . ." Still chuckling, she shook her head and bundled Isobel's skirts and bodice into an untidy roll, tying it with twine from a ball she found on the floor.

Isobel was glad to hear Adela's laughter and wished she might hear more of it. Having borne the burden of managing the household at Chalamine since Cristina had married Hector, Adela had aged beyond her years. Her laughter reminded Isobel that Adela was only four years older than she was.

"You must go to Kirkwall, Adela," she said firmly. "I mean to, I promise you, for we shall never see such an event again in our lives. The King of Scots has said that a Norse prince, even one Scottish by birth, cannot demand royal treatment in Scotland, that here he will be just another earl. But in Orkney, he will be a prince, so I want to see that ceremony, and you must not miss it. Moreover, think of all the men who will be there, excellent prospects for husbands, every one of them! Except the married ones, of course," she added conscientiously.

"I thought you didn't want a husband."

"I don't," Isobel said. "But you do, and you shall have one. You will make some man an excellent wife—a fine mother for his children, too."

"Bless you, no man will want me. I've no looks left, and few social graces."

Isobel made a rude noise. "You are as much one of Macleod's beautiful daughters as the rest of us, my dear, and as to social graces, you lack practice, that's all. Hector and Cristina are going to Kirkwall, as are Lachlan, Mairi, and Father. And you may be sure that Aunt Euphemia will go, too, for she says it is to be a grand historic event. Sakes, even Ian Dubh Maclean may go, because he will think the same as Aunt Euphemia, and he is quite mad about history."

"Ian Dubh is Hector's father, is he not?"

"Aye, and although he must be nearly as old as his grace, he is not decrepit. We shall make a grand party, I warrant, and travel in a most imposing flotilla!"

"We'd best be on our way, m'lady," Matthias called from outside.

"We're coming," Isobel said, giving Adela a quick hug.

Michael hid a smile when Lady Isobel strode from the hut in Ian's leather breeks and a shirt that looked several sizes too big for her. She had belted it with cording and had wisely retained her own well-worn boots. She carried her cloak over one arm and the rest of her clothing in a bundle tied up with twine.

He and Matthias had decided that for Adela's safety and that of Michael and Isobel, Adela should retreat with Ian, the flock, and the dogs to the high pasture. Later Matthias and Ian would escort her home or to Eilean Donan when they delivered his message to Hugo.

Informing Adela of this decision, Michael added gently before she could refuse, "You'll be safer with Ian, my lady. None will seek you there, and few will know you if they stumble upon you, particularly if you plait your hair and strive to act like a common lass. You must know how much you resemble your sister. I noticed it straightaway, and the ones who seek us may do so as well. I believe them capable of anything, and you must not risk your safety."

"Then I should go with you!"

"Two men and a lad in a fishing boat crossing the Kyle

will draw little notice," Matthias said. "'Twould be a different matter an they see a woman wi' us. Moreover, ye dinna want t' go to Mull, and your father would be vexed if ye did."

"But I could come back with you. Isn't it just as dangerous for Isobel?"

"Not as dangerous as it would be with four in our boat," Michael said. "We'll make better speed with only three, my lady, and the men after us are inlanders. I doubt their skills can match Matthias's against a strong current."

"But what of your skills?" Adela demanded. "Do you ken aught of boats?"

"Enough, my lady, to do as Matthias bids me," Michael said evenly.

She glowered at him but said no more about it. Nevertheless, she was still visibly fuming a short time later when Michael and Isobel left her with Ian and followed Matthias, who had slung Isobel's untidy bundle over his shoulder.

Michael was surprised at the older man's rapid pace. He seemed to make no allowance for the lass, nor did she seem to expect him to.

That she had not complained the day before about losing her horse and having to walk had impressed him. She seemed to view the whole situation as an adventure, and he realized that had she been more like her darker-blonde sister, he would not have considered anything more than finding somewhere safe to leave her while he took to the hills to hide until he could arrange to meet Hugo.

That Isobel had been willing to help him and able to suggest alternative plans had made things easier. Indeed, had he been alone, cut off from Eilean Donan, he might soon have found himself at a standstill, but now she was determined to see it through and seemed eminently capable, so he was willing to let her take the lead. In fact, he would be reluctant to part with her, although he was fairly certain that his reception at Lochbuie would not be what she expected.

He was grateful that Matthias asked no questions about his identity. Having accepted the man's help, he was reluctant to lie to him but likewise reluctant to share information unnecessarily. Having learned discretion from birth, he found it hard to break the habit at the best of times, which this certainly was not.

They had been walking for some time when Matthias slowed and muttered, "Four below, riding south, where this track meets the one along the water."

"Keep walking," Isobel said. "If they have seen us, our stopping will alert them. Can you tell who they are, Matthias? They may be Macleod men."

"Nay, they carry twa banners, my lady, such as them the lad told me about."

"Two?"

"Aye, he said he didna ken either o' them. One bears a white cross."

Isobel looked over her shoulder, her gaze meeting Michael's. He said nothing, and the riders had disappeared toward Glenelg by the time their small party reached the shore. Turning toward the north end of the Kyle, they found Matthias's boat beached under trees where the lush woodland met the high-water mark.

Across the water and to their left, the village of Kyle Rhea lay peacefully in the midday sunlight, no more than a few scattered cottages near the shore.

Tossing Isobel's bundle into the bow of the coble,

Matthias said in the same voice he used when he spoke to Ian, "Get ye in, lad, and be ready t' hoist yon sail as soon as we launch her. Ye'll ha' t' be quick, ye ken."

Nodding, she obeyed without a word, moving agilely to the mast at the center of the boat. Noting Michael's look of astonishment as he watched her, she grinned at him, pulling knots free on the furled sail as she said, "I've been out in boats since I learned to walk, sir, so don't look so amazed. You can trust me to know what I'm doing."

"'Tis a gey stiff breeze," he said. "Blowing from the northeast, too."

"Aye, but a strong wind is what we need," she said, still smiling. "The current flows hard from the south, so a north wind will help us fight it as we row. Since we need go less than half a mile, I doubt we'll be swept into Loch Alsh."

"Keep your voice down, m'lady," Matthias warned quietly. "Ready, sir?"

"Aye," Michael said. "Let's away with her."

With that, they shoved the boat onto the water and jumped in, grabbing oars and using them to turn it toward the opposite shore as Isobel quickly hoisted the sail and whipped its line around the cleat. Getting in position to row was a scramble, but both men managed deftly and soon were pulling hard for the opposite shore. Each manned a pair of oars and put his back into his strokes, making Isobel wonder how Michael could stand such exertion when his body must still be fiery with pain.

She crouched between them by the mast in case the wind shifted and she had to turn the sail. The canvas billowed one moment and flapped noisily the next as the little boat tossed and rolled on the turbulent water, but they made steady headway.

Gripping the mast to keep from being thrown into the

water, and despite the icy spray and seawater that spilled over the gunwales, soaking her each time the boat pitched, Isobel inhaled the fresh sea air and grinned wider than ever. She loved being on the water, danger or no danger. Moreover, she mused, if the outlanders were watching, she could be confident that they would not suspect any "lad" who had hoisted a lug sail so neatly of being anyone they sought.

The coble boasted a stern rudder, but without a fourth person to man it, it was not much use, although Matthias took the first opportunity to fix it to its peg and tie it in position. With the wind and current so strong, and both men clearly experienced oarsmen, the sail was more useful than the rudder for such a short journey.

The current was fierce indeed, pushing north harder than the wind pushed south, but it was nevertheless not long before they beached on the opposite shore.

Michael was first out and extended a hand to Isobel. As she grasped it and stepped onto the thwart to jump out, Matthias exclaimed, "Look yonder!"

Looking over her shoulder, she saw a boat coming toward them at speed from Glenelg Bay with at least four oarsmen rowing hard.

Chapter 5

Jerking her hand from Michael's as she jumped, Isobel exclaimed, "If they saw you helping me, they'll guess I'm female!"

Matthias scrambled ashore to help Michael drag the coble onto the shingle, saying dryly, "They'll be sure of it now, seeing ye pull away like that. But, as few boats as there be on the water, I'm guessing they'll want a close look at each one."

"They're coming this way, and at a speed considerably greater than ours was," Michael said, eyeing the approaching boat with concern.

Matthias glanced narrow-eyed at it again. "Dinna fret, sir. If ye make haste t' the village, 'tis my guess they'll no catch ye there afore ye find help."

Isobel watched the oncoming boat. "By heaven," she exclaimed. "I believe they've misjudged the current or failed to consider the additional momentum of a boat carrying so much weight."

Complacently, Matthias said, "Aye, sure, I thought they would."

"Still, they're already coming about, so they won't be swept into Loch Alsh. We must hurry. Matthias is right, sir," she added. "The village will provide safety."

"Matthias had better come with us," Michael said.

"I will then, as far as the village," Matthias said. "I've a kinsman there who will row back wi' me, and the men in the village will tell those villains the boat belongs to the laird. I doubt they'll demand any answers from him."

Accordingly, they hurried along the shingle to the village, where Isobel requested an armed escort for herself and Michael to the home of MacDonald's kinsman, Donald Mòr Gowrie. Matthias made his own arrangements, and knowing they could trust the villagers to delay their pursuers, Isobel thanked him for his help and went confidently up Glen Kylerhea with Michael and their escort.

Michael watched Isobel stride up the narrow track with her bundle of female clothing slung jauntily over one shoulder, apparently perfectly at ease in her unfeminine garb. Ian's breeks fit tightly across her hips, and he found himself imagining what she would look like without them. Mentally taking himself to task for allowing his mind to wander, even down so enticing a path, he fixed it instead on what course they might take should this kinsman of Mac-Donald's refuse them assistance.

He soon learned that she had placed her confidence well, however. The journey up the glen to a square tower looming over the river took only thirty minutes, and their host received them in his hall. Donald Mòr Gowrie was a lean, salt-and-pepper-haired man of fifty summers with a long face and eyebrows so thick they jutted out over his eyes. He greeted Isobel with the warmth he might have accorded one of his own kinswomen, and she explained the situation to him briefly, showing a gift for glibness and a lack of detail that Michael appreciated more than she could know.

Gowrie remained silent as he looked from Isobel to Michael. Then, with a twinkle in his blue eyes, he said, "I warrant ye've no told me the whole tale, lass, and I'd supposed ye'd share our midday meal, but wi' such men after ye, ye'll no want to wait. I'll ha' ponies saddled and food packed, and take ye to me harbor at Loch Eishort. Ha' your pursuers their own boats, lad?"

"No, sir," Michael said. "That is, if they do, I am unaware of it."

"Well, no matter. First they'll ha' to learn where ye be, and folks here will say nowt to them, nor will the villagers." His eyes narrowed, and Michael knew he had let his skepticism show. "What makes ye think someone might speak o' ye?"

"The men following me have no scruples, sir. They are extremely dangerous."

"Even so, I'm guessing they willna want to anger the Lord of the Isles," Gowrie said. "I'm thinking, too, that they dinna ken who fosters our lass here."

Michael nodded but did not comment, aware that Macleod might have told Waldron about Hector but uncertain that it would make much difference if he had. To be sure, a foster daughter of Hector the Ferocious held value for Waldron only if he controlled her. That same foster daughter free of his clutches, protected, and traveling under the golden banner of the Lord of the Isles with its familiar little-black-ship device was another matter. However, her escape, not to mention Michael's own, would infuriate Waldron and thus make him more dangerous than ever.

"We should make speed, sir," Isobel said to Gowrie. "Our journey to Mull could easily take us twelve hours or more."

"Aye, lass, I'm willing," he replied, "but it'll take me lads a few minutes yet to saddle the ponies. Meanwhile, I'd suggest ye pay your respects to me lady wife and let her assist ye to change into more feminine garb for the journey if ye ha' some, unless o' course, ye mean to travel all the way home in them breeks."

Michael was astonished to see the lass redden and nibble her lower lip, but she rallied quickly.

"Thank you, sir," she said to Gowrie. "I'll do so at once."

Less than twenty minutes later, the cavalcade proceeded at a good pace up the glen. Gowrie rode with them, and a large contingent of armed men followed. The journey to the gray waters of Loch Eishort took less than thirty minutes, but when Michael noted aloud that the tide had not yet finished turning, Gowrie said curtly, "Ye'll no want t' be dawdling, lad. Me captains and oarsmen be always ready, lest his grace needs them, so they'll be off wi' ye at once, and God speed."

Seeing at least a dozen galleys and longboats in the harbor, Michael held his peace, and soon they were aboard one with three dozen well-armed oarsmen. Another with a similar number of men aboard was making ready nearby.

As Gowrie took leave of them, he said to Isobel, "I'm sending two boats to make sure ye arrive safely, lass. Shall I tell them to make for Duart or Lochbuie?"

She hesitated, then said, "Lochbuie is farther, but—"

"Sakes, twenty miles willna matter. Wi' the wind from the northeast, and as strong as it be, me lads will get plenty o' rest, and I'll ha' them break their return journey at Ardtornish to see if his grace has commands for them."

"Then tell them to make for Lochbuie if you please, sir. I'd as lief not have to explain all this to Lachlan Lubanach and then again to Hector."

"I warrant ye would not," he agreed, laughing. "Ye're a braw lassie, m'lady. I'd be that proud to ha' ye for me own daughter. 'Gainsay who dare!'"

They got underway then, and as the galleys neared the mouth of the loch and the open sea, the helmsman's beat increased their speed.

Michael faced Isobel in the bow, his seat on the port side of the stem post, hers on the steerboard side. He still wore Matthias's jerkin and shirt, but she wore her blue riding dress and gray cloak again. He did not try to talk to her, because with the noise of the helmsman's gong, the wind rattling the sail against its mast, and the rhythmic slap and splash of the oars, conversation would be difficult at best.

As their journey progressed, Isobel huddled in her cloak, clearly unable to sleep, and Michael recalled that by the time they had beached near Kyle Rhea village, she had been wetter than either he or Matthias. His protective instincts stirred, and he wondered if her sister's warnings echoed in her ears as they did in his.

Isobel pulled her cloak tight around her, wishing she had worn a warmer gown than her old blue stuff one for her ride the previous morning. The galley's high bow offered some protection, but the chill of the northeast wind came from behind them.

She was so tired that even the chilly sea air could not keep her awake. Her head kept falling to one side, waking her when it struck the gunwale or when fear that it might startled her awake. At last, though, exhaustion claimed her.

When she stirred to wakefulness again, her head seemed to have found a comfortable spot, and she felt warmer, so doubtless someone had draped an extra sail or heavy cloak over her. Drowsily, she realized that the cacophony of splashing, flapping, and clanging had ended. All she heard now was the wind, intermittent creaking of the mast, and the hushing sound of waves breaking around the galley.

Without opening her eyes, she knew that the oarsmen had shipped their oars, letting the strong wind blow the boat along while they rested.

A gull's cry sounded as if it came from only a few feet away.

Blearily, she opened one eye, expecting to see Michael sitting across from her as he had been when she fell asleep, but he was not there. Instead, she saw two gulls flying alongside the galley, hopeful of food. She stirred more, and the object she leaned against stirred as well. Startled, she sat up with a jerk.

Michael smiled drowsily at her. She had been sleeping with her head against his broad chest, his right arm around her shoulders.

"Close your mouth, lass," he murmured. "Did you enjoy your nap?"

"Faith, sir, what are you doing?" she demanded. "I hardly know you!"

"You did not let that disturb you last night," he said.

Her eyes widened. "What are you talking about?"

"You curled up next to me and slept like a kitten," he said.

"I did not!"

"Aye, you did. I awoke before you and got up when I

heard your sister approaching the hut. Had I not, she would have been able to tell you so herself."

Isobel shuddered at the thought and glanced warily at the oarsmen. Michael had spoken quietly, however, and with their backs to the bow, none of the men paid them any heed. If the helmsman had seen them, he showed no sign of it.

"I was afraid you'd topple off the bench in your sleep," Michael went on. "If you had, you might have hurt yourself, so I decided that only a villain would allow that to happen when he could so easily prevent it."

"Aye, by waking me!" She glanced at the oarsmen again, then the helmsman. The latter's apparent lack of interest no longer fooled her. He had undoubtedly taken notice when Michael switched seats to hold her, and might easily tell the others. "Only think of what they will say about this!" she exclaimed, gesturing toward the men.

"Nay, for Gowrie told me his men are discreet," he said. "You trust him. Why should I not?"

"Even so," she muttered.

He turned her to face him, looking directly into her eyes. "Tell the truth now, lass," he said. "Do you really know so little of me?"

"How can you think otherwise? We met only yesterday. I do not even know your whole name."

"Nonetheless, you do know me," he said. "And I know you. I feel as comfortable with you after these two days as I would if I'd known you all my life."

Oddly, she felt the same, but it was daft to feel so about a man she scarcely knew and one, moreover, who had required constant direction—until now. At the moment, though, the way he held her, making her look at him, stirred unfamiliar sensations that she could not define. But she did not try to pull away.

"What can you know of me besides my name?" she asked, wondering why she sounded breathless even to her own ears, and why his smile—faith, just his voice—stirred her senses so.

"I know that you are a beautiful woman with an adventurous spirit, that you face life boldly, and that you don't let adversity daunt you. I would have us be friends, lass. I have not so many that I cannot use one more."

"I suppose we could be friends," she said, relaxing and wondering how a person could feel relief and disappointment at the same time.

He pulled her closer, murmuring, "I have wanted to do this since I awoke this morning, and now that we have agreed to be friends . . ."

Although a voice in the back of her mind shouted at her to resist, she did not. She did nothing to encourage him either, staring into his eyes as his face came closer and closer until he kissed her.

With a moan, she melted against him, letting him embrace her as his lips explored hers, tasting them softly, gently, until she could think of nothing else. His arms tightened around her, and her awareness of the other men vanished as she savored the sensations that his touch stirred throughout her body.

Never before had she felt so free of authority. That sensation alone was heady, encouraging her to press harder against him, to put her arms around him.

The tip of his tongue stroked first her upper lip, then the lower one. One of his hands slipped beneath her cloak and began gently stroking her back. When her lips parted, his tongue darted inside, and the moan that escaped her then sounded loud to her. She stiffened, certain that at least some of the others must have heard.

"Gently, sweetheart," he murmured against her lips. "Don't leap out of your skin, or they'll think I'm forcing you, and that would not do at all."

She wanted to say that he *was* forcing her, that somehow he had rendered her both witless and unable to defend herself. It was certainly not the first stolen kiss she had enjoyed, but none of the quick pecks on a cheek or friendly busses on her lips had stimulated her senses the way this one did.

Without looking away, he released her gently and straightened her hood, retying the ribbons at the neck of her cloak as if that were the only reason he had turned her to face him, as if such movements would fool for one minute any of the men supposedly not watching them. Trying to glower at him, to let him and them, too, know that she disapproved of his methods, she discovered when she saw the twinkle in his eyes that she wanted to laugh instead.

"Don't look at me like that, sweetheart, unless you want me to do it again," he murmured, his eyes still dancing.

Straightening, she struggled to regain her dignity, saying sternly—at least, she hoped she sounded stern—"You have taken a great liberty, sir. I would warn you to have a care. And you must certainly *not* call me 'sweetheart.'"

"You are right to warn me, lass, but you do invite such liberties, you know."

She opened her mouth to tell him he was daft to think such a thing, but when his eyes narrowed as if he welcomed the chance to argue with her, she shut it without saying a word. He was right, and she knew it.

She knew, too, what Hector and her sister would say about the risk she had run by interfering in the scene at the cave, particularly since she had been alone. Despite Cristina's habit of taking solitary rides before she married

Hector, both she and her formidable husband would surely agree that Isobel should never do such a thing. The freedom she constantly sought, and often demanded for herself, was not common to young women of her station in life. Indeed, at Lochbuie, she never rode alone. She did so at Chalamine only because she could safely ignore her father's commands. She dared not ignore Hector Reaganach's.

"Relax, lass," Michael said. "'Tis better, I think, if you go back to sleep. We'll soon enter the Sound of Mull, and the wind is so strong that the helmsman has said he expects us to make Lochbuie Bay shortly after Compline."

She shook her head. "I am rested, sir. Moreover, these men will require supper before they leave Lochbuie, and they will spend the night, and—"

"Gowrie said they carry their own rations and need sleep only a few hours on the beach before departing for Ardtornish," he said. "Their mission is to make sure you arrive safely, nothing more."

She nodded but insisted that he return to his former seat. Nor did she sleep, wanting to be certain both galleys passed Ardtornish Castle, seat of the Lord of the Isles, and Duart Castle, the seat of Lachlan Lubanach, without stopping.

She had never been more sincere than in telling Gowrie she did not want to explain the situation more than once, so it was not until they had left the Sound of Mull behind them that she let herself doze for the rest of the journey.

Despite the late hour when the oarsmen rowed into Lochbuie Bay, the sun was just sinking below the western horizon, painting the waves in the bay with fading rays of golden light. At this season, the dusk that followed would linger past midnight.

As usual, numerous galleys and longships rested at anchor in the harbor, but their own boats put in alongside the long stone-and-timber pier, and as they did, Isobel saw a surge of activity on the ramparts of the castle at the top of the rise.

Soon men descended the hill, the guardsmen above having easily recognized MacDonald's little-black-ship banner.

Within moments, Isobel was thanking Gowrie's men and happily greeting the Lochbuie welcoming party, most of whom were old friends she had counted as family for years. She introduced Michael as a cousin from the north desiring to pay his respects to the Laird of Lochbuie, thus giving her excellent reason to return home betimes.

If a few skeptical looks greeted this explanation, she paid them no heed, knowing none of her audience would question her—not so publicly, at all events.

Gowrie's men saw to their galleys, lowering the sails and putting up the oars for the night in racks along the centerline of the pier, as Isobel led the way to the castle where she had spent the happiest years of her life, with Michael a step behind her. Certain as she was that Hector and Cristina would understand the necessity for bringing him to Mull, she was nonetheless a bit nervous about explaining it to them.

Michael had been quiet for some time, and she wondered if it had occurred to him that Hector was likely to be impatient with his secrets and demand a full and immediate explanation of the incident at the cave.

"Lass," he said so quietly that the word reached her ears alone as they neared the castle entrance, "about that tale you spun Donald Mòr Gowrie . . ." He hesitated.

"Aye, what about it?"

"We cannot employ such a strategy with Hector Reaganach."

Impatience stirred, and not for the first time. The man

was as handsome as any she had ever met—more handsome than any mortal man should be. Moreover, he was exactly the sort of man she had always insisted she would prefer a man to be. He listened to her when she spoke, never dismissed her opinions or showed the typical masculine tendency to patronize or correct her. Indeed, he seemed not to have a domineering bone in his body. So why, she wondered, did he so often stir a desire to box his ears, shake him, and demand that he think for himself?

With more patience than she felt, she said, "I am not such a noddy, sir!"

"I never meant to imply that you were," he said, his voice still low and calm. "It just occurred to me that since you did spin that tale, and since Hector is likely to meet Gowrie at some point in the future—mayhap quite soon—"

"Aye, sir, and for that very reason I shall tell him exactly what I said to Gowrie. Indeed, I mean to tell him everything that happened. He will perfectly understand why I told Gowrie as little as possible, I promise you."

"I hope so, but I fear he may not as perfectly understand why you have done me the honor to concern yourself so deeply in my affairs."

"Of course he will," she said. "I have only to tell him exactly what happened to us. Gowrie's men will say naught of what hap—"

"Aye, lass, but will he listen?" He spoke louder, and she cast a guilty glance at the Lochbuie men nearest them, realizing that she had nearly said more than she should. But the men were talking amongst themselves and paid little heed to her or to Michael, who added, "I have grown increasingly certain these past hours that I shall walk into the hall at Lochbuie beside you only to hear Hector order me cast into a dungeon or carried off to the nearest hanging tree."

"Hereabouts," Isobel said dulcetly, "felons who deserve such punishments are cast from the highest cliff to certain death in the sea."

"Just so," he said. "I must say, though, that that information does not reassure me." He sounded serious, but she saw his lips twitch.

Then, as their eyes met, he smiled, and as always, his smile warmed her to her bones. Her impatience melted, but she shook her head and said, "I do wish you would hearten yourself more, sir. Indeed, I do not know how you get on in life when you are always so sure the worst will happen. Why, you put me forcibly in mind of Adela when you speak like that."

"Do I? Is that such a dreadful thing?"

"Of course not. I just wish you would be more resolute."

"Do you want me to explain our coming here?"

"No, no, I'll do that," she said. "I know exactly how to manage Hector. I do hope, though, that he and Cristina are alone tonight, because it will be best if I can make things clear to him at once. Rory," she said, raising her voice to draw the attention of the nearest guardsman, "the laird *is* at home, is he not?"

"Aye, m'lady, and he said for ye to go straight to the hall. That is to say, he told us to bring whoever be sailing into the bay under his grace's banner to him straightway. I'm thinking he'll be that glad to see it be yourself."

Assuming from those words that Hector and Cristina were alone, she saw no reason to stir curiosity among his men by asking if they were. That she heard no minstrels or chatter as she hurried up the narrow, winding stone stairway to the great hall reinforced that assumption, so she entered that cavernous chamber confidently with Michael just behind her, only to stop a step later in sharp dismay.

Except for one gillie who tended the roaring fire on the great hooded hearth in the east wall near the candlelit dais at the far end, the lower hall was dark and empty, but the dais certainly was not.

Despite the hour, Hector and Cristina lingered at the high table, but they had moved from their customary places midway along the board to the end near the fire, and they were not alone. Four others sat with them. Lachlan Lubanach and his wife, Mairi of the Isles, sat with their backs to Isobel, but she recognized both instantly. Facing her were her aunt, Lady Euphemia Macleod, and Lady Mairi's mother, the princess Margaret Stewart, daughter of Robert, High King of Scots.

"Mercy, Isobel, is that you?" Cristina exclaimed, jumping up and peering toward her through the lower hall's gloom. "I'm delighted to see you, darling, but what are you doing here days before your time? Is aught amiss at Chalamine?"

Michael had almost run into the lass when she stopped so abruptly. Glancing at her, he saw that she had paled, but she regained her composure quickly and, hurrying forward, said, "Nay, Cristina, all is well, and Father is preparing to travel north with the girls—and Adela, too, I hope. I am sorry if our unexpected arrival startled you into thinking otherwise. I did not mean to frighten you."

Michael noted that she glanced more than once at the large man who rose to stand beside Lady Cristina, and he easily recognized Hector Reaganach. Not until the others turned toward them did he recognize Hector's twin brother,

Lachlan Lubanach, Lord High Admiral of the Isles, and Lachlan's lady, Mairi of the Isles.

Then, to his further surprise, he saw that the woman sitting across from Mairi was her mother. He had no idea who the thin, middle-aged lady next to Princess Margaret was, but it had already become abundantly clear to him that matters were about to become more complicated than either he or Lady Isobel had anticipated.

Hector opened his mouth, but the lady next to Princess Margaret forestalled him, saying, "Really, Isobel, you are growing to be quite as thoughtless as our Mariota used to be. You ought to have known that it would frighten Cristina to see you so unexpectedly and at such an hour. What else was any of us to think but that you'd brought bad news from Chalamine? And who is that fellow with you? Surely, you did not travel so far with only a manservant to look after you. So inappropriate! Wherever is your maidservant?"

Hector's steady gaze shifted to Michael, stirring a chill of guilty discomfort that he had not felt since before his father's death. He straightened his shoulders much as he would have in older times, bracing himself to meet that look, and for the first time since leaving Glenelg, he gave thought to his clothing, wishing he had had something other than a shepherd's shirt and jerkin to wear with his breeks.

Isobel dismissed her lack of a maid with an impatient gesture, saying, "Michael is not a manservant, Aunt Euphemia."

"Then who is he, lass?" Hector asked in a deceptively calm voice.

"He . . . he is Michael, sir," she said, evidently realizing that anything more she might say about a man she called only Michael would be insufficient to satisfy them. "If you will let me explain, I can make everything clear."

"When did you last eat?" Cristina demanded.

Again, the lass dismissed the question with a gesture as she replied, "Sometime around midday, but that does not matter, because I must tell you—"

"Come and sit down, Isobel," Hector said in a voice that brooked no refusal. "Take that seat beside Mairi. As to your companion, I'd prefer to talk to him without your explanations. You will not mind engaging in a brief conversation with me, will you, lad? Privately, and at once?"

"I welcome the opportunity, my lord," Michael said, belatedly remembering his manners and bowing to the table at large.

He nearly made a separate bow to Princess Margaret but decided against it, since no one had made him known to her. He had seen Hector and Lachlan more than once before, but no one had ever formally presented him to them, either, and he doubted that they would remember his presence at any of several overcrowded events they had chanced to attend at one time or another.

Hector crossed the dais, saying, "We'll adjourn to another chamber, I think."

"Do you want me?" Lachlan asked, raising an eyebrow.

"I'd prefer that you stay here," Hector said. "Isobel, your transport consisted of two of his grace's galleys, did it not?"

"Yes, sir, but the men will rest and leave by morning. I *can* explain," she added.

"I have no doubt that you can, and your oarsmen are welcome to camp below, but I still want a word with your companion before you explain anything. You may order food whilst I talk with him, but first tell me from whom you had those ships."

"From Donald Mòr Gowrie of Kyle Rhea," she answered.

He nodded. "Very well. Welcome home, lassie. I neglected to say I'm glad to see you, but you need have no doubt of that. Sit down now. We'll not be long."

Michael waited patiently as Hector stepped from the dais and came toward him. He had always thought himself a tall man, but Hector the Ferocious was both taller and broader. With a touch of relief Michael noted that he was not carrying the legendary Clan Gillean battle-axe that men said accompanied him everywhere.

"Isobel, do you not think that you should change your dress?" Lady Euphemia asked. "You have been traveling all day, child, and you look it."

Michael watched Hector.

Lady Cristina, chuckling, said, "She has no need to change, Aunt Euphemia. I want to hear all the news from home. Ivor," she said to the gillie at the hearth, "pray tell them in the kitchen that Lady Isobel has come home with a guest. Ask them to bring supper for them both straightaway."

"Aye, m'lady."

Hector's gaze had not left Michael, and Michael was aware that Lachlan likewise kept his eyes on him, as did Isobel and doubtless the others as well.

Hector gestured toward a doorway in the west wall. "We'll talk yonder, lad."

Michael nodded, realizing that he was to precede him, which told him that Hector did not trust him. Although under the circumstances he could scarcely blame the man, the knowledge did give him pause. The next few minutes, no matter what conversation took place, were bound to be uncomfortable.

Since the lass had kept her dirk, he lacked even a weapon to protect himself, not that he would attack any man in his own castle, or that he could be certain he would prevail against Hector the Ferocious. To be sure, Hector was nearly fifty years old and doubtless no longer as skilled as when he had acquired his nickname, but he wielded sufficient power to be a formidable adversary, and Michael had already drawn more enemies than any man could want. He wanted no more.

Hector followed him into a small chamber containing little more than a heavy table, two joint stools, and a back stool—clearly a room where he dealt with lesser men. Shutting the door, he moved to the far side of the table, folded his powerful arms across his chest and said sternly, "Now, lad, suppose you tell me what game you've been playing, traveling about with Lady Isobel as you have?"

In the most diffident manner of which he was capable, Michael said, "I give you my word, my lord, that her ladyship suffered no ill at my hands. I found myself in great jeopardy, and Lady Isobel risked her own safety to intervene. Fortunately, we were able to escape and, with Gowrie's help, we came directly here. That is all."

"Is it?"

Hector spoke the two words gently, but they stirred a tingling chill at the base of Michael's spine. Clearing his throat, he said, "Mayhap you would like to ask me something more, my lord."

"Aye, I would," Hector said. "Does the lass ken who you are?"

His warning tone told Michael that it was past time to speak plainly.

"No, my lord. Without knowing whom else she might tell, I deemed it safer under the circumstances not to tell her. I collect, though, that you do know me."

"Aye, of course I do."

"Does Lachlan Lubanach also know?"

"I believe so. Of the two of us, it is my business to know such things so that he need not concern himself, but instinct tells me that he also recognized you."

"I have never formally met either of you," Michael said.

"So you assumed you could continue to play your game here, did you?"

Feeling a sudden, urgent need to prevent his believing that for a moment longer, Michael said, "You misunderstood me, sir. I meant only that since no one had ever formally introduced us and since we've attended but three or four large gatherings in common, I hoped I might have a short time in which to weigh what options I had before confiding the little I know about this matter to anyone here."

He realized that he had braced himself again for censure or worse, and tried to relax, but Hector did not berate him. Instead, he stood for a long moment, gazing at him thoughtfully, until Michael, accustomed to more volatile men, began to wish he would speak.

At last, with a slight smile that was anything but reassuring, Hector said, "I believe that your own actions have limited whatever options you may have had."

"Have they, sir?"

"Aye, because they've left you no choice now. You'll have to marry the lass."

"I believe—"

Indeed, sir," Michael said sincerely, "I have no objection to
marrying Lady Isobel if she will agree to it. I believe she'd
make me an excellent wife, because she is the most intrepid
woman I've ever met, the most fascinating, and the most
beautiful. But she has made it abundantly plain that she has
no wish to marry, ever."

"You can safely leave it to me to persuade her otherwise."

Unable to resist, Michael smiled as he said, "She tells me
she knows exactly how to manage you, sir."

Hector chuckled, surprising him. "Does she now? Well,
we'll see."

Relaxing, astonished at the sense of satisfaction those
words gave him, Michael said, "May we sit, sir? I own, my
energy tonight is not what it usually is."

"We've no need to dally here any longer," Hector said. "I
wanted to speak to you privately only because, once Isobel
made it plain that she either could not or would not identify
you properly, I wanted to forestall any inclination you
might have had to deceive us and to learn what had brought

you to such a pass. You must tell us, you know, but you may elect to tell me now, or speak openly to us all."

"I believe—"

Hector stopped him with a gesture. "I'd advise the latter course because I have no secrets from my brother and few from my wife. Lachlan and I likewise trust Mairi. And as to Lady Euphemia, we can send her to her chamber if you like, but for all that she may seem like a chattering magpie, she is not."

"I will reveal as much as I can to you, sir, and as much as you think I should to the others," Michael said. "I still believe, however, that Lady Isobel, and indeed the other ladies, should know as little as possible, lest my enemies come to believe the women know what they want to know. When they learn that I have been here, as they will, they may suspect everyone here of having that information."

Hector frowned. "Just who are these enemies of yours?"

"One is my cousin Waldron of Edgelaw."

"I do not know him."

"He's the bastard son of one of my father's cousins, who sent him to be raised in France with a branch of our family there before allowing his return to Edgelaw, near Roslin, about ten years ago. Waldron resents our wealth and his baser position, despite the generosity of my father and his cousin, and now that of my brother. He believes he can improve his estate by aiding a greater enemy of ours."

"And that enemy . . ."

"The Kirk of Rome," Michael said. "Apparently, his Holiness Pope Urban—like Pope Gregory before him—and certain others, as well, believes that something was taken from the Kirk that must be returned."

"Sakes, lad, stop talking in riddles! What did you take?"

"I took naught, sir, for the incident happened nearly a century ago. Indeed, I do not even know exactly what is missing," Michael added. "I've known all my life that we guarded a secret, but my father died before telling us what it is. Rumor suggests, however, that great treasure is involved, and my cousin thinks I know its location, but I swear to you on my honor that I do not have the slightest notion."

"I see," Hector said. "In that case, I understand your concern, but we must get back to the others soon, or they will all be down upon us. Not even my brother possesses enough patience to sit out there quietly whilst you and I discuss this matter more thoroughly. We will talk more of it, however. That I promise you."

"Aye, sir, I'm agreeable. I could use a strong ally in this business."

"Have you no friends involved in it now?"

"The only one who knows or suspects the whole is my cousin Hugo Robison, who is presently in Kintail. I arranged to get word to him, so I expect he'll turn up here tomorrow or the next day. I . . . I let Lady Isobel think him a servant of mine."

"I see," Hector said. "You may come to regret much of what you led her to believe. However, I'll let you deal with that. For now, I suggest you tell us all how you came to meet her, what you can of how she aided you, and what exactly brought you here. You should be able to negotiate any obstacles that arise in discussing those points, and I'll help you where I can. If you step into truly deep water, I'll end the discussion. And, sithee, lad, if the Kirk be involved in this, I agree that the less our womenfolk ken of your treasure the better it will be for us all."

Michael nodded, relieved.

"We'll have to tell them who you are, though, and that straightaway."

"Yes, sir."

"Since I'll tell Lachlan all that you have told me, you should know that he is likely to want to take part in any future talks we have."

"I have no objection to that."

"Then you and I are agreed on the matter of your marriage to Isobel, but what of your family? Might they have objections?"

Meeting that stern gaze, Michael said dryly, "My brother may have other plans for me, sir. He often does, but I have not seen him in months, nor have we discussed any alliance in particular. In any event, I am my own man. The decision as to whom I shall marry will be mine."

Hector's eyes twinkled. "You put me in mind of myself at your age, lad. However, Sir Henry is your liege lord, is he not?"

"Aye," Michael said. "And, as such, he commands my loyalty. But I made it plain to him long ago that I would choose my own bride. Whether he chooses to recall that or not may prove another matter, but it can make no difference. Indeed, my mother will be more difficult than Henry, but I have as much confidence in my ability to manage her as Isobel had when she said she could manage you. I'll wager my record speaks better for itself, though," he added with another smile.

"Very well, then," Hector said, offering his hand. "Now we have only to inform Isobel of the great honor in store for her."

Michael followed his host back into the hall, but although he smiled as he thought about Isobel, he could not pretend to be as confident as Hector.

The lass had made her position clear.

Earlier, when Hector and Michael left the hall, Isobel had watched them go, lending only half an ear as Cristina explained that Princess Margaret had accompanied Mairi and Lachlan because MacDonald was ailing and they were unsure that he would be able to travel north with them to celebrate the installation of the new Prince of Orkney.

Mairi said, "Because it is to be such a grand occasion, if he cannot attend, we are agreed that she will go with us to represent him. And since we had already planned to spend the night here tonight, she elected to come with us." Smiling at Isobel, she added, "I think it is delightful that you were able to return whilst we are here, my dear. We've missed you dreadfully."

"Did you think to ask someone to bring up your baggage?" Cristina asked.

"I brought none," Isobel said with a shrug as she returned Mairi's smile. "I had no opportunity to pack, Cristina, because one doesn't during an adventure. I mean to tell you all about it, but we should wait until Hector and Michael return."

"He is very handsome, your Michael," Mairi said.

"Mairi!" Cristina exclaimed as Isobel gasped.

"Mercy on us all, madam," Lady Euphemia said in the same breath, "I trust you are jesting. Our Isobel is not so lost to her own worth as to think we would let her marry a man like that. Why, he is . . ." She hesitated, clearly at a loss.

"He is one of the handsomest men I've ever clapped eyes on," Mairi said. Twinkling at her husband, she added, "Not counting anyone here, of course."

"I should hope not," Lachlan retorted with a loving

smile. The smile vanished, however, as he turned to Isobel and said, "Where did you meet him, lass?"

Having been about to declare that she had no intention of marrying anyone, let alone Michael, Isobel recognized the same deceptively gentle tone in Lachlan's voice that she had heard so often in Hector's. Stifling the denial on her tongue, she said politely, "Near Glenelg, sir."

"When?"

Wishing she had the nerve to tell him it was none of his business, or even that she did not want to have to explain everything twice, she said, "Yesterday."

"Yesterday!" Cristina and Lady Euphemia exclaimed in one voice.

Unable to suppress her resentment, she glowered at Lachlan but relaxed a little when she detected a twinkle in his eyes. She braced herself nonetheless, knowing that he had opened the door to sharper interrogation.

Cristina and Lady Euphemia both began talking at once, whereupon Lady Euphemia said apologetically, "I beg your pardon, my dear Cristina. I know that I should hold my tongue. She is your sister *and* your foster daughter, of course, so you should be the one to demand that she explain herself."

Before Cristina could do so, Mairi interjected with a laugh, "Have mercy on the poor child, both of you. Would you force her to explain everything to us now only to have to repeat it all as soon as Hector and her Michael return?"

"I warrant Hector is getting the full tale as we wait," Lachlan said dryly.

"Not if he knows what is good for him, he isn't," the wife of his bosom said roundly. "I want to hear it all without anything left out. Come and sit beside me, child," she added. "I have much to tell you, and I want to hear all about your sisters. How does Adela fare? Has she tired yet of running your father's household?"

Isobel sighed, fearing that tempers would rise before the night was over and feeling grateful for Michael's milder temperament. Even as she reassured herself, however, she wondered how he could possibly defend himself against four such unyielding personalities—five if one counted Lady Euphemia, as indeed one had to these days. She had long since abandoned the meek, overly compliant disposition she had assumed years before, while living in her brother's household at Chalamine.

Mairi soon turned the conversation to her children and those of Hector and Cristina, reciting for Isobel a number of amusing things they had done during her absence. In this manner the time passed swiftly until Hector and Michael returned.

As the two approached the dais, Isobel tried to judge how much Michael had suffered from whatever Hector had said to him. He gazed directly at her, but although he smiled and appeared to be his usual calm self, he did look a bit wary.

Hector, however, was smiling broadly. He walked up to Isobel and rested a hand gently on her right shoulder as he said to the others, "I have excellent news for you. Sir Michael St. Clair, Master of Roslin and brother to Sir Henry St. Clair, soon to be installed as Prince of Orkney, has done Isobel the great honor of asking for her hand in marriage. I have agreed, and they will therefore be married as soon as we can make the arrangements."

"No," Isobel gasped, attempting to jump to her feet and set matters right.

Hector's hand remained firm on her shoulder, holding her in place.

Long experience having taught her that it was useless, even foolhardy, to defy him, she simmered but remained obediently still, biting her tongue to keep from shouting at them all that they could not coerce her into marriage, not to any man.

Lachlan arose, held out his hand to Michael, and said in a reflective tone, "I thought you looked familiar, St. Clair." Then, looking with barely concealed amusement at Isobel, he added, "'Tis a good match you propose, but I'm guessing that our lass here did not even know your proper name until now."

"Nay, my lord, she did not," Michael admitted, also looking at her.

Isobel did not trust herself to meet his gaze. She wanted to leap up and tell him, and Hector, too, exactly what she thought of such an absurd proposal, but with Hector's iron hand still clamped to her shoulder, that option was out of the question. She noted that Cristina stared at her as if she would like to say something, but she remained silent, too, so Isobel knew she would gain no support from that quarter.

The news had apparently rendered Lady Euphemia speechless.

Even Mairi, for once, was silent.

"Sit down, lad," Hector said genially, indicating the place next to Lachlan as he took his own seat at the end of the table, thus neatly using his brother and Mairi to separate Isobel and Michael. "I know you have much to tell us, but first I should present you properly to the Princess Margaret, and to my lady wife and my brother's wife, as well—and to Lady Euphemia Macleod, my lady's aunt."

Lady Euphemia, finding her tongue at last, said, "To be sure, we are honored to meet you, Sir Michael, but I hope you will forgive my bewilderment—indeed, *our* bewilderment.

For how can this be, Isobel?" she added, shifting her gaze from Michael to her grandniece. "Indeed, since you traveled here together today without benefit of any other female to lend even a semblance of propriety to your journey, we must be glad that you traveled with a man who desires to take you to wife, but 'tis nonetheless quite improper and all very sudden. Is it not?" she asked the others in general. "I do not even want to think of what Murdo will say to this!"

Isobel nearly smiled at the expression on Michael's face as he remembered that she had a father, and one, moreover, who would most likely have a good deal to say about the suggested marriage of his daughter to a man he did not know.

Turning to Hector, she said stiffly, "You cannot suppose that my father will be pleased about this notion of yours, sir. Surely, he must give his permission."

Hector's eyes narrowed in that annoying way they had when something she said or did, or the tone she used, stirred his displeasure, but this time she did not care. He was trying to dictate her future, and she had every right to speak her mind on that subject. She held his gaze until, surprisingly, his expression softened.

Gently, he said, "When your father agreed that you should foster here, lass, part of that agreement was that I should bear the responsibility of providing you with a suitable husband. Thus, he has already given his permission, and since he has declared more than once that we have spoiled you beyond reason, I doubt he will be much amazed to learn that you have chosen your own husband."

"But I didn't!"

"Aye, but you did, Isobel," Lachlan said. "Whatever were you thinking, to travel here in a galley full of men with Sir Michael as your sole protector?"

As she tried to think how best to answer him, several servants entered from the buttery behind the dais, carrying trays, and with a frowning glance at them, Hector said, "We will discuss that journey further after the lads have served Isobel and Michael their supper. Then, I think, we will let them begin at the beginning so that we can hear the whole tale."

He waited only until Isobel and Michael had trenchers, platters of meat and vegetables, and goblets of claret before them. Then, dismissing the servants, he said, "The hour grows late, so I would ask that we begin now, and with you, Sir Michael, since doubtless you ken more about what happened than the lass does."

"Aye, sir, somewhat more, but I can tell you only that I was visiting a friend in Kintail, who told me of a cavern in the vicinity. I have long had an interest in such places, so when I awoke betimes yesterday morning, I went in search of it. I had just come upon its entrance when six men descended upon me, took me captive, and demanded that I give them certain information that I do not possess. They were expressing their disbelief of that fact when Lady Isobel providentially intervened."

"What information?" Mairi asked.

"Just one moment," Hector said. "How did you come to intervene, Isobel?"

A silence fell, and Isobel stared at the trencher of food before her, wishing that Michael had taken longer to reach her part in their adventure.

Lady Euphemia said with a sigh, "You know perfectly well how that came about, my lord. Out riding alone, she was, I'll warrant, just as she always does at Chalamine—aye, and as you did, too, Cristina. Do not claim that you did not."

"No, Aunt Euphemia, I shan't deny it," Cristina said. "Usually it is perfectly safe. What happened, Isobel?"

Sending a grateful look her way, Isobel said with feeling, "They were whipping him! They had tied him by his arms, stretched him between two trees, and torn off his shirt. His screams drew me to them. They were horrid, all six of them!"

"Merciful heavens," Mairi exclaimed. "You confronted six men by yourself?"

"Aye, sure, for they were on Macleod land," Isobel said. "But when I ordered them to stop, they hustled us both deep into that dreadful cave, tied us up, and left us there whilst they went to see if I'd left a party of armed men anywhere nearby."

"You certainly should have had an escort," Lachlan said sternly.

"Let her get on with her tale," Mairi said. "Obviously, you escaped them."

Michael smiled. "We did indeed, madam, thanks to her ladyship."

"Thanks to Hector," Isobel said, smiling at that gentleman. "I had the dirk you gave me, sir, when I turned thirteen—in its sheath on my leg. The only difficulty lay in getting my hands on it with my arms bound behind me and my ankles tied."

"Faith, how did you accomplish such a feat?" Lachlan demanded.

Cristina laughed. "Do not tell me you can still contort yourself as you did years ago when you startled poor Kate out of her liver and lights!"

Isobel smiled at Michael and received a smile in return when she said, "It is astonishing what one can do when fear drives her. I thought I heard them returning."

Between the two of them they related nearly all that had happened, including the tale Isobel had told Donald Mòr Gowrie, omitting only the interlude between them on the ship. "So you see," she concluded as she came to the end, "anyone would understand that we did only what necessity demanded. Therefore, no good reason exists for me to marry Michael even if I did travel with him."

"*Sir* Michael," Hector reminded her gently.

She saw Cristina grimace and exchange a look with Mairi.

Princess Margaret had not said a word beyond an occasional exclamation of astonishment or horror, but it was she who said now, "You must know that is not the case, Isobel. Word travels with amazing speed here in the Isles, my dear, and you can be sure that everyone will soon hear of your adventures if only because news having anything to do with the new Prince of Orkney simply leaps from every tongue."

"But Gowrie's men will say nothing! They won't, not even about—"

Realizing she had allowed herself to say more than she had intended, she stopped abruptly. Glancing toward Michael, she was not surprised to see him tilt his head down and put a hand over his eyes. He appeared to be biting his lower lip.

"About what?" Hector prompted.

"Nothing," she muttered. "It was nothing."

"I do not agree," Michael said gently. "Not at all."

"I see," Hector said.

"Well, it doesn't matter," Isobel said grimly. "I won't be made to marry anyone. I am sorry, madam," she said hastily to Margaret. "I do not mean any disrespect to you, but the law of the Isles will support me. No one can force a woman to marry if she does not want to do so."

"That is true throughout Scotland, my dear," Margaret said. "But you are not thinking clearly, because brutal reality is quite another matter. If people believe, as they will—and, everyone, pray forgive me for putting this so bluntly—if they learn that you have spent time alone with Sir Michael, not just in that galley, coming here, but also in the wee hut you spoke so casually about . . ." She paused, then added in a rush, "In plain words, you have admitted spending the night with this young man, sleeping in the same bed with him for all we know, and as a result, no other reputable man will want you, because your reputation for chastity will be shattered."

"But I don't want a man," Isobel protested.

"Oh, but that is not all that the loss of one's reputation means," Cristina said. "You do enjoy going to court, Isobel, and taking part in other social activities. But if we allowed you to do so after this particular adventure of yours, people would be shocked and offended. They would say horrible things to you, and to us."

"Then I won't go anywhere," Isobel declared. "I'd rather be ruined than married, and that's the plain truth of the matter. I don't want a husband forever telling me what to do, what to say, and how to think!"

"Is that what you think husbands do?" Lachlan asked.

"Isn't it what most of them *try* to do?" his wife asked demurely.

A look from him silenced her, but he, too, said no more.

Hector said, "You would have to miss the prince's installation, Isobel."

"I don't care!"

Michael cleared his throat. "Forgive me, all of you, but I will have no part in forcing myself upon an unwilling bride. I am more than willing to marry Lady Isobel if she will agree to it, but I will not abet any scheme to force her agreement."

Feeling tears prick her eyes, Isobel stood up, bobbed a curtsy in the general direction of Princess Margaret, and turned blindly toward the stairway, saying gruffly, "Since the matter is now settled, I will bid you all a good night."

She got only a few steps away before Hector said sternly, "Not just yet, lass."

She stopped but did not turn.

He was beside her the next moment. "We're going to have a talk, you and I," he said, urging her toward the same doorway through which he had taken Michael.

Michael watched her go, marveling at the gentleness in the huge man walking beside her. Although men throughout the Isles might fear Hector the Ferocious, plainly his women did not.

Michael's own father would never have stood for a daughter of his speaking as forthrightly as Lady Isobel had, but neither Hector's size nor his fierce temperament had intimidated her. Indeed, Michael wondered if anything did.

"You need not fear for her, sir," Mairi of the Isles said. "He will do no more than try to make her understand what she faces if she does not marry you."

"I do not fear for her safety, my lady," he said. "I have seen that lass with a dagger in hand, calmly contemplating the murder of the villain who had captured her. She would not thank me for believing she required protection from any man."

"Faith, sir," Lady Cristina said with a wry smile. "I believe you understand my sister better than she understands herself."

"I make no such claim, madam," he said, smiling back. "Nor did I understate my position before," he added with a direct look at Lachlan Lubanach. "If her ladyship does not come to me willingly, I will take my leave of you and head north as soon as my men arrive. My brother did ask me to join him several days before his ceremony, doubtless to lend additional consequence to that drab occasion."

"Do you mock the honor your brother claims?" Princess Margaret asked.

"Nay, madam, although I own, I do not take it as seriously as he does. His grace, your royal father, has declared that no man outside the Scottish royal family may claim to be a prince within the Kingdom of Scotland. Therefore, Henry will hold the rank of Earl of Orkney here, although he will retain the princedom's right to issue his own coins and to exercise judicial authority on his domains, including the powers of the pit and the gallows."

"Will he insist that his brothers be addressed royally?" Margaret asked.

"Mercy," Lady Euphemia exclaimed. "If he does, then our Isobel will be Princess Isobel. I warrant she has not thought about that. What an honor, indeed!"

"So it would be if that were so," Michael said. "I stand as heir apparent now, but Henry's wife expects a child soon, and in any event, after the earldom becomes official here, my title will be simply Lord Michael St. Clair of Roslin. If Lady Isobel does agree to marry me, she will still be no more than my lady wife, I'm afraid."

His brief experience of her assured him that she would hold firm and that he would therefore be wise to accept her refusal with dignity and let her go. However, the notion of

Isobel as his wife had taken a stronger hold on his imagination than he had realized, and he found himself wishing that she could bring herself more easily to submit to Hector Reaganach's decree.

A vision slipped into his mind's eye of Isabella of Strathearn's likely reaction to such a union, especially if he presented it to her as a faît accompli at Kirkwall just before Henry's installation ceremony. Even the fact that Isobel's name was similar to his mother's would not weigh with Isabella—not positively, at all events.

Maybe Isobel was wiser than she knew.

In the small chamber that Hector used to deal with unimportant visitors to Lochbuie, Isobel watched warily as he shut the door, closing out the rest of the world. Usually such discussions as the one about to take place filled her with trepidation, for he was a stern man when displeased, and thanks to her independent, freedom-loving nature, she had displeased him often over the years.

His scolds always left her feeling limp, because she loved him far more than she loved her father and hated to disappoint him. But an inner spirit often drove her to defend her need to be herself. She had defended it against five older sisters, two younger ones, and her father before coming to live at Lochbuie. To Hector's credit, he had not tried to change her nature, only to teach her discipline and self-protection.

Thus, instead of always punishing her harshly when she taxed his patience, he had given her a dagger, taught her how to use and care for it properly, and had taught her many other, nearly as useful things, as well.

Nevertheless, he did not tolerate defiance from anyone, and she was certainly defying him now, so she knew she ought to be as nervous as she usually was, if not more so. Instead, she felt numb, as if nothing he said or did to her would matter.

To her surprise, he did not begin his tirade the moment the door was shut. Instead, he left her standing just inside while he walked around the table. Even then he did not speak but pulled out the back stool and straddled it, folding his arms across the top of its back and gazing silently, even speculatively, at her.

Grimacing, she looked down at the floor.

"Don't look away, lass," he said.

A tear trickled down her cheek, and her nose began to run. She sniffled and wiped her arm across her face, trying to deal with both details and to look casual about it as she forced herself to look up at him.

He continued to watch her, his gaze as uncomfortably penetrating as it always was. He knew her well, and she wondered if he knew what she was thinking, although she did not really know that herself.

She wished he would speak, would get it over with.

As if she had spoken the thought aloud, he said, "Your attempted departure from the hall just now was a trifle unmannerly, don't you agree?"

Her throat ached, and more of the tears welling in her eyes threatened to spill over. She could not imagine why she wanted to cry. Hector rarely had that effect on her, at least not until he had thoroughly scolded her, or worse.

"What is it, lassie?" he asked gently. "What has upset you so?"

She swallowed hard, exerting herself not to look down again.

He remained silent, patiently waiting for her to speak.

At last, drawing a deep, quavering breath, she said, "I don't know, sir. Maybe I'm just tired. I slept on a hard floor last night, but I also slept much of the way here, so . . ." Remembering how and where she had wakened, she left the sentence unfinished and, feeling heat in her cheeks, hoped he would not ask what memory was making her blush.

"Marriage is not such a dreadful thing, Isobel. I cannot imagine trying to get on in life without your sister at my side. 'Tis clear that the lad cares for you," he added. "He made no objection to marriage. Indeed, had I not suggested it, I believe he would have done so himself. He clearly sees the wisdom of such a course."

"I don't believe he would have made an offer on his own," she said. "I have found him most biddable, sir. Indeed, he accepts whatever course one suggests to him. For a man, he seems singularly inept at making decisions about what he must do. He always imagines that the worst will happen—always!"

"Does he? I own, I did not take such measure of him when we spoke. But if you believe that, I own I'm surprised that you object to marrying him. Not only do you make him sound the exact opposite of men you say you despise as husbands, but he said exceedingly complimentary things about you."

"Did he?" That Michael had spoken well of her gave her a warm feeling, but she forced herself to ignore it. "He is a kind man, a gentle man," she said. "But although I know you love Cristina, sir, I have seen little else to recommend marriage, and I do not want to marry a man merely because he thinks he has ruined me and must set things right. I know you believe others will shun me or be ashamed of me, but I won't care. I am content here. The children will be delighted if I stay with them, so I won't mind missing Sir Henry's installation. Moreover, Adela has said that she would like to visit me. Perhaps you will say she cannot, but—"

"I'll say no such thing, lassie. Your sisters are welcome at Lochbuie any time they choose to visit here."

"Thank you."

"You are adamant then about rejecting this marriage?"

"Aye, sir, I am."

"Very well, then you may go off to bed and I will make your apologies to the others. I'll also tell Sir Michael that your decision is firm. Since he expects his men to catch up with him here tomorrow, I warrant he'll depart soon afterward."

"Aye," she said, thinking that it would be exactly like Michael to do that.

Having slept poorly and awakened far too early, Isobel arose and dressed without troubling to send for a maid. It occurred to her to wonder how her woman would manage to return from Chalamine to Lochbuie and to hope Adela would somehow persuade Macleod to send her, but she knew she would be wise to find someone else to tend her needs for a while.

These thoughts and others of their ilk soured her mood to the point that she had no wish to inflict her company on any other person, let alone on the multitude of those who were currently disappointed in her. So after she donned her shift and an old gown that fastened up the front, she put on boots stout enough for a long walk, took her cloak from its hook, and set off to seek the morning sun and solitude.

Half expecting to meet Hector or Cristina, especially since the latter frequently arose early when Lochbuie entertained visitors, she was grateful to escape the confines of the castle unnoticed by anyone except a gillie or two, one guard on the ramparts, and the solitary sentinel at the postern gate. To the sentinel, she explained that she was going to walk along the shore near the harbor. Since she frequently did so, and since guardsmen on the ramparts commanded a wide view of the area, the gate guard made no objection.

Breathing deeply of the freedom she felt outside the curtain wall, she hurried down the path to the bay. MacDonald's galleys were gone, and the tide on the turn, so the water was at its lowest point, and the muddy, rock-strewn shore stretched into the bay halfway to the far end of the long pier that began at the bottom of the path. Galleys, longships, and smaller craft rocked gently on incoming waves.

At this time of year, the morning twilight that began not long after midnight lasted hours, just as dusk did. Thus, land and sea were as visible as on any overcast day, although the sun's first rays were peeking over the eastern hills. Puffy pale-pink-and-gold clouds drifted overhead in what promised soon to be a bright azure sky.

A lad coiled rope on the pier. Another fished from a rocky outcrop on the sharp eastern point at the mouth of the bay, but Isobel saw no one else about.

Catching up her skirts, she hurried along the shore toward the bay's western knolls, scattering shore birds as she went. A streaky-brown curlew that had been contentedly probing the mud with his long, curved beak in search of breakfast screamed a curt *"kvi, kvi, kvi,"* as he took flight in protest at the intrusion and as warning to his fellow scavengers.

As she smiled at the bird's outrage, her mood lightened, and she remembered why she loved the sea with its ever-changing moods. Breathing deeply of the salty air, she felt a stir of pleasure at sight of nearly hidden pink blossoms of thrift and sea spurge peeping from the short-cropped, grassy foliage of the knoll ahead. At this time of year, even the sandy, nearly barren shore exploded with color.

Avoiding sprawling, gray-green clumps of spiny sea holly, she climbed the knoll and paused at the top to watch a gray seal swimming just off shore. A moment later, a colony of puffins floated into view, their triangular orange bills as large as their faces. Moving carefully, so as not to startle them into flight, she found a flat rock and sat to watch them.

Michael will most likely leave today.

The thought entered her head unbidden, and with it memory of his warm smile, the twinkle in his eyes whenever she said something that amused him, his calm acceptance of all that had occurred, and the way his sensual, honey-smooth voice could arouse physical sensations deep within her body that she had never felt before meeting him. If he left, she would never see him again or learn his secrets, for surely it was not only his relationship to the future Prince of Orkney that made men want to flog information out of him. There were other mysteries to solve, too, not least of which was the effect he had on her after such short acquaintance.

What was it about the man, she wondered, that brought thoughts of him to fill her mind so often and so completely? At least once during her restless slumber the previous night, she had dreamed she slept beside him, so close that his body enveloped her with a fiery warmth that had all but consumed her, making her want to touch him, even to caress him, and to beg him to do the same to her.

Not that she would ever beg any man for anything.

In any event, as she had reached for him, Lady Euphemia had loomed before her, demanding—in a voice exactly like the shrill, raucous piping of an indignant oystercatcher guarding its supper—to know if she had lost her mind. Rather than answer that question, Isobel had awakened.

After that, she had lain in bed, sternly fixing her thoughts on the walk she would take as soon as the day brightened enough so that she could go outside without causing anyone to wonder at her doing so. She had carefully avoided contemplating this second suggestion of her aunt's, albeit dream-inspired this time, that she had gone mad. And she did not want to consider madness now.

Nor had she changed her mind about Michael or about marriage.

A deep groan, almost a growl, startled her out of her reverie.

Blinking at the fat little puffin that had strolled up to inspect her, followed by two of his chums, she marveled as she had many times before at how unbirdlike the chubby little creatures sounded and how human they looked, as if they wore white shirt fronts with black jerkins and breeks, and red or yellow stockings. Their eyelids opened and closed as human eyes did, giving them a most comical expression.

More clouds were gathering in the west, promising rain squalls by afternoon, and she saw that other puffins from their colony had come ashore. They stood about now, very upright on their sturdy legs, looking like a group of plump, dignified courtiers enjoying a social conversation.

When the one closest to her cocked its head as if to ask what she was thinking, she said, "You look as if you would offer me advice, sir, just as everyone else does. But at least you will not urge me to marry Sir Michael."

The bird tilted its head the other way, as if it would hear more.

"Who are the St. Clairs, anyway?" she asked him. "I warrant you know no more about them than I do. To be sure, his brother is to be a prince, but what manner of Scotsman

would be a Norse prince? And although Sir Michael is re-
freshingly *un*-domineering, I have discovered that his in-
ability to think for himself is nearly as maddening as is the
propensity of other men to make every decision without regard for one's wishes. Well, not maddening," she muttered.
"Annoying, though, and who'd *ever* have thought that it
could be?"

Her audience was no longer listening if, indeed, it ever
had been. The chief puffin ruffled its glossy feathers and
wandered off with its chums to join the others, their unhur-
ried, rolling gait making them look no less humanlike from
behind.

As she turned away, distant movement to the east caught
her eye, and a large galley with exceptionally graceful lines,
looking golden in the sunlight, hove into view around the
eastern point of the bay. Spray from its flashing oars danced
in the sunlight like tiny jewels. A flapping banner waved
from its mast.

The distance was too great to discern the banner's device, but she suspected that Michael's men had arrived. If
so, they had wasted no time, because certainly Ian MacCaig
could not have reached Eilean Donan before sundown the
previous day, if not later, to deliver his message.

Glancing toward the castle ramparts, she observed increased activity there and knew that if Hector Reaganach
were not already astir, he soon would be, and others as well.
With a sigh, she stood and shook her skirts free of sand or
grit they might have picked up. An impulse stirred to run
away as fast and as far as she could go, but curiosity stirred,
too, to see what Michael's man was like. Moreover, she told
herself, courtesy demanded that she at least bid Sir Michael
a polite farewell.

Walking back down the knoll, she reached the muddy

shore again and was picking her way through various bits of flotsam washed up by the tide when she noticed a figure striding down the path toward the pier. Easily recognizing Michael, she stopped where she was, thinking he had not seen her.

If he was in such a hurry to leave that he rushed to meet his men, she decided that she did not care that he had failed to notice her. The galley approached the pier at speed and in grand style. Every helmsman and oarsman took pride in his skills and loved to show them off, but she could not deny that it made a fine picture.

She heard the helmsman shout for his rowers to "hold water!" and then to "weigh enough!" The oars plunged into the water, sharply curtailing the galley's speed. Then, while the nearside oars stayed in—sculling powerfully, she knew—the bank of oars on the pier side flashed straight up and the boat drifted in until it gently touched the wood pilings and lads rushed to catch its lines and make it fast.

Expecting to see Michael hurrying along the pier, she looked for him.

Footsteps crunching on shingle nearby warned her that he had turned along the shore instead and was nearly upon her.

"Good morning, lass," he said.

"And to you, sir."

"You are up early."

"Aye." She eyed him warily, wondering if he would say, as so many men would have, that she ought not to have come down to the shore alone.

"'Tis a splendid morning, is it not?"

She nodded, feeling strangely shy. Then, damping suddenly dry lips, she said, "I thought that must be your boat, but I suppose it is too soon for it to be here."

"That's the *Raven*, sure enough," he said. "But I saw you walking over here and wanted to speak to you before you meet Hugo."

"Is Hugo your man, the one who was staying with you at Eilean Donan?"

"Aye, in a manner of speaking," he said with a warm smile. "But here he comes now, nearly on the run, so I expect we should go to meet him."

The man striding toward them along the pier did not resemble any manservant Isobel had ever seen. He was as tall as Michael and looked a lot like him. With the rising sun behind him, his light-brown hair danced with red-gold highlights, and as he drew near, she saw that his eyes were the same cerulean blue as Michael's.

She looked up at the latter, noting that a muscle twitched near the right corner of his mouth as if something had disturbed his usual calm. Although he did not look at her, she sensed that he knew she was looking at him.

"Michael, lad!" the other man exclaimed. "How fortunate you are that I find you safe! Whatever were you thinking, to disappear like that?"

Not a manservant then. Menservants did not address their masters in such a familiar way. Clearly, she had been wise to refuse marriage to a man who evaded the truth as Michael so clearly had.

"Well met, Hugo," he said, reaching to grip the man's outstretched hand and to clap him on a shoulder as well. "I'm sorry to have put such a fright into you, but I collect that our courier reached Eilean Donan in good time."

"What courier? If you mean that young scamp Ian Mac-Caig, we met him in Glen Mòr along with a lovely young lass who was arguing with him about which direction they should take. Ian would have whisked her off the path at our approach, but the lass stood her ground as if she owned the place."

Isobel pressed her lips together at hearing this disrespectful description of her elder sister. She said nothing, though, curious to see how far the man's sense of humor would take him.

Michael said calmly, "Take care how you speak, Hugo. My lady, I hope you will forgive my cousin's bad manners and allow me to present him to you." Without waiting for yea or nay, he went on, "Little though he has recommended himself, this is my cousin Sir Hugo Robison of Strathearn."

"I'm pleased to meet you, sir," Isobel said. "I did not know Sir Michael had a kinsman hereabouts. He told me only that he'd left a manservant at Eilean Donan."

Sir Hugo raised his eyebrows and said with a mocking look at Michael, "Manservant, eh? You overstep the mark, lad, if you think I'll serve you with anything but what you deserve for such an impudence."

To Isobel's surprise, Michael chuckled. "You may try, of course. But I do sincerely apologize to you, my lady, for my prevarication."

"I am sure it is of no consequence, sir," Isobel said with the same politeness she had shown his cousin. "You had no reason to confide in me. Indeed," she added, gathering dignity close so her true feelings would not reveal themselves, "I am sure you must have private matters to discuss. I will take my leave of you."

"Wait, lass," Michael said, putting a gentle hand on her arm as she turned away. "Tell me first if you are still of the same mind as you were last night."

"Indeed I am," she said. "You have merely given me further reason to believe I chose the right course."

"Very well," he said. "Then we'll depart as soon as the

tide turns again, for I see no reason now to delay sailing to Kirkwall. However," he added when she started to pull away, "you need not hurry on ahead. We'll escort you properly."

"Indeed, Lady Isobel," Sir Hugo said when she hesitated, "you must not run away, because I am charged with all manner of messages from Lady Adela. I should have realized from your strong resemblance that you were her sister." His eyes danced. "I do hope you will forgive me. I vow, I meant no disrespect."

Smiling flirtatiously at him and ignoring Michael, Isobel said, "If you met Ian and Adela in Glen Mòr, sir, I assume that you were there searching for your cousin. That also explains how you managed to arrive here so quickly. I'm only sorry that you could not arrange to bring my maidservant with you."

"Lady Adela did suggest such a course," Sir Hugo said with a reminiscent gleam. "*And* practically handed me my head in my lap when I told her I could not delay even the single hour she insisted it would take me to fetch the lass, because I knew that Michael would expect me to lose no time catching up with him. Had I known he was enjoying himself and not keeping nervous watch lest his seekers find him before I did, I might have dallied longer."

"You chose the wiser course," Michael said dryly. "Come now, let us go up. Doubtless, the men on the wall have already announced your arrival and the fact that I came down to meet you. We do not want to annoy Hector Reaganach again."

Hugo's eyebrows shot up again. "Faith, *have* you annoyed him? I own, I'm eager to meet him, for although I've often been in his presence, it has always been in a crush at court or some like occasion, so I have never been presented to him."

"Well, you shall soon have that honor," Michael told him. "Doubtless, he will also present you to his lady wife, who is another of Lady Isobel's sisters, as well as to Princess Margaret Stewart, her daughter Mairi of the Isles, and to Lachlan Lubanach Maclean, Lord High Admiral of the Isles."

"You find yourself in most exalted company, do you not?" Sir Hugo exclaimed. Grinning at Isobel, he added impudently, "My lady, you do not know what you have done by introducing this rascal to your family. They should instantly have consigned him to perdition."

"Well, they did not," she retorted. "Indeed, they want me to marry him."

She was not sure what demon had impelled her to blurt out the last bit, but Hugo did not exclaim or even look surprised.

He merely regarded her more narrowly as he said, "Do you mean to say that you have been wise enough to elude that fate? Pray tell me that the reason he means to leave Lochbuie at once is that you had the good sense to reject him."

"Well, I did," she said. "But in truth, sir, I do not know that sense had much to do with it. I don't want to marry any man, and my kinsmen want me to marry him only because they think he has somehow compromised my reputation."

"Oh, I doubt that is the sole reason, my lady. If I think a moment, I should be able to come up with at least one or two others to explain their position. But since you had the wisdom to spurn him, I shall hold my peace."

His twinkle was difficult to ignore. Conscious of Michael's sudden oppressive silence beside her, she grinned at Sir Hugo, and when he offered his arm, she accepted it and allowed him to escort her through the gate and upstairs to the hall.

Michael made no comment regarding his irrepressible cousin's notion of humor, letting the two go ahead of him and wondering only why Hugo's reflexive flirtation with Lady Isobel did not annoy him more. From their earliest years, he and his cousin had competed against each other in everything, particularly when it came to their flirtations. They were as close as brothers, and in some ways closer, for at times they seemed almost to read each other's minds.

They had nearly come to blows over women in the past, but now he felt only gratitude to Hugo for making Isobel smile again. If he was irritated with anyone, it was with her for flirting back, but he had no right to feel irritated about that.

She was a mystery to him. He had never known a woman whose thoughts morning and night were for anything other than marriage, household, social events, or children. Women who did not marry were generally thought to be sad creatures, but Isobel clearly was not, and she was already well past the age that most fathers insisted on finding husbands for their daughters. Lady Adela was older yet.

If he recalled correctly, Isobel had said there were eight of them and that she and three others were still unwed, so he had assumed that Macleod had managed to find husbands for only half of his daughters, perhaps because he lacked wealth enough to endow them all well. But if they were all as beautiful as Isobel and Adela, the man would have to be a fool to assume they would require large tochers.

As he followed Hugo and Isobel into the hall, he saw that the others had gathered there, evidently to break their fast. He had been in the process of dressing when he chanced to see Isobel outside, and had finished quickly and hurried down the spiral stone stairway that led from his small bedchamber to the kitchens on the first level, below the hall, without entering that chamber. No sooner had he stepped outside the wall than he had had a clear view of the *Raven* rounding the point into the bay. Realizing that he had little time remaining to explain Hugo to Isobel before she would meet him, he had hurried to intercept her, but the galley had arrived too quickly to allow a detailed explanation.

Hector Reaganach was on his feet. "More guests, Isobel?"

"This gentleman is Sir Michael's cousin, who has come to fetch him," she said, taking her hand from Sir Hugo's arm and stepping back.

When Hector shifted his gaze to Michael, he took the hint and went forward, saying, "He is indeed my cousin, my lord, Sir Hugo Robison of Strathearn."

"You are welcome at Lochbuie, Robison," Hector said. "I believe you must be a connection of Isabella, Countess of Strathearn and Caithness, are you not?"

"I have that honor, my lord," Hugo said, making his bow.

Hector made the other introductions, formally presenting Sir Hugo to Princess Margaret before inviting the two men to join the family at table.

As they accepted the invitation, Hector added, "I trust your men will join us. Doubtless, our people have already told them they are welcome."

"Aye, my lord, they will be eager to do so," Sir Hugo

said. "They won't enjoy much rest, however, as Michael informs me that he wishes to depart with the afternoon tide. Doubtless, they had hoped—"

"Mercy me," Lady Euphemia exclaimed, "your men *should* rest, sir, after such a long journey. Sir Michael, surely, you do not mean to leave so soon!"

"You are kind to concern yourself, my lady," he said. "But I must not linger. Had circumstances been different . . ." He fell silent, looking for Isobel to be sure she had caught his meaning.

But Isobel was not where she had been only moments before. He saw but a glimpse of her skirt as it whisked out of the great hall to the stairway.

Realizing that she would be unwise to sit down at the table with her sister and aunt, not to mention Princess Margaret, in the old, rather shabby gown she had donned to walk on the shore, Isobel opted to break her fast later and took the opportunity afforded by Hector's conversation with Sir Hugo to slip away.

Since no one had objected, she doubted that anyone had seen her go or would miss her if she did not return. Indeed, Cristina had given her a sharp look, warning her that she must at least change her clothing before she did return.

Meeting a maidservant coming down the stairs, she asked the girl to bring bread and ale to her bedchamber.

"Aye, m'lady, straightaway."

"I'll want your help to dress, too, Ada. In this dress, I dared not stop to break my fast with the princess Margaret."

"Och, nay, m'lady," the girl said, twinkling. "Ye've sand

on them boots, and your hair's in such a tangle, it looks as if demons ha' been dancing through it."

Isobel had not spared a thought for her hair. If it was in a tangle, it was partly because she had not bothered to do anything more than to smooth the thick plaits with her fingers before going outside. The plaits themselves had loosened in the stiff breeze, however, and she could not doubt Ada's evaluation. No wonder Cristina had given her such a look.

Ada soon joined her in her bedchamber, bringing sliced ham as well as the bread and ale, and quickly made her presentable while Isobel ate.

"The hall be full o' men now," Ada confided. "They do say they willna be staying, though," she added with a sigh of disappointment.

Isobel realized that she shared Ada's regret and tried to tell herself that it was only because she found Sir Hugo amusing and wanted to know him better. That thought, however, led only to remembering that she would have little opportunity to enjoy socializing with young men in the future, because she would be ruined and therefore unable to take part in all the social events she had enjoyed in the past.

Although she told herself that it would not matter in the least, that such events were unimportant, and that she would enjoy the solitude, those arguments were less convincing than they had been before that fate loomed so largely before her.

"Be Sir Michael truly a prince, then?" Ada asked.

"He is not," Isobel said.

"But I heard that his brother be one, and if one brother be a prince, be they not all princes?"

"You should not be gossiping about the laird's guests,"

Isobel said sternly. "In any event, even his brother is not a prince yet."

"Aye, sure, but when he does become one, will not—?"

"Enough, Ada. That will do."

She did not want to talk of Michael or the man about to become Prince of Orkney, but she wished that she had paid more heed when Hector and Lachlan, and even their father, Ian Dubh Maclean, had discussed the ceremonies that would soon take place in the far north. She had cared only that they would see a Scotsman who had become a Norse prince, not about more trivial details. And she wished now, more than she had thought she would, that she would see that ceremony.

Since she had already decided that she would not rejoin the others, she was not as happy as she might otherwise have been when her sister entered the room a few minutes after Ada had left it. It occurred then to Isobel that she might have been wiser to seek her solitude elsewhere.

"Good morning, love," Cristina said, moving to embrace her. "I would have come to you last night, but Hector said he was sure you wanted time to think."

"His way of saying *he* wanted me to have time to think," Isobel said.

"Aye, but I did want to talk with you, and I was certain from the way you slipped away just now that you would not return. I was right, was I not?"

"Aye," Isobel admitted. "I realized I must look a fright, and then once I was away . . ." She spread her hands. "I hope you do not mean to try to persuade me to marry him."

"No, of course not," Cristina said, moving to gaze out the narrow window overlooking the courtyard.

"Good," Isobel said. "Because I have not changed my mind."

"Have you not, dearling? Are you perfectly certain that you could not be happy as his wife? They say the St. Clair family is enormously wealthy, you know."

"Are they? Then doubtless that is one of the reasons his cousin thinks Hector wants me to marry Michael," Isobel said with a sigh. "Sir Hugo said he could think of reasons other than to prevent my ruination."

"Did he?" Cristina sighed. "But the fact that Sir Michael could make you more comfortable than most men could is hardly a bad thing."

"Well, I don't think Michael has so much," Isobel said. "He does not look like a rich man, or act like one. Moreover, I should think all the money belongs to his brother. He is to be a prince, after all, and princes should be wealthy."

"Mairi says the entire family lives more royally than her mother's family does," Cristina said. "The St. Clairs have at least three castles, she said. A liaison like that would benefit more than just you, Isobel. You might think about Adela, Sorcha, and Sidony. Just imagine what such a connection could mean to them."

"Let one of them marry Michael then," Isobel said tartly.

When Cristina gave her a look, she said with a sigh, "I ought not to have said that, but I'm not going to sacrifice myself, for I am not noble, Cristina, nor do I want to be. I was afraid of this, although I did not know that wealth entered into it."

"What do you mean?"

"I expect that everyone, not just Hector, you, and Aunt Euphemia, but also Mairi, Lachlan, her grace the princess Margaret, and doubtless even Ian Dubh, will try to talk me into marrying that man. Not to mention our father," she added, as she realized what Macleod's likely reaction would be to learning that a man of wealth was willing to marry her. "Faith, I'll have to enter a nunnery to find any peace."

"I'll be happy to leave you to your peace," Cristina said, walking to the doorway. She turned as she reached it, adding, "But you should know that we care about you, Isobel, all of us. If we express our concern about your future, you should know that is but one of the consequences awaiting you if you continue in this stubborn refusal to understand the life that you are creating for yourself."

When she had gone, shutting the door with a snap behind her, Isobel stared at that door for a few moments before following. The last thing she wanted was to spend the day entertaining a string of well-intentioned advisers. Only to Cristina did she dare speak her mind freely. To the others she would have to be more respectful, and she knew she could not endure many such conversations before erupting.

Accordingly, with the intention of resuming her interrupted walk, she avoided the great hall by taking the service stairway that led to the kitchens, only to stop on the landing above them when she heard voices below and realized that Michael was talking with his cousin.

Although she could not see them, their voices floated clearly up to her through the narrow, spiral stairwell.

She turned swiftly, thinking they must be on their way up, but Sir Hugo's next words stopped her with her right foot on one step, her left on the step below.

"So you've told the lass naught of your quest, have you?"

Isobel could not have stirred another step then if her life had depended on it. Good manners were one thing, overriding curiosity quite another.

Chapter 8

Michael said firmly, "Not here, Hugo."

"No one in the kitchen is paying us heed, Michael," Hugo said, "and we have privacy here that we might not have if we try to talk in your chamber. 'Tis why you wanted to take this stairway in the first place, is it not? You thought Hector Reaganach or one of the others might pursue us otherwise, to ask more questions. But 'tis only to me that you need give answers now. Whether you choose to talk about her ladyship or not, I want to know why you slipped away to that cave."

Michael sighed, wishing, and not for the first time, that Hugo would remember that although he was a year Michael's senior, he was neither his parent nor his older brother. Hugo had sworn fealty both to him and to Henry, and consistently displayed that loyalty by acting as a boon companion and even as a bodyguard when necessary. But that was all. He held no authority over Michael.

"Hugo," he said, "I know you are angry that I went to the cave without you, but at the time you didn't believe I'd meet danger in going, and nor did I. Moreover, you have shown no interest in my belief that a cave somehow figures in our family secrets, so I decided to let you sleep rather than argue any more with you."

"Aye, sure, you were ever the thoughtful one," Hugo said sardonically. "Did you likewise neglect to warn me that Waldron was in the vicinity?"

"Here at Lochbuie?"

"Don't push me too far, cousin."

"What makes you suspect that Waldron is involved?"

"Who else would be leading men to find you? Lady Adela said a number of men were hunting you. She said two of them called you criminal and accused you of abducting Lady Isobel. She also said they took a whip to you. Is any of that true?"

"It is all true," Michael said. "Nonetheless—"

"Faith, lad, what were you thinking to involve two innocent lasses in this?"

Michael chuckled. "You know nothing about it, cousin, or about Lady Isobel, who involved herself and is the only one concerned in this business. But if you will cease berating me as if you were my father, who was much better at it than you, I'll tell you all about our adventure. First, though, come upstairs with me. I do not like talking in stairwells, and I warrant I can protect you from Hector and his minions."

Hugo reached for him but stopped halfway, cocking his head to listen.

Michael had heard it, too, a soft footstep above. Putting a finger to his lips, he listened for further sound but heard none. "A servant most likely," he murmured. "There are small chambers off the stairs all the way up, which is why I'd prefer to talk in my chamber, so come."

He led the way, and Hugo followed without further protest.

Isobel made her way quickly but as silently as possible up the stairs until she reached her bedchamber. Being as certain as she could be that the two men would not follow her to a level known to be family quarters, she waited until she could be certain they had gone elsewhere before going downstairs again and outside.

Carefully avoiding family members, she slipped out through the postern gate again, telling its guardian that she was going for another walk. "The one I took this morning ended before its time when our visitors arrived."

"Aye, sure, m'lady, but they'll be off again by afternoon tide, they say. It'll be coming on to rain afore long, too," he warned. "Look yonder."

Noting the still-darkening clouds in the west, she nodded, saying with a smile, "I won't melt if it does rain." Then she hurried off down the path, having no wish to linger when it might mean being seen and called back to bid a proper, respectful farewell to their departing guests. Mairi, Lachlan, and Princess Margaret would doubtless be leaving on the afternoon tide, too.

Not that it was necessary to await the tide. Oarsmen could row a galley against its force and often did, but most captains would not begin a long journey by unnecessarily pitting their men's strength against an incoming flow. Hector would not, and neither, apparently, would Michael or Sir Hugo.

With curiosity burning a hole in her mind, she wasted no time communing with the few denizens of a shoreline considerably diminished since her earlier visit. Seawater now covered the mud, leaving only a strip of shingle between breaking waves and the high-water mark. Along this strip, she strode, keeping a wary eye out for more powerful waves as she tried to create order from her scattered thoughts.

The tide would begin turning before the castle folk sat down to their midday meal, and the men would want to be off soon after they dined. But she could not share that meal with Michael and Sir Hugo without attempting to elicit answers from them that she knew they would not give, so it was better that she walk.

Still, she could not go just anywhere on the island. There were rules against that, and she needed to think, which she could do more easily if she did not have to worry about inadvertently wandering beyond sight of the ramparts.

Topping the knoll where she had seen the fat little puffin and his friends, she walked on toward the low western promontory of the bay's mouth. The puffins had gone, but two otters played offshore and gulls wheeled overhead, shrieking. A stiffening breeze blew her from behind, whipping her cloak and skirts around her legs, but although she knew it was blowing the rain-dark clouds closer, she loved the sense it gave her of being at one with the elements.

She told herself she need not spare a thought for what was happening at the castle, that everyone would be glad not to have to concern themselves with her or with the trouble she had stirred. Only when she heard the bell clanging the hour did she stop and turn. Seeing nothing to make her think anyone was searching for her, she was about to turn back when she realized that except for a lad running toward the castle, doubtless fearful of missing his dinner, the pier was empty.

The golden galley awaited its master near the end, bobbing on the waves, and a smaller one that she recognized as Lachlan's bobbed near the landward end.

No one watched either boat.

Apparently, all the men had gone inside to eat, trusting those on the ramparts to keep watch. Even the ramparts looked deserted, although she knew they were not. Lochbuie was always carefully guarded.

She began walking back toward the castle without giving thought to why she did. Not until she glanced up as she walked along the shingle, and saw the lone guardsman pacing his course behind the castle parapet, did the thought form fully in her mind that she wanted a closer look at Michael's ship.

She looked up once, saw no one, and told herself that she need not look again, that she was doing nothing to which anyone could object. No one would mind in the least if she wanted to look more closely at a boat tied to Lochbuie's pier, and no one could be surprised that she might want to examine one that dared to be larger than the one belonging to his grace's Lord High Admiral of the Isles.

Accordingly, she strolled past dozens of oars standing blade-up in the racks down the center of the pier, straight to the golden galley with its banner waving in the breeze. She remembered that Michael had called it the *Raven*, but she could see its device now, and it was not a bird but a black cross on silver cloth. The thought flitted through her mind that, although the cross was black rather than white, the device was similar to what Matthias had described on the strangers' banner.

She counted fifteen highly-polished oarsmen's benches and realized that with the usual minimum of four men per bench, two to alternate rowing with each oar, Sir Hugo must have come with at least sixty oarsmen, and might have half again that many, since each bench looked as if it could seat six men, maybe even eight. Hebridean galleys normally boasted only thirteen benches and twenty-six oars. Hector rarely required more than fifty-two oarsmen even on long trips, but she knew that his lead galley could carry eighty.

A kittiwake's easily recognizable cry sounded right overhead, startling her, and she glanced at the castle again. The lone guard walked the parapet, but although he had surely seen her, she did not think her presence on the pier would concern him enough to report it. When he rounded the corner, she stepped over the gunwale onto a bench. Moving from bench to bench, she saw that the galley was as tidy as any of Hector's boats. Michael's men clearly knew their business well.

The high bow blocked the breeze, still blowing from the northeast, and the sun's rays were warm. She pushed her cloak off her shoulders to savor the warmth as she sat on the portside foremost bench, which served as one of two forward storage lockers for extra sail canvas, oiled raingear, and other equipment. Leaning against the oak planking of the galley's high bow, she shut her eyes, enjoying the movement of the boat as it rocked on the waves, and the warmth on her cheeks and eyelids.

Not until approaching voices and a steady thunder of footsteps on the pier startled her did she realize that her restless night after the exhausting previous day had tired her so that, in the seductive warmth, she had fallen into a doze. Recognizing Mairi's voice, and Lachlan's, she felt momentary panic and remembered Mairi's insistence on calling Michael *her* Michael. The last thing she wanted was to have to explain to either Mairi or Lachlan what she was doing on Michael's boat.

The thudding footsteps and murmur of men's voices told her that Lachlan's oarsmen accompanied them. They were going home to Duart Castle.

Mairi and Lachlan had no cause to walk any farther once they reached their galley, especially if Princess Margaret was with them, as surely she must be. But if the midday meal had ended, the others would soon be coming, too—if, indeed, Michael's men were not right behind Lachlan's.

Hoping that was not the case but determined to avoid teasing questions or worse if Lachlan took it upon himself to scold her for making free with another man's boat, she looked for somewhere to conceal herself. The only places showing the least promise were the storage locker on which she sat and its mate opposite.

Quickly opening the first, she saw that it would not do, for it was top-full with brass rowlocks and other heavy items. The second, however, held rolled canvas and was otherwise nearly empty, leaving plenty of room for her. Without another thought, she stepped in, curled up, and eased the lid shut.

Strolling behind the Lord High Admiral and his lady, Michael watched the far shoreline in hope of catching a glimpse of the lass. When she had not appeared at dinner, Hector Reaganach had sent a servant to look for her. But learning that she had gone outside the wall again to walk on the shore, he had merely nodded to the gillie who relayed that information, and had gone on eating his meal.

Michael admired the man's restraint. The lass had tested it a good deal since their unexpected arrival at Lochbuie, and he had rarely met a man of power who was able to withstand for long such blatant flouting of his wishes.

Bidding one's guests farewell when they departed was not merely a duty but a strict obligation of courtesy. Doubtless

Isobel would face rebuke, if not stern reprimand, for her bad manners. That thought stirred mixed emotions.

On the one hand, he hoped Hector gave her all she deserved. On the other, he hoped he would not be too harsh. And whatever Hector did, Michael hoped he would change his mind about allowing her to attend Henry's ceremony.

Pausing only to bid the princess Margaret, Lachlan Lubanach, and his lady farewell and to see them aboard their boat, he left his host and hostess to finish their own farewells and returned to his musing as he moved on to board the *Raven*. He knew he was indulging in false hope by thinking Hector might change his mind. If the lass were to go, she would face not only scandal but the Countess of Strathearn, and Michael could not wish his mother's displeasure on anyone.

It struck him now that he, too, would face that displeasure if the scandal of his having spent a night alone with Isobel should spread to Orkney or Caithness, and he wondered if it had occurred to Isobel that if such a scandal did erupt, he would figure in it as the villain. He doubted that even that knowledge would change her mind about marrying him, however, and he found himself wondering, as Hugo took charge of the men, if anything could.

Although he had told himself it did not matter one way or the other—that he owed her his protection, but the decision to marry or not was hers to make—he had not realized how disappointed he would be at her refusal. Still, it was for the best, because marriage to him would make them both more vulnerable to Waldron's endless scheming, and he did not want her to become a pawn in that game.

His oarsmen boarded swiftly and took to their oars. Well fed if not rested, they would fare well enough until they put in somewhere for the night where they could hunt and fish for their supper. He had no reason to keep them at their stations through the night, nor did he want to. They could easily make Skye by dusk and could perhaps seek hospitality from Gowrie of Kyle Rhea.

He said as much to Hugo, who nodded and moved aft to inform Caird, the helmsman. Still thinking of Isobel, gazing at the far shore, hoping to spy her walking there, Michael noted with half an eye that the two men in the stern conversed longer than the simple relaying of his order would require.

Hugo explained when he returned, saying, "It occurred to me that if Waldron was able to commandeer a boat at Glenelg, he might also have acquired a galley or longboat. If he did, he will have managed by now to learn your direction."

Michael nodded, knowing it was pointless to mention that Gowrie had promised his men's discretion. If Waldron wanted information and knew where to come by it, he would have it. That his men had seen them crossing to Skye had surely provided him with sufficient information to lead him to the rest.

"What do you and Caird suggest?" he asked.

"That we head west rather than returning as we came through the Sound of Mull. We can sail near the coast of Ireland and miss anyone lying in wait for us at the west end of the Sound."

Michael nodded again and signaled his assent to the helmsman before taking his seat on the larboard storage locker.

"Did you get any sleep last night?" Hugo asked.

"Not much," Michael admitted. He had spent most of the night with images dancing through his head of Isobel lying next to him as she had the night before, kissing him as she had on the boat. His back still gave him a good deal of pain, too.

"I suspected as much," Hugo said. To an oarsman approaching with two satchels containing their extra clothing, he said, "Leave those. I think Sir Michael may want to use one as a pillow before long, and I may use the other one, myself."

"Aye, sir," the man said, setting them down and moving to take his station.

Waiting until their host and hostess had bade farewell to their other guests, and for Lachlan Lubanach's galley to pull away from the pier, Michael stood on the nearside locker to shake hands again with Hector, then moved aside for Hugo to do the same. With farewells over and the laird and his lady turning toward the castle, he sat down again on the offside locker.

The *Raven* headed for open water beyond the mouth of the bay.

Isobel scarcely dared to breathe. She hated the darkness and the confining space, but she was more frightened now of revealing her presence. She thought she could handle Michael easily enough, since he seemed consistently willing to submit to her lead. And perhaps she could manage Sir Hugo, who accepted Michael's authority to some degree, at least, and was after all only another flirtatious male such as those she was forever meeting at court and elsewhere. But managing Hector would be another matter, for if he should learn that she had left Lochbuie concealed in the *Raven*'s storage locker . . . The thought made her shudder.

They were on open water, because the boat rocked more and she could hear wind in the sail. She had heard them say they would head west, that they thought Waldron might be following them. She could not imagine how he could be, since neither Gowrie nor Mackenzie was likely to lend him a galley and Michael had not suggested that Waldron knew anyone else in Kintail or Glenelg. Macleod certainly would not give him one.

The men continued to talk, but to her disappointment, they did not speak again of Michael's so-called quest or other secrets. Their comments grew briefer until only rhythmic sounds of the helmsman's gong, and slapping, splashing oars filled her ears.

Sometime later she startled awake to thumping movement and a curse from Hugo. "Rain, Michael! It's going to pour in a minute. Let's have that canvas out."

Even before Isobel had digested his words, the lid of her storage locker flew open and spatters of rain struck her cheek. She shut her eyes.

Ignoring the spattering rain, Michael stared at her in shock, then glanced at Hugo in an attempt to suppress the jolt of fury that threatened to overcome him.

The twinkle in Hugo's eyes did not help, and clearly sensing as much, he quickly looked over his shoulder, but Michael knew the oarsmen were pulling hard, their backs to them, unaware that anything was amiss. The rain would not disturb the men or chill them. Their minds and bodies concerned themselves solely with rowing, and so it would be until the helmsman issued new orders.

"Tell Caird to put in to shore," Michael snapped, wishing

Hugo would turn that smirking look back toward him for just one little moment.

But Hugo had better sense. He took a step forward, ignoring the increasing downpour as he shouted the command to the helmsman.

Without further ado, Michael reached down and grabbed Isobel by an arm, hauling her out of the locker and onto her feet.

She straightened her shoulders, giving him look for look. "I can explain," she said with a calm that he was certain she had to force.

"Not one word," he snapped. Putting his face close to hers, he added grimly, "I have much to say to you, my lass, but you may wait until we have privacy to hear it."

Isobel stared at Michael in dismay, putting her hood up against the rain and drawing her cloak more closely about her. She wished that she could recover her dignity as easily, but that was impossible, because when a man jerked a woman unceremoniously from his storage locker, she could scarcely put her chin in the air and insist that she had belonged there.

At least Michael had stopped glowering, had shifted that heart-poundingly dangerous, ice-filled gaze away from her, but he was undeniably furious, and she had not expected fury from him. Surprise, perhaps, even dismay—and worry, too, that Hector Reaganach might blame him for what she had done.

Michael did, after all, seem to make a habit of expecting the worst.

She had expected to have to explain that Hector would

correctly blame her for the incident, and she had thought Michael's generally mild nature would let him accept her word about that. But now his anger swirled ominously around her, overpowering her senses and frightening her. She dared not move or speak, lest the result be something even worse.

"There," Michael said, pointing. "That beach yonder will do, Hugo."

Without looking at Hugo, Isobel knew he made some gesture of protest, because Michael's expression hardened more, sending a shiver up from the base of her spine and reminding her of the look he had shot her at the cave that first day. She did not like the idea of beaching the galley, but she knew that if they did not run too far onto the sand, the oarsmen could easily pull the boat off again.

Hugo gave the command, and several of the men glanced back, clearly sensing something amiss. Although more than one mouth dropped open, no man let his gaze linger.

"You'll want the towboat lowered," Hugo said.

"Just put out a plank," Michael said.

"It's too shallow here to get close enough. You'll get your feet wet."

Michael did not reply. The rain had settled into a steady gray drizzle.

"Do you want me to go ashore with you?" Hugo asked.

"Nay, only the lass."

"Sakes, sir," Isobel exclaimed, unable to keep silent a moment longer, "do you mean to put me ashore and make me walk back to Lochbuie?"

"You'd be well served if I did," he said curtly. "You deserve much more, but I'm not lost to my own responsibility in this business, believe me. Nonetheless, when I'm finished

with you, you may wish that I'd thrown you overboard and
let you swim back."

He said the last so calmly that another splinter of ice shot
up her spine, and she realized that she had badly misjudged
him, that she did not know him at all.

The boat ground onto sand and shingle, and without
comment, ignoring Isobel's protest that she could easily
walk, Michael lifted her and waited impatiently for them to
put out the gangplank.

She felt small and defenseless in his arms as he walked
down the plank with her but safe, too, which, considering
that he was ready to murder her, seemed odd indeed. When
the plank ended in knee-deep water, he began striding
through it toward shore, and when she opened her mouth to
speak, he cut her off, saying curtly, "My temper is on a tight
rein, lass. I've had no sleep for two nights, these boots were
new a fortnight ago, and I'm nigh to wringing your neck. So
hold your damned tongue, or by heaven, I'll let impulse rule
my next actions."

Isobel pressed her lips tightly together, but the temptation to tell him exactly what she thought nearly overpowered her. She had long felt pride in her ability to hold her
own against anyone, even against Hector the Ferocious,
most of the time. But to her surprise, she had no desire to
test Michael St. Clair, at least not just now.

He carried her easily and swiftly to the shore, but he did
not put her down until he had carried her a short distance

into the beech wood above the high-water mark. When he did stand her on her feet, she felt no relief, only profound wariness.

That the men on the galley could no longer see them she thought both a blessing and a strong reason for her growing fear of what Michael meant to do. At least the thick canopy of leaves overhead protected them from the rain.

His hands clamped to her shoulders. "Are you mad?" he demanded. "You want no more to do with me, so what demon possessed you to hide on my boat?"

"I didn't!"

He gave her a shake. "Of all the useless lies you might utter, that is the most foolish. How can you say you did not when I found you hiding in that locker?"

"Please, Michael, let me explain."

"I'm listening," he said grimly, his fingers still gripping her shoulders so hard she knew they would leave bruises.

She swallowed hard, feeling tears well into her eyes. "It wasn't like that. I was just curious. I wasn't trying to hide from you, or even trying to hide on your boat. I wanted to look at it, because I love boats and the *Raven* is yours, and because it is even bigger than Lachlan's."

He did not speak, and she wondered if it pleased him at least a little bit that she had noticed the greater size of his boat. Men always took pride in their boats.

When his eyes narrowed ominously, she added hastily, "I didn't want Mairi to catch me there, because . . ."

"Why not?" he demanded when she hesitated. "If you were doing nothing wrong, why fear Lady Mairi?"

She nibbled her lip, recalling that Hector would say she had no business to be on Michael's boat, and that if Hector would say it, Lachlan would say it, and by the look of him, Michael believed the same thing.

She sighed. "I thought you would not mind if I looked at it, but I suppose I was wrong. I do know that Hector would say I should not have got aboard, and—"

"And you feared that Lachlan Lubanach or his lady would say the same."

His voice was gentler, his usual calm apparently restoring itself, and an impulse stirred to tell him that was exactly what she had feared. But even as she opened her mouth to say the words, they froze on her tongue and honesty prevailed.

"I . . . I did think that about Lachlan," she admitted. "He nearly always does agree with Hector, but if you must know, Mairi—last night—called you *my* Michael, and I knew she would tease me more if she saw me on your boat. I won't deny that I also feared that Lachlan would not approve and that I knew Hector would not. I did think you would not mind, but when I heard them coming, I just wanted to hide, so I did. Then you came aboard, and I could not—"

She broke off, biting her lip, trying to think how to explain those feelings.

"You could not trust my good nature enough, or that welcome you say I would have offered you, simply to tell me you were there," Michael said in a flat tone that made her wish she could deny his assessment. "Instead, you kept perfectly silent until we were well away from Lochbuie and I discovered you myself."

"I didn't think—"

"That much is true, lass. You didn't think," he said bluntly.

"You don't understand."

"That is true, too," he agreed, but his tone turned his agreement into yet another accusation. "I don't know what manner of game you are playing with me," he went on. "But whatever it is, I'd advise you to take greater care. You do not know enough about the business in which you meddle, or about me, to understand the danger, but you soon will if you play me any more such tricks."

"If you would just tell me—"

"Had you agreed to marry me, I would have told you all I could," he said. "But your refusal rendered that step unnecessary. In any event, we are not discussing me or my secrets now. You have already made it clear that your ruination is not of primary concern to you, so we need not consider that either. What did you expect me to do when you did finally emerge from that locker?"

She hesitated, trying to gauge his temper, wondering if his calm had reasserted itself sufficiently to let her speak freely.

He gazed back at her, waiting. His stillness in so isolated a place seemed more formidable than most men's anger, and she hesitated a moment longer.

"When did you mean to show yourself?" he asked in that oddly gentle way.

"I don't know," she said more abruptly than she had intended. "I did not have any idea what to do, if you must know. It is all very well for you to stand there, saying I should have told you I was there, but it did not occur to me. When you and Sir Hugo and all those oarsmen came aboard, I just froze where I was and hoped the earth would swallow me before I had to deal with the consequences."

"Then let me put my question this way," he said, his manner still as calm as if hers had matched it. "What do you expect me to do with you now?"

His hands remained on her shoulders but were no longer bruising her. His demeanor was respectful and calm. Taking courage in hand, she said, "I know you do not want to go all the way back to Lochbuie, sir, so perhaps you may find it more convenient just to take me north with you."

His fingers twitched on her shoulders, but he continued to look directly into her eyes, his gaze searching hers as he said, "Just what do you expect to happen, lass, if we should arrive at Kirkwall together?"

"Surely, Sir Henry would offer me his protection."

"Aye, sure, and why not, although 'tis the bishop's protection you should seek rather than Henry's, since we will all be staying at the bishop's palace. But doubtless, as a man of the cloth, his eminence will be generous, and doubtless, too, my mother will happily offer you her protection, as well."

"Do you think so?" she asked doubtfully.

"No, my dear, exasperating innocent, I do not think anything of the kind. My mother would eat you alive. What I *do* think is that you have lost your wits. Do you honestly think so little of me that you believe I would do more than I have already done to aid you in your own destruction? No, don't answer that, because I don't want to hear any more nonsense, and I have much more to say to you.

"It is my firm belief," he went on when she bit her lip, "that someone should have taken a stronger hand with you long ago to protect you from yourself. That your father did not do so does not amaze me, because he had eight daughters and no man could prevail against so many. That your foster father did not *does* surprise me, but it is nonetheless his duty now to try to rectify that omission. How do you think he would respond to finding you at Kirkwall? He'll soon be a guest of my brother himself, you know. Do you expect Henry to protect you from Hector?"

That thought was not one that she wanted to dwell on,

nor did she think such a question deserved an answer. Nevertheless, his reproaches were beginning to make her squirm, and she wished he would stop.

"You seem to think that you may just do as you please," he went on in that same conversational tone. "And that is another thing that Hector Reaganach must deal with, because I do not have the right. If I did, you would find yourself across my knee right now, learning a hard lesson. As it is, you will return to Lochbuie."

"But I thought you would help me! You kissed me, so I thought—"

He caught her hard again, and when she looked up in surprise, he captured her mouth with his and kissed her hard, his arms sliding around her shoulders, holding her tight against him as he pressed his lips against hers and thrust his tongue between them into her mouth.

She sighed, put her arms around him, and kissed him back.

Roughly, he caught her by the shoulders again and set her back on her heels. Then, still holding her shoulders, he said sternly, "As you see, you can easily entice me to kiss you, lass, but kisses have nothing to do with the matter at hand."

"But you—"

"Did you think to change my mind with kisses? You won't do it. I do want to help you. Indeed, I have come to care more for you in two days than I thought I could care for any woman in a lifetime, although I swear I do not know why I should. But the fact that I do is what provides me now with a nearly overwhelming urge to beat you until you cry for mercy."

"But, then—"

He held up a hand, silencing her. "I won't make you

walk back to Lochbuie, Isobel, but you are going to return and face Hector Reaganach. And because I do care deeply about what happens to you, it is my urgent hope that he will do what I am so fervently longing to do to you now."

"Do you think I hid aboard your boat just so that I could go to Kirkwall?" she demanded, her senses still whirling from both the kiss and his unexpected declaration. "I promise you, I did not. It all happened exactly as I said it did."

"How it happened matters not one whit," he said. "What matters is that you continued to conceal yourself long afterward, rather than do what was right, and thus we both find ourselves in this predicament. It is for that that you deserve punishment, my lass, but you may try your explanation on Hector Reaganach with my goodwill. Mayhap you will find him more understanding."

Chapter 9

The return to Lochbuie seemed to take considerably less time than it had taken them to reach the point where Michael had found Isobel, and the journey seemed very fast to her despite her discomfort both physically and emotionally.

For one thing, although the rain had eased to no more than heavy mist, and although the men had broken out oiled canvas cloaks for those who wanted them, everyone was wet and uncomfortable. For another, Michael's last words to her still rang in her ears, because he had not said another word to her since, even during their return to the boat when he had picked her up again rather than making her walk through the low-rolling surf and up the narrow gangplank.

She doubted that Hector would give her much time to explain anything, nor would it matter even if he demanded an explanation, because she had none that would satisfy him. For the short time that she had been able to persuade herself that a simple impulse had led her to do something foolish but of little consequence, she had retained a certain confidence, but Michael's reaction had destroyed that.

Even now she did not know what demon had stirred her to suggest that he take her with him to Orkney. The moment the words jumped from her lips, she had known the idea was thoughtless, but Michael's reply had shaken her nonetheless. It still rankled that he had fixed on the one major flaw in her argument about having acted out of momentary panic, and had reprimanded her for not having had the courage or integrity to reveal herself to him before they left the harbor.

His nearness and his fury had enveloped her so completely while he hurried her back to the galley that she could not think of a single counterargument. But once they were aboard, with the boat headed back toward Lochbuie, thoughts of what might have been had consumed her. If only she had said this or done that, she told herself, the outcome would have been different.

But as emotions eased their influence on her thoughts, common sense stepped in, until each argument that had presented itself sounded weak, even stupid. None would do for Hector, certainly, and she had a feeling that making her peace with him would be far easier than doing the same with Michael.

Suddenly, she wanted with all her heart to make peace with Michael.

He stood there, apparently unaffected by the rolling motion of the boat, leaning a shoulder against the bow's high-curved stem-post, his arms crossed over his chest, staring grimly, blindly sternward. His anger at the change in his plans that her actions had forced was nearly tactile.

At least, she mused, the oarsmen could rest now, because with the wind in the larboard quarter, they could ship their oars. Even the lads manning the huge sail's shrouds and braces had less to do. But she knew that the journey west, sailing against the wind, had taxed them all, and they had enjoyed little rest at Lochbuie. The men would be looking forward to starting the trip over again even less than Michael was.

As the mouth of Lochbuie Bay hove into view ahead, she did not know which worried her most, that he would simply put her ashore on the pier and leave her to make her explanations alone, or that he would not, that he would go with her to meet Hector and tell him exactly what she had done.

As it happened, Hector's appearance on the pier before the galley landed rendered that choice unnecessary. Isobel saw him striding toward them, oblivious of the drizzling rain, and she nearly flinched, because every movement of his tall, broad warrior's body revealed his anger with her.

She wished then that she could dive back into the storage locker, and when he loomed over her as Michael helped her onto a bench so that she could step onto the pier, she felt both men's anger envelop her, and fought back tears at the thought of having managed with one small, stupid incident to infuriate the two men she cared most about in the whole world.

The thought caught her unawares. That she could link them in her mind like that seemed extraordinary. She had known Michael less than three days. Why should she care so much what he thought of her?

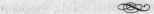

Michael saw Isobel's tears, recognized her struggle to control them, and an unexpected wave of compassion washed away much of his anger.

Hector looked as one might expect Hector the Ferocious to look under such circumstances, and although Michael believed Isobel should face a reckoning, he feared from Hector's expression that he might punish her too harshly. None of the gentleness the man had displayed the previous evening was in evidence now.

He looked straight at Michael and said, "I have no need to ask whose fault this is, lad, so don't look so worried. I know you did not try to abduct her."

"No, my lord," Michael said, noting that Hector kept a firm grip on Isobel's upper arm and showed no intention of releasing her. "I'm thinking, though, sir," he added, "that since my oarsmen have had little rest today, mayhap we should stay the night now at Lochbuie, with your permission."

"Granted, and not just out of hospitality, for I saw that you headed west when you left," Hector said, adding in a sterner tone, with a gimlet look at Isobel, "Our lass may have done you a kindness by stowing away, as I suspect she did."

"I'd be interested to know how that can have been a kindness," Michael said, ignoring a temptation to shoot just such a look at her himself.

"You told me that your enemy has connections to the Roman Kirk," Hector said. "You should know that the Green Abbot of Iona is of that ilk and a sworn enemy to Clan Gillean. Any allies the men following you may have hereabouts will be Mackinnon men. And if they know you came here, the Mackinnons of Mull will be watching your every move now, so 'tis just as well that you did not go ashore or sail near the Holy Isle, where men might recognize your banner."

"Her ladyship and I did go ashore briefly an hour or so west of here, but we did not linger," Michael said evenly.

"I see," Hector said, looking from one to the other. "I

think we had better get out of this rain. After Isobel and I have had our talk, I want to discuss these troubles of yours further, lad. Your men will take supper in the hall with us."

"Thank you, my lord. You are generous."

"Sakes, lad, the lady Isobel is my responsibility, and the necessity for you to stay is her doing," Hector said. "For me to offer you and your men a hot supper and dry beds seems small payment for the trouble she has caused you. Her ladyship's own payment," he added grimly with another look at Isobel, "will be more taxing."

Isobel stood stiffly, determined to retain the shreds of her dignity if it killed her but certain that Hector was angrier with her than she had ever seen him. His grip on her arm was viselike and would leave bruises similar to the ones Michael's fingers had doubtless left on her shoulders, and Hector's tone of voice whenever he mentioned her name left her in no doubt of what he intended to do.

He had put her over his knee more than once since she had come to live with him and Cristina, but such episodes had been quickly over. She had a feeling that this one would be worse than the others. That Michael was in agreement with him made her punishment inevitable, though, so it would be best just to get it over with.

Accordingly, she made no protest as she hurried along beside Hector, although he made no attempt to shorten his long strides to accommodate hers. Her cloak billowed in the chilly wind, but halfway to the castle entrance the rain stopped, so she could at least be grateful for that.

She had heard Michael tell his cousin to supervise the men as they put up their oars and prepared the *Raven* for the night, so although she did not look back, she knew that he followed them now. The knowledge that he was aware of exactly what Hector meant to do was humiliating, and Hector's intended punishment even more so, but when they reached the hall, she realized that yet more discomfort lay ahead.

As they entered, Cristina rushed to meet her, exclaiming, "Oh, my dearling, I feared that something dreadful had happened to you. Where have you been? You're all wet! Did you fall? Did you run into Mackinnons? I cannot tell you how worried I've been since the men on the wall told us they had lost sight of you!"

Before Isobel could reply, Hector said, "I promised you I would find her, sweetheart, so you need not have worried. She merely took the bit between her teeth again, but this time she has inconvenienced Sir Michael and his men, and I mean to make my disappointment in her behavior very clear to her."

Lady Euphemia, close on Cristina's heels, exclaimed, "Mercy, Isobel, what can you have done to inconvenience Sir Michael? His ship left hours ago!"

With both women staring at her, clearly expecting an explanation, and with Hector and Michael silently flanking her, the former still gripping her arm, clearly meaning for her to answer the questions herself, Isobel pushed back her hood with her free hand and said, "I . . . I was on his boat, Aunt Euphemia. It happened quite by accident, I assure you, but—"

"But how could you have done it by accident?" Lady Euphemia demanded. "That is not a thing anyone does inadvertently, Isobel. One either boards a boat or one does not. I declare, my dear, you grow more and more like our poor Mariota every day. I thought we were finished with such inexplicable matters when she—"

"We have finished with them, madam," Hector interjected. "I am about to make certain of that, so if you will excuse us, I will settle this matter with Isobel at once. You are welcome to come with us, St. Clair," he added abruptly.

To Isobel's shock, Michael said calmly, "Then I will, sir, thank you."

Michael knew that Hector had issued the invitation out of courtesy, because the behavior for which he was going to punish Isobel had greatly inconvenienced a guest. He knew, too, however, that Hector had not expected him to accept, because the same courtesy that led to such an invitation nearly always led to its rejection.

Discipline, although a solemn duty of a lass's father, foster father, or husband, was not a scene for an audience, and Michael could not have said exactly why he had accepted the invitation, only that instinct had stirred him to do so. But he rarely ignored that instinct, and he did not ignore it now.

Isobel was pale as Hector urged her toward the small chamber where he and Michael had conversed the previous night, but Michael did not think her pallor stemmed from fear of punishment. Until only moments before, she had seemed resigned to her fate if not altogether accepting of it.

Her cheeks had reddened when the two women scolded her, and only toward the end of that scolding had she paled. She had looked wan then but had turned nearly white when Michael said he would join them, making him suspect that she had known Hector might include him and now feared much greater humiliation.

He was sorry for that, but instinct was instinct, and

things happened because they were supposed to happen. He would see the business through, wherever it led.

Hearing the door shut, and feeling Michael's presence loom behind her, Isobel faced Hector numbly and hoped he would say what he wanted to say and do what he was going to do quickly so that she could escape to the blessed solitude of her bedchamber and shut out the rest of the world.

Instead of going around the heavy table as he did when he meant only to scold her, he sat on the front edge of it, folded his arms across his chest, and looked long and hard at her.

She stood still, making no effort to avoid his gaze.

"I'm disappointed in you, Isobel," he said softly.

He had said as much to Cristina, but hearing it again brought an ache to her throat as she strove to think of an acceptable reply. She could not protest, because she knew she deserved to hear the words. She nearly looked away but thought better of that, too. She would not cry either, not with Michael there to see it.

"By heaven," Hector said with a sigh after a moment or two, "I seldom find myself at such a loss, but I do not know what to say to you. 'Twas bad enough when you interfered in a dispute between men without thought for your own safety, and I have already expressed my disapproval of your lack of judgment in spending the night alone with Sir Michael, but apparently to no avail. I've no idea now of how to make sure you understand that this latest start of yours deserves stern punishment."

When he paused for breath, she said quietly, "I know I

was wrong, sir. I have already said as much, and truly, I can explain how—"

"I don't want to hear explanations or excuses," he said curtly. "Before I proceed, however, I do want to hear you accept responsibility for your rash behavior and make a sincere apology for the trouble you have caused Sir Michael."

She swallowed, but the ache in her throat remained. She could not look at Michael, but to Hector she said, "I do apologize. I know you will say I should not have set foot on Sir Michael's boat, and although I did believe he would not object, I was wrong to let panic drive me to hide when I heard the others coming, and wrong to keep silent after he came aboard. I never meant to make anyone angry. I just . . ." Her throat closed, words failed her, and she fell silent.

"You must realize that one at least amongst his men or ours will talk of this," Hector said. "You could not have done anything more certain to nourish the scandal you have already stirred. Take off your cloak, lass. You have left me no choice . . ."

Paying no heed to his hesitation, she untied the cloak strings, shrugged it off, and braced herself, certain that she knew what was coming.

". . . unless, of course . . ." He paused again, waiting, one eyebrow raised.

No more than she could have flown could Isobel have stopped the words that flew off her tongue: "Unless what?"

"I was just thinking that, although this incident may stir greater scandal, it becomes naught but a romance if the ending includes marriage," he said dulcetly.

Isobel stared at him, the ache in her throat stronger than ever.

"Well, lass? Are you still determined to refuse him, or . . . ?"

She shut her eyes, and Michael's presence behind her loomed even larger until she opened them again and murmured, "I doubt that he still wants me, sir."

"St. Clair?"

The name floated past her, stopping the breath in her throat until Michael said calmly, "I am still of the same mind, my lord."

"You'll need to take a firm hand with her," Hector said. "But if you're still willing, I'll leave the rest of this to you. I'd recommend a strap or a stout switch."

"Thank you, my lord. I can deal with her."

"Then I'll leave her to you and see what I can do to arrange a speedy wedding for you," Hector said, straightening. "Come to me when you've finished, and we'll talk further." He left the room, shutting the door behind him.

"Look at me, lass."

Isobel could not move. Indeed, she could scarcely breathe.

"Look at me, Isobel," Michael repeated.

After a long moment, she turned slowly, her face ashen.

He opened his arms to her. When she hesitated, he thought for a moment that she would ignore their invitation. But then she glanced down at her wet cloak, stepped over it, and walked silently into his embrace.

The top of her head barely reached his chin, and she buried her face against his chest. He had given his own sodden cloak to a gillie upon entering the hall, but although he suspected that his doublet was damp, too, she did not seem to mind.

Holding her close, he could smell rain in her hair, could

feel the supple warmth of her body; and a knot of uncertainty that he had not even known lay deep inside him relaxed into a sense of unfamiliar but nonetheless welcome contentment.

Moments later, she stirred, and her hands gingerly touched his waist.

"Put your arms around me, sweetheart," he murmured into her hair.

"Sweetheart?" She spoke against his chest.

"Aye," he said.

"He expects you to punish me," she said. "Are you going to?"

Instead of answering, he said, "Do you understand why he is angry?"

She nodded.

"Do you think he is wrong to be?"

She shook her head.

"Look up at me, Isobel."

She obeyed, her expression wary.

"Did you agree to this marriage between us because you thought such an agreement would spare you from deserved punishment now?"

She hesitated again, sighed, and said, "You *do* mean to beat me."

"Answer my question."

"Why should I? You will say either that I am lying or that I'm just saying what I think you want to hear. After all, you offered to marry me only because you think you must assume responsibility for what happened between us."

He felt a strong desire to tell her that she had attracted him from the moment she intervened with Waldron, to try to explain that her determination to kill the man in the cave if necessary had sealed that attraction, and that everything she had done since had simply reinforced it. But common sense stopped him before he uttered the words, because it occurred to him that to give so headstrong a lass such a weapon to use against him might not be wise.

The truth was that he did not care why she had agreed. He was just glad that she had. If part of him was also relieved to know he would not be leaving her behind to face alone the consequences of a scandal they had brewed together, he thought that was only natural. To have earned Hector Reaganach's good opinion was also important, but he would not beat her simply to retain it.

He said gently, "Do you think I ought to punish you?"

"He expects you to, so I suppose you will say you have no choice."

"I have managed to stay alive on several occasions that might well have proved fatal by *not* doing what others expect of me."

"Faith, sir, Hector will not kill you if you do not meet this expectation."

"So I'm hoping," Michael said with a smile.

She wrinkled her brow and gazed searchingly at him. "I do not always know what to make of you," she said at last. "Will you ever share your secrets with me?"

"Perhaps," he said. "You do need to know more about them, to be sure."

"Will you tell me about your quest?"

He stiffened, recognizing Hugo's word on her lips.

Isobel felt his reaction, cursed her folly, and dampened suddenly dry lips.

In a voice that raised the hair on the back of her neck, Michael said, "You were listening on that stairway."

She lifted her chin, saying with careful dignity, "I was taking that stairway to go back outside, and I chanced to overhear your cousin's question. Surely, you do not count that as 'listening on that stairway.'"

"Aye, sure, I do," he said uncompromisingly. "An innocent person continues downstairs. She does not stop to listen or turn and creep silently back upstairs when she fears discovery. That you did both makes me wonder now if you hid in that storage locker in hopes of overhearing another such conversation. Indeed, I'd not be amazed to learn that you agreed to marry me now not only to avoid punishment but also because I said that had you agreed to it before, I'd have told you what I know."

She opened her mouth to deny it, but he put a finger on her lips and said, "Take care, lass, for you have made no secret of your curiosity. Indeed, I think it is what most frequently lands you in trouble. So I'll tell you this, and you'd better heed my words. I'll not tolerate a wife who lies to me or who listens at doors and on stairways."

Hastily, barely giving him time to move his finger, she said, "I won't then."

"I want your solemn promise."

"I promise," she said. "And I did not board your galley hoping to hear more. Truly," she added, suppressing memory of her disappointment when he and Hugo did not reveal more information about what Hugo had called Michael's quest.

He was silent for a long moment, looking at her, increasing her tension.

Her skin had begun prickling the moment Hector had left her alone with him, Michael's open arms had done little to ease that, and now it felt as if her skin were afire. Not only had she wondered more than once why his voice alone could stir such disturbing feelings in her body, but he could make her more uneasy with a look than Hector at his most ominous could.

Michael seemed to look straight into her soul. Tracing a line along her jaw with one finger, he said gently, "I am not entirely persuaded by your assurances, sweetheart. I sincerely hope, however, that you are persuaded by mine."

Trying to ignore the shiver that shot up her spine, she nodded and leaned into him, sighing when his arms went around her again and he drew her close.

Marriage would soon link her forever to this man who stirred her fears and other less familiar sensations so easily and so inexplicably. But she had known the moment Hector asked if she would change her mind that she could not let Michael St. Clair sail out of her life again if anything she could do would stop him.

Michael had no idea if her sigh denoted relief that he would not punish her or something deeper, but he was content for those few moments to hold her and let her feel safe, if that was what she felt.

A drop of water trickled down his neck, reminding him that his hair was still wet. The lass's, protected as it had been by her hood, was merely damp and curling as it dried. They both needed to change into dry clothing before supper, and he doubted that she would go willingly upstairs before she knew what he would say to Hector Reaganach, and Hector to him. He had never known a woman so filled with curiosity, but since it had brought her into his life, he would not condemn it. He would, however, do his best to control it, lest it lead her into more danger.

At the moment, curious about something himself, he asked the question he had wanted to ask since they had left the hall: "Just who is Mariota, lass?"

She tensed, then drew an audible breath and pulled a little away, looking up as she said, "She was my second eldest sister, sir. She died in a fall some years ago."

Her eyes sparkled with tears, and he was unsure if they were new ones or remnants of her earlier distress. When she continued to watch him, he realized that she did not want to talk about Mariota. But he wanted to know more about her.

"What does Lady Euphemia mean when she says you are growing more and more like her? She has said that twice now," he added when she hesitated.

She licked her lips, sending an unexpected jolt of desire through him. Then, with a tremulous smile, she said, "Mariota was extraordinarily beautiful, sir, but impulsive. No one has ever suggested that my looks are a match for hers, so I'd wager Aunt Euphemia means that I tend to be as impulsive as Mariota was."

He waited, hoping she would say more, but she met his gaze solemnly and remained silent. The thought crossed his mind that she might be waiting for him to reassure her that no one could be as beautiful as she was, but he sensed wariness rather than yearning for compliments. Moreover, he was nearly certain that her earlier pallor had begun with the mention of Mariota. But he could not press her more now. Hector was waiting.

Michael pulled her close again, tipped her chin up with a finger, and kissed her gently.

When she moaned and pressed her lips hard against his, he tightened his embrace and kissed her more thoroughly, smiling when she allowed his tongue into her mouth to explore its soft interior. His body responded instantly, and he knew that if he did not control himself, he would take her right there in Hector's chamber. As he eased himself away from her, he smiled again.

"You stir my passions too easily, lass. I think we'd best wait until we are safely married before continuing along this course."

She caught her lower lip between her teeth, then gently disengaged herself and bent to pick up her cloak. The look in her eyes when she straightened again told him that a thought had occurred to her that she was reluctant to share.

"What is it?" he asked.

"My demon curiosity," she said ruefully. "It stirs again."

Michael chuckled. "This time, sweetheart, I believe it augurs well for us both. But come now. Hector awaits us."

"What will you say when he asks if you punished me?"

"He won't ask," Michael said. "You are as good as mine now, lass, and no gentleman probes into private matters between another man and his woman."

She looked doubtful, but she need not have worried. When they returned to the hall, they found a veritable hive of activity there.

Hector strode to meet them. "You took long enough, lad, but you should both change into dry clothes, and quickly. I've had word that ships are blocking the mouth of the Sound near Mingary. We depart for Duart directly after we sup."

"Do we, my lord?" Michael said without bothering to conceal his amusement. "My men are going to be sleeping at their oars, I fear."

"Nay, for I've told my captains to select a contingent of good, strong oarsmen for the *Raven*, so that your lads can rest. We'll scatter them amongst mine in the other boats, and they need not lift a hand. I've already given the orders, and I've informed your cousin, as well, so you may refresh yourself without concern."

"What about our discussion?" Michael asked.

"You'd only have to repeat the details to Lachlan at Duart," Hector said. "We'll put it off until we get there."

Feeling Isobel stiffen beside him, Michael said, "Lady Isobel should hear the whole, my lord. If you will object to her presence when we talk at Duart, I'll need enough time here before we leave to discuss it with her privately."

Hector frowned, and to Michael's surprise, Isobel made no attempt to persuade him. Indeed, he thought, she was unusually quiet.

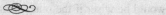

Isobel was speechless.

Both Cristina and Lady Mairi were strong women with minds of their own. But although she knew Hector and Lachlan nearly always gave their wives general information about their comings and goings, if the women wanted to know more, they generally met first with strong resistance if not outright refusal. If they pressed harder, sometimes they succeeded in learning more, but they also risked censure, and often received stern rebuke instead of the information they sought.

That Michael would inform Hector that he meant to tell her as much as he would tell Hector and Lachlan was the last thing she had expected. But that was exactly what he had done, and she was not about to say anything that might change his mind or stir Hector to forbid it.

Although Michael had said that Hector would not demand

to know if he had punished her, she knew that Hector made his own rules. If he wanted to know, he would ask, and if he did not ask Michael, he would ask her. And if he learned that Michael had not, he might still do so himself. She was not afraid of punishment. Indeed, she almost wished that Michael had obeyed Hector. The things he had said to her instead had made her feel dreadful, and they kept echoing through her head. Punishment, although physically more painful, was nearly always quickly over.

Hector was looking at her, but when she met his gaze, his eyes began to twinkle, and she relaxed. "Aye, lad," he said, turning to Michael. "'Tis a good notion, that. She's a sensible lass most of the time, and she should know the truth."

Michael nodded but said, "Aye, however—and I do not mean any disrespect by this, my lord. But I do still think it would be wiser if the other women—"

"I agree," Hector interjected. "Isobel is to be your wife, so she must know enough to keep her safe. The others have no reason to know your secrets, and may even be put at more risk if your enemies have reason to think they do."

Michael relaxed visibly, giving Isobel to wonder how much more he knew, and if he truly intended to tell even Hector everything. But he said only, "Then we'll go now and change, my lord."

"Wait," Isobel said as he turned to offer his arm. To Hector, she said, "What about the wedding, sir? You said it should be speedy. Are we to marry at Duart?"

"We have no chaplain here, lass, as you know, and since you will want a proper wedding, I mean to arrange it with his grace's chaplain at Ardtornish."

"Will not such haste create more comment?"

"Nay, for no one will wonder that you want to marry quickly, not with his grace in poor health and Sir Michael's brother expecting him straightaway at Kirkwall. Even if he were willing to wait a few days and go with us when we had planned to go, local parsons would not have sufficient time to proclaim your banns. But that will not trouble his grace's chaplain, and in any event, unless our arriving a few days early will trouble Sir Henry, I think we had all better go north together."

Michael said, "Guests never trouble my brother, sir, be they ever so many. He revels in company, and will welcome all who come, whenever they come."

"Then that's settled," Hector said. "Go now, and do not tarry."

Michael accompanied Isobel to the door of her bed-chamber, kissed her lightly, and said, "If he or Lachlan Lubanach should object to your presence at our discussions once they begin, lass, do not fret, for although I may decide that I cannot tell them all I know of this matter, I will tell you. You have my word."

"I won't fret, sir. Hector has given his word, too, and he does not break it."

"Nor do I, lass; don't forget that," he murmured, cupping his hand behind her neck and pulling her face close to his. His hand felt warm and strong.

"Dress warmly," he added before he kissed her again.

When he released her, she hurried into her chamber, feeling breathless and filled with wonder at the abrupt turn the course of her life had taken. Then it dawned on her that she had too little time to pack properly, not only for a long journey and the installation of a prince but also for her wedding.

Chapter 10

Isobel was astonished at how quickly everyone was ready to depart. She had scarcely begun searching for suitable clothing to take when Cristina entered and said that her own maid, Brona, had already packed much of what Isobel would need.

"Knowing that you would return barely in time to leave, and not knowing if you'd think to have new gowns made up at Chalamine, I had several made for you here," she said. "You will doubtless want to try them on, but Brona or Mairi's Meg can attend to any adjustments for you at Duart or Kirkwall."

"Thank you," Isobel said. "Adela did arrange for me to have three new gowns made up at Chalamine, but I left them behind with my maidservant."

"Aye, well, I have been preparing for this journey all summer," Cristina said. "So at least you'll have a new dress for your wedding as all brides should."

"To assure them of good fortune in marriage," Isobel said with a grin. "You sound nearly as superstitious as Father."

"Most people are superstitious about something, and nearly everyone is when it comes to weddings," Cristina protested. "At ours, Aunt Euphemia gave Hector a silver coin to put in his shoe, and she rarely pays heed to such stuff."

Isobel chuckled. "Much good the coin did him."

Cristina smiled. "He may have thought as much then, Mistress Impudence, but I do not think he thinks so anymore. Now," she said, "I've had Brona see to your packing, but you will want to look through your things to be sure we're leaving nothing behind that you will need." She smiled and gave Isobel a hug as she added, "After all, I was not expecting you to marry before we journeyed to Kirkwall."

With another hug, she left Isobel to her tasks and went to hurry the others. In little more than an hour, thanks to Hector's habit of being always ready to respond to trouble, twelve ships and their passengers were ready to depart, and in the swift galleys, the journey took little more than three hours. As they approached the small harbor below Duart Castle, they heard bells ringing the hour of Compline.

The wind had died to near stillness less than an hour before, and the clouds had likewise dissipated to reveal an oval moon high overhead. The castle, on its high promontory where the Sound of Mull converged with Loch Linnhe and the Firth of Lorn, looked silvery in the dusky gray moonlight.

Despite the late hour, the harbor and the hillside above it teemed with armed men, and galleys patrolled the waters of the Sound and the Firth.

They found their host and hostess still up, and after Hector explained that new circumstances warranted discussion, Lachlan nodded, saying, "Mairi can take the women upstairs and get them settled, whilst you and I and Sir Michael adjourn to my inner chamber, where no one will disturb us. I trust that you have all supped."

"Aye, hours ago," Hector said. His gaze met Michael's, and he added, "Isobel will stay with us."

Lachlan looked from one to the other, then nodded without comment.

"Mayhap we should all stay," Mairi suggested.

This time Lachlan exchanged a look with his twin before he said, "Nay, lass. You'll do more good by seeing that our lady guests and their maids are comfortable. I've a notion that at least some of us may be leaving for the north in the morning."

"Aye," Hector said. "I'm thinking we'll want as large a flotilla as possible."

Lachlan nodded again, then said to his wife, "Tell the lads to begin making ready, and find someone to send a message to Ardtornish. If your mother does not wish to depart with the flotilla, she need only say so and I'll make special arrangements for her. What?" he asked, turning again to face Hector as if that gentleman had spoken.

"Before you send any message to Ardtornish, you should all know that our Isobel has accepted Sir Michael's offer of marriage. In view of his grace's ill health, and the fact that the lass would do better to travel north as Sir Michael's wife, the sooner their marriage can take place, the better it will be."

"Aye, that's true, for it will hush the rumormongers," Mairi said, hurrying forward to hug Isobel. "I'm pleased that you made this decision, my dear."

"If they are to marry before going north, they must do so at Ardtornish or here at Duart," Hector said. "I thought his grace's chaplain might oblige us."

"An excellent notion," Lachlan said, adding to his lady, "Go along now, lass. Send your Ian to Ardtornish with those messages, and tell one of the lads in the hall to see that we are not disturbed." He glanced again at Hector. "What of Macleod? Does he know about this wedding?"

"Nay," Hector said. "I'm thinking we'd best stop at Glenelg on the way."

Lachlan nodded, and before Isobel had time to absorb their matter-of-fact reaction to her news, she was sitting between Hector and Michael at the long table in the inner chamber that Lachlan generally used to meet his many informants and to confer with the friends and allies of Mac-Donald of the Isles.

Lachlan sat at the head of the table, saying, "You've heard, I expect, that there are strangers about, several galleys at least, lying just outside the west end of the Sound near Mingary."

"Aye," Hector said. "Sir Michael was going to sail west because he feared that his enemies might be lying in wait, but I did not think it wise for him to go so near the Holy Isle, so we all came here."

Isobel noted another look between the twins. She knew from past experience that Lachlan suspected that Hector was leaving out details, and from the warmth in her cheeks, she realized that her blushes would tell him that those details pertained to her and thus probably to her sudden decision to marry. But he made no comment other than to say, "You were wise to bring them here."

"Aye, sure," Hector said.

Lachlan turned to Michael and said, "I had thought to deal with the intruders myself, but since you'd told Hector earlier that your enemies believe you possess something that the Kirk insists should be returned to Rome, I thought perhaps I'd wait to learn more. I'm hoping you can oblige me."

"Aye, sir, I'll do my best," Michael said. "'Tis true that they suspect my family possesses such a thing."

"And you have said that you know not what that item is."

"That is also true, my lord. I do know, however, that whatever is missing has links to the past, because my father said we had a solemn duty to keep St. Clair business within the family, to guard our secrets well. He said that my grandfather of heroic memory laid that duty upon us, and in truth, I doubt that my father would approve of my confiding even what little I have to you and Hector Reaganach."

"We are honored by your confidence, sir, and give you our word that nothing you tell us will go farther unless you grant us express permission. Am I to understand that the secrets you spoke of begin no farther back than two generations?"

"I believe so, but I know only that such secrets exist. I do not know what they are, nor does my brother."

"Are you certain of that? Henry is the elder, after all, and your father's heir."

"Aye, sir, but I would know if he were lying to me. He has a strong sense of honor. Moreover, he told me that our father said once that when Henry came of age, he would have to bear the responsibility of keeping those secrets, that our father would explain them then. But he died before that day came, and anyone else who may know or suspect what the secrets are has not shared his knowledge with us."

"I see." Lachlan frowned thoughtfully.

Isobel easily followed that train of thought, however, and said eagerly, "You are thinking of your father, are you not, sir? Michael, I'm sure I told you about Ian Dubh's interest in historical matters. Most likely, he knows more about such things than all of us together and may well have an idea about what it is you seek."

"My father is here at Duart now," Lachlan said, getting to his feet. "He is Chief of Clan Gillean, and I must tell you, I took the liberty this morning of briefly describing your troubles to him so he might ponder them, but you can trust him as you trust us. With your permission now, I'll invite him to join our discussion."

Looking from one earnest face to the next, Michael felt as if things were quickly spinning beyond his control, and he was by no means sure he liked it. However, even Isobel's curiosity was no match for his where the subject of the family's secret was concerned. He assumed it was something hidden, some object that bore importance to St. Clairs and to others, too, but what exactly it was and where it might lie hidden were matters beyond his ken. Moreover, despite Lachlan Lubanach's courtesy, that gentleman clearly assumed that Michael would agree.

"I'd welcome Ian Dubh's advice, sir," he said. "Please ask him to join us."

Isobel shifted her weight beside him, stirring other thoughts in his head and feelings in his body that had nothing to do with his family's mystery.

While Lachlan went to the door to ask the gillie outside to fetch Ian Dubh, Michael casually moved the hand nearest Isobel to his lap and then to her thigh, startling her. He was amused to note that although her leg jumped, her expression gave nothing away. But his amusement quickly shifted to a suspicion that she had flirted with other men in just such an inappropriate manner. He remembered, too, the ease with which she had flirted with Hugo and even with the villain Fin Wylie in the cavern.

Firmly reminding himself that the flirtation with Fin Wylie, at least, had been a matter of self-defense, he told himself that she was too much of an innocent to have dabbled beyond flirtation with Hugo or any other man, not to mention that she was too fond of her own freedom to have enticed others to think she might willingly have accepted their advances.

Her hand touched his just then, but a moment later an elderly man entered, and Michael quickly arose with the others to greet him. Ian Dubh's quick stride and upright posture belied his gray hair and apparent age. He was thin and neither as tall nor as broad as his sons, but Michael saw at once that he was no milksop.

"This is Sir Michael St. Clair, Father, the gentleman I mentioned to you this morning," Lachlan said. "He has offered for our Isobel, and she has accepted him. We are hoping that you can help him solve this puzzle of his."

Ian Dubh's grip was firm, his smile welcoming. "'Tis a good match," he said. "You are Master of Roslin, are you not, and grandson of Sir William St. Clair, who accompanied Sir James Douglas and Robert Logan on their ill-fated attempt to carry the Bruce's heart to Jerusalem?"

"I do have that honor, sir," Michael said.

"But I heard that Sir Henry's *father* was the one who carried Bruce's heart, sir, and fought beside him at Bannockburn, too," Isobel said.

"Nay, lass," Michael said. "Henry wasn't born until fifteen years after Bruce's death, and my grandfather's, come to that. Our father died thirteen years later."

"Many make that mistake, Isobel," Ian Dubh said. "When a man is famous, it is natural for those who talk of him to paint him in ever more glorious ways, as if boasting of such knowledge somehow links them more closely with him. Sir Michael's father was also Sir William St. Clair. He died in a fall from a horse."

"He was a soldier, too, though," Michael said.

"Indeed, he was, like his father and grandfather," Ian Dubh said. He looked as if he would say more, but he glanced at Lachlan and Hector instead, then back at Michael, before he said, "I think perhaps you will want to speak more of this alone, lad."

Michael looked at Hector and Lachlan, too, hesitant to agree if it might make him appear rude to them.

Isobel had been watching Michael carefully, and she understood his discomfort in the face of his growing audience. Nevertheless, it took nearly all the strength of mind she possessed to speak now. Quietly, she said to no one in particular, "It is Michael's secret, after all. Mayhap he should know what it is, if indeed Ian Dubh can tell him, before we all share in it."

Hector had stiffened at his father's suggestion, and her words only made him stiffen up more. Lachlan, too, looked about to protest.

Before either of them could say a word, Ian Dubh said in a tone Isobel had rarely heard from him, "I will speak to Sir Michael alone."

"Isobel must stay, sir," Michael said firmly.

Looking annoyed, Ian Dubh said, "As she is to be your wife, that is your decision to make, lad, but I would caution you. Such secrets are not the province of women. Not only might she inadvertently betray you, but should these enemies of yours suspect that she shares your confidence, her life might be in danger."

"I believe she will be safer knowing, sir. Moreover, I gave her my word."

"Then there is no more to be said. You two may leave us, however," he said to his sons.

Without another word, they left the chamber.

Isobel watched in wonder until the door had shut behind them.

Ian Dubh said evenly, "You are surprised that they left, lass?"

She nodded and then, recollecting herself, turned back to him and said, "Yes, sir. I did not think they would go, or that they would allow me to stay if they did."

"I am still Chief of Clan Gillean, Isobel, for all that Lachlan has taken over most of my duties these past years. I allow you to stay only because Sir Michael commands your presence and, as I understand it, has every right now to do so."

"Do you think you know what my enemies seek, sir?" Michael asked.

"Before I answer that, I think Isobel should know that your father, like his before him, was not just a soldier but a Knight Templar and thus a very fine soldier indeed. One must suppose that you and Sir Henry are Templars, too, are you not?"

Despite long experience, the rush of dismay that Michael felt was such that for once he failed to control his features, and his mouth dropped open before he could prevent it. Warily, he said, "The Order of Knights Templar no longer exists, sir. It ceased to do so long before I was born. Moreover, I am a man of peace."

The old man's blue eyes twinkled. "Sakes, lad, you need not hide your teeth with me, unless you do so for the lass's sake, in which case, I apologize, but you did say she was to hear all."

Michael glanced at Isobel, saw her eyes narrow, and said hastily, "I have no wish to hide anything from her ladyship. But nor will I make any claim to be a Templar. My grandfather had that honor, as his tombstone at Roslin Castle attests, and my father was a fine soldier, thanks to similar training. But I was only five when he died, scarcely old enough to benefit from his skills."

Ian Dubh looked speculatively at him, but Michael had himself in hand again and met the look easily. He had said nothing that was untrue, and the exchange did not affect his promise to Isobel.

Isobel looked from Michael to Ian Dubh and back again. Clearly, the older man did not believe Michael, but Michael seemed sincere. She had heard of the Knights Templar, because both Lady Euphemia and Ian Dubh had occasionally spoken of them in describing historical events, but she knew little about them.

Ian Dubh took a seat on the other side of the table from them and gazed thoughtfully at Michael before saying, "You may disclaim the connection, lad, but I believe the information you seek lies in the history of the Order."

"But the Pope declared the Knights heretics, ordered their arrest, and disbanded the Order more than seventy years ago," Michael said.

"Those arrests took place primarily in France, at the order of King Philippe le Bel," Ian Dubh said. "He'd already done away with two popes and controlled a third, but he did not control the Knights Templar. He owed them a vast amount of money that he did not want to repay, which is why he sought to control the papacy."

Michael said, "With respect, sir—"

But Ian Dubh went on firmly, "The Order was never dissolved in Scotland because the papal bulls dissolving it were never proclaimed here. Even if they had been, how much sway do you think the Bishop of Rome commanded here, especially since he had excommunicated Robert the Bruce the year before?"

"Probably none," Michael said, "but we have little time for history lessons if Lady Isobel and I are to marry before we head north, sir, and my enemies are lying in wait for us even now. With respect, what is it that you believe they seek?"

"They seek the treasure, of course," Ian Dubh said.

Isobel gasped. "What treasure?"

"Besides being the best soldiers ever known, the Templars also provided the world's largest banking organization," Ian Dubh explained. "Men could deposit funds with them in Scotland or England, and with no more than a letter, could draw equivalent funds from the Order in countries as far away as the Holy Land. Thus, they did not have to carry their riches with them. The Templars could provide such a service because their temples and preceptories safeguarded much of the world's wealth as well as the Order's own wealth, amassed throughout its history."

"But if they were heretics . . ." She glanced uncertainly at Michael, knowing that she spoke not just about Templars in general now but also his grandfather.

Ian Dubh said, "'Twas not their heresy that undid them, lass, if such heresy ever existed. 'Twas the huge loans they made to world rulers, men such as Philip of France, who did not want to repay them. At the time of the Templars' downfall, Philip controlled Pope Clement as completely as if His Holiness had been a puppet rather than a man. The moment he received word that Clement would cooperate, Philip ordered the arrest of all Knights Templar in France and sent his men to seize their Paris treasury. But the treasure had vanished, along with most of the French Templars. Their great fleet at La Rochelle had vanished, as well."

"Where did they go?"

He smiled. "Most would say that no one knows."

"You will not say that, however," she said confidently.

"I cannot say that I *know* more than that," he said. "But I can tell you that when I was very young, my father was constable of Tarbert Castle, and late one dark, mist-filled night when I was supposed to be in bed, I saw a number of strange ships moving so silently on the loch that they looked like ghosts, because towboats pulled them. I learned that my father knew of their presence, and therefore I believed that I would learn more myself, but when the sun arose the next morning those ships had vanished, and my father not only denied knowledge of their presence but punished me for having slipped out during the night without permission."

"But where could they have gone?"

"Sakes, they could have gone anywhere, but you will perhaps recall that, for years, I've studied documents pertaining to matters from Robert the Bruce's time."

"Aye, of course," she said.

Turning to Michael, he said, "I'll show you some of those documents. They provide only vague references to the

Paris treasury but suggest that your grandfather assumed its guardianship and arranged for its transport to Scotland with the permission of his grace's father, Angus Og. Angus Og had won fealty from many Isles clans by then, particularly south of the Isle of Skye. Little occurred in these waters that he did not learn about as quickly as Lachlan Lubanach's vast network of informants collects information now for his grace. He would certainly have known of any strangers' ships, especially since the most likely route for them to have taken to Loch Tarbert would have taken them first through the Sound of Isla, near Angus Og's primary seat at Finlaggan. Had those ships not been welcome, he would have dealt with them before ever they reached Loch Tarbert."

"And such an incident would be widely known now, in bards' tales and the like, so he must have welcomed them and kept it quiet," Michael said thoughtfully.

"Aye, and Robert the Bruce welcomed military aid from Scottish Templars, including members of your family. No Scottish Templar was ever executed or imprisoned, because Bruce, being excommunicate, had no reason to comply with orders from Rome, if such orders were even issued to excommunicates."

Isobel had been thinking about the Templar treasury. "Much of the world's wealth, sir? Could even a fleet of ships have carried so much?"

"Their fleet was said to be enormous, lass. Documents show that at least eighteen were at La Rochelle, whilst many others were going about their business elsewhere and did not return."

"But where could they all have gone?" she asked.

"Templar ships provided transport for many goods that the people of the Isles export, particularly for our petrol oil, which has for years been used throughout Britain, Europe, and elsewhere as sacred oil in the kirks. Ships that provide that transport now are often St. Clair ships," he added with a pointed look at Michael.

"But why would the Templars bring such a treasure to the Isles?" she asked Michael. "Was your grandfather an Islesman?"

"Nay, he lived at Roslin Castle, in Lothian, ten miles south of Edinburgh."

"True," Ian Dubh said. "But recall that at the time the English controlled Scotland from Edinburgh south. Bruce had not yet vanquished them, so it would have been safer to hide the treasure here in the Isles then and move it inland later."

Michael sighed. "But I'm guessing from what you've said that your documents say naught of where they hid it or where it might be now."

"Nay, but what about your own? Every noble family possesses muniments, documentation of titles, grants of land, and so forth. Have you examined yours?"

Michael nodded. "Henry and I have read everything we could find at Roslin. In truth, not much is there beyond the grant for the castle, documents pertaining to the barony, my mother's marriage settlements, and a few decisions of the baron's court. Henry is also Baron of Roslin," he added in an aside to Isobel. "My title, Master of Roslin, is merely a styling that will redound to Henry's son when he has one."

"For that matter," Ian Dubh said with a smile, "your title will change when Henry officially becomes Earl of Orkney, as he'll be known here. As I understand it, that was part of the arrangement Henry made with the King of Scots."

Michael nodded.

"What sort of arrangement was that?" Isobel asked.

Michael remained silent, but Ian Dubh said, "Sir Henry

will retain many of the privileges that accompany a princedom, lass. For example, he will be able to issue his own coins and exercise judicial authority within his realm. Sir Michael, as his brother and a potential heir, will be known as Lord Michael St. Clair of Roslin."

"That is not important, however, because Henry will soon produce his own heirs, and I have no wish to be a prince or Earl of Orkney," Michael said.

"You are wise, lad, for such titles come with more responsibility than one might suppose," Ian Dubh said. "Moreover, there were other claimants to the princedom, and the Norse King demanded a promise of loyalty to himself, not to mention payment of an amount that is far more than most men possess."

"The princedom is Henry's concern," Michael said. "Mine appears to be this supposed treasure. Can you tell me more about it, sir? Of what does it consist?"

"I don't know," Ian Dubh admitted. "I can tell you only that any number of Islesmen must have known about the ships that carried it here, if not more about the treasure itself. That no one speaks of it now is testament to the influence that both Angus Og and Bruce had, and to the loyalty that Islesmen extend now to his grace. If you like, you may come to my chamber and have a look at those documents. I have made fair copies of several, which I will give to you, but I warrant your best hope of discovering the whole truth lies at Roslin. I doubt you'd find anything in Caithness, since that property came to your family through your mother."

Michael turned to Isobel. "Do you want to see the documents, lass?"

She shook her head, unexpectedly overwhelmed by all she had learned. Ian Dubh's explanation of Michael's position revealed that she had not perfectly understood it before. The plain fact that he was brother to a man who would become a Norse prince had meant little to her. Even learning of his brother's wealth had not fazed her, because a man's wealth did not necessarily mean that his siblings were likewise wealthy. Moreover, never having felt its lack, she had little interest in money. But to learn that Michael was potentially heir to that princedom and that his children might likewise inherit it, however small that chance might be, was another matter entirely, and one that she needed to think about with great care.

She knew that she ought to tell him at once of her concern, but he and Ian Dubh were discussing the latter's documents in greater detail, and she did not want to interrupt, especially to discuss the subject now foremost in her mind.

"If you will excuse me," she said, standing, only half aware that she had inadvertently interrupted Ian Dubh midsentence, "I will bid you both a good night, because tomorrow looks as if it will be a long and perhaps difficult day."

Both men stood when she did, and Michael said, "I'll escort you to your chamber, my lady, before I meet Ian Dubh in his."

"Pray do not trouble yourself, sir," she said. "I share a room with my aunt when we visit Duart, and I know my way."

"Nevertheless, I will escort you," he said firmly. Turning to Ian Dubh, he said, "I can easily find someone to direct me to your chamber, sir, so I shan't keep you waiting long."

"I'm a patient man," Ian Dubh said. Then, giving Isobel a measuring look, he added, "Sleep well, lassie. If Lachlan has taken over the arrangements for your wedding, I warrant it will take place soon after you wake in the morning."

"Aye, sir," she said, making a brief curtsy, afraid suddenly that if she tried to say more, she might cry.

As Michael reached for her hand and tucked it firmly into the crook of his arm, it occurred to her to wonder when, exactly, he had changed from the man who so amiably followed her lead to one who seemed determined now to ignore it. But she remained silent as they made their way to the main stairs.

After the first flight, the spiral stairway narrowed and she went ahead. But when they arrived at the chamber she shared with Lady Euphemia and she reached for the latch, he stopped her by catching her hand and drawing it back.

"Wait, lass," he said quietly. "I would know what has disturbed you so."

"Ian Dubh awaits you, sir, and we should not stand here talking where my aunt may hear us."

"Ian Dubh will wait, and we can hear Lady Euphemia snoring. What is it?"

"Nothing of consequence," she said, feeling guilty as the words tripped glibly from her tongue but feeling, for once, utterly incapable of explaining herself in a way that would make sense to him without betraying her family.

He stared into her eyes for a long moment in the way that made her most uncomfortable. Then, as she felt heat creeping into her cheeks, he said, "You might like to think up a different answer, sweetheart, one that I am more likely to believe."

Much as she wished she could elude his stern gaze, she could not seem to do so, but neither could she blurt out the truth to him, not the whole truth, certainly.

He seemed content to hold her gaze, to make her squirm in her guilt as he had done earlier that day, until at last she said, "This marriage is happening too fast, that's all. I'm thinking we should wait longer, not marry so quickly. It cannot matter if we wait. It is not as if we will be traveling alone together again, because if Hector and Lachlan have their way, they'll surround us with protectors of all sorts, a vast flotilla of galleys full of oarsmen and family. Moreover, sir, you don't even want to marry me. You know you don't. You feel as constrained to do so as I do, myself."

His fingers on her shoulders found the earlier bruises, making her wince. Immediately, his grip eased, but he did not take his hands away as he said, "That answer is no better than the first, lass. We are going to be married just as soon as a priest presents himself to say the words. So unless you can give me truly good cause, I will not call it off, nor help you to do so. We need to make speed, Isobel. Henry himself may be in danger."

"How could he be? Surely, he has surrounded himself with protectors."

"Aye, but they will make little difference to Waldron."

"Waldron waits at the other end of the Sound," she reminded him. "He is no threat to anyone else whilst he stays there, not when Lachlan knows he is there."

"We know only that his galleys lurk there, not who is aboard them. And Waldron is always welcomed in Caithness, and at Roslin, for that matter."

"Mercy, why should he be?"

"He is my cousin despite the circumstances of his birth," Michael said, lowering his voice to a near whisper. "He is also a prime favorite of my mother's, because he has always been most charming to her. I had not thought about all this before, because he said naught to me about Henry or his ceremonies and I knew naught of any treasure. Waldron just insisted that I should tell him where 'it' was, and since 'it' was a mystery to me, I thought only about his stubborn refusal to accept that I did not know what was missing. A treasure of any size complicates things. Moreover, Ian Dubh said there are other claimants to the princedom."

"Are you saying that Waldron may be one of those claimants?"

"He cannot be a true claimant, because he is baseborn and he comes from the French branch of our family. Henry's claim originated not only through our mother, who is cousin to the Norse King, but also through Henry's first wife."

"He was married before?"

"Aye, his first wife was the Norse King's daughter. They were very young, and she died soon afterward. Her father helped ours arrange Henry's second marriage."

"But none of this will matter once Sir Henry is made Prince of Orkney."

"That's true, and I believe it is too late now to contest it, in any event. But since Waldron believes it is God's will that he should have whatever he wants, he may try to claim the princedom anyway, either by guile or by force."

Isobel's head was whirling, but she tried to return his thoughts to the subject at hand. "Even so, I warrant your brother can take care of himself, and we—"

"No more now, lass. You need to sleep, and I must not miss this opportunity to learn what I can from Ian Dubh. We'll talk more in the morning."

Her mouth opened in protest, but he had his hand on the door latch, and before she could think of anything to say that might sway him from his decision, she found herself inside the bedchamber with the door swinging shut behind him.

As she took off her gown and, in her shift, slipped quietly into bed beside Lady Euphemia, she promised herself that she would make everything clear to him, somehow, before anything else happened the next day. She could not allow him to marry her if she might taint his children with the same demon that cursed her.

Chapter 11

With the help of a gillie who directed him, Michael found Ian Dubh's chamber easily. When he entered, the older man was reading a parchment, weighty with red wax seals, at a table lighted by a number of candles and cressets. Other such documents, neatly rolled, lay in a tumble nearby.

"Come in, lad," he said, looking up. "I trust all is well with your lass."

"Aye, sir," Michael replied, shutting the door. "But I do not want to keep you up longer than necessary, so pray, let us proceed at once to the matter at hand."

"I have the documents here," Ian Dubh said, gesturing toward the tumbled pile of rolls on the table. "You may peruse as many as you like, and I'll give you fair copies of the two that pertain particularly to the St. Clairs. The one suggesting that your grandfather helped arrange for the Templars to come here is most interesting. You will find, however, that he spelled his name differently from the old style."

"I know, sir; he spelled it 'Sinclair,' the way one pronounces it," Michael said. "My mother prefers the French spelling, however, and Henry indulges her preference just as our father did."

"Does he? I had heard as much, but believing that your esteemed grandfather's wishes must prevail, I own, the news did surprise me."

"It would not if you had enjoyed the privilege of meeting my mother."

"I see. Well, come round here, and I'll show you the references to Sir William. Before I do, though, there is one other detail that you should know."

"Indeed?"

Ian Dubh nodded. "I left one thing out of my tale about the ghost ships," he admitted. "Sithee, I was not alone that night."

"No?"

"I was but six years old, and I own, I'd not have had courage enough at that age either to defy my father or to sneak out after I was supposed to be in bed."

"But you did both."

"Aye, but to follow someone else, someone I greatly admired."

"An older child?"

"Aye, a close cousin, and one whose father had even more right than my own to order things at Castle Tarbert."

With a tingling sense of anticipation, Michael said, "If, as you told us, your father was constable at Tarbert, he yielded authority to only one man."

"Two, if one counts the King of Scots," Ian Dubh said, "but in view of the controversy that raged over who *was* king at the time, we need consider only one."

"His grace's father, Angus Og. So the cousin you followed was . . ."

"His grace, of course," Ian Dubh said. "In view of his

illness now, I took advantage of your interlude with our Isobel to intercept the gillie Lachlan has arranged to send to Ardtornish, and conveyed my own orders to him."

"May I ask what they were?"

"To see that his grace becomes acquainted with your presence here. I think that you should speak with him, if he agrees. Sithee, but for having seen the ships myself, and knowing at the time that Angus Og was aware of their presence in West Loch Tarbert, I have learned no more than what little I have read of the matter. Indeed, when I pointed out the existence of these documents to his grace, he refused to discuss them, saying that what lies in the past should remain in the past."

"Then why do you believe he would speak with me?"

"Because I also told the lad to say that your life has been threatened. His grace has a great fondness for Isobel, so I believe he will want to meet you in any event, to give your marriage his blessing. Then we shall see what we shall see."

With that, he proceeded to acquaint Michael with the documents and to explain more about them than Michael had energy to absorb. The hour was late before he got to bed, and he fell at once into a deep sleep.

Isobel's first glimpse of the new day was Mairi's smiling face, as that lady leaned over her and said cheerfully, "Wake up, Isobel. The priest is here, and I have come to help you dress for your wedding."

From that moment, Isobel felt as if all control over her life had fallen to others, that she retained none for herself. Being checked, restricted, and compelled were constraints that she resisted with every fiber, but the people who commanded her were those she was least accustomed to disobeying, so when they massed against her, as they did now, she found it impossible to protest with her usual energy.

Not that she did not try.

As Mairi whisked her out of bed, Isobel said she was not by any means certain that she wanted to marry just yet.

"Nonsense," Mairi replied briskly. Then, to her maid, she said, "Brona, it is the moss-green silk we want."

Isobel tried again. "But, Mairi—"

"Cristina is even now gathering your flowers for you, my dear. I know many consider it bad luck for anyone but the bride to gather them, but I know too that you care as little for such superstitions as Cristina does, so you will be grateful to have one less task to perform. You know that neither Hector nor Lachlan is blessed with much patience, and if I judge your Michael correctly, he possesses little more than they do. Moreover, it has been my experience that once men have determined upon a course of action, they do not happily brook delay."

In this manner, she kept up a running discourse that allowed Isobel time only to reply to such questions as her ladyship fired at her from time to time almost midsentence. Did she want her hair up or down? Did she think the moss-green silk would look well with a dark-blue-and-yellow shawl? Did she not think that perhaps she would prefer to wear stout shoes rather than flimsy slippers with her wedding dress, since they would be taking ship for the north directly after the ceremony?

It occurred to Isobel only as she was answering the last question that doubtless Mairi was attending her rather than Cristina, whose right it was as her elder sister, because the latter believed Isobel was unlikely to offer Mairi resistance, let alone outright defiance. If that had been Cristina's reasoning, Isobel admitted—if only to herself—she had been right. As for declaring her independence to Lachlan or to his grace's priest, who had clearly arisen betimes to travel from Ardtornish for the sole purpose of performing her wedding, or insisting that she would wait a while longer to marry, she could not bring herself to do either.

Thus it was that she went meekly downstairs with Lady Mairi to the great hall, where she discovered that nearly all the inhabitants of Duart Castle had gathered to see her married. Hector and Lachlan stood near Michael on the dais with the thin, grizzled parson. Sir Hugo, standing beside Michael, smiled and winked at her. When she smiled back, Michael glanced at Hugo, but Hugo ignored him and winked at Isobel again.

Cristina moved forward to give her the bouquet of flowers she had gathered. As she did, she plucked two pink roses from it and put them in Isobel's hair, which Isobel wore in loose flaxen waves down her back. Standing back to judge the full effect, Cristina said, "You look more beautiful than ever, dearling."

"'Tis true," Lady Euphemia agreed. "None of the rest of you will ever match our Mariota for looks, but I'm thinking that today our Isobel draws close."

"Thank you, Aunt Euphemia," Isobel said, but even to her own ears, her voice sounded weak, because the last thing she wanted was to be like Mariota. Catching Michael's gaze on her, she suppressed a grimace, straightened her shoulders, and tried to believe he deserved whatever he got from their marriage.

The priest stepped forward, spread his arms to silence everyone in the hall, and directed Michael and Isobel to the makeshift altar at the front of the dais. From that moment, the proceedings took on the semblance of a dream, and it seemed only minutes later that Isobel heard him say, "I present to you Sir Michael and Lady St. Clair. You may kiss your bride now, sir, if you choose."

Michael grinned, and before the entire Duart household, he put an arm around Isobel to draw her close, tilted her face up to his, and claimed her lips in a kiss that heated her to her toes. As she felt herself melting toward him, she collected her wits, became fully aware of her audience, and stiffened abruptly.

Michael held her closer, and in prolonging his kiss, he touched the tip of his tongue to her lips, but he did nothing else other than to kiss her right cheek and then her ear. As he kissed her ear, he murmured, "It is done, sweetheart. Do not forget that you have promised to obey me and to be meek in my bed and at my board. I shan't be a harsh husband, but neither am I one to relish feminine fits of temper."

"You said we would talk first," she muttered, trying to ignore the fluttery sensations that heated her body, and surprised as she had been before that he could read her mood so well. She hoped that no one in their audience was doing the same.

"Aye, well," he said, "events moved faster than my brain did this morning, and, too, I saw no sign from you that you objected."

Not wanting to give him the satisfaction of hearing her admit that she had allowed similar events—or Mairi—to sweep her right to the altar, she kept silent.

Servants swiftly produced a simple breakfast of bread, meat, and ale, and afterward, Hector slung Lady Axe, his legendary battle-axe, over his shoulder. The others gathered up their belongings, and everyone who would join the flotilla descended the steep path to the harbor and boarded galleys to begin their journey.

Five miles later, when the ships turned into Ardtornish Bay, Isobel, lost in her own thoughts, glanced at Cristina in vague surprise that they were stopping so soon. But Mairi said with a grin, "Surely, you remember that we sent word to my mother yestereve of our intent to depart today. She sent her reply with the parson this morning, promising to be ready, but we are all to go up to the castle first, because my father desires that you present your new husband to him."

Isobel had forgotten all about Princess Margaret, but glancing at Michael, she noted his lack of surprise, and guessed that he had known all along that they would stop at Ardtornish. He smiled, and although his smile had the same effect on her that it always did, she vowed to herself that, one way or another, he would pay dearly for having put her in such a position.

Then he stood and reached a hand out to her. Taking it, feeling it enfold hers, and looking into his smiling eyes, she recalled with a start that one other aspect of marriage existed to which she had given much too little thought.

Michael had only begun to savor his success in winning Isobel. He had thought her beautiful from the start, but seeing her now, dressed as she would be for court, with her smooth, rosy cheeks, her blue-gray eyes showing only gray today, her flaxen hair hanging like a gilded sheet nearly to her waist, and her low-cut gown framing pillow-soft breasts, he thought no one could be more beautiful, and he wondered again what the oft-mentioned Mariota had been like.

Well aware that this was no time to indulge his curiosity further, he and his lady led the way up steep steps carved into the cliff from the harbor to the great black-basalt castle on its jutting promontory above. Inside, they continued up more steps to the great chamber, then through it to a smaller one beyond.

The inner chamber contained a great blue-curtained bed, its drapery exquisitely embroidered with red, green, and white birds and flowers. In the bed, propped up against cradling pillows, lay MacDonald, Lord of the Isles.

Clearly weakened by his illness, he looked gaunt and, to Michael, much older than Ian Dubh. His hair was thin and white, his pale blue eyes watery and reddened, his face gray and shadowed with stubble. As they entered, he straightened on the pillows, and as his gaze caught Michael's and held it, Michael found himself enduring a shrewd, measuring gaze and hoping that he would not fall short.

Ian Dubh had stayed at Duart, and Lady Euphemia remained in the hall with the waiting women, so only Hector, Lachlan, and their lady wives had accompanied the newly-weds into his grace's presence.

Mairi stepped forward, and when he extended a hand to her, she grasped it as she bent to kiss his cheek. "Good morning, sir," she said. "I have brought Isobel and her new husband to meet you before we all depart for the north."

"Aye, lass, I see that," he said, and his voice was strong despite his illness.

"I warrant I should present them to your grace properly, as Sir Michael St. Clair and his lady wife," Mairi said with a grin.

Michael bowed and Isobel curtsied as MacDonald said, "Step forward, the pair of you. I would learn more about this hasty wedding."

Mairi opened her mouth to explain, but Michael forestalled her by saying calmly, "I regret the necessity for haste, your grace, but I must be at my brother's side when he is installed as Prince of Orkney, and it seemed wiser to take my lady wife with me than to leave her behind. My enemies know we have been together long enough for her to learn something of my affairs, and although I know less than they believe, I want her safe and will worry less if I keep her with me."

MacDonald's eyebrows rose. "Do you think us unable to protect her, sir?"

Michael smiled and waited for an answering gleam before he said, "I know you can protect her, your grace, but although I've arranged settlements with Hector Reaganach, I warrant you will agree that such matters arrange themselves better after marriage than before. You see, I want her protected in more ways than one."

"You make an excellent argument, lad," MacDonald said, adding bluntly, "Does that mean that you've already bedded the lass?"

Noting Isobel's flaming cheeks, Michael suppressed another smile as he said, "Not yet, sir. We have felt some need for haste today."

"It will not hurt your enemies to wait an hour or so longer," MacDonald said. "Whilst she retires with Mairi and Cristina to the bedchamber my lady has set aside for her, and prepares herself for you, you may remain here and bear me company."

This time, Michael did not risk looking at Isobel. Her gasp had been enough to tell him that she had not yet wholly accepted this duty of marriage, and he had no wish to stir her to rebellion in his grace's bedchamber. Nevertheless, he was relieved when Ladies Mairi and Cristina took command of her and led her from the room.

Hector and Lachlan clearly hoped to stay, but Mac-

Donald dismissed them with a gesture, and Michael found himself alone with him.

"Draw up that stool, lad," MacDonald said. "I'll wager Ian Dubh told you the pertinent facts of our history, since his message to me, although cryptic, made it clear that he wants me to speak to you of what the two of us saw that night."

Michael obeyed the request to draw up a stool and sit but did not reply, seeing no sense in pointing out that, regardless of what message Ian Dubh had sent, the decision lay entirely with MacDonald as to whether he would speak.

"Both of us suffered for our sins that night," MacDonald said with a small, reminiscent smile. "I'm guessing he told you all he knows of the matter, augmented by what little his prized documents have revealed of it since."

"Aye, sir, he told me about the four ships he saw when he followed you to the shore below Castle Tarbert. He said they disappeared by morning and the two of you could learn no more about them."

MacDonald chuckled. "I made the mistake of deciding when they vanished that I'd keep my tongue behind my teeth, but my daft wee cousin had less sense and suffered the same overweening curiosity then that plagues him to this day."

And him not even a Macleod, Michael mused.

"What makes you smile, lad?"

Recollecting himself, Michael said, "It has recently come to my notice, my lord, that such curiosity seems to abound in the Isles."

"So it does," MacDonald said, twinkling. "I know Isobel well. Indeed, I'd ask you to tell me how you met and all about your brief courtship, but I know you are aching to consummate your union, so I'll not keep you. Doubtless you want to know anything I can tell you about those ships."

"Aye, sir, an it please you."

"I think that, with enemies threatening, you need to know at least as much as I do, but I may not know as much as you hope." He was silent for a moment, gathering his thoughts. Then he said, "What I do know derives more from my long rule as Lord of the Isles than from direct knowledge of the facts."

"I collect from what you said about Ian Dubh's curiosity as a child that he spoke out of turn and thus drew attention to your disobedience."

"Aye, that's true, but that earned us naught but a fine skelping. In time, my father did come to explain some few things to me that may prove helpful now. I do not know what, if anything, you know about the Knights Templar."

Since this time Michael had expected the reference, he did not react except to say, "I know that my grandfather was a member of the Order, your grace, as many other Scottish nobles were. I know that Pope Clement ordered their disbanding and the arrests of all members. Ian Dubh said Clement was a pawn of Philip of France."

"Aye, and supposedly following Clement's edict, Philip commanded the arrest of every Templar in France. We ignored the edict here, of course. Edward of England was creating nuisances throughout Scotland, particularly along our coasts—here in the west as far north as Isla, and along much of the west coast of Ireland, for that matter—but even Edward lacked the authority to enforce Clement's edicts here. And of course Robert the Bruce had no inclination to do so."

"But surely, in time, with such an edict in place . . ."

"Even now, the only one hereabouts who heeds the Pope

is the Green Abbot of Iona, and he does so only when it suits his purpose, as I suspect it does now."

"Then you, too, believe the abbot may be involved with my trouble."

"I do," MacDonald said. "He overstepped his mark years ago when he and some of his minions attempted to assassinate both me and the King of Scots in one traitorous act. The King ordered him to keep to the Holy Isle for the rest of his days, and for the most part, he has obeyed that command. But Fingon Mackinnnon is his own man, and should he ever show himself to you, I'd warn you to take great care. Your lady knows she must not trust him, but he knows her, as well."

"What happened to those four ships?" Michael asked, believing MacDonald was rapidly tiring, and hoping to learn more before he had to let him rest.

"I cannot say for certain, because my father believed as I do that the fewer people to know such details, the safer it was for everyone," MacDonald said. "He said men who wanted me to know they had been party to that affair would tell me themselves. None has, but I do know that the most likely places for those ships to have offloaded cargo were Castle Sween, Kilmory, and Kilmartin, all places where your grandfather and the Bruce wielded influence. I also know that the Templar fleet comprised more than four ships and that Sir William, and subsequently your father and brother, developed what amounts to a St. Clair navy that can match or surpass that of any ruler in Europe or Britain."

"Aye, we do control a good many ships," Michael agreed. "But surely, most of those that came here from France must be old or have fallen apart by now."

"Perhaps," MacDonald said. "But ships do not just crumble to dust, lad, not if they're well cared for, and your family makes a practice of caring for theirs. Of course, their great wealth allows them to refit more than most shipowners can."

Michael could not pretend to ignore the implication this time. "Faith, sir, do you think my grandfather took that treasure for himself? Because if you do—"

"Stand easy now," MacDonald said. "I make no such accusation. I know your grandfather's reputation for honesty and integrity, and I do not for a moment believe he'd have done such a thing. Moreover, I know that your family wealth derives primarily from your father's marriage to Isabella of Strathearn."

"But?"

"Aye, well, surely you've noted yourself that your family is even wealthier than hers, wealthier even than the Norse King, by most accounts. 'Tis one reason, I suspect, that that wily gentleman agreed to let your brother Henry assume what Henry chooses to call a princedom, and not just any princedom, I might add, but the highest in all of Scandinavia, save that of the Norse King himself."

"Ian Dubh told me how much Henry is paying for it," Michael admitted. "Nonetheless, there apparently were and still are other claimants to the title."

"As there are other Templars who must know of the treasure's existence, if not its exact contents."

"But do not most people believe that the Templars no longer exist?" Michael asked, wondering if MacDonald would reply the same way as Ian Dubh had.

"Aye, sure, here in Scotland they became Knights of St. John instead," MacDonald said, eyes twinkling again. "One thing my father told me is that nearly all Templars who fled arrest in their own countries—knights, sergeants, and minions alike—came to Scotland, even from Ireland, where none was arrested until seven years after the Paris incident. Thus, hundreds came to Scotland, and you must realize that they all knew their Order had controlled vast wealth, and most must have realized or learned at some time or other that the treasure had gone missing."

"So Scotland offered refuge to all who would come," Michael said.

"Aye, of course. By the time Philip tried to confiscate the Paris treasury, Robert the Bruce had been King of Scots for over a year, although he endured five more years of struggle to unite Scotland and rid it of Edward's English army before our victory at Bannockburn finally settled things."

"And the Templars played a part in that."

"A large part," MacDonald said, "because not only did Bruce welcome such finely trained soldiers, but most of them had managed to flee with their equipment and weapons. So as far as he was concerned, *they* were his treasure. My father was one of his closest friends, and between them, with your grandsire's help, they made certain that Templars everywhere knew Scotland welcomed them. To be sure, they did not all come at once, but they came in large numbers and small for years after that awful Friday in Paris. And they turned the tide at Bannockburn."

Michael nodded, saying, "Then what happened afterward?"

"I fear I know little more that can help you, for although I suspect a number of men of having played a part in guarding the treasure, as I said, none has admitted as much. However, if your grandfather controlled it, it lies safely hidden, and I'd warrant its hiding place is on St. Clair property—and property that has been in the family a long time, because such property is least likely to leave St. Clair control."

"Then most likely it lies at Roslin, but Henry and I have searched the whole castle."

"All the old Templar holdings are controlled by others, so I'd suggest that you search again. But meantime, lad, I'd advise you not to keep your bride waiting any longer. Our Isobel has a temper, you know, although she rarely indulges it."

"I doubt she has displayed it to you, my lord."

"Nay, but news travels with speed through the Isles, as you will see."

"If one desires a rose, your grace, one must respect its thorns."

MacDonald chuckled, looking ten years younger. "So I have been told, lad. Indeed, your father told me years ago that that is an ancient Persian proverb."

"My father?"

"Aye, and as I recall, he recited it to me just before he married your mother. Now, go to your wife with my blessing, sir. I wish you both well."

"Thank you, your grace," Michael said sincerely as he bowed and left the old man to his rest. He liked MacDonald and could easily understand his popularity, but once outside the bedchamber, Michael's thoughts were for no one but his bride.

Isobel had never felt more constrained than she did as she waited with Cristina, Mairi, their maids, and her aunt for Michael to claim her as his own. She had scant knowledge of what that meant, living as she had, first in the household at Chalamine, motherless from her third year, and then at Lochbuie, where the laird and his lady enjoyed the luxury of a private bedchamber.

She wished she dared command everyone to leave her and go about their business, but she knew that although the two maidservants might obey, Cristina, Lady Mairi, and Lady Euphemia would not. Moreover, lying naked beneath a blanket that was not even hers, she felt more vulnerable than usual.

At last, though, unable to keep silent any longer, she said, "I have only the vaguest notion of how men and women couple. Should I not know more about it?"

Cristina said guiltily, "I suppose I should have talked with you about what to expect, dearling, but everything happened so quickly that I didn't think of it."

"Nonsense," Mairi said. "You will find that you know exactly what to do, Isobel, and if you have any doubts, Michael will show you." With a grin, she added, "If my own experience was typical, you will enjoy it very much."

The maidservants giggled, and Isobel wished she had not spoken. But then the latch clicked and the door opened almost before awareness set in that it was her husband who walked in so unceremoniously. On his heels came the priest.

Michael said, "I'd take it as a kindness if you would lose no time in blessing this bed, parson."

The priest smiled indulgently. "All bridegrooms are impatient, sir, but you will want everything as it should be." Nevertheless, he was efficient, and Hector and Lachlan appeared in the open doorway as he was finishing the brief ritual.

Michael observed their arrival with visible wariness. "I'm grateful for your assistance, my lords, but I would be alone with my lady wife if you please."

The two men glanced at each other, eyes mutually atwinkle, and Isobel had a sudden fear that they would insist on bearing witness to her conquest, or at least on assisting Michael to prepare for bed, as she had heard was frequently the fate of bridegrooms. But Michael turned to Lady Mairi and said, "I warrant the princess Margaret would welcome your assistance with her preparations, madam, and that of the lady Cristina and your maidservants, as well."

"Aye, sure, she will," Mairi said, chuckling and taking firm hold of her husband's arm. "Come along, you men, and let the happy couple get on with their important business, so that we may all depart for Kirkwall as soon as possible."

Within moments, the chamber was empty, and Isobel watched with mixed relief and wariness as Michael barred the door.

He turned and smiled. "I have faith in them, but I believe you will feel more comfortable if you know that no one can walk in on us."

"Comfort is not a word that springs to mind just now," she muttered.

He strode to the tall window and yanked the curtains shut, dimming the light inside to what little could slip through the narrow opening where they met. Then, moving to the curtained bed, he seemed to loom over Isobel.

"You need not fear me, lass," he said gently as he began to unfasten his doublet. "I will take the greatest care not to harm you."

"Will it hurt?" she asked.

"It may hurt a little the first time," he said.

"Will what you do give me a child?"

"Do you want a child?" he asked, smiling again.

Noting that the thought seemed to make him happy, she felt a prickle of concern but pressed the point nonetheless. "Will it?"

"I cannot say. It may."

"Then we should wait until we can talk more about certain things," she said.

"Nay, lass, it is my sacred duty to consummate our marriage quickly. I would see you protected as my wife, and to that end, I want to be sure that no one else can have any cause to contest our union."

"We can just tell them that we consummated it," she said reasonably.

"Could you tell such a lie to Hector and the others?"

The thought sent a shiver through her. Lying to Hector was never a good idea, but if such a lie were necessary, for Michael . . . "I think I could," she said.

Even in the dim light she saw his eyebrows shoot upward. "Does that mean you would tell lies to me?"

"I don't lie," she said, squirming a little. "Sometimes, if it is necessary, I may shade the truth a little or neglect to tell the whole truth."

He sat on the bed, and she started to ease a little away from him, but he stopped her with a light hand on her bare shoulder. His hand was warm, but the look in his eyes was cool. "Could you lie to a priest who asked if we had consummated our marriage, or to his grace?"

She had been about to insist that she could lie to the Green Abbot without a single twinge of conscience, but his grace was another matter. "Nay, not to his grace."

"Do you recall my reaction to finding you on my ship?" he asked softly.

His tone sent another shiver through her, but she said, "I do not know why you must bring that up again, sir. That incident lies in the past."

"Aye, it does," he agreed, stroking her bare arm. "But

you would do well to remember that I do have a temper, sweetheart, and take care not to rouse it again."

She frowned. "Do you mean you'd be angry if I refused to couple with you?"

"Nay, lass, you have as much to say about that as I do, for I do not believe in forcing women. I will insist that we consummate our marriage, but I would ask for your submission. I have no wish to bed an unwilling wife. My warning just now had to do only with your apparently casual attitude about lying to people other than his grace. I would have you understand that it will be as dangerous for you to lie to me."

"Then I will try not to," she said. "It is only that sometimes one feels obliged to lie a little. For example, if someone asks one for an opinion of a new dress or hat, or asks other such questions, lying may be the only tactful way to reply."

Taking her chin firmly in hand, he made her look at him as he said, "If I ask you a question, Isobel, I want an honest answer."

"And will you give honest answers to my questions, sir?"

"I will," he said. "If I cannot, I will tell you that I cannot, and I will try to explain why. Sometimes secrets belong to other people, and when someone entrusts me with a secret, I am obliged to honor that confidence."

"Mayhap I, too, have such secrets."

"Do you?"

She could not meet his gaze. "Not just now," she admitted. "I was only thinking that I might one day. If I told you that that was the case—"

"A woman should not keep secrets from her husband," he said flatly.

"I see," Isobel said. "Only husbands may keep secrets."

He sighed. "That is not what I meant to say. Nor have we sufficient time now to talk this matter out as we should. I agree that we must discuss it further, because you make a good point, but right now we have an important duty we must fulfill."

"Consummating our marriage," she said. "Perhaps making a baby."

"Aye," he said, proceeding to take off his doublet.

As she watched him unlace his breeks and kick off his boots, she nibbled her lower lip silently. But when he stood and faced her, clearly ready to claim her, she said, "There is one secret you must know before we couple, sir. Mariota was mad."

Chapter 12

Michael paused in the act of removing his nether garments and straightened again to look down at Isobel, his most trusted instincts warring against each other. On the one hand, instinct told him she was telling the truth as she knew it. But a similar reliable instinct had told him he could trust Hector Reaganach, the admiral, and the Lord of the Isles. Logically, either the Maclean twins and Mac-Donald knew naught of this madness, or Isobel was mistaken.

Wondering how patient the others awaiting them would be, he glanced at the door, but he had securely barred it, and he did not think they would interrupt him without better cause than their own impatience. Deciding that that did not matter anyway when it was his life and hers that were at stake, he held his peace long enough to finish undressing and to climb into bed beside her.

When she shrank from him, he said, "I was mistaken, sweetheart. 'Tis clear that we need to discuss this matter further before we proceed, but I would like to hold you, if I may, whilst we do."

"Then you believe me," she said on a note of relief that reinforced his judgment that she believed what she said.

"I do. Now, come here to me." He stretched out his arm invitingly, remaining silent until she had scooted closer and laid her head in the hollow of his shoulder. Drawing her nearer yet, he stroked her bare arm with his fingertips, delighting again in the silky smoothness of her skin and hoping she would soon lose her tension and be at ease with him. Quietly, he said, "Tell me again how Lady Mariota died."

She hesitated as though choosing her words, then said, "There is a cliff above the castle."

"Above Chalamine?"

"Nay, here at Ardtornish. They call it *Creag nan Corp*."

"Aye, sure, I've heard of it," he said. "'Tis MacDonald's punishment rock, but surely, your sister was no felon cast to her death on the rocks beneath it."

"No," Isobel said. "We . . . we were on the cliffs one day—Cristina, Mariota, and I—and . . ." Her hesitation this time lasted longer, but he waited, then grimaced when she added in a rush, "Mariota and I fell off. We caught hold of shrubbery, but Cristina could only reach me. Mariota . . ." She fell silent again, her lips pressed tightly together as if she dared not trust her voice any further.

He shuddered at the thought that he might so easily never have met her. Turning to his side, still holding her close, he looked into her eyes and wished he had left the curtains open so that he could see her expression more clearly. He had a feeling that his change of position made her uncomfortable, but he did not think that discomfort stemmed from sexual fear of him.

Her gaze shifted from his, and knowing that the subject was uncomfortable for her, he said only, "That must have been terrifying for you."

"Aye, for I was but twelve at the time."

He waited, letting her choose her pace, knowing she would be more likely to tell him the whole tale if he did not press her.

He was watching her so intently that she could scarcely breathe, but although she had decided that she had to share her worry about Mariota's madness with him, she could not seem to get the words out. The few that had come had spilled from her tongue easily enough, but they danced around what she wanted to say without saying it. A nagging voice in her mind warned that she was betraying her family. Still, she knew he could tell that she was not giving him the whole truth, and in light of his warning earlier, his steady gaze made her nervous. In other circumstances, she might have invented a reason to postpone the discussion, but postponement now could so easily lead to much worse things. She exerted herself to meet his gaze, wishing that he would say something.

"I . . . I cannot think how to tell you about it," she admitted at last.

"Why were you so dangerously near such a cliff?" he asked.

Heat flooded her cheeks, making her grateful for the dim light as the voice in her head said jeeringly that she ought to have known he would not so easily accept her glib description of Mariota's fall. His curiosity was as active as hers, and his determination to find answers was, if possible, even more intense.

Resisting the strong temptation to evade his piercing

stare, she said, "Mariota was already at the top of the cliff, and Cristina, too, when I rode up to them."

He frowned. "Were you not all three riding together?"

"Nay, I had followed them."

"So, even at twelve, you took your own road."

"Aye, sometimes." She grimaced, then said more sharply, "Pray, do not quiz me, sir. Telling you about this is difficult enough."

"Very well," he said. His tone was amiable, as it usually was, but she easily detected the slight edge that told her he wanted her to get to the point, and quickly.

Closing her eyes so that she need not watch that amiable expression change to one of horror, she said, "Mariota had threatened to throw herself off the cliff, and when Cristina tried to reason with her, Mariota tried to push her off instead."

"How did you come into it?"

His tone was so gentle that she opened her eyes, wondering if he had misunderstood her, but when she saw his expression, she shut them again and swallowed hard before she said, "Mariota had told me what she was going to do, and I told Cristina. That's why Cristina went after her."

"She is the eldest, so mayhap I can understand that, although she ought to have told Hector, or you should have. And if you followed only out of curiosity—"

Knowing how consistent men were in believing that women could not handle crises without their assistance, she interjected hastily, "I got frightened, and rightly, too, because when I arrived, Mariota was daring Cristina to stand at the edge with her. I could see that something was dreadfully wrong, and I shouted at Cristina not to do it, but she always wants to think the best of people, particularly of Mariota, because she loved her, so she told me to be silent and did as Mariota asked. But I jumped off my pony and ran closer. Neither was paying me heed, because Mariota was intent on cozening Cristina into doing what she wanted her to do and Cristina was trying to persuade her to return to the castle. Then Mariota grabbed her and tried to push her off, and I ran and caught hold of Cristina and tried to pull her back, but Mariota would not let go, so I tried to push her as I pulled Cristina, and . . ."

". . . and you and Mariota fell over the edge," he said when tears she had not noticed before choked her into a watery sob. His voice seemed strangely hoarse as he added, "Don't stop there, sweetheart. Tell me what happened next."

Despite the gruff tone, his calm steadied her, and she said, "Cristina tried to reach us, but she couldn't, and when Mariota realized that although Cristina might succeed in rescuing me, she could not reach her, she . . ." She gulped, hardly able to believe it herself even now but forcing the words out. "Michael, she grabbed my foot and tried to climb right up me, but I . . . I kicked her and . . . and she fell."

The sobs came then, wracking her body, but Michael gathered her close and held her tight. He did not speak until the worst of the storm had passed, but then he murmured, "Just cry, sweetheart, until you can cry no more. It will all be easier then."

But commanded to flow freely, the wellspring of her tears dried up instead, and she was able to regain control of herself within a minute or two.

He was gently stroking her hair, and the sensation of his warm hand against her scalp was comforting. She sighed deeply and let herself relax against him.

"Better?" he said.

"Aye," she muttered. "But I don't understand why I lost

control like that, because I don't think I cried that hard even when she died."

"Do you think that by pushing her, you were responsible for her death?"

Her throat and stomach tightened at so blunt an expression of the very thought that had flitted through her mind as she had described what happened, that she *was* responsible, but common sense stirred quickly. "I never described it to anyone in just those words before," she said. "Hector came, and it was he who rescued me, because Cristina was only able to hold on to me, not to pull me up, and we—Hector and I—were more worried about her than anything else. But you can see, sir, can you not, that Mariota must have been mad to do what she did."

"Sweetheart, what I see is that at twelve, you were as brave as you are now, and if our children are lucky enough to inherit such bravery, I'll be a proud man."

Her heart swelled, but she looked searchingly into his eyes, trying to see if he spoke the truth or merely felt obliged to say such a thing because his pride refused to allow him to reject her so soon after marrying her.

He met her gaze steadily and then bent his head to claim her lips in a warm kiss. When she realized that the kiss was quickly becoming more demanding, she pulled away. "But she was mad," she said. "She must have been!"

"I'm thinking 'tis more likely that she was badly spoiled, that if she was so beautiful, she was used to getting her own way and was just trying to do that when everything went amiss," he murmured. "Even if she was mad, though, you have six other sisters and a host of kinsmen, sweetheart. How many of them are mad?"

"None that I know about," she admitted. "But surely you

would care very much if by marrying me you introduced madness into the St. Clair family."

He chuckled. "What will happen, will happen. Besides, you have not met Henry yet. When you do, you may change your mind about who is introducing madness into the family, and indeed, doubt your own wisdom in marrying me."

"Faith, sir, Henry will be a prince! But *our* children . . . what if—"

"Our children will inherit bravery and strength of mind from their mother," he said firmly. "Those two qualities will overwhelm any tendency to madness."

"Are you sure?"

"I'm sure," he said in that same firm tone. "Now then, lass . . ."

Three sharp knocks on the door made them both jump, and Hector's voice thundered through the wood paneling: "The tide has turned, you two, and time is fast fleeing. If you want the advantage to be with us when we meet your enemies, you'd better stir yourselves out of that bed, and right swiftly."

"We'll be with you shortly, my lord," Michael said.

"Faith, sir, how can we be?" Isobel said. "It is my fault, I know, but—"

Michael silenced her this time simply by placing a finger to her lips. "We are not going to consummate our marriage with a hasty coupling, sweetheart. It would be too easy for me to hurt you, for one thing, and for another, I want to enjoy my bride at some leisure when we do."

"But what can we tell them? I'm sure they will see that I've been crying."

"Aye, and if they do, they will blame me," he said. "If you would please me, you will offer no information to them about this conversation. I think your sister may ask you if all is well, but you need only say that it is, and she will not pry further. That is one good thing you will discover about being a married lady. People will usually respect the slightest hint that they tread close upon an impropriety."

She found that hard to believe, because none of her sisters had ever hesitated to ask her anything they wanted to know, but he was already getting up and reaching for his clothes. When she hesitated, he looked over his shoulder at her, grinned, and tossed her shift at her.

"Slip that on, lass. I'll help you do everything up when I've got my breeks on. Unless you'd prefer that I send for your sister's maidservant."

"No, thank you," she said, knowing she was blushing at the thought of him helping her. But it would be worse to have Brona fussing over her.

She dressed as quickly as she was able, and Michael fastened the buttons and tied the ribbons at the back of her gown. When she would have opened the door, he stopped her with a gesture and then, to her astonishment, drew his dirk from his boot and casually made a shallow cut in his upper forearm.

"What are you doing?" she exclaimed.

He smiled. "They will expect to find blood on those sheets. If they find it, no one will ask questions. Have you something with which I can bind this up after I attend to that?" he asked.

"Trust a man to think of binding only after he's bleeding all over the carpet," she said dryly as she took his dirk from him and used it to cut a strip from her red-flannel underskirt. "This will have to do. I hope your doublet sleeve will cover it."

He chuckled, moved to the bed, and carefully rubbed blood onto the sheet.

"Faith, that is fine linen belonging to his grace and Princess Margaret," she exclaimed, horrified to think they would believe the blood was hers.

"So it is," he said, grinning. "Are you going to tend my wound?"

They bound up his arm and smoothed the doublet sleeve over the binding. Then, after looking around the chamber to be sure they had collected all their belongings, he draped her cloak over her shoulders and tied its strings under her chin. She moved again toward the door, but he drew her close and kissed her.

"Thank you for telling me, sweetheart," he said. "That took courage, I know, but I hope you will always find the courage to tell me what you think I should know."

She looked into his eyes again, wondering if she would ever understand this man she had married. But she had no more time to think, because Hector banged on the door again.

This time, Michael opened it, put his arm around her, and said, "We're ready, sir. We'll just follow you if you please."

Hector looked at Isobel, and in her guilt at the deception they had created, heat surged to her cheeks and she had to exert herself to manage a smile.

But, as Michael had predicted, Hector asked no questions. Turning to Brona, who stood behind him with a bundle of clean sheets, he said, "Tend to the bed, lass, and hurry. The women's boat will wait for you, and for her grace's women, too."

As he headed toward the stairway, he added over his shoulder, "I thought you'd prefer that Brona attend to the bed, rather than his grace's people."

Michael gave her a squeeze, and she hid a smile as they followed Hector downstairs, outside, and down the steep cliff steps to the waiting galleys. She had long since learned that men enjoyed pointing out their cleverness to women.

On the pier, Hector said to Michael, "We have fifteen boats now, so we've decided to put our ladies and their maid-servants in two near the end of the flotilla, with one other boat following as rear guard. We've plenty of men armed with bows, arrows, and their dirks, and other weapons at hand if they prove necessary. But we want to keep the women as safe as we can, and away from any action."

"Aye, 'tis a good notion," Michael said. "And with respect, sir, I'd suggest that you, the admiral, Hugo, and I ride separately."

Hector said, "But we may find need to confer from time to time."

"Aye, sir, but I know my cousin Waldron's methods. He believes in cutting the head off any beast that attacks him, so I believe that if he sees us all in one galley, he may ignore the other boats and send all of his forces to destroy that one."

Hector nodded. "'Tis not the usual way of battle, to be sure, being suicidal for those who attempt it. But 'tis true that if a commander be willing to sacrifice boats full of men to defeat one ship out of a flotilla, he could well succeed."

"Aye, because a headless beast dies quickly," Michael said. "Or so Waldron says. You need not worry that Hugo or I might put ourselves forward to countermand orders that you or the admiral may issue to the men in our boats," he added diffidently. "Although Hugo is a fine soldier, and understands Waldron as well as I do, we also know how to follow orders. Moreover, we both know the pair of you to be outstanding commanders."

Isobel, long adept at reading Hector Reaganach, noted the shrewd look he shot Michael as he said, "I don't worry about insubordination, lad. Instead, I'd say that if either of you sees an opportunity to affect the outcome of whatever confrontation befalls us, you will have the good sense to follow your instincts."

"Thank you, my lord."

Isobel shifted her gaze to her husband, wondering how many personalities existed within the man. When he spoke to Hector he did not in any way resemble the man who had so easily followed her lead at the cavern and afterward. If anything, he sounded as if he had agreed to follow Hector only because he already knew and respected Hector's reputation as a soldier.

"I'll take you to the other women, lass," Michael said.

"I don't want to ride with them," she said, certain that although Brona and Mairi's woman, Meg Raith, might respect her new status long enough to forget they had known her since her arrival at Lochbuie, and might therefore refrain from quizzing her about her marriage bed, Cristina and Mairi would not.

"That is not a point for discussion," Michael said. "We may well find ourselves embattled as soon as we reach the opening of the Sound. At such a time, a lead galley is no place for a woman."

"Do you honestly believe that any cousin of yours would attack a boat with a woman in it?" she asked.

"Aye, I do," he said. "You heard what I told Hector Reaganach, and you have met Waldron yourself and should therefore understand that he sees only the goal he seeks. He would not have hesitated to hurt you at the cave, because he believed he could make me tell him all I knew if he did."

"But you have said you know nothing that would help him."

He looked at her. "Exactly so," he said. "I might even have been able to persuade him of that fact—in time."

She turned away, looking across the water as she digested his words. Understanding was neither pleasant nor persuasive.

"We have fifteen boats, several fitted with battering rams," she said. "They cannot possibly have so many. Nor, despite what you say, can I believe that your cousin's oarsmen will have so little regard for women, even if he does."

"Make no mistake about Waldron," Michael said, his tone harsher than she had yet heard it. "He has no one working for him whom he does not trust implicitly to obey him, and his men know well the penalty for disobedience. They will die for him, lass, without question or pause, or he will kill them himself."

"Faith, what manner of man is he?"

"He is an assassin at heart, a soulless killer of men. Remember that."

"I do not know that word, 'assassin,'" she said, frowning.

"'Tis a word from another language," he said, "a word I learned from my father that he learned from his. One can only hope it never becomes so common here that everyone knows it, but you must understand it to understand Waldron."

"But what language? I thought he was your cousin, a man of your own clan."

"He is, but from the French side," Michael said. "Members of our clan came to Britain from Normandy with William the Conqueror. Waldron speaks both English and Gaelic fluently because he learned both languages, and

French, from birth, and other languages that were a part of his training as a soldier. But we have no time for more of this now," he said, looking past her into the distance.

"But that word 'assassin' is not Gaelic, English, or French," she protested.

"Sakes, lad," Hector boomed behind her, "have done with your trifling and get the lass aboard that boat. We've others to load as well, and little time for it."

"Aye, sir," Michael said with a rueful smile. "I apologize, although I warrant you know the source of my lethargy. Behave yourself, lass," he added, kissing her soundly and handing her into the women's boat before she could think of a retort that would not instantly make Hector wonder things she did not want him wondering.

Welcomed enthusiastically as she took her place on the cushioned bench between her sister and Lady Mairi, she noted that their women sat in a second boat, likewise boasting twenty-six oars and flying the little-black-ship banner of the Lord of the Isles over that of Clan Gillean.

She noted, too, that Michael went at once to the *Raven* to confer with Sir Hugo, who greeted him with a broad smile and a clap on the back. They talked for only moments, however, before Michael made his way to Hector and Lachlan, who were talking at the end of the pier nearest the cliff stairs.

To her relief, Mairi and Cristina said nothing about her bedding, talking quietly of other, trivial matters instead and generally leaving her to her thoughts. A short time later, she saw Princess Margaret and her two waiting women making their way down the cliff stairs. It seemed no time after that before Lachlan handed her grace into the women's galley and saw her settled near the stem-post with her women seated opposite her, the three of them thus occupying the seats most sheltered from wind and spray.

"I do apologize if I have caused any delay," Margaret said. "His grace sent for me because he desired to know that the embroidered sail he is sending as a gift to Sir Henry for his lead galley had got safely aboard. It had, of course." Smiling at Isobel, she added, "This must seem a strange way to begin a marriage, my dear."

"Oh, no, your grace," Isobel assured her. "I love adventure, you see, and to travel so far north in such a company for such an event seems most exciting."

"I see. Well, Lachlan Lubanach informs me that we should make Skye tonight if those ships lingering near Mingary do not delay us overlong. He will send a boat on ahead of us once we are clear of danger, he said, to warn Macleod of Glenelg and Gowrie of Kyle Rhea to expect us, and invite them to join our flotilla."

Isobel nibbled her lower lip.

"What is it?" Cristina asked her in a low tone. "Are you all right?"

"Oh, aye," Isobel said hastily. "I was just thinking that Father will soon know that I have married. What he will say I don't even want to imagine."

"Sakes, do you fear he will be displeased?"

"Aye, sure," Isobel said. "Any plan that is not his own displeases him."

"Your marriage into the St. Clair family will not, however," Cristina said. "Hector has told me they possess wealth beyond one's imagining. Such a connection can only increase the power of the Macleods, Isobel. Not only will Father approve but so will Macleods throughout the Isles."

Isobel frowned. "I have heard that, of course, and mayhap Sir Henry is wealthy, but I still don't know that

Michael is. To be sure, he seems to have his own galley, or at least the use of one of his brother's, and he is Master of Roslin Castle, but that is only a styling. 'Tis Henry who owns the castle."

"Hector told me that Sir Michael was most generous in your marriage settlements and that Sir Henry has naught to say to them unless he wishes to add to them," Cristina said. "No one, least of all our father, will condemn your marriage."

Her voice had risen, catching the attention of Mairi, who had been conversing quietly with her mother but who turned now and grinned at Isobel.

"Cristina is right," she said. "No matter what else happens today, Isobel, you need not worry about your father's reaction to your marriage. My father has had much to say about him over the years, but he has ever agreed that Macleod is nearly as practical a man as his grace is himself, and few men are more practical than he. Is that not so, madam?" she asked Margaret.

"You and Lachlan Lubanach certainly found him so," Margaret said dryly.

"Aye," Mairi said with another grin. "And so you will find Macleod, Isobel."

It crossed Isobel's mind then that even if Macleod did approve, she was by no means certain that she had been wise to marry Michael St. Clair. She would know the truth of that only after she came to know him better, assuming of course that he survived the encounter that lay just ahead.

Michael dozed lightly on and off in the galley to which Hector had directed him. The helmsman had his orders, and the galley's own captain was in command, giving Michael to hope that he need have no hand in whatever took place when they reached the western mouth of the Sound of Mull.

The rhythmic beats of the helmsmen's gongs drummed in his ears, but he found the rhythm soothing. Although he was as relaxed as a man could be in a moving vessel on sheltered, if swift-moving water, his eyelids rarely shut all the way, allowing him to watch enough through his lashes to catch the occasional smile of a resting oarsman who glanced back at him, and he had no doubt that others he did not see smiled, too. That they did so did not disturb him.

He also kept watch on the twin sons of Gillean in the two lead boats. Hector's boat, he noted, rode some distance ahead of Lachlan's, as one might expect, since it was Hector's duty to protect the Lord High Admiral. Michael noted, too, that Lachlan stood near his helmsman and seemed to watch the north shore of the Sound rather than the water ahead. More than once, Michael saw signals flashed from hilltops there, either lighted torches waving back and forth, or reflective materials that caught the sunlight.

At one point, the admiral's oarsmen eased their pace to allow the *Raven* to move alongside, and Michael heard Lachlan shout to Hugo, "Six ships, not four! They wait in ambush a short distance west of Mingary."

Hugo waved, and Michael did, too, to let Lachlan Lubanach know that he had heard. The admiral's boat continued its slower pace as if expecting him to catch up, too, and he was tempted to do so if only to make certain Lachlan understood that six ships posed a great threat even against a dozen if their commander was Waldron of Edgelaw. But he had taken the measure of the Maclean twins and, certain that neither man left such details to chance, he waved

Lachlan on. He could now see Mingary Castle dead ahead, where the Sound curved sharply to the west.

Looking back to make sure the women's boats lagged well behind, and noting that rather than just one boat following them, two others had slowed, so that three well-armed galleys now protected them, he knew he need have no concern. Their own captains had orders to turn about at the slightest hint that the leaders might fail to control the conflict ahead, and to make all speed back to Ardtornish.

Nor need he worry that Isobel might try to take matters into her own hands. Even she would not be so bold as to defy Princess Margaret, let alone try to sway his grace's oarsmen, helmsmen, and five captains from their sworn duty.

That the battle group had thus reduced itself to ten ships did give him pause, but as the lead boats neared the mouth of the Sound, all looked serene ahead. Just four gongs beat now, but Michael watched Lachlan's boat, and when a third banner, bright red, suddenly shot up its pole to join the other two, he looked for the three boats fitted with battering rams.

Although the beat of the four gongs continued without changing, oarsmen in the three ramming boats increased their pace to double-time, quickly passing leaders that fell in behind them, their own speed increasing to match the rammers. The men, taking their cues from their captains' silent hand signals, rowed their boats into formation, and Michael knew that anyone listening but unable to see the ten galleys would hear only the gongs from four.

The area for miles around—including the Ardnamurchan Peninsula to the north, the north coast of Mull to the south, and the Isle of Coll to the west—was MacDonald's territory, firmly controlled by the Lord of the Isles and his loyal followers. Therefore, chance was slim that any spy other than MacDonald's own lurked near enough to see that the boats numbered more than twice as many and were moving twice as fast. But Michael had long since learned not to count Waldron out if the slimmest chance existed that his cousin might out-think him.

As that thought flew through his mind, memory stirred of Hector's warning that the Green Abbot of Iona and other members of Clan Mackinnon would be likely to support Waldron if only because he claimed to represent God and the Vatican.

The Isle of Mull contained not just MacDonald's people and members of Clan Gillean but also a good many Mackinnons, any number of whom might be watching from the south shore of the Sound, just as Lachlan's men watched from the north. And those Mackinnons might be as deft at signaling each other, and might even manage to signal Waldron's boats, which could easily lurk to the south, out of sight, in the sea lane between the Holy Isle and the west coast of Mull.

Michael made certain that his dirk was ready to hand in his boot, and that his small sword and targe lay nearby. The likelihood that he would need the targe was better than that he would need dirk or sword, because arrows posed the greatest threat in a sea battle, but he liked to be prepared for any possibility.

It irked him to linger behind the vanguard, especially since Hugo and the *Raven* had moved ahead, but he had agreed to maintain the role he played when Hugo had reminded him that, because of it, Waldron tended always to underestimate him, which might provide an advantage in any future confrontation between them.

As they turned west, eight boats preceded his, drawing swiftly together. And not before time, he decided as they rounded the headland. He watched the sea, rougher now as it opened to the south, but shouts drew his attention to two ships moving toward them from the headland of Ardnamur- chan to the north. Even as he noted the two, two more hove into view from the south and two more from behind him, near Oronsay. Waldron had hoped to confine them in a circle of his warriors.

As the ships flying banners of the Lord of the Isles con- tinued to draw together, all six of the enemy ships aimed for the *Raven*, which had drawn a little away from the others. He realized then that whoever commanded the enemy had orders to take his boat and that the enemy commander as- sumed he was aboard her. He saw, too, that Hugo stood in plain view on the stern-post, holding on to the rope that led from the post to the mast. From a distance, he knew, he and Hugo looked much alike.

Shouting followed, and bowmen in the lead boats shot a rain of arrows at their attackers, who returned fire. Michael's boat increased pace to join the others, and he saw that they were closing quickly. Oars flew upward as one larger galley—Hector's, he thought—drew perilously near the largest of Waldron's boats.

Grappling hooks flew as men rapidly lashed the boats to- gether. Two others from their flotilla closed in and began lashing, too, no easy task on waves from the open sea that rolled the ships about and broke against their sides.

The others in the flotilla joined swiftly in a wheel for- mation, stem-posts out, stern in, creating a huge defensive raft with the *Raven* now in the center. More men took up bows and began shooting a rain of arrows at the enemy boats. Other men boarded two of the enemy boats before Michael's galley was lashed to the rest, and he saw one of Waldron's ships already speeding away.

Stones followed the arrows, and someone from the flotilla threw one so hard that the man it hit toppled backward into the sea. His mates managed to grab him and haul him back aboard, but he was dead or unconscious, for he did not move.

Michael's weapons were out, and the moment his boat was close enough to let him leap to the next, he hurled himself into the fray.

Chapter 13

Isobel watched the battle in horror. It had erupted so quickly and had gone from swarming boats to a raft of moving bodies and flashing swords so swiftly that one moment she had seen the galley that carried Michael and the next it had merged with the others so that she could not tell which one it was. She could identify only the *Raven* in the center and Lachlan's ship, because their banners differed from all the others. She realized that she was standing on her bench, gripping the gunwale so tightly that her knuckles were white, but she had no memory of jumping up there.

All the women were on their feet, watching, all showing varying degrees of the tension Isobel felt. Despite Michael's continued insistence that he was a man of peace, she knew that he was in the thick of the fighting. Men seemed to jump right over one another and from ship to ship as they fought. She saw spears flying and swords flashing, heard battle cries and screams of the wounded. Already, though, the noise had lessened. The Lord of the Isles' boats were larger than their attackers, with higher sides, and they numbered more than half again as many.

Glancing toward the three galleys that had lingered behind to guard the women's boats, she knew from the expressions of the men aboard them that they felt left out, and she could sympathize with their frustration. Although she had no wish to fight, she wished fervently that she were closer and could see better. As it was, the captain of their boat ordered his men to back water, to keep the galley in place and ready to depart at the least hint that the tide of battle might turn. Isobel did not fear that fate, however, only that Michael might suffer injury or worse.

Cristina, too, seemed worried, but Mairi did not, and if Isobel could not make herself feel as relaxed as Mairi looked, the older woman's confidence did ease her anxiety. Observing that one of the attacking ships had managed to slip away and was heading south at speed, she wanted to shout at the other boats to catch it. She looked to her own captain, but although he watched the departing boat narrowly and with visible annoyance, he gave no indication of wanting to follow.

Minutes later, the battle was over, and although another of the enemy boats had disengaged by then, evidently Hector and Lachlan were content to let it depart, too. Thus, two of the six had escaped, but four had not.

"Do you see Hector or Sir Michael?" Cristina asked. "I cannot see them."

"Hector's boat is just drawing up to Lachlan's now," Mairi said. "Don't worry, I'm sure they are all safe."

Isobel had no idea where Michael was. "I don't know how you can tell them apart," she told Mairi. "They all look alike to me, save the admiral's and the *Raven*."

Mairi just smiled, but she kept watching, and Isobel suspected only then that she was not as confident as she had wanted them all to believe.

She hoped they had captured the wicked Waldron, but she could not be easy again until she knew that everyone she cared about was safe.

They had boarded the four remaining enemy boats and quickly taken control of them, and Michael was as certain as he could be, both from the hasty retreat of two that had fled when they saw how greatly the flotilla outmatched them, and from the rapid surrender of the others, that Waldron had not commanded them. He strongly suspected that at least the two fleeing galleys belonged to the Green Abbot of Iona, but he wondered where Waldron might have come by the others.

When Lachlan found him moments later and told him they would give the men who had yielded the usual opportunity to swear fealty to the Lord of the Isles, he said, "With respect, my lord, I'd counsel against that. 'Twould achieve naught but to admit Waldron's spies to your midst. Indeed, I had wondered why he would attack a force so much larger than his, but mayhap his goal was just that, to add his men to ours, knowing that victors nearly always make such offers to the losers."

"'Tis a good point you make," Lachlan said. "Hereabouts, one can trust the word of even an enemy if he swears fealty to his grace, but your cousin's men apparently practice different customs."

"They do, sir," Michael said. "They give loyalty to no one but Waldron."

Lachlan nodded. "Then we will inform his grace accordingly."

He spoke quietly to one of his men, shouted to the captain of another boat to go on ahead of them at speed to Glenelg to warn Macleod of their coming, and then directed his helmsman to ease away. When the ships were all un-lashed, they turned toward the Ardnamurchan shore, where crews from the captured vessels, having to a man sworn full faith and loyalty to MacDonald of the Isles, were set ashore with instructions that if they made their way to Ardtornish, they could swear fealty to his grace in person and join his service.

"Meantime," Lachlan said to them, "we will unburden you of your galleys and weapons, so that you need no longer trouble yourselves with them. 'Tis small penalty for attacking ships belonging to MacDonald of the Isles."

Then, assigning crews to the extra boats with men from all the others, they set off again, now a flotilla of nineteen. As they left Ardnamurchan behind, Michael wondered if Lachlan had remembered that he'd intended to warn Mac-Donald about Waldron's men. Recalling the many signals earlier to the admiral's ship from the north coast of the Sound, and the man to whom Lachlan had spoken, he smiled, certain that the admiral had everything well in hand.

Isobel was astonished that the men, despite having fought a battle, seemed refreshed rather than exhausted and were able to continue their journey at much the same pace as they had set through the Sound of Mull. She had seen Michael, had even waved to him, but oddly, knowing he was safe, instead of relieving her seemed to annoy her. He looked as if he had been having fun, not as if he had been in danger of losing his life. Clearly, the battle had been a tame one.

They stopped to take a midday meal but did not beach the vessels, lashing them together again instead, so the oarsmen could rest while others kept watch. They had cold meat, bread, and ale that they had brought with them for the purpose.

She would have liked to do as many of the men were doing, and jump from one boat to another, if only to ask Michael if, now that the battle was over, she could join him in his boat for a while, where it would be more interesting.

But when she stood and started to step onto her bench again, Cristina said sharply, "Don't you dare, Isobel. You will remain here with us like the lady you are and not go traipsing along from boat to boat like a hoyden."

Isobel lifted her chin. "I am a married lady now, Cristina. I will thank you to remember that and cease giving me orders as if I were still a child."

"Nay, lass, she's right," Michael said from behind her.

She had thought he must have joined Sir Hugo aboard the *Raven* by now, and that boat's banner was clearly visible to her right, so his sudden appearance from her left startled her. She turned and said irritably, "I am perfectly nimble, sir, and I want to hear all about the battle. From where we waited, one could scarcely see what was happening."

"I'll be happy to describe it to you in detail, sweetheart, just as soon as we can enjoy some private time together. But for now, you will remain here with Princess Margaret, Lady Mairi, and your sister."

His obvious assumption that he need only give the command for her to obey it nettled her more, and she opened her mouth to say so, but as she did, the echo of his words reminded her that Princess Margaret would hear, so she said only, "Then pray do not forget this time that you have promised me a discussion, sir."

"Nay, lass, I'll not forget," he said.

Despite an edge to his voice that suggested he was not merely reassuring her but warning her as well, she turned away from him and took her seat again. If he expected to act the tyrant over her after promising that he would never do such a thing, he had to learn that tyrannical behavior would incur consequences.

"Isobel, you make me blush for your manners," Cristina hissed at her. "You should not talk to him so, and whatever did you mean, 'this time'?"

Taking care that her words would not travel to the others, she murmured, "Surely, propriety forbids prying into personal affairs between a wife and her husband, Cristina. Must I actually answer that question?"

"No, of course not," Cristina said apologetically. "Forgive me, dearling."

Her swift apology made Isobel feel guilty but not so guilty that she was willing to explain. Nevertheless, she said contritely, "There is naught to forgive. I should not have spoken as I did either."

Amiable relations between them being thus restored, the rest of the day passed slowly, for as much as Isobel loved being on the sea, the scenery was exactly as it had been just days before. Even the cushioned bench grew hard long before they reached the Sound of Sleat, which separated the western Highlands from the east coast of the Isle of Skye.

Recognizing their location, Isobel said in surprise, "Are we not going to harbor in Loch Eishort? 'Tis a much more sheltered harbor than any in the Sound."

"Nay," Mairi said, "because the shortest route north from here is through the kyles and the Inner Sound."

"Have you traveled to the Orkney Islands before, then?"

Mairi laughed. "Nay, but I quizzed Lachlan until he drew maps for me, showing me exactly how we'd go, and why."

They scarcely had time to beach the women's boats and set anchors for the others before a welcoming party from Chalamine appeared at the top of the hill path down to the bay. Michael and the other men of their party rejoined them shortly before the riding party arrived.

"There is Father, and Adela is with him, but Sidony and Sorcha are not," Cristina said. "I hope he is not expecting us to stay longer than the one night."

Hector said, "Lachlan sent word ahead to him about the battle, and doubtless the captain will have told him we'll need oarsmen for the extra boats we have as a result and that we mean to continue at dawn. 'Tis a long journey we have ahead."

The burly, rather grizzled Macleod greeted her grace and Lady Mairi with formal politeness, and his daughters with brusque affection, before turning to Hector and Lachlan to say that he had set sentries to keep watch for them.

"Your messengers made it plain that ye'd be wanting to make an early start tomorrow, so I kent fine ye wouldna want to be riding an hour to get to your boats afore then," he said. "Moreover, I've come to tell ye I'll be joining me boats wi' yours, if I'll no be putting Sir Henry out by the doing."

"You won't, sir," Michael said.

When Macleod looked askance at him, Hector laughed and said, "Allow me to present your new son to you, Macleod, and your new brother to you, Lady Adela," he added as Adela joined them. "This is Sir Michael St. Clair, Isobel's husband, and brother of the same Sir Henry who is to be our host at Kirkwall."

"Aye, sure," Macleod said, putting out a hand and

shaking Michael's with obvious enthusiasm, although he continued to speak to Hector. "Yon messenger said there'd been a wedding, and Adela here told me summat o' Sir Michael. 'Tis pleased I am to welcome ye to the family, lad. So, ye believe a few extra bodies arriving early willna vex Sir Henry, but be ye sure o' that? Sithee, I'll ha' Adela wi' me, as well. Doubtless her sisters and aunt will look after her, but since she's said she wants to go, I've decided we'll leave the two younger ones at home in hopes o' finding her a husband. Then, too, three o' them be too many for anyone to watch."

Smiling, Michael assured him that Sir Henry would be delighted.

"Then we'll join ye here for supper," Macleod said. "Me lads ha' brought a fine lot o' mutton chops, manchet loaves, and roasted haunches o' good Highland beef that we can spit over fires to warm up a bit if ye've summat to use as spits and lads to turn the meat whilst we talk."

This being agreed, they rejoined the others to prepare for the night.

Delighted to see Adela and to learn that she would join them on the journey, Isobel invited her to sleep with her in one of the women's tents.

Dusk had set in before the men finished building the cooking fires and setting up tents along the hills near the bay, well above the high-water mark. Two large tents were set up for the six ladies and their tirewomen, and others of similar size for the oarsmen, but a number of the latter elected to sleep in the open with the long woolen wraps they called "plaids" to ward off the chill.

Isobel described her wedding for Adela, who seemed shocked by its hasty arrangement but accepted her assurance that haste had been necessary for the very reasons that

Adela herself had foretold at the shieling. Isobel said nothing of her reluctance to marry and invited Adela to accompany her while she collected her cloak and a comb from a satchel of belongings that she had left on the boat.

Learning that Adela had brought the dresses she had left behind, although she had been unable to persuade Macleod to include Isobel's maid in his party, Isobel said, "I shan't miss her. I've grown quite accustomed to sharing Brona and Meg Raith."

They were returning to the ladies' tent to arrange their sleeping places when a firm hand on Isobel's arm and a familiar voice speaking her name stopped them.

"You'll sleep with me tonight," Michael said.

"I wish you would not approach so silently," she said irritably. "You always seem to appear out of nowhere."

"Come with me now, and I'll show you where we will sleep."

"If I must travel with the women, I'll sleep with them, too," she said.

"Nay, lass, for we'll have but one or two nights on this journey that we can spend together. We'll take advantage of them when they come."

"I thought you said we would discuss things," she said. "You just throw orders at me like any other man would."

"Isobel, really," Adela exclaimed. "What a way to speak to your husband!"

"I did say we'd have a talk, and we will do so tonight in my tent," Michael said, adding, "Lady Adela, I think Lady Cristina is looking for you."

"I'll go to her at once," Adela said, casting Isobel a reproachful look as she fled.

Watching her go, Isobel said, "Is Cristina really looking for her?"

"I don't know," he said.

She looked at him then.

In the same even tone, now beginning to grate on her nerves, he said, "Since you make a point of remembering what I say to you, madam wife, doubtless you will recall that I also said I do not easily tolerate fits of feminine temperament."

"Then you had better stop hurling orders at me, sir. I don't like it."

The words leaped forth before she knew she was going to speak them, and she realized instantly that she ought to have held her tongue. Expecting the sort of tirade that usually followed impertinence on her part, she shut her eyes and waited for the flood of words to engulf her.

Again, Michael surprised her. Putting an arm around her shoulders, he touched a finger to her chin and tilted her face up.

Startled, she opened her eyes.

With a smile, he kissed her. He did so thoroughly, and when she relaxed and began to respond, he raised his head to murmur, "I don't like fratching with you, sweetheart. Can we not declare a truce long enough to talk, mayhap even to sleep?"

"Aye," she agreed with a rueful smile. "I have been bored all day, sir, except during the battle and talking with Adela. Fratching at least stirs the blood."

"So it does," he said, kissing her again and pressing his body against hers. Then, with a twinkle when she pressed back, he said, "Are you sure you're hungry?"

"I'm famished," she said firmly. "Moreover, we are going to talk first."

"We'll see," he said. "I suppose we should eat before we do anything else."

Isobel ground her teeth but said nothing more as they headed for the ring of cooking fires and the long boards set up on trestles nearby to serve as the high table.

When Michael stepped away to talk with Sir Hugo, Cristina moved nearer, saying in an undertone, "You must smile, dearling, lest you give rise to the sort of gossip that stirs scandal. You look like a thundercloud ready to storm, and whatever has vexed you surely cannot be as bad as that. Only think how fortunate we are that none of our men suffered grievous harm today. Only a few arrow cuts and one head lump from a sadly well-thrown rock. Our husbands suffered no injury at all, so you should be giving thanks, not frowning."

"Aye, sure, but sithee, I never asked for a husband. Moreover, he is behaving exactly as I expected a husband to behave, and marriage is forever and ever, Cristina." She sighed. "Forever is a *very* long time."

Glancing around, Cristina said, "Keep your voice down, Isobel. Whatever else you do, you must not make a gift of your feelings to the whole world. What do you mean, he is behaving as you expected a husband to behave? Husbands are husbands, after all, and marriage is much the same for everyone."

"But I thought he was different from other men," Isobel said with another sigh. "He seemed much more reasonable, more willing to hear what I had to say, even to take my advice rather than dismissing it as woman's talk. In fact," she added, remembering, "at times I grew impatient with him, believing he did not bother to think for himself. But now he flings orders at me just as other men do."

Cristina chuckled. "Men are men, Isobel. I do not know why Sir Michael behaved as he did before, but I would remind you that he comes from a powerful family and is therefore doubtless accustomed to command. He certainly has shown no inclination to let either Hector or Lachlan overwhelm him, and they are, as you know well, exceptionally intimidating men."

"Aye, but you did not see him earlier. Even after we arrived at Lochbuie, he was content to let me say my say."

Cristina pressed her lips together for a long moment as her eyes darted back and forth in the wary gaze that told Isobel she still feared their being overheard. Then she said quietly, "You should not be discussing this with me, dearling. If you do not understand Sir Michael, you must discuss that with him. He is your husband now, and as you say, he will remain so until death parts him from you."

"Well, I don't think I want him after all," Isobel said. "What if I were to tell you that he has not yet consummated our marriage?"

Cristina gave a choking sound and quickly covered her mouth. "Isobel, you must not say such things where others might hear you! Moreover, if you were to tell me that tale, I would not believe you, because Brona saw evidence to the contrary with her own eyes. Did you think she would not tell me? Good evening, Father," she added, hastily stepping past Isobel to greet Macleod.

It was as well that she did, because warmth had flooded Isobel's cheeks at the thought of Brona telling Cristina that the newlyweds had successfully coupled. Knowing that Macleod would demand explanations if she did not quickly join them, she drew a long, steadying breath and did so.

He greeted her with a wide smile and open arms, and although she could not remember the last time he had hugged her, she went into them willingly.

"I feared you would be displeased, sir," she said. "You had every right to expect an invitation to my wedding."

"Aye, sure, but Hector Reaganach explained the sore need for haste, and a connection to a royal prince be nowt for any man to sneer at," he said, releasing her. "Who'd ha' thought ye'd be the one to do such a grand thing?"

"Sir Henry is not really royal," she pointed out. "The King of Scots has declared that only members of the Scottish royal family may claim that honor, so Sir Henry will be only Earl of Orkney here in Scotland."

"Aye, aye, and 'tis proper so," Macleod agreed. "Still and all, though, the man be heir to a royal princedom, albeit a Norse one, and powerful into the bargain. The connection can do us nae harm. I willna deny, though, I were gey displeased when that villain Waldron o' Edgelaw invaded Chalamine, looking for ye."

"Invaded, sir? I heard that he spent one night and left the next day."

"Aye, he did that, but whilst he were there, he accused your Sir Michael o' criminal acts. He said, too, that he'd either abducted ye or ye'd run off wi' him."

"Michael did no such thing," Isobel declared. "Nor did I. We had to flee, because Waldron wants something from Michael that he does not possess to give him. I warrant the villainous man did not tell you that."

"Aye, well, ye're out then," Macleod said. "He did tell us that Sir Michael's family had taken summat during the Crusades that the Holy Father in Rome wants them to return now to the Kirk. If that be so . . ."

"Sakes, sir, even if it were, the Crusades were over and done nearly a century ago. How could Michael know aught of such doings?"

Macleod shrugged. "I'm thinking it might be interesting to ask him."

"Ask me what, sir?" Michael said as he came and put an arm around Isobel.

"We were talking of Waldron," she said, wondering if she could attach a small bell to his hat to warn her of his approach. "He told my father that your family took something during the Crusades that he wants to return to the Kirk," she added, hoping her expression would reveal nothing of what she knew about the matter to her father or Cristina.

"Did he?" Michael said, turning with a smile to Macleod. "I warrant, sir, that being clearly a man of insight, you saw straightaway that my cousin seeks only to enrich himself. Somehow he has come to believe that tale and prates it to anyone who will listen, but I give you my word that he is misinformed. To believe him, you would have to believe that my grandfather, best known for dying in his attempt to fulfill a promise to the Bruce, was a man of exceedingly bad character."

"Aye," Macleod said, frowning. "'Tis true I'd ha' to believe the one thing to believe the other. Nobbut what I disbelieved it all from the outset, lad, and so I tell ye to your face. 'Tis welcome ye are at Chalamine whenever ye choose to visit."

"Thank you; I am honored," Michael said. "But if you will excuse us now, it has been a tiring day, and I would see my lady wife fed and well rested. I came only to tell her that I have arranged for us to enjoy a more private supper in a tent."

He held out his arm to Isobel, and with her father beaming at her, and Cristina silently watching, she sighed and let him take her from the company.

As they walked along the narrow band of shingle, she saw that with the tide on the turn, the Kyle was as flat and calm as if it never swept boats into Loch Alsh.

"We'll need to wait until it is calm like this again to get all these boats safely through the narrows," she said.

"Aye, so the admiral said," Michael told her. "We'll be able to sleep the night through though, because he is waiting for word from men he left behind to question the captives we took today. Mayhap they will have learned something to help explain the reason for this morning's battle."

"Did you see Waldron?" she asked. "Was he in one of those other two boats?"

"Nay, and that worries me, as does the fact that those two boats turned back. I'm thinking that wee battle was no more than a diversion to slow us on our way, and I'm wondering why Waldron would arrange such a thing."

"The boats that turned back may have been the Green Abbot's," she said.

"Aye, they were, but if Waldron sought his help, he had reason."

"Mayhap he had no other way to acquire boats for his purpose. The Green Abbot is ever willing to make mischief for MacDonald and Clan Gillean."

"Aye, perhaps."

But she could tell he retained his doubts.

He guided her up the slope to a tent set well apart from the others. Nearby someone had turned a large, flat rock into a supper table complete with linen cloth.

Smiling, Michael said, "Our food is likely cold by now, because I told the lads we'd serve ourselves, but that way, we can talk."

She gave him a wary look. "Does that mean you will really discuss things with me or that you mean to scold me for the way I spoke to you earlier?"

"Sit down, lass. I'm weary to the bone and in no mood

for fratching. If I say we'll talk, that is what I mean. I know you are angry that we did not do so before the wedding this morning, but if you can tell me what I might have done, or what we together might have done to alter that course of events, I'll certainly listen."

She grimaced as she took her seat on a rock that someone had thoughtfully padded with soft pelts. Squares of linen covered a bowl of apples and their bread trenchers, protecting the sliced mutton and beef on the latter from raiding flies and other insects. Mugs of claret and a manchet loaf likewise had protective coverlets.

Michael had thought of everything.

Spreading the linen square from her mug across her lap to protect her skirt from meat juices, she said, "When you put it so, I have to agree that neither of us could have done much to stop the proceedings—not when the others were so set on having their way, but still—"

"One of us might have stopped it," he interjected. "But not I."

She cocked her head. "Are you so easily led then, sir? I own, I once thought you were, but I have seen enough now to know you don't follow anyone blindly."

"At times, as you will see, I play certain roles that have served me in the past," he said. "I may sometimes appear witless to you, but I am truly a man of peace, Isobel—at least, when I'm allowed to be—and I am not such a fool as to refuse to follow when I can trust my leader. I trusted you to know your own land better than I, and to know the best way for us to elude Waldron and his men there."

She sipped her claret and set down the mug. Then, meeting his gaze, she said, "I thought you had no ideas of your own. I even grew impatient with you."

"Aye," he said, smiling. "I know."

"How do you know? How is it that you can read what I am thinking when I can never read you?"

"Ah, but you could if you'd put your mind to it, sweetheart, and it will grow easier in time. I am not mysterious to those who know me well. 'Tis only that few know me, but I am confident that you will become one of those few."

"How can you know that?"

"I just do."

She thought about what he had said. "I misunderstood you when you said you could not stop the wedding, didn't I?"

"You did," he said. "Only think how I would have looked had I insisted on delaying those proceedings so that we could talk more. Hector Reaganach already knew of your reluctance to wed, but he likewise knew you had agreed to marry me, so any delay I requested would have looked as if I were the reluctant one. A gentleman simply cannot put off his wedding without looking like a scoundrel."

"I suppose that's true," she admitted.

"Eat your supper, sweetheart. I grow impatient to claim my bride."

Heat surged to her cheeks, and elsewhere, but there was more she wanted to know. "May I ask you something?"

"You may ask me anything you like—later," he said. "I hope you will always speak your mind to me."

She nibbled her lower lip thoughtfully, then grinned. "I doubt you will always like what I say to you."

"I'm sure that is true, sweetheart, but I'll always listen. Now, eat your supper."

They ate silently, but Michael ate swiftly, and Isobel knew his thoughts were not on his food. He looked often at her, and often he smiled. As their meal progressed, his gaze tended to linger on her body, even to caress her, and her body began to respond to those looks until she could scarcely attend to her food.

She had picked up the remains of her mutton chop and was tearing the last bits of meat from the bone with her teeth when his gaze caught hers. With the bone still in her mouth, she hesitated, watching him, and then slowly drew the bone out again. Pausing with it inches from her mouth, she continued to watch him as she licked the meat juice from her lips.

Believing she must look demented, gaping at him as she was, she tore another piece of meat from the bone and chewed it, watching him watch her. Then she started when he reached out and took the bone from her hand.

"We'll go now," he said, his voice deeper, huskier than usual. Putting down the bone, he reached for a cloth and began to wipe each of her fingers with it.

"There's a wee burn yonder," she said, surprised to find her own voice unpredictable. "I . . . I can wash my hands there."

"Later," he said, casting the cloth aside and standing.

"But what about the rest of this food?"

"Leave it." He held out his hand, and she took it, unusually aware of its warmth as it closed around hers. That warmth seemed to spread from his hand all through her as they walked the short distance to their tent.

The tent was little more than a low, rough shelter, but Michael had angled it so that the shrubbery around it would protect their privacy. And inside, he had spread furs to lie on and thick plaids to cover them. But Isobel could not imagine how he expected her to undress in such a tiny space.

Isobel looked wide-eyed as she said, "I am not accustomed to undressing with anyone about but our women. Do you expect me to do so here in the open, sir?"

He smiled reassuringly at her. "No one will bother us, sweetheart, and I want to see my bride, as much of her as I can see, that is, in this dim light. I'll gladly help you undress and do my best to block anyone else's view."

She licked her lips again, clearly having no notion that each time she did, a jolt of lust shot through his body that stirred base, primeval instincts, reminding him that in the past men had been less civil than they were expected to be now in more chivalrous times. He wanted to rip her clothes from her, throw her down on the furs, and ravish her. But even as that thought stirred, he knew he wanted much more from his spirited bride than base conquest. He wanted to watch her respond, to see her pleasure, and to learn what would please her. And he wanted to teach her to please him and show her how to enjoy herself in the pleasing.

Exerting iron control over his desire, he set out to stir hers.

Chapter 14 _____

Isobel was tense, and as Michael reached for her bodice laces, his fingers brushed the side of her left breast, making her gasp. She could not believe how quickly her body had come alive at so light a touch. Every nerve tingled and grew hot, lighting rivers of unfamiliar heat all through her.

She looked up into his eyes, trying to see if he felt what she felt, but before she could discern anything other than his smile and the way his eyes crinkled at the corners, he caught her hard against him and his lips crushed down on hers.

She responded at once, pressing close to him, savoring the warmth of his lips on hers, welcoming his tongue when he thrust it into her mouth, teasing him with her own as he explored inside.

One hand held her close, but the other worked swiftly to untie her laces and free her breasts from their confinement. He made small work of her shift, untying the bow at the front and spreading the gathered cambric off her shoulders, out of his way.

"Ah, sweetheart," he murmured as he bent to kiss her breasts, "you cannot know what being so near you does to me."

"Sakes, sir, you make it sound as if I'm torturing you."

"That's it exactly." He looked up with a grin. "Can we push all this material off you and just let it fall to the ground?"

"Aye, sure," she said, "but if you get these clothes dirty, you'll have to order new ones made for me."

"I'll order you anything you like if you let me choose the patterns," he said.

Chuckling at the thought of any man choosing a woman's dress pattern, or knowing the least thing about such matters, she opened her mouth to make a flippant retort, but his lips claimed hers again before she could. The next thing she knew, her skirts and shift lay in a tangle on the ground, and the breeze was caressing her bare body.

She reached for the top fastening of his doublet. "If I must stand bare in this dusky moonlight, sir, you must do likewise."

He laughed then and patted her bare backside. "Go inside the tent, sweetheart. Suddenly, I don't want to take the smallest risk of sharing this time with anyone else, unlikely as the possibility is that anyone would dare watch us."

She went willingly, glad to be out of sight, and when she lay down on the furs, she discovered they were even softer than she had expected, and stirred her already heightened senses more. Then he stood at the opening, watching her, his broad-shouldered, slim-hipped body outlined against the darkening sky, making her wish for the first time for more light so that she could see him more clearly.

Then he was inside, stretched beside her, his skin cool against hers until he gathered her close to him and pulled one of the plaids up to cover them. As his lips sought hers, his free hand cupped one breast, and his thumb brushed its nipple.

She kissed him hungrily, stirred to greater passion as he stroked her breasts and body, stiffening only when his hand crept lower to the joining of her legs, and cupped her gently there.

"Easy, lass," he murmured. "I've no wish to hurt you, but as I told you, the first time may be painful. I would do what I can to make it less so."

"You seem to know much more about this than I do," she said.

He chuckled. "I promise, I'll teach you all I know."

The hand cupping her moved, and she lost interest in sparring with him, devoting all her energy to savoring the wonderful feelings his touch stirred in her.

His body felt hard against hers, even more muscular than she had known it to be, but his fingers and lips were gentle and tender, his sensual voice even more entrancing to her ears than the songs of the sea that she had always loved so.

The plaid had slipped away, leaving them both exposed to the night air, but Isobel barely noticed. Every sense and sensitivity concentrated on what he was doing to her, and when one warm finger slipped inside her, teasing and exploring parts of her that she had never touched herself, she moaned softly and wondered if she were somehow being wicked to care only for the wonders he stirred. Surely some people would believe behavior that gave her such pleasure must be wicked.

She gasped again when he slid lower and took one taut nipple into his mouth, sucking and licking it as if it wore a coating of nectar.

Her hand found his hair surprisingly springy to the touch, its soft curls twining round her fingers as if even the hair on his head would possess her. Her body began to writhe beneath his, feeling an urgency that she did not understand until he moved again, this time shifting himself so that she could feel his tumescence beside his busy hand and know what he meant to do next.

Her heart seemed to stop beating, and although he still murmured softly to her, she could not take in the words, having no thought or understanding of anything save the movement of his body against hers, particularly that portion of it that now was seeking entrance to hers.

His lips claimed hers again, and his tongue thrust deep inside her mouth as, below, he eased himself inside her. The ache that his entrance caused radiated through her from top to toe, a feeling unlike any she had felt before, overpowering, all-consuming, speeding passion to the wayside as her body struggled to adjust to his.

Her gasping moans sounded different now to her, but at least she could hear him again and could make out his words.

"This is the only time it will feel painful, sweetheart, and the pain will pass quickly," he said softly. "Or so I'm told."

The obvious afterthought made her smile, but then he moved again, easing himself almost out of her before thrusting into her again, making her cry out. The pain was greater, but he did not stop. She could see that his eyes had shut, and he seemed somehow more distant from her, because he said nothing more but moved faster and faster until he seemed frenzied, pounding into her, until at last, with a soft moan of release, he relaxed heavily atop her.

Although his weight seemed as if it would crush her, he remained so for only a moment or two before he eased himself aside, holding her as he did, so that she turned with him onto her side.

"Don't pull away, love," he said as she moved to do so.

"I want to stay inside you, to enjoy your velvet softness a wee bit longer."

The aching had eased as soon as he stopped moving, and the feeling that came now was pleasant and more comfortable. She felt safe with him, and protected in a way she did not remember feeling before, except perhaps when she was small, before her mother died and she learned that her world could change drastically overnight. A niggling thought stirred that perhaps such contentment was dangerous, that perhaps it was how husbands controlled wives, but she pushed the thought away, curious to learn what he would do next.

In that instant she learned something new about her body, that it could go from painful aching to an aching for pleasure in a very short span of time. She stirred beside him and put a hand on his bare chest, enjoying the feeling of the soft, curly hairs there against her palm.

He hugged her and kissed the lobe of her right ear. "Say something, love," he murmured. "I would know what you are thinking."

She smiled. "I'm thinking there are many things about myself that I did not know and wondering how many more I will discover with you."

The sound he made was half chuckle, half sleepy murmur, but he said only, "I look forward to that journey."

A moment later, she realized he was asleep.

She lay still for what seemed a very long time, not wanting to waken him but uncertain what to do. The stickiness between her legs was beginning to itch and feel most uncomfortable, and she vaguely remembered a conversation she had overheard once between Cristina and a new bride. The bride had talked of blood from her first coupling, and how it had frightened her nearly witless, thinking she was dying. Cristina had laughed but admitted that she had been glad her husband had explained matters to her, else she might well have feared the same.

Doubtless mothers explained such things, Isobel thought, glad that she had overheard the two women, although she had risked punishment to do so. Hector Reaganach took as dim a view as Michael did of people who listened at doors.

Surely Michael, who seemed to know all there was to know about coupling, had known about this, since he had known to leave blood on their sheets at Ardtornish. Did he expect her to lie there all night suffering sticky discomfort?

He snored softly, and she felt a sudden, almost maternal sense of amusement that made her next decision easy. She had no reason to stay there, after all. She was a married woman who had never had trouble making decisions for herself before. Admittedly others had often disapproved of them, and doubtless Michael would dislike many of them, too, but in fairness to him, he had already shown a respect for her ability to think for herself that was greater than even Hector's.

On that thought, she eased herself gently away from him and out of the tent, gathering up her shift and underskirt from the ground outside. Donning both, she found her shoes and pulled them on as well, wincing at their roughness without her hose but determined to attend to the more urgent problem without further ado.

The night had darkened, and stars dotted the sky. The moon peeked over the horizon, so she could see easily enough to make her way to the stream that trickled down the hillside, pausing only to collect several of the cloths that had covered their mugs and trenchers for supper. Bracing herself against the icy chill of the stream's swift-flowing water, she dampened a cloth and began carefully to clean herself.

A night bird's call sounded in the distance, and below her the tide was running again, its waves against the shore making more noise than the bubbling water beside her. Had she not chosen to turn her head just then and look up at the sky, and had the watchers below her not chosen that moment to shift their positions to the other side of the stream, she would have missed seeing them.

"Michael, wake up!"

He heard Isobel's voice as if from a great distance, and his struggle to waken felt much as if he had to dig his way from deep inside the earth to its surface, but then her voice came again, more urgently.

That urgency hastened his wakening as every instinct for danger stirred.

"What is it, lass?" he demanded, sitting bolt upright.

"Men below on the hill, in the streambed. They were looking down at the others, so I doubt they saw me, but they are creeping downhill, and I saw none of our guards. I didn't know whether to shout an alarm, or what to do, so I came to get you."

"Good lass," he said, getting up and grabbing his breeks. "Find my jerkin, will you?" As she turned to obey, he reached for the sword and dirk that had lain near him, beneath the furs. Shrugging on his leather jerkin as soon as she handed it to him, and without bothering to find shirt or doublet, he shoved his feet into his boots, slung the sword strap over his head, and shifted the weapon into place at his hip.

"Don't follow me, lass, and don't wait here for me. Climb higher, and take care that no one sees you before you find a place of safety. Under no circumstance are you to show yourself until I call for you to come to me."

He made sure his tone left no room for argument, and she was wise enough to say only, "I will, sir, but what do you mean to do?"

"To determine exactly what the threat is, and then I will decide," he said. "But I'll be safer if I need not worry about you."

"I know," she said. "Go now, and hurry!"

But he was already gone, like a wraith, moving as he always did, so quietly that he seemed to vanish into the darkness. It was odd that she could see one of the watchers darting from shrub to shrub but could no longer see Michael.

As the thought crossed her mind, Isobel realized that if the watcher had taken that moment to look up at her, he would doubtless have seen her as plainly as she saw him. Having no wish to draw such attention, she snatched up a plaid to cover herself, then followed the stream up the hill, taking care to walk only on grass or mud, and keeping far enough from the water to avoid slipping on loose stones or a damp rock.

Even as she congratulated herself for being an obedient wife, her curiosity threatened to undo that obedience, because she had heard no sound from below, and she could not bear the suspense.

By following the stream, she had perforce been in a declivity of the sort coastal Scots called a combe. In order to see more, she would have to climb to the flanking ridge on one side of the stream or the other. Noting thick shrubbery on the far bank, she chose to stay on her own side and scrambled up the little hill, keeping low as she did and taking cover behind a huge boulder at the top.

To her relief, she had a clear view of the landscape below, could see even the reflection of the moon on waves in the Sound, but she could see nothing else moving and could hear nothing. The fear that whoever was creeping up on the sleeping men must have seen Michael, and somehow had overpowered him before he could give the alarm, sent a chill through her that stirred an impulse to dash down the hill herself, or at least scream a warning to the men sleeping below.

All that held her silent was the fact that she had no idea how many invaders there were, or how well armed they were, or even where they were—that and a strong if inexplicable instinct that she could trust Michael. And if she screamed, she might precipitate matters before time, and make everything worse for everyone.

She would count slowly to one hundred, she decided. If naught had occurred before then, she would ease her way down the hill and find Hector or Lachlan.

She had reached eighty-seven when the hillside erupted with noise and activity. Seeking frantically for Michael, she saw Hector first, recognizing him because of the great battle-axe that he held aloft, its blade gleaming silver in the moonlight. Lady Axe was famous, for she had been with Clan Gillean for over a hundred years, an ancestor having first wielded her to legendary effect at the Battle of Largs when, with the help of God and four stormy days, the Islesmen had kicked the invading Norsemen out of the Isles forever.

Carefully, Isobel crept closer, wondering where the other

women were. Mairi was bound to be where she could see what was happening even if all the others had managed to take shelter in one of the boats with men to guard them.

There! She had already spied more than one man wearing no more than a sleeveless leather jerkin and breeks, but only one looked like Michael. At first, she was certain it was he, but as she watched, she grew less certain that it was not Sir Hugo. The man she watched seemed to be here, there, and everywhere, slashing, constantly moving, cutting down anyone who attempted to fight him. Surely, Hugo.

Then it was over, and she heard Hector's voice echo across the landscape with MacDonald's war cry. Others followed, including those of clans Gillean and Macleod. They had routed the enemy. Delighted at the victory, she hurried down as fast as she could, and saw boats crossing from Kyle Rhea as she did. By the time she joined the others, Donald Mòr Gowrie was there, too, with a score of men.

She searched the crowd for Michael, then heard Hector shout his name and saw Michael striding to meet him. Picking up her skirt with one hand and holding the plaid with the other, she ran as fast as she could in shoes too loose and uncomfortable without proper hose inside them.

As she approached, Hector clapped Michael on the shoulder and said, "Good lad! Had you not seen them after they disabled our guards, and managed to alert the rest of us, we might have been slaughtered in our beds."

Isobel stopped where she was, wanting to shout that it had been she who had seen them but knowing that she'd do better to hold her tongue.

Then she heard Michael say in his usual calm way, "You do me more honor than I deserve, sir. 'Twas not I but my lady wife who gave the alarm. She was"—Isobel felt fire surge to her cheeks in embarrassment that he would tell

Hector what she'd been doing when she saw them—
"wakened by them, and awakened me."

Hector saw her then and smiled at her approach. "We
owe great thanks to you, lass, although I cannot imagine
how you were able to hear that lot when our own
guardsmen did not. You must have ears of a sharpness I'd
not imagined."

She could think of nothing to say, for she could not lie to
him, but Michael said with a touch of amusement, "I had
not thought how unlikely it was that she could hear them
from our tent. Doubtless she got up to answer a call of nature and is shy about saying so, or perhaps fears to tell us
she did so without waking me. You must not go out alone at
night like that, lass," he added gently. "The danger whilst
Waldron seeks us is too great to take such a risk."

She glanced at Hector, expecting him to say more, but he
did not. Evidently, Michael had been right and even people
accustomed to taking one to task forbore to do so if one had
a husband, so perhaps they could be useful creatures, after
all.

Michael said, "I doubt you need us any longer, my lord,
so we'll leave you and the others to attend to our captives
and seek out their boats."

"Aye, you've done enough, the pair of you," Hector said.
"Get some sleep now, because tomorrow will likely be another long day."

Michael draped an arm around Isobel's shoulders and
gently urged her back up the hillside toward their tent.

When they were beyond earshot, he murmured, "I
thought I told you not to stir from your place of concealment until you heard me call for you."

His tone was the one that always stirred tension in her
body, but it also stirred memory of the demon swordsman

she had watched, the man she had first believed was
Michael, then Hugo, cutting down every foe that stood in
his path.

Certain now who it was, she said, "I thought you were a
man of peace."

"Would you have had me let them attack the camp?"

"Nay, of course not, but neither did I know you could
fight like that."

"When one must do a thing, one should do it well, but
you are trying to change the subject, lass. I must be able to
trust you."

The sudden prickling of tears caught her by surprise, and
when she choked back a sob, he caught hold of her and
turned her abruptly to face him.

"I hope you don't think to unman me with tears. They
will avail you naught."

"Nor would I attempt such a thing," she said indignantly
as several tears spilled down her cheek. "I don't know why
I'm crying, but it has naught to do with what you said to me.
At least," she added honestly, "I don't think that it does."

"Then what?"

"I'm not sure, but I was so worried about you, thinking
first that you might have been caught out there and killed or
hurt, and then thinking I saw you in the midst of it all and
. . . and not being sure. I had to know, Michael. I *couldn't*
wait."

His hands gripped her shoulders tighter. "That isn't good
enough, Isobel. I ken fine that you don't know me well yet,
but I tell you now that you can trust me with a weapon in
my hand. I don't flaunt my skill, lass, but I am an able
fighter with almost any weapon."

"You are certainly able enough with a sword," she
agreed.

"Aye, well, it was the wish of my grandfather and my father that their male children learn the skills they themselves knew. Henry also has the ability, but he, too, conceals it. 'Tis an odd thing about men, that many of them, when they know another man possesses skill with weapons, yearn to test theirs against his, and will challenge him for no cause other than to test him. Therefore, I was taught, and Henry likewise, to keep our abilities to ourselves whilst constantly striving to improve them."

"Was Waldron, too, taught in such a way?"

"He was, albeit not by the same people, and with at least one other important difference. You heard Hector Reaganach speak of the Knights Templar."

"Aye," she said.

"They were known throughout Christendom as the world's greatest military force. 'Twas proficiency similar to theirs that I learned from my foster father."

"Where did you foster?"

"One day I may take you there," he said. "As to Waldron, although his training in weapons was much the same as mine and Henry's, I think he selected only what suited him from the many philosophies we studied, and ignored the rest. He was always greedy, and although my father insisted on seeing him well educated and trained, Waldron's greed has colored everything he's done."

"How so?"

"The combination of his skills and his belief that everything is permitted to him inclines him to believe that he can do as he pleases and take what he wants."

"But how can any man believe such a thing?" Isobel asked. "No one can simply do whatever he wants."

"Aye, well, now that Waldron has allied himself with the Kirk of Rome, he believes that any battle he fights allies him with God. And he is not alone in that belief. Many believe, as he does, that God protects all soldiers of Christ, including the Templars, and will absolve them of any sin they commit. That is why Waldron believes that he can do as he pleases."

"But if you trained as he did, do you not believe the same thing?"

"I do not," he said. "Such training produces excellent soldiers, and soldiers are often needed quickly, without sufficient time to train them. That is why my father arranged for us to train as we did. He believed that since Scotland will not be safe until the English agree that we are an independent nation, we are likely to need good soldiers again. But you keep changing the subject, lass. I want your word that, henceforward, if I give you an order in the midst of a crisis, you will obey it."

She hesitated, uncertain what to say and aware that in his own way, he was also seeking to change the subject, but he waited patiently. At last, she said, "I understood that you wanted me out of harm's way, and I did obey you without question. But I do not think it is right or fair to insist that I should have waited for you to collect me after the battle. What if you had been killed?"

"Eventually Hector or someone would have called you," he said.

"Aye, when it finally occurred to someone that I was missing," she said.

He did not answer at once, but then he said evenly, "Had we lost the battle, you would have been safer up here on the hillside."

"Had we lost the battle, I would not have dashed down to find you," she said, uncertain even as she said the words that they were true. She knew that even then she would have wanted to know if he were injured or dead and, if he were injured, would have wanted to be with him. Lest he see the contradiction in her expression, she added quickly, "You said before that you trusted my judgment at the cavern, Michael. Surely, you could at least try to trust me not to do anything so dreadfully foolish as to rush into the heat of a battle to find you."

"Aye, lass, you're right," he said. "I'll try to remember your words. But you must understand, too, that I have been taught that protecting women is my solemn duty because they are weaker than men and not skilled in weaponry."

"But I am neither weak nor helpless," she pointed out.

He smiled. "Your wee dirk gives you confidence beyond what I believe to be wise, and although I do trust you not to run foolishly into danger that you can see and understand, I also know that you can be impulsive and may rush into danger you don't recognize when it stands before you."

She opened her mouth to insist that she was not such a fool, then remembered how they had met, and shut it again.

He grinned. "Aye," he said. "I've seen your impulsiveness for myself, and whilst I cannot say now that I am entirely sorry for it, knowing that it exists does give me pause. I'll try not to leap to judgment of your behavior without more cause than you gave me tonight, and to treat you instead more as I would a lad with similar knowledge and training."

"Thank you," she said with sincerity.

"Aye, well, but woe betide you if you show poor judgment and run yourself into danger because of it. If a man under my command foolishly risked his own life or the lives of others, I'd punish him severely, and you *are* under my command. Do not doubt that, for when you agreed to marry me, you gave me that authority, and I do not want to hear you say that you did not mean to do so, because that is ir-relevant now. In the eyes of the world—aye, and by my own instinct and training—I do bear responsibility for you, and the authority that goes with it. So do not ask that I shirk that responsibility or surrender it to you or to anyone else, for I will not."

For once, she could think of nothing to say, and his tone, not to mention his surprisingly reasonable reaction to her previous protest, made it impossible to argue with him. Even so, his warning gave her pause, because she hated re-strictions and knew that she tended to resist them with all her might. She considered explaining that to him but de-cided she would be wiser not to try to do so just now.

They had reached their tent, and Michael moved ahead to straighten out the furs and plaid again. When she joined him there, he drew her close enough to make her wonder if he meant to make love to her again, but he only kissed her, gave her a hug, and the next thing she knew it was morning.

The boats got underway as soon as the tide flowed in far enough to make it safe for them to pass through the narrow kyles, and after that the flotilla followed the Inland Passage north, keeping careful watch for enemy ships. They saw none, and although their journey took several more days, the time passed more swiftly than Isobel had expected. When Kirkwall's U-shaped harbor appeared at last, the number of ships she saw there astonished her. She had thought the Lord of the Isles' fleet was large, but clearly, that of the St. Clairs was larger yet.

They could see the great yellow cathedral and sprawling bishop's palace as they debarked into smaller boats that carried them ashore, and from the landing, Michael escorted her up a path and into the palace, to its cavernous great hall. The hall was well appointed, comfortable looking, and boasted roaring fires in two huge fireplaces to offset the chill that enveloped the Orkney Islands even in midsummer.

Their host, awaiting them on the dais with two women, looked like an older version of Michael, although Sir Henry's hair was much lighter. Watching him as he greeted Princess Margaret, Isobel thought his manners pleasant, his welcome sincere.

He presented the ladies with him as his mother and his wife, and then motioned Michael forward. Since Michael's hand grasped Isobel's firmly, she went with him, and as he shook hands with Sir Henry and presented her to him, and to their mother, Isobel made her curtsies, noting that although Sir Henry and his lady smiled warmly at the news of Michael's marriage, his mother did not.

Isabella of Strathearn, a willow-slim, elegantly attired woman of apparently much greater haughtiness than Princess Margaret, seemed to glower at Isobel, making her feel a distinct chill.

Sir Henry, clearly unaware of his mother's demeanor, said cheerfully, "Your taste has always been excellent, Michael, and I believe our father would approve. I certainly do. I trust your journey was not too taxing, my lady."

"Not at all, sir," Isobel said, returning his smile. "I love being on the sea, however long the journey might be."

"I, too," he said. "One day I mean to sail to the edge of the earth if not beyond."

"Beyond the edge?" She was shocked. "How could anyone do that?"

"I once saw a map, my lady, that suggested the earth is as round as a ball."

His mother made a slight, impatient sound, and after a guilty glance at her, he added with a twinkle, "But we can talk more about that later. I am wont to get carried away on the subject, and I do not want to spoil Michael's surprise."

"Surprise?" Michael said, frowning.

"Indeed, my son, and a great honor, too, as I am sure you will agree," Isabella, Countess of Strathearn and Caithness, said, smiling at last.

"Prithee, madam, not another word," Henry said with an indulgent chuckle. "You promised that this surprise would be mine to unveil. Michael, I know you will share our delight when I tell you that someone we have not seen for too long a time has come to help us celebrate my installation. Moreover, he has brought another with him who will doubtless confer great consequence upon your marriage by giving it his blessing. Come out now, cousin, and show yourself."

Feeling Michael stiffen beside her, Isobel had sufficient warning so that she did not cry out or otherwise reveal her dismay when Waldron of Edgelaw stepped from the shadows of the fireplace inglenook onto the dais. However, when Fingon Mackinnon, the Green Abbot of Iona, followed him, her mouth dropped open and she turned to Michael to warn him.

But his hand squeezed hers hard, and understanding him, she kept silent.

Chapter 15

Praying that his generally outspoken bride would continue to hold her tongue, Michael kept a firm grip on her hand as he nodded silently to Waldron.

Then, as his cousin continued toward him, he added coolly, "I own, I did think we might find you here. Am I correct in believing that your companion who offers his blessing is the fabled Green Abbot of Iona?"

Although his blue eyes were alight with laughter, Waldron did not offer to shake hands as he said, "Faith, lad, art still at outs with me? I had thought all such disgruntlement long buried in the past." Casting an oblique look past Michael at their audience, he added, "He still harbors resentment because I could so easily best him at weaponry when we were youngsters."

A slight shuffling of feet was the only response, and since Michael did not take his eyes from Waldron, he could not tell if the words had stirred any other reaction among his fellow travelers from the south.

The silence lengthened, but Waldron still looked amused and willing to wait for a reply, so Michael said evenly, "'Tis not I but you who stirs coals from the past, cousin. Moreover, you have not answered my question. Is this man Abbot Mackinnon of the Holy Isle?"

"He is," Waldron said. "And, as he is a good friend, I've brought him to bless the installation of our intrepid prince, and now your marriage, too. You and Henry bring great honor to the St. Clairs, and such acts should be sanctified. It remains only for our Hugo to do something of note, but Macleod has many daughters, has he not?"

Isobel's hand twitched in Michael's, and he realized that he had stiffened up again. But he did not need her warning to know that he had to tread lightly. Waldron had also noted his reaction, because the gleam in his eyes revealed as much. Let him smirk, Michael decided, saying, "I believe you've met at least two of Macleod's daughters, cousin, but if you were courting, I doubt they knew as much."

The gleam vanished, but Michael could scarcely count the hit, because his mother said sharply, "Whatever can you mean by that, Michael? I do not understand you. You should be making your bow to our honored guest, Abbot Mackinnon, and thanking him for his kindness if he does offer you his blessing on this marriage of yours. Mayhap he will bestow it upon you during tomorrow's High Mass."

"Indeed, Countess, I should count it a pleasure," Fingon Mackinnon said, bowing slightly in her direction. "Indeed, I admire Lady Isobel's good sense."

Isobel's fingers tightened until Michael thought she might cut off her own circulation if not his, but she did not rise to the bait.

Knowing it was only a matter of time before one of the two men would goad her into saying something better left unspoken, he said amiably, "You honor us, sir, but I hope you will all forgive us if we beg permission to retire now to our chambers to refresh ourselves. Our journey, as you know, has been long."

He turned back to Henry then, bowing but holding his brother's gaze as he did. For all that Henry delighted in playing the fool and idly prating of mythical ventures, he possessed a formidable intelligence, so although he gave no sign of any message passing between them, Michael knew that one had.

With his pleasant smile, Henry said, "Doubtless all of you just arriving at Kirkwall will be glad of such an opportunity. And since I know that my people, and those of his eminence the Bishop of Orkney, have made chambers ready for you either in the palace or in a comfortable hall-house nearby, pray go with them now. We will all take supper here shortly after Vespers."

As palace servants moved among them, Isabella said, "I would take it as a great favor, Abbot Mackinnon, if we might converse a bit longer. We so rarely see anyone of such importance from the Kirk."

"Faith, madam, we are currently enjoying the hospitality of his eminence the Bishop of Orkney, and have our own chaplain with us besides," Henry said. "We are scarcely bereft of spiritual guidance."

"It is not the same," Isabella said.

The Green Abbot made her another bow and said, "It will be my pleasure to spend an hour with you, Countess, and I will rejoin you shortly, but I did promise to meet briefly with his eminence before Vespers, and I should do that first."

Ignoring his mother, the abbot, and Waldron, Michael turned with Isobel to leave the dais. The first thing he noted as he did, however, was how grim a number of his companions were looking.

Isobel had all she could do not to glance back at Waldron as Michael led her away from the dais. She did not want to give Waldron the satisfaction of knowing how much his presence disturbed her, but curiosity warred with wisdom, making it almost impossible not to watch to see what he would do next. He seemed to think he was as welcome at Kirkwall as Michael was, and indeed, if the countess was any measure, he was certainly more welcome there than Michael's bride.

In the moment before Michael turned to escort her from the dais, Waldron looked right at her, his expression changing slightly to one that she often encountered at court, where young men who had indulged too heavily in brogac, the potent whisky of the Isles, sometimes grew too amorous for their own good. Waldron's expression resembled those drunken leers but seemed more ominous. He looked hungry and as if he expected to fulfill that hunger.

As she and Michael faced the others, she saw that Hector looked ferocious and Lachlan studiously calm. Mairi had put a hand on Princess Margaret's arm, and Lady Euphemia looked distressed. Princess Margaret's two women, middle-aged sisters whom Mairi had always referred to as the Weed and the Rose, fluttered around their mistress, stiffening sharply when the abbot walked past Michael and Isobel, nodded at Princess Margaret, and said, "Madam, I hope we see you well."

Margaret nodded back without speaking, and the abbot walked on, passing through a doorway near the back of the hall, clearly at ease in the bishop's palace.

Expecting Waldron to follow him, Isobel glanced back at

the dais when he did not. Not seeing him, she said in surprise to Michael, "Where did he go?"

"With my lady mother, I expect," he said, following her glance. "Doubtless they retired to her chambers, which I'll wager lie somewhere beyond that door at the back of the dais." To Hector, he said, "Do you expect my cousin or the abbot to cause trouble here, my lord? I believe they will not. My cousin values my mother's good opinion and would not willingly relinquish it."

"I agree that they will behave," Hector said. "Mayhap they did hope to cause grief to your brother, because from all you say of Waldron of Edgelaw, he covets what the St. Clairs possess. Had he seen his way clear before now to claiming the princedom for himself, I'll warrant he'd not have hesitated to do so."

"I was more concerned that he might attempt to harm Henry," Michael said.

"Too many factors argue against that possibility," Lachlan said.

All those galleys in the harbor, for one, Isobel thought, although she did not put herself forward to the point of saying so aloud, knowing that Princess Margaret would disapprove of her entering such a conversation.

However, to her surprise, Lachlan said, "A primary factor is the thousand gold pieces your brother will pay the Norse King at Martinmas. I doubt that your cousin could pay such a price. Even if somehow he could, you would still be Henry's heir. Therefore, he cannot even try to win the princedom unless he is willing to do away with three people—Henry, you, and Henry's visibly pregnant wife— an iniquity that would damn him forever in the Norse King's eyes. Mark you, Waldron may once have thought it possible, but by now he will have realized his error. Not only does Henry have too many protectors, but if Waldron has not already learned the terms of Henry's agreement with the Norse King, he will do so soon enough."

"Since he believes God is on his side, he may not care about iniquities," Michael said. "Moreover, any setback will frustrate and anger him, and when he is angry, he grows even more dangerous."

"But he will not flaunt his frustrations here," Lachlan said, extending one arm to Princess Margaret and the other to his lady wife. "Now then, I suggest that we take advantage of Sir Henry's excellent hospitality to rest before supper."

Nodding, Michael tucked Isobel's hand in the crook of his arm and they moved with the rest of their party to follow a pair of palace servants upstairs to their chambers. When Isobel saw Sir Hugo offer his arm to Adela, she glanced at Michael, wondering how he would react. But he paid them no heed, and she was not surprised to see her sister accept Sir Hugo's escort with a smile.

After seeing Adela safely inside the room she would share with Lady Euphemia, Hugo walked on with Michael and Isobel to theirs. Isobel expected Michael to send him away, but when he did not, she realized that the two men must have communicated in some silent manner before then.

Inside the small, rather barren chamber, Hugo shut the door firmly and moved past the curtained bed to look out the narrow window beyond it. "Is it safe to talk here?" he asked Michael.

"For now," Michael said. "But I'm thinking the sooner we see the backs of that precious pair, the safer we will be."

"That won't be until after Henry's ceremony," Hugo said. "And that's still two days away, is it not?"

"Aye, on Sunday."

"You'll take care until then, lad," Hugo said, his gaze shifting pointedly to Isobel and back as he did.

"Aye," Michael said, resting his own gaze on her as he added, "Lass, you must be wary, as well, and take special care never to be alone with Waldron. By that I mean you must not wander anywhere alone. Seek escort from me or from Hugo, or from Hector Reaganach or the admiral. If none of us is at hand, send for a gillie or one of Henry's menservants. You will know them by their tunics. They are gray and bear the black St. Clair cross."

She would have liked to tell him there and then what she thought of his issuing such orders to her in front of Sir Hugo, but she restrained herself until after that gentleman had departed. The moment the door snapped shut behind him, however, she said tartly, "Do you think me feeble-minded, Michael?"

His thoughts had clearly moved on to something else, because he regarded her blankly for a moment before his eyes focused and he said, "I don't think anything of the kind. Why would you think so?"

"If you do not think me witless, then why did you feel obliged to act the protective husband in front of Sir Hugo?"

"Because I wanted you to know that he will expect you to request his protection if you need it. I did not want you to think for a moment that by making such a request to him you might somehow be imposing on his good nature."

"In other words, you did not want to leave me any opportunity to offer that as an excuse for taking my own road, as you once described my tendency to trust my own judgment and make my own decisions."

"Aye, sure," he said with a grin, clearly pleased that she understood him so well. "And now that we have come to agreement on that subject, I propose that we explore other agreeable entertainment until we must dress for supper."

"We are supposed to be refreshing ourselves," she reminded him. "Changing our clothing or attending to other such necessities before supper."

"Aye, that's what I meant," he said, reaching for her bodice lacing.

She stepped back. "I don't want to."

His reaching hand stopped, hovered in midair. "What?"

"You heard me."

"Aye, I did, but I'm your husband, lass. You are my wife."

"You said you would not bed an unwilling wife."

He sighed. "I won't, sweetheart. I know our first coupling hurt you, and that what happened afterward may have put you off coupling for a time, especially since we failed to find other opportunities before now. I can understand, too, that a few doubts may have lingered to fester in your mind, but—"

"It is not a matter of pain or festering, sir, but of trust," she said flatly.

"Trust?"

"Aye, yours in me. You have asked me again and again to trust you, from the day we first met, when we were finding our way out of that cave and we could not see our hands in front of our eyes. You even asked me to trust that you could not tell me more about what Waldron sought from you."

"But I could not."

"That does not matter. My point is that you did ask me each time to trust you. I'm just naming all the occasions, sir."

He looked down at the floor then, and she thought he was biting his lip. Whether it was to keep himself from roaring or laughing at her, she could not tell, but that did not matter either. She meant to have her say.

"All my life people have told me to use my own judgment and then scolded me when I did, or they simply ignore the fact that I possess any judgment to use," she said. "The main reason I have hitherto avoided taking a husband is that I did not want another person in my life always telling me what to do and how to act. You said you would not, but you do. You expect me to trust you all in all, but you choose when you will trust me, and I am trying to tell you that for me to give you the complete trust you ask for, I must know that you believe in me, too."

He drew a deep breath then and looked her straight in the eye as he said, "Isobel, although I feel as if I have known you all my life, I have not, and we still have much to learn about each other. I do trust you. Moreover, you know that I do. I can provide a list, too. I trusted you in the cave whilst you were freeing yourself and when you suggested how we should handle Fin Wylie, that lout of Waldron's who came to collect us. I trusted Matthias and Ian MacCaig with no more than your word that I might. I trusted your decision that we should cross the Kyle and make for the Isle of Mull to take shelter with a man I scarcely knew, whose reputation is fearsome. And when you told me that I could trust Donald Mòr Gowrie, I trusted him, too. I even trusted your considerable knowledge of boats and the sea."

"Perhaps, but you did *not* trust me when I explained how I got onto your boat," she said. "And you did *not* trust me to have sense enough not to dash into a battle to find you," she added hastily when she remembered exactly what he had said on his boat, and how angry he had been. "Nor did you trust me to be sensible just now, and simply tell me to ask Hugo if I needed an escort."

He was silent, but she had no doubt that he was controlling temper rather than his sense of humor. Well, he could just bellow at her if he wanted to, she told herself. It would not matter one whit. She wanted him to understand that this was important, so why, she wondered, did she feel as if she were going to cry?

Michael struggled to control himself. He wanted to shake her, but he wanted even more to make the discussion go away so that he could make love to her. He had been thinking about that in the boat before they landed. It had even crossed his mind in the great hall before he clapped eyes on Waldron and the Green Abbot. If the truth were known, the notion that he soon could take his wife to bed again had flitted through his mind as he sparred verbally with Waldron, and her proximity afterward in the bedchamber had made him want nothing more than to push Hugo out the door and bar it against him and anyone else who might dare to interrupt.

But although he could counter nearly every argument she had launched at him, he could tell from her intensity and demeanor that the subject was of great importance to her, and he knew he would rue the day if he did not deal with it now.

Accordingly, he drew another deep breath, called on skills he had learned in his training, kept his hands at his sides, and said calmly, "Sweetheart, I do trust you. Moreover, you must know that some items on that list of yours are spurious. I won't repeat what I said to you on the boat, because I know you remember as well as I do. I know it rankled that I did not accept your explanation, but I explained why, and I would guess that if you did forget all I said, you have remembered it now."

He paused, in case she wanted to respond to that, but she did not.

"Likewise," he went on, "we talked about my need to know that you will obey me in a crisis, and you agreed—or I thought you did—that you would do so henceforth. Since I have no idea what mischief has brought Waldron and the abbot here, I do count their presence as something of a crisis. You are right, though, that I should have discussed the matter of your safety with you before I brought Hugo into it. He followed us because he knew I would have orders for him, and I took advantage of our all being together to make sure you knew that he would expect you to call on him if necessary."

A tear spilled down her cheek, and he reached out and brushed it away with his thumb but made no other move to touch her.

"You are right about another thing, too," he said, his voice as gentle as he could make it. "Total trust is something that one person grants to another, but likewise must it be earned, one *from* the other. No one should give or expect trust blindly, because like anything one builds to last, trust requires a foundation, and a good foundation needs time to grow strong. Therefore, incidents of partial trust must occur, to test it, before it can be offered freely. As to my having perhaps chosen when to trust you implicitly and when to doubt, you may recall things that you've said or done that make it hard for me to say you have earned my unreserved trust, but in fairness, lass, I too have been at fault."

Another tear and a hastily suppressed sob were her only response.

"Look at me, sweetheart."

She looked up, her eyes swimming.

"Do you understand me?"

"Aye, you think that because I said I sometimes don't tell the whole truth, you cannot trust me, but I don't lie, Michael, or at least not to those I . . . I care about, and moreover, I think you can tell when I'm shading the truth or not telling you everything. You get a certain look . . ."

"Aye, I can tell, I think, but don't you see that I cannot be sure I will always know? I've promised to tell you the truth and to tell you if, for good reason, I cannot. I do not think I have broken that promise. Can you not make me the same one?"

She bit her lower lip, then said, "I don't know. I usually just say what is in my head, and sometimes, it just doesn't seem sensible to blurt out the whole truth. If someone asks what I think of a hat or dress, for example, and I loathe it . . ."

"You know that is not what I mean."

"But many things seem like that to me, Michael. Moreover, words don't matter as much as actions do, such as when you and Hugo seemed to confer without words *before* you told me to apply to him if I needed an escort."

He chuckled then, clearly surprising her. "Sweetheart, Hugo was asking me if I wanted him to involve himself. You should know that we have always been very competitive, and in the past we have had a few disagreements over women. If you will recall, you flirted with him outrageously when he first arrived at Lochbuie."

"I did not!"

"Isobel."

She grimaced. "Well, not any more than I flirt with anyone. One does, you know, and it means nothing—just a smile or a look."

"Married ladies should not indulge in such behavior," he said.

"Sakes, at court married ladies are the worst offenders," she retorted.

"Whether they are or not makes no difference to me," he said. "I will do you the courtesy of trusting you to behave more circumspectly."

She thought about that for a moment before she said, "Doubtless you think you have been very clever to use the subject of this discussion to manipulate my behavior rather than just ordering me not to flirt, but your doing that makes me wonder if you truly meant what you said earlier."

He felt as if she had slapped him, and as if he had deserved it.

"I did mean what I said," he said ruefully. "But you are right to take me to task, lass. I fear I may prove a jealous husband, and that was partly the point I was trying to make about Hugo. He did not want to seem to be giving orders or even advice to my bride, whilst at the same time he felt it necessary to make certain I would not act the fool where Waldron is concerned, so he took it upon himself to remind me that I should be sure you understood the danger in which we stand."

"I do," she said. "Do you really feel as if you have known me all your life?"

He smiled with profound relief, believing he knew exactly what course her thoughts had taken to make that leap. "Yes," he said. "I've told you so before. Don't you feel the same way?"

꧁ꙮ꧂

Isobel thought about the question. Michael did not know what an advantage the effect of his voice on her gave him in any discussion like this one, but especially when he made her feel as if he truly listened to what she said to him. He seemed to have an uncanny knack for doing that whenever she began to think he was like every other man. She wanted to believe he would always listen, although experience told her it was unlikely. It occurred to her then that trusting him to do so might be exactly the sort of thing he had meant when he said that sometimes they would just have to trust each other to see what happened, and hope the foundation grew stronger.

He was waiting patiently, so she said, "I know you would like me to say that I feel as you do, sir. I do understand what you mean, because I seem able to talk to you as easily as I can to people I have always known, but, in truth, just when I think I am coming to understand you—who you are and what you think—I discover I don't know you at all. You have been at least two different men since we met, and I don't know which one is the one I should trust."

He touched her arm and she felt the warmth of his fingers through the thin fabric of her sleeve. "In time you will learn that you can trust them both." he said gently, tilting her chin up and kissing her lightly.

"Perhaps," she said, meeting his gaze, "but I expect to test that, sir."

The hand on her arm moved to tug the front lacing of her bodice loose. "I, too, have some tests in mind," he said. "I noted one or two particularly sensitive points on your beautiful body. I would test them to see if that sensitivity can be increased."

Heat surged through her, and she reached up and put a hand behind his head, curling her fingers into his hair, pulling him toward her to kiss him soundly.

With a low moan in his throat, he slid both arms around her and pulled her close, fitting his body against hers and moving his hands caressingly down her back to cup her bottom cheeks and pull her closer yet.

She could feel his body seeking hers, pulsing against her.

His fingers were back at her lacing. The bodice was a simple one of pale rose-colored silk, constructed like a man's jerkin and laced tightly at the waist, with each front half ending in a point below the tie. In a trice, he slipped it off her and dropped it to the floor. His fingers moved next to the pink ribbons of her gathered, low-cut cambric shift. As he slipped its sleeves down her arms, baring her shoulders and the tops of her breasts, she felt as if the shift confined her, but for once confinement seemed only to heighten her passion as she waited to see what he would do next.

He paused, gazing down at her, and then, extending his right index finger, he dipped it into the space between her breasts and, slowly, began to draw the cambric lower and lower.

The light rat-a-tat-tat on the door startled both of them as much as if it had been a thunderclap.

"That's Henry," Michael said.

Dismayed, she said, "You were expecting him?"

"Aye, albeit not so soon. I'll tell him to go to the devil."

"Sakes, sir, you cannot do that! Help me get my bodice back on."

"Nay, sweetheart, I should speak to him alone."

"Had he wanted to speak to you elsewhere, he'd have sent for you, would he not?" she demanded.

"Aye, perhaps," he said, but his frown told her he had just realized she was right. "I forget that this is the bishop's palace rather than Henry's own."

"I won't pretend I don't want to hear what you have to

say to him, since I know you will talk about Waldron and all that has happened, but if I must go, tell me now. Don't send me away in front of him."

"Let's see what he has to say first," Michael said. "If you have to leave, sweetheart, it will be by his command, not mine. I keep my promises."

He said in a quiet but nonetheless carrying voice, "One moment, Henry."

There was no response, but Michael picked up Isobel's bodice and helped her put it on, tightening the laces for her but leaving her to tie the bow while he went to let Sir Henry in.

Henry said nothing until he was inside with the door shut. Then, with a rueful look at Isobel, he said, "I apologize for disturbing you, my lady, but I think your husband wished to speak privately with me, and with so many housed here just now, privacy is scarce. My mother and her tame abbot are currently occupying the chamber I customarily use as mine own, so I'd hoped I might intrude here rather than try to evict them."

"You are most welcome, sir," Isobel said, smiling at him and receiving a warm smile in return. Taking heart from that warmth, she said, "I hope you do not mean to turn me out. Michael said I must go if you say so, and I will, of course, but I was party to nearly all that has happened to us since we met, and I must confess, I'm a curious person and will likely force him to tell me everything eventually."

She held her breath when he turned to look at Michael, wondering if either gentleman would object to her boldness.

Michael said nothing, and Sir Henry turned back with another smile. "Faith, madam, if you can winkle things out of him that he'd as lief not tell you, I welcome you even more heartily to our family, and hope you will teach me how you do it."

"You lack her weapons," Michael said, chuckling. "Find a seat now, Henry, for I've much to tell you and things to ask you, and I know we have only a short time. The window embrasure may be wide enough," he added when Sir Henry looked around the bleak chamber and frowned at the low joint stool that seemed to be the sole piece of furniture other than the plainly curtained bed and washstand.

Finding that he could sit on the narrow windowsill, if not fit his broad shoulders into the space as well, he leaned his elbows on his knees and said, "I must say, you did not look nearly as amazed to see Waldron as I'd expected."

"I wasn't surprised," Michael said, and proceeded to tell him why.

Isobel remained silent, fascinated by the details he included, as if he remembered every single thing that had happened. He told Sir Henry exactly what had taken place at the cave and afterward, everything until they reached the Isle of Mull. Then, he told him only that Hector had been unhappy about their having traveled together with only oarsmen to chaperon them but that he regained his good humor when Michael offered for Isobel and she accepted him.

She had not realized until then that she had feared he would reveal all that she had said and done, but when she sighed her relief, Sir Henry looked at her, his expression reminding her of Michael's when he peered into her soul.

Henry made occasional exclamations of amazement or annoyance as Michael's tale unfolded, and at the end he said, "Waldron has always taken his own road, but I never thought he would turn against one of us in such a dastardly way. Shall I send him away?"

"Nay," Michael said. "'Tis better to keep him close enough to watch."

"Aye," Isobel said. "MacDonald of the Isles says one should treat one's enemies as houseguests and watch over them tenderly lest they steal the silver."

Henry laughed. "We'll leave his welcoming to my mother, I think, but your tale, Michael, makes me think that perhaps I should show you Father's letter."

"What letter? I thought we had both seen everything of his at Roslin."

"Not this," Henry said with a grimace. "I have never shown it to anyone, because certain things he wrote in it were not things that I wanted to share with anyone else, even you. Faith, you least of all! But I think I must now."

"Yes," Michael said. "I think you must. Where is it, at Roslin or St. Clair?"

"It is right here," Henry said, reaching into his doublet. "It never leaves me."

Chapter 16

Michael took the letter, which was folded horizontally into quarters, and carefully unfolded it. One could tell that Henry had carried it about with him for some time, and since their father had died more than two decades before, it was somewhat the worse for wear. However, Sir William had written with a good quill and brown-gall ink on thin, well-scrubbed and chalked calves' vellum, rather than on less durable paper, which told him as clearly as it would anyone else that Sir William had intended his eldest son to keep his letter.

Glancing at the date under the signature, Michael said, "He wrote this shortly before he died."

"Aye," Henry said. "Whilst we were all at Dunclathy."

"That's Hugo's home in Strathearn," Michael told Isobel.

Henry said, "Mother received the letter when she got word of our father's death, for the bearer of those sad tidings delivered it to her. She intended to give it to me straightaway but forgot, so I did not read it until weeks later."

"Forgot?" Michael said skeptically.

"Aye, or so she said. I've long suspected that she read it first and thought it would be kinder not to give it to me just then, because he'd written it after receiving a report from Sir Edward of some mischief I'd committed. So, as you'll see, the first half of it is a lecture on the responsibilities of any heir to the bounty of St. Clair, which he spells as one pronounces it, rather than in the French way. That may be another reason she did not give it to me straightaway, since she always insists on the French spelling and might have feared I'd change it. But I'd wager 'twas its content. Not pleasant reading, certainly, but I've kept it to remind me that a good reputation is more valuable than money, and to live every day as if it were to be my last."

"Does he include both maxims?" Michael asked.

"Aye."

"That last one rather gives one chills if this was his last letter."

"I believe it was," Henry said solemnly. "You will see for yourself why I thought it had no bearing on the family secret we have sought so long to understand, but 'tis possible that a few words of that last paragraph may prove relevant. I own, I have never understood them, but perhaps he expected trouble from Waldron or his ilk. I just thought 'twas more of the scold that precedes it."

Michael read swiftly, understanding why Henry had not wanted to share such a letter. Its searing contents made him curious to know what mischief his brother had embroiled himself in at the age of thirteen to receive such a reprimand. Still, their parents had raised them to have solemn respect for duty and honor, and Michael had received his share of reprimands and worse, if not from their father, who had died when he was only five, then certainly from their foster father.

He came at last to the pertinent paragraph, and found it disappointingly brief. *And so*, Sir William had written, *if aught should happen to prevent my return, you must be prepared to take full responsibility for yourself and for our beloved family. Therefore, keep these my words with you, and study well the philosophers that your tutors present to you. When you seek answers, follow the direction of the bearded men, who will ever reveal the path of truth. May the Almighty watch over you at Roslin, my son, and keep you safe from harm. Your affectionate father.*

Michael read Sir William's signature and the date once more, then looked up. "I see why you were loath to share this letter, Henry," he said. "What I do not see is why you think it may prove at all useful to us."

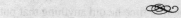

Isobel had been striving to contain her impatience, not to mention her bursting curiosity, but Michael's last comment was too much to bear.

"But what does it say?" she demanded. When Henry looked startled and Michael's lips twitched, she realized that she had sounded just a trifle shrill and added quickly, "If you do not mind sharing that information with me."

"Not the whole letter," Sir Henry said quietly.

"Nay," Michael agreed. "Only the last paragraph, since it is the only part you believe may pertain to our situation. See if it seems likely to you, lass."

After he had read the passage aloud, Isobel asked him to read it again. When he had done so, she said to Henry, "Is it that he mentions a path of truth, sir? For I must agree that it does not otherwise seem at all useful."

Sir Henry stood as he said, "I don't know why it came to

mind just now. When you and I have read other letters of his that we found, Michael, searching for answers, I've sometimes felt a twinge of guilt at not having shown this one to you, but only because I'd wondered occasionally if he'd had a premonition of his death."

Michael said, "It has always seemed odd that he left no specific instructions for you to follow if he died. He knew he'd most likely go into battle, and if he did have such a premonition, surely he must have feared that the secret, whatever it is, might be lost forever if he failed to share it with you."

"Sakes," Isobel exclaimed, "just traveling is dangerous enough! I'd think that if your father knew something important that he had not shared with anyone else, something passed to him by his father, that he expected to pass on to you, Sir Henry, surely the first time he did anything that put his life in peril, he would have seen to it that you had knowledge of where that information lies, or how to find it."

Michael grimaced. "One might argue that his not having done that means only that our grandfather failed to pass the information on to our father before setting out for the Holy Land with Robert the Bruce's heart."

"Aye, sure," Henry agreed, "but Father must have known. After all, you just told me that Ian Dubh's documents strongly suggest that our grandfather arranged for the Templars to find sanctuary here in Scotland. If he accepted responsibility for something as valuable as the Templar treasure, he would have made certain that our father knew about it. Father was, after all, an adult by then, and we know he believed the family bore heavy responsibility for something, because he spoke of that responsibility many times, directly and indirectly."

"Very true," Michael agreed. "Moreover, Isobel is right. He

would have found a way to pass it on, particularly if that responsibility was entrusted to our grandfather by other Templars. Mayhap Father expected you to learn of it from someone he trusted; perhaps someone who helped conceal it."

"Then surely I'd have heard by now," Henry pointed out dryly. "I'm four-and-thirty and have been head of our clan for twenty years."

"But what if that trusted person also died unexpectedly?" Isobel said.

"Then we are back to this letter of Henry's," Michael said. "I do not recall seeing any other document that he directed to you personally, Henry. Were there other such letters?"

"No," Henry said, visibly struck by the question. "He included other messages for me in letters he sent our lady mother. In truth, when he was away from home, the mendicant friars usually delivered his less personal messages orally. Aside from those letters to our lady mother, I know of no other personal messages to anyone amongst the documents I've seen."

"Well, I doubt that he would have given such information either to the friars or to our mother," Michael said. "I don't remember much about their relationship myself, but you have often commented on how prickly it was."

"That is true, but I agree that he would have made every effort to be sure I had any information I needed," Henry said, clearly thinking aloud. "Others may exist who know the secret—or some of it—particularly if the treasure Ian Dubh described forms part of a larger secret. Our father's personal responsibility, however, would have weighed most heavily on him. We know he did not share it with Sir Edward, although he trusted him so deeply that he trusted him with most of our training."

"But we know, too, that he was unlikely to have risked entrusting the whole tale to a lad as young as you were then, in a letter or otherwise," Michael said.

"Even had I been the sort who consistently applied myself to my studies and weaponry," Henry said with a rueful smile. "That letter you're holding, therefore, contains the only instructions of any sort directed personally to me that we have found, and I cannot imagine why I did not realize that long before now."

"Because we have been searching for formal instructions labeled as such," Michael said. "We assumed that he must have left something of the sort, but I begin to think he simply refused to think that he might die before he could tell you himself, as I'll warrant his own father did with him."

"An error I will not make," Sir Henry said. "But I'm thinking we need to look more narrowly at this letter now. As your lady noted, it does mention a path of truth, and 'tis the only reference that you and I have seen to a path of any kind."

"May we make a fair copy of that final paragraph, sir?" Isobel asked.

"No need, lass," Michael said. "I have memorized it, and you should likewise commit it to memory, if you will. There can be no harm in Henry's continuing to carry the letter on his person, since he has done so for years without incident, but I'd as lief we create no other copies to put at risk."

She nodded, knowing he was right, but Henry looked upset.

Guessing at once that he disliked the risk of sharing the letter's embarrassing contents with her, she said, "I promise, sir, I will read only the last paragraph."

He glanced at Michael, who said, "You may trust her,

Henry. Indeed, had I not believed that, I would not have introduced this subject in her presence."

Isobel's heart warmed, but she suppressed her delight and continued to gaze solemnly at Sir Henry.

He said, "Aye, well, I own, I feel most uncomfortable sharing this matter, but since Waldron has apparently learned more about it than we know ourselves, and has already thrust it upon the two of you, you are both party to it now whether you want to be or not. I will trust you, my lady. Give her the letter, Michael."

He did, and Isobel paid little heed to their conversation after that, exerting herself instead to commit the contents of the final paragraph to memory. As she did, a thought struck her. "Did your father have a favorite philosopher, Sir Henry?"

He shrugged. "If he did, I know not who it might have been."

"Hector and Aunt Euphemia like Publius Syrus," she said. "Both of the maxims in this passage are his, I believe, but I have heard my aunt speak of other Roman philosophers. Surely, Rome did produce the best-known ones."

Sir Henry and Michael exchanged a look.

"What?" she demanded. "I wish you would not speak to each other without words. You and Sir Hugo do that, too, Michael, and it is most irritating."

Sir Henry's eyes twinkled. "My mother complains of that whenever we are all together in the same place, so I do apologize most sincerely, my lady. 'Tis only that we studied a host of other philosophers, many of whom were not Roman, and I warrant that my father did, too."

"Mercy, were there so many of them, then?"

Michael said, "Hundreds, I expect. We cannot tell you many details about our training, lass, but since you may hear things that will confuse you, particularly since the Green Abbot has involved himself in our affairs, you should know that the Kirk of Rome considers much of what we studied, including certain Judaic, Islamic, and Gnostic philosophers, to be heresy."

Isobel grinned. "I'm not sure what those words mean, but my father complains that the Pope does not understand simple matters of Celtic life, that he condemns anything that disagrees with Kirk teachings or gives one pleasure, and also foolishly claims that a wise respect for superstition is naught but heresy."

"I have heard that Macleod of Glenelg is a gey superstitious man," Sir Henry said with an answering gleam.

"Aye, he kisses his thumb to seal a promise. He avoids travel on Fridays, particularly if that day should fall on the thirteenth of the month, and he insisted that my sister Cristina marry before any of his other daughters could, because he believed that if she did not dire things would befall Clan Macleod. That is how she came to marry Hector," Isobel said, adding quickly when the two men exchanged another look, "I mean only to say, however, that I am not quick to condemn all that the Kirk thinks is wrong. Indeed, I would like to learn more about such things."

"The Holy Kirk certainly teaches that men who study the philosophies of Jews, Muslims, and Gnostics are heretical, my lady," Henry said. "I shudder to imagine what his opinion would be if we introduced such ideas to our lady wives. But my father and men of his ilk simply called it education. They believed that if men would just seek creative unity among world races and religions, and attempt to fuse the philosophies that underlie Roman, Greek, Islamic, Christian, and Judaic thought—they would find that we all have much more in common than otherwise."

"Are the philosophers all bearded men?" Isobel asked.

Sir Henry and Michael looked at her in surprise, then at each other.

"Why do you ask that?" Michael asked.

"Because he underscored those two words," she said, showing him.

He looked briefly and smiled. "Certainly not all philosophers had beards, lass. Beards were but matters of fashion as they are now. I should say that he meant to emphasize certain phrases in his letter. Recall that he was angry when he began it. He has rested his pen a few times, too, as you can see by the dots of ink here and about."

"Some are just spatters," she said. "Only a few phrases are underscored."

"Many men do that, though," Sir Henry told her.

Nodding, she continued to study the last paragraph, hoping both men would believe she needed the extra time to memorize its contents. Trying not to be obvious, she skimmed over the rest of the page, taking care not to read more but looking for other underscored or dotted words. She saw none other than in the one paragraph.

"Listen," she said, interrupting Michael. "These are the words he underscored or put dots under in that last paragraph: *'Keep these my words with you. Study well. Follow bearded men. Path of truth at Roslin. Keep safe.'*"

"Let me see that again," Michael demanded, holding out his hand.

Sir Henry moved nearer so that he could read it as Michael did. The latter finished first. "By heaven," he said, "I believe my lass has found your message."

"Aye," Henry said, scratching his head. "It seems obvious now. How could we not have seen it before?" His eyes narrowed as they shifted back to her.

Isobel chuckled. "I am no witch, sir, I promise you. Michael said your father must have left you some instructions, and you both agreed that this is the only letter he ever directed to you alone. I merely accepted both of those statements as fact and tried to figure out how he might have included a message in this letter that anyone reading it would not instantly recognize. The lines and dots are not nearly as dark as the words they mark, and perhaps they are darker now with age than when he put them there, and thus noticeable to one seeking a message. I warrant you would have noticed them yourself before long."

"You are kind, my lady, and generous, but I still feel like a noddy to have carried such a thing with me all these years without deciphering its true meaning."

"You'd best keep deciphering, my lad," Michael said. "Because if you know the meaning of those words, I do not. I own, I did wonder why he should pray for you 'at Roslin' rather than simply offer a prayer for your safety."

Henry grinned suddenly. "I recall wondering if it meant that he did not trust Sir Edward," he said. "That he was advising me to look elsewhere for answers than to his cousin. Fortunately for me, I never suggested as much to Sir Edward."

"I understand that he is your foster father, but who is Sir Edward exactly?" Isobel asked.

"Sir Edward Robison of Strathearn is Hugo's father," Michael said.

"But I thought Sir Hugo was a connection of your mother's," she said. "I am sure that is what he told Hector."

"And that is also true," Sir Henry said, "because he is a double cousin. His mother is a St. Clair, our father's youngest sister."

"If Sir Hugo's mother had the same father that your father did, does that mean that Hugo is a Knight Templar, too?" she asked.

Sir Henry looked at Michael, but this time Isobel did not object. She looked at him, too, and waited.

He rolled his eyes, but he smiled, too. "Hugo's father was, and we all had the same training, lass. But if you would please me, you'll not mention the Templars to anyone even when it seems safe, as it does here, for there are ears everywhere."

"Aye, there are, indeed," she said, remembering the many times she had eavesdropped as a child.

"You know, Michael," Henry said, "many of the carvings at Roslin portray bearded men."

"That thought had occurred to me also," Michael said. "Every lintel, pediment, and pillar contains different carvings, however, as do most of the door panels, but I have never paid any particular heed to their details."

"The message does seem to refer to Roslin," Isobel said.

"Aye, and I'm thinking that the sooner we can search for a pattern amongst those carvings, the better," Michael said.

"You cannot leave here before the ceremony," Henry said with a sigh. "I would not mind in the least if you did, especially if you can find the key to this puzzle, but our lady mother—"

"Say no more," Michael interjected hastily. "I've no wish to infuriate her any more at present. I could see at once that my marriage displeases her."

"I cannot think why," Henry said, smiling at Isobel. "Pray, do not take offense at her megrims, my lady. Much as she may think she commands all in her orbit, she does not rule at Kirkwall, or at Roslin."

"She will not trouble me, sir," Isobel said confidently.

Michael put his arm around her. "It must be nearly time

for supper, Henry," he said. "Had you better not go and prepare yourself to receive your company?"

"Aye, for my Jean will be fearing that our mother will blame her for my tardiness. I must therefore make haste, but put your wits to work, Michael. It will not do for you to declare that you are bound for Roslin. Waldron will be hot on your heels if not well ahead of you if he suspects that we have learned something new."

Michael nodded, and Isobel made her curtsy, but Henry caught her hands and pulled her up again, planting a firm if brotherly kiss on her cheek. "Welcome to Clan St. Clair, my lady," he said warmly.

"I do not think he is at all eccentric," she said when he had gone. "He seems most pleasant and kind."

"Aye, he is a good man," Michael said. "For all that he believes he can sail a ship to the edge of the earth and beyond."

"He said he had seen a map," she reminded him.

"Aye," he said. "But I'm thinking he dreamed it, for I have never seen such a thing, nor do I think anyone else has. And right now," he added in a warmer tone, "I am recalling that Henry interrupted us at a most inopportune moment. Shall I untie your laces for you, madam?"

Feeling the surge of heat that particular tone always stirred in her, she grinned saucily and said, "You may loosen them for me, sir, but if you do not want to anger your mother, I'd suggest that you attempt no more just now."

He raised his eyebrows. "I warrant you think you have found the one weapon that will win over all of mine, lass, but you are mistaken. My mother does not terrify me, although I own, she does try. I am my own man."

He reached then for her laces, and she did not attempt to dissuade him, neither when his fingers wandered more freely about her body than the changing of her clothes for supper warranted, nor when he stripped her clothing from her and carried her to the bed.

As he quickly disrobed, she murmured, "We'll be late."

"Aye, perhaps."

She chuckled low in her throat as he climbed into bed with her, but moments later, she was moaning. She had forgotten how swiftly his mouth and fingers could stir her body's responses. She did remember the aching pain she had felt at Glenelg Bay, however, and that memory made her wary.

When his fingers touched her between the legs, she tensed.

"Relax, sweetheart," he murmured. "Touch me."

She had been kissing him and moving against him, stirred by his caresses, but she had kept her hands near his sides or back, uncertain what else to do with them. Remembering certain things he had done that she had found particularly pleasurable, she began to experiment, scooting lower to kiss his nipples, and lick and suck them as he had done with hers. When he gasped, she smiled, and as his hands continued their explorations, her body responded more and more fervently.

She felt no pain, only desire, and when he shifted his body to possess hers, she welcomed him, finding it easy to match the rhythm of her responses to his thrusts. As their passion increased, she stopped thinking of everything but the sensations he stirred and what she could do to stimulate equal feelings in him.

With no more than a change in his breathing to warn her, his rhythm altered to a more urgent pace, but her body responded with equal fervor. The sensations she experienced then overwhelmed her, giving her a sense of soaring higher and higher until her mind seemed to have entered a place filled with sunlight, where she felt warmth and joy unlike any she had ever known.

With a groan, Michael collapsed atop her, his face buried between her shoulder and her neck. Gently, he kissed her just below her ear and murmured, "Ah, sweetheart, that was wonderful."

Gasping, almost sobbing, she tried to draw a deep breath, but he was too heavy. Choking back a bubble of laughter, she said, "It was splendid, sir, but if you do not move, you will render yourself wifeless and thus unable to repeat it."

"A dire fate," he said with a chuckle as he shifted his weight off her. "I collect that you found this experience more enjoyable than last time."

"Aye," she said, "It was wonderful, but I don't understand how a body can go from having so much energy to so little." She felt languorous and content to stay where she was. Even as that thought drifted through her mind, though, another trailed behind it, reminding her of the time. "Mercy," she exclaimed, sitting bolt upright, "we *are* going to be late for supper!"

"Very likely," he agreed, his tone of voice mirroring the feelings she had had before the unwelcome reminder presented itself.

"Well, don't just lie there," she said, tugging at one muscular shoulder. "Get up and get dressed—and make haste about it, too!"

"Gently, lass," he said. "We'll not starve, even if we are late."

"Now, you listen to me, Michael St. Clair. Your mother already looks at me as if I were something she'd scrape off her shoe. I don't want to do more to irritate her before she has even come to know me. Up, sir, or you will not need to suffocate me to render yourself wifeless in bed."

"Heaven forfend," he said, laughing but getting out of bed nonetheless.

The others were all at their places when Michael and Isobel entered the great hall, but she noticed straightaway that Sir Henry's chaplain had not yet spoken the grace before meat. One seat was empty on the ladies' side of the high table, between Cristina and Adela, and another was empty on the gentleman's side, between Lachlan and Sir Hugo. Princess Margaret occupied the ladies' place of honor, next to Sir Henry's wife, Jean, with Mairi beside her. Macleod of Glenelg sat at the far end of the table on the men's side, and Waldron sat at a central table below the dais with a number of men she did not know. She saw Michael eye them narrowly, but she did not see the Green Abbot, so perhaps he was late, too.

The meal passed quickly and without incident. The food was excellent although plainer than what Isobel was accustomed to at Lochbuie, and the claret flowed freely at both ends of the table. Minstrels played throughout the meal, and when servants presented the banquet of sweets, a troupe of players ran into the center of the lower hall. A space had been cleared for them there, and a fool emerged to direct their antics. Jugglers and acrobats displayed their skills first.

Many travelers in Isobel's party were covering yawns before the jugglers had finished. Isobel had had but one goblet of wine, but although she still felt the aftereffects of her interlude with Michael, she was not tired. Cristina clearly was, however, and Lady Euphemia, and before long, Princess Margaret stood, thereby announcing her intention to retire.

Everyone else stood until she and her ladies had departed from the hall, but then others prepared to leave, including Lady Euphemia, who paused beside Adela and Isobel to say, "I shall not presume to tell you when you should go to bed, Isobel. Now that you are a married lady, you are at your husband's beck and bay, but you, my dear Adela, will come along with me, and go straight to bed."

"Oh, pray do not take me away so soon, Aunt. I promise you, I am not at all sleepy, and I want to watch the players. See, they are even now taking their places."

Lady Euphemia looked as if she would insist, so Isobel said, "She can stay with me, Aunt. Cristina is still here, too, so we'll see that she gets back safely. Indeed, I cannot imagine what could happen to her in a bishop's palace."

"Nor can I, my dear, but there are a good many young men here, and young men, by their very nature, cannot be trusted to behave. Do not go anywhere alone tonight. Indeed, you should not go anywhere without a good strong, trustworthy gentleman to accompany you. But I warrant Sir Michael will look after you both, so I shall leave you now and bid you goodnight."

Adela chuckled when Lady Euphemia was safely out of earshot. "Faith, I did not think she'd give in so easily. Is this what it is like at his grace's court, Isobel? I never had interest in such things, you know, but I hope there will be dancing tonight. I fear I have grown quite sinful of late. Sir Hugo has not gone yet, has he?"

Isobel looked at her. "Do you like him?"

Adela shrugged. "He is very merry, is he not? But I do

think he ought to be more serious about some things. He seems to laugh at everything."

"He does have a cheerful disposition," Isobel agreed. "Still, I think he takes his duties seriously."

"Oh, aye, indeed he does," Adela said, frowning. "I had forgotten that. Do you know he refused to ride with me to Chalamine to collect your maid? And he had no way to know at the time that we would be seeing you again so soon. Indeed, I did not know that myself. And he might have taken her with him quite easily."

"It all came right in the end," Isobel said soothingly. "Yes?" she added, when a gillie wearing the St. Clair gray tunic with its distinguishing black cross stepped up to her and made his bow.

"Beg pardon, madam, but the princess Margaret has asked that you and the lady Adela join her in her chamber at once. I am to escort you there."

"Just Lady Adela and me?" Isobel asked.

"Aye, madam."

Adela paled. "What do you think we have done?" she asked.

"I cannot think of anything," Isobel said. "But we had better not tarry."

They got up at once, and when Cristina turned with a questioning look, Isobel said, "Princess Margaret sent for Adela and me. I cannot think why, but we'll be back in a trice, I expect. If Michael asks, tell him we have a St. Clair gillie with us."

Cristina nodded and turned to relay the information to Mairi.

They followed the gillie out of the hall, along a corridor to the main stairway, and up two flights to another corridor. Halfway along, he stopped at a door and rapped. The door swung inward, revealing the golden glow of candlelight within, and he gestured for them to precede him.

Adela went first, but Isobel bumped into her when she stopped just inside the door and cried out in surprise. Before Isobel could see what had startled her, a hard hand pushed her into Adela, and the door snapped shut behind them. Hearing a bar thud into place, she turned and saw the gillie who had accompanied them standing in front of the now-barred door, fists on his hips, grinning at her insolently.

"Sakes, what do you think you are doing?" she demanded.

"Don't blame him," a familiar voice said. "He just followed my orders."

Adela stepped aside, and Isobel found herself face to face with Waldron of Edgelaw. Beyond him stood the Green Abbot of Iona, the flickering light and his vulpine features making him appear even more predatory than his companion.

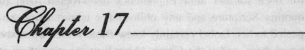

Chapter 17

How pleasant to see you both," Waldron said with a deep bow.

"Where is Princess Margaret?" Adela asked, looking bewildered.

Isobel grimaced. "I warrant she is in her bedchamber, preparing for bed, and would be most astonished to learn that she had sent for us. What do you want with us, you villain?"

Waldron looked amused. "What I'd like most, Mistress Wasp, is to have the schooling of you long enough to teach you a woman's proper place in this life."

"Indeed, Isobel, lass," Abbot Mackinnon said dulcetly, "a wiser woman wouldna speak to any gentleman in such an impertinent way. She'd show more respect, and forswear enmity, for good manners are the bulwark of civil behavior."

Isobel met his harsh gaze and said evenly, "'The path of the just is a shining light,' or so I once heard you say, my lord abbot. If you are in league with this man, mayhap 'tis because you do not know his wicked ways."

"Such evil words corrupt good manners," the abbot said sternly.

"But truth is great and will endure," she retorted, grateful for once for her aunt Euphemia's deep-rooted habit of quoting Scripture and any philosopher whose words appealed to her. Isobel certainly knew Bible verses when she heard them, and if the Green Abbot kept spouting them at her, she would just spout them right back. "This man took me prisoner just a short time ago and threatened to let all his men have their way with me," she went on. "You once claimed friendship with my family, sir. Do you condone such fiendish treatment of your friends?"

Waldron snapped, "Enough of this farce. Abbot Mackinnon knows I serve the cause of God, His Kirk, and His Holiness the Pope. Therefore, I am without sin."

"If your god forgives what you do, he is no god of mine," Isobel snapped.

Adela gasped. "Isobel, you speak sacrilege!"

"You do, indeed," the abbot said. "Moreover, Isobel, Waldron is right. God forgives all who battle in the name of Christ and His Kirk, and He would want you to tell Waldron everything he wants to know."

"I'll tell him nothing," Isobel said disdainfully.

"Aye, lass, you will," Waldron said. "One way or another."

"Mercy," Adela exclaimed, clearly frightened. "Tell him, Isobel!"

"Even if I could, I would not, but I cannot, for I don't even know what they are talking about."

"This gets us nowhere, my lord abbot," Waldron said. "Take the lady Adela out of the room with you for a few minutes. I shall talk privately with Lady Isobel, because I believe I can quickly persuade her to tell me what I want to know. If I cannot, you must bring Lady Adela back, and we will see if certain of my more persuasive methods, when applied to her, will not loosen Lady Isobel's tongue."

Isobel glanced at the abbot to see if such ominous words would persuade him of Waldron's evil ways, but if they had any effect, she saw no sign of it. Clearly Hector and his grace were right, and the Green Abbot had long since lost any claim to goodness—if, indeed, he had ever had any.

Mackinnon took a firm grip of Adela's arm, and still doubtless respecting his office if not the man himself, she allowed him to escort her from the room with no more than a helpless glance over her shoulder at her sister.

As Isobel watched them go, she turned slightly away from Waldron and moved to slip her hand through the slits in her skirt and underskirt to the dirk in its sheath. But to her shock, she found no slit, for the gown was one that Mairi had ordered for her. Having found that it fit her well, she had not thought about slits in her haste to dress for supper. Feeling a distinct chill of fear, she turned slowly back to face Waldron.

"Come here to me, lass, and we will see just how brave you are," he said with a smile that she was sure emulated the devil's own.

Raising her chin, she straightened her shoulders. "I am not afraid of you," she said, hoping she could persuade herself of that, and quickly. As she held her ground, her steady gaze continuing to challenge him, she wondered briefly if Michael trusted her enough yet to believe her when she told him that she and Adela had not left the hall alone—if, indeed, she survived to tell him anything.

With a look of annoyance, Waldron moved toward her, and she backed away step for step, without taking her eyes off him, until she had backed into the wall.

"You see, my dear, there is no escape," he said with another of his horrid smiles as she looked frantically left and right and saw no weapon to help her, only two wall sconces of candles that burned with irritating cheer. "Now, we will begin."

Michael was quietly talking with Hugo and the High Admiral at the high table when Isobel and her elder sister left the great hall. Watching them go, and noting their escort's St. Clair tunic, he had returned to his conversation, thinking they must have decided to pay a visit to the garderobe tower, or even to take a short stroll outside to clear the claret fumes from their brains, as many others were doing.

Hugo sat on his right and Lachlan on his left with Hector Reaganach just beyond Hugo. Hector had been conversing with the gentleman on his right, but he turned now and caught Michael's eye.

"I'm guessing you saw your cousin depart some few minutes ago with our irritating, unmitered, and rebellious abbot," he said quietly.

"I saw Waldron and others from his table leave," Michael said, "but in watching them, I failed to note the abbot's departure. In truth, he looks unlike any abbot I've ever met, since he does not wear clerical garb. He blends into the crowd."

"Aye, few who do not know him well would recognize Fingon for a man of the cloth, even at home," Lachlan said. "Not only does he pay no heed to the dictates of Rome in his personal life, having lived with the same woman for years and sired a number of children with her, but he always wears the expensive clothing of a courtier. Moreover, as you have seen, he thinks nothing of disobeying a royal command by leaving the Holy Isle when it suits him. I warrant he believes his grace's illness foreshadows his demise, or he hopes it does. I know you look upon Waldron as your chief enemy. Still, you should pay closer heed to the abbot."

"I will indeed, sir, thank you," Michael said, chastened.

Hector began to say something, but Lachlan interrupted him to ask Michael if he had recognized the gillie who had spoken to Isobel.

Michael frowned. "*He* addressed her? I assumed that she had sent for a St. Clair gillie to escort her and Adela to their destination, but I saw them all only as they were leaving the dais. I never had a clear view of his face. Did you, Hugo?"

"Nay, because I could not see Isobel or Adela from here any earlier than that, myself, not without leaning well forward and looking down the table. Hector Reaganach's height clearly gives him an advantage over lesser mortals."

A tingling at the back of Michael's neck brought him to his feet, but his voice was calm as he said, "I believe I'll take a stroll myself, my lords, if you will excuse me."

"Nay, lad, we'll all go," Hector said, leaning down to pick up the famous Clan Gillean battle-axe from beneath his chair.

"You may go," Lachlan said, smiling lazily at his twin. "However, you must not all depart at once. 'Tis better if only Sir Michael and his cousin leave now. You may follow them, but it would be as well to have some idea first of their direction."

Hector nodded as Michael said, "You wait here, Hugo, whilst I ask the ladies Mairi and Cristina if Isobel or Adela said aught to them of their intentions."

He moved at once to the ladies' end of the table, where both women quickly apprised him of what they knew.

Cristina looked worried, but Mairi said, "They can scarcely come to grief with my mother, sir, and even if they have left her already, you need not fret. Your lady is perfectly capable of looking after herself *and* Adela."

"Under most circumstances I would agree with you, madam, but I do not trust my cousin. If he managed to lay hands on her—" He broke off, unable to continue because for once his emotions threatened to betray him. The thought of Isobel in Waldron's hands was too much to contemplate. "If you will forgive me—"

"Wait," Lady Cristina said. "Surely, he would not harm her! He must know she has powerful protectors."

"I will see that he does her no harm, madam, but I must go at once." With a hasty bow, he returned to Hugo, saying quietly as he bent to collect his sword and scabbard from beneath his own chair, "The gillie told her that Princess Margaret had sent for them. Lady Mairi said they thought it odd, because her mother had left the hall, intending to retire, and she rarely entertains anyone after supper."

Hugo got up then, found his sword, and moved to stand next to Michael.

Michael told Hector they would seek the women first in Waldron's chamber, after which the two men wasted no time leaving the hall. Once away from the crowd, each slipped the long leather strap of his scabbard over his head and across his chest, then shifted his sword high onto his back, where he could more easily reach over his shoulder to draw quickly.

"If they came this way, would Isobel not have realized they were going in the wrong direction?" Hugo asked when a gillie directed them to a wing at the opposite end of the palace from their rooms, as well as the princess's chamber.

"Nay, how could she?" Michael asked. "We went right to our own chamber, where Henry joined us. Isobel would have no knowledge of her grace's location, and would trustingly have followed any gillie she thought to be one of our own."

They hurried up the spiral stone stairway to the next level and along the long corridor upon which it emerged.

"This cannot be right," Michael said a moment later. "These doors are all too close together. Unless each room here has two entrances, Isobel would not believe that Henry had put her grace into such a small one. Moreover, it is too quiet." His heart pounded as if he had been running a great distance at top speed.

"You go up to the next level," Hugo said. "I'll continue on here to make sure, then join you upstairs. I warrant Hector Reaganach will be along soon, too."

Michael did not wait to hear more but turned and ran back to the stairway, taking the spiraling stone steps two by two and hoping he did not meet Waldron on the way. As with most such stairways, the builder had given the advantage to a right-handed swordsman at the top rather than to an invader at the bottom. Thus, it twisted counterclockwise, putting Michael's sword hand near the oiled-rope banister. A man coming downstairs, the banister at his left, could hug the wall, thus using the widest portion of the steps and leaving his sword hand free.

Emerging at the next level, Michael saw that the doors were farther apart, indicating more spacious rooms. Furthermore, the corridor was wider and boasted a bank of tall windows along the outer wall, overlooking the front courtyard. More important guests would be housed here than on the lower floor. Indeed, the only sign that this was a bishop's home rather than that of a wealthy nobleman was

the holy-water font at each end of the corridor for the convenience of his eminence's guests.

As Michael hurried along the corridor, Lady Adela
emerged from a room near the end. She looked distressed,
and a tall man with shoulder-length gray hair emerged behind her, holding her left arm in what most people would
consider an inappropriate manner for a man not closely
related to her. He retained his hold on her as he shut the
door behind them and turned toward Michael. It was the
abbot.

Although tempted to reach for his sword, Michael resisted the impulse, letting his hand rest easy at his side as he
watched their approach. Knowing that Waldron had ears
like a cat's, he did not want to make any noise until he had
to, and the bright golden, dust-mote-strewn light from a sun
low in the west made it unlikely that the abbot had recognized him or would fear one man approaching them. Lady
Adela was another matter. She would know him at once.

She did. He saw as much in her eyes, but she did not
speak. Still, she must have stiffened or otherwise given her
captor warning, because he hesitated. He wore a long jew-
eled dirk in a sheath on his left hip, which told Michael that
the abbot was right handed, but although Mackinnon shifted
the weapon slightly as if to move its hilt more readily within
reach, he did so with his left hand, his right still tightly gripping her ladyship's arm.

Careless of him, Michael thought. Waldron would not
have made that error. Praying that the abbot would assume
only that Adela had hesitated at seeing another person in the
corridor, and that he was more concerned that she would cry
out for help than he was about the lone gentleman, Michael
continued toward them.

He heard hasty footsteps on the stairway, knew them for

Hugo's, and a moment later, saw the abbot's eyes widen. The hand near his eminence's dirk moved slightly away from it, but he did not ease his grip on the lass's arm.

Michael went on as if naught were amiss. Hugo, too, remained silent, but Michael knew from his rapid footsteps that his cousin was moving up behind him.

Keeping his face expressionless, he strode on, moving to his right as if to give room for the pair coming toward him. Although he avoided looking directly at Adela, who was near the window wall and well to his left, he could see that she was not watching him as carefully as she watched Hugo. He noted that the abbot's hand tightened on her arm as they neared.

Knowing he had judged his timing well, he gathered himself mentally.

Two strides later, his right fist came up from his side and connected solidly with abbot's chin. Mackinnon reeled backward and went down so swiftly that Michael nearly failed to catch him. As it was, the abbot's head hit the floor with a thump loud enough to make Michael glance back at Hugo with a rueful grimace.

Hugo shook his head to indicate that he did not think the sound had been loud enough to carry far. His left hand was up, index finger at his lips, reminding Adela not to speak. She had not cried out when Michael had struck the abbot, and she nodded her understanding now without comment.

Michael signaled Hugo to look after their captive and the lass, then turned and strode silently to the door of the room from which the pair had come. Pausing there, he reached back for his sword.

Having heard the door shut behind her, Isobel watched Waldron carefully, trying to forget all that Michael had said about his cousin's prowess and remember all that Hector Reaganach had taught her about how to defend herself. Waldron was tall, muscular, and clearly menacing, but Hector the Ferocious was taller, broader, and surely more powerful. Not that she had ever actually bested Hector, but she had thrown him once, quite by accident, simply by following his instructions.

She had known without his telling her that only the great difference in their sizes had caused that absurd fall. Standing close behind her, he had bent over her, showing her how to grasp his arm and elbow and explaining how she should position herself. As he talked, she had suddenly thrown her hip into his thigh in the manner he had shown her only a few moments before. To her great delight and astonishment, and to his own, as well, he had toppled right over her to the ground.

She could not, however, expect Waldron to be so innocently cooperative. Nor would she voluntarily turn her back on him.

He was still about four feet away when she reached up, snatched one of four candles from the sconce above her right shoulder, and hurled it at him.

He knocked it to the floor, even paused to stamp out its flame, then look another step toward her.

"Don't come any closer," she snapped, grabbing another candle. "I am not afraid of you."

"You should be afraid, lass," he said grimly. "You should be very afraid, because I am already angry that you are putting me to this trouble. If you don't drop that at once, I will not only punish you for your insolence a few minutes ago, but I'll make you even sorrier for having the impudence to wave that thing at me."

She could see for herself that he was angry, and his anger was frightening, but his voice did not stir the hairs on the back of her neck the way Michael's did when he was angry. Waldron reminded her more of her eldest nephew, Cristina's son, who at the age of six, balked of something he wanted, had thrown a tantrum in the hope that pure fury would gain it for him. Remembering how Hector had handled that incident made her wish she were three times Waldron's size and could simply take a strap to his backside to teach him manners. Despite the gravity of the situation, her lips twitched at the ludicrous thought.

"By the Rood, woman, do you dare laugh at me?" he demanded, closing the distance between them in less than a heartbeat.

She brought the candle upward as hard as she could, the way Hector had taught her to use her dagger, but Waldron struck like lightning and sent it flying. It hit the wall and went out before she was entirely aware that she no longer held it.

Gripping her wrist so tightly that she cried out, he yanked her to him and slapped her hard across the face.

Her ears rang, but her free hand flashed up and fisted itself as it lashed sideways hard across the end of his nose, and she had the satisfaction of hearing him grunt. His hand went up to strike again, but at a whisper of sound from the doorway, he flung her aside instead and snatched his sword from its scabbard.

Landing hard on a hip, she looked up to see Michael in the doorway, his long sword out before him in both hands, at the ready. He did not glance her way. Indeed, she thought both men had already forgotten her existence. Their gazes locked, they circled slowly, each waiting for the other to attack.

She opened her mouth to shout at them to stop, to remind them that they were in a house of God, or near enough to count as one. But realizing she might distract Michael and thus give Waldron a chance to kill him, she held her tongue.

Michael's usual calm had enveloped him the moment he saw Waldron shove Isobel away. Watching him closely, he wondered which his cousin wanted more, the location of the treasure or Michael's death. If the former, Michael might have an edge. If the latter . . . He realized in that instant that it did not matter a whit which it was, because whatever his cousin's intentions had been at the outset, the moment the two swords clanged together, Waldron would care only about besting him, for so it had always been. Once begun, the competition was all that mattered.

Waldron feinted, but Michael had known he would and did not address the feint. Instead, he waited a split second until Waldron was pulling back, and then he thrust hard and straight. But the parry came as quickly, and his fingers vibrated as his sword did, its steel ringing from the clash.

He did not want to kill Waldron in front of Isobel, but he believed he would not have to, because Hugo would hear the noise and come. He need only fend off Waldron's attack until then.

The thought gave him pause, because he knew that such thinking did not augur well for his own safety. He must put the lass out of his mind completely, a task he had already discovered to be much harder than one might think.

Movement beyond the swordsmen caught Isobel's eye just then, as a small door at the back of the room opened.

"Michael, look out!" she cried.

Two men stepped into the room, swords drawn, but Michael seemed to ignore them, for he did not take his eyes off Waldron.

"I'll deal with him," Waldron snapped. "Take the lass!"

Leaping to her feet as the men turned toward her, Isobel darted toward the doorway through which Michael had come. As she reached it, Hugo appeared before her, grabbed her, and pulled her through it, stepping past her with drawn sword as he did. Hector was a short distance beyond him in the corridor, bent over the Green Abbot, with Sir Henry, of all people, peering interestedly down at them.

Hector finished tying a knot, saw Isobel, and stood. The clanging sounds in the room behind her increased in both number and volume.

"Oh, hurry, sir," she cried. "There are three swordsmen in there against just Michael and Hugo."

Sir Henry smiled. "Sakes, lass, that will but give that pair a bit of exercise."

Hector cocked his head. "If I'm not mistaken, the noise within has already ceased. Also, however, Fingon appears to be stirring at last, so if you'll keep an eye on him here, Sir Henry, I'll just have a look in there."

Isobel noted that, despite Hector's confidence and the sudden silence, he removed his battle-axe from its sling as he approached the doorway. Then Adela rushed forward to hug her, and Isobel spent the next few moments reassuring her sister that she was quite unharmed.

"It all happened so fast that I scarcely had time to be afraid," she said. "It seemed as if you had just walked away with the abbot when Michael arrived. It is the first time I've been glad that he walks as silently as a ghost."

"Aye, he does move like a wraith when he wants to," Henry said.

"He ran to that doorway, though," Adela said. "His face was white, Isobel. I think he was truly frightened."

With a gimlet eye on the abbot, Sir Henry said, "Lady Adela has already described how you were tricked into coming here, my lady. I am most displeased that you should have been treated so whilst a guest in this household, and by a member of my own family. Pray be so kind as to accept my profound apology."

"Oh, thank heaven, there they are now!" Adela exclaimed.

Isobel had already seen them. So relieved was she to see Michael safe that she wanted to run and hug him, but she was not sure he would appreciate such a display of affection, or so much as a hint of her previous concern. She had noted before that men seemed to take such behavior as an insult to their skill. Moreover, had he not said that she need never worry when he had a weapon in hand?

Waldron and his two minions, weaponless now, walked together, with Hector, Michael, and Hugo following them. As they approached, Henry said, "What the devil do you think you have been doing, cousin?"

"I?" Waldron shrugged. "You would do better to ask your impulsive brother how it is that he dared to strike down a holy man who is very likely the most powerful man of the Kirk anywhere in the Isles and western Highlands."

Instead of rising to this bait, Henry regarded him shrewdly and said, "It appears that he struck you, too, cousin, or did you forget and walk nose first into a door before you opened it?"

Waldron's face reddened, and he shot Isobel an evil look.

Michael moved to stand beside her, and as he did, his hand brushed hers.

Welcoming its warmth, she smiled at him.

Henry said, "Although, plainly, you do not want to answer my questions, cousin, you have abused my hospitality, both of you, making me think little of you, my lord abbot, or your so-called holiness. A holy man does not trick young women into danger. Nor does any man who thinks himself a gentleman, Waldron, and until now I believed that you at least made some pretense to act as one."

Waldron shrugged again, saying, "You speak well for a thief, Henry. But, as you will learn, thieves never prosper."

Henry shook his head. "Michael told me about this fancy of yours, but since to believe it, I must likewise believe our revered grandfather was the thief in question, or— No, 'tis worse than that, is it not? He had to have been one of a gang of thieves, if your version of events is true. But we know he was an honorable man."

"It matters not whether he believed he was guarding the contents of the Templar treasury or stealing them," Waldron snapped. "Our present Pope, like his predecessors, has commanded that every item that vanished when the Templars fled Paris be returned to the custody of the Kirk. Do you dare to defy His Holiness?"

"The Pope wields no power here," Henry said softly. "Nor do I believe that we ken the whereabouts of anything that belongs to the Kirk of Rome. What I do believe, however, is that I have come to the end of my patience, Waldron. You are no longer welcome here, nor at castles St. Clair or Roslin. I shan't order you out on the instant, but neither may you continue to roam freely about this household."

"You hold no authority over me," Waldron said.

"Nor over me, certainly," the Green Abbot declared.

"You are both wrong," Henry said in a harder, colder tone than any Isobel had yet heard from him. "On Orkney, gentlemen, I am the *only* authority."

Waldron laughed. "Faith, Henry, you are not even Prince of Orkney yet, and will not be until your precious ceremony on Sunday!"

"Again you err, cousin. I have been Prince of Orkney since the second day of this month, when the Norse King officially installed me at Maestrand in Norway. That ceremony was small, because his grace King Haakon preferred it so, and also because we could not expect many of my new subjects to journey to Norway, but he likewise agreed that a much grander ceremony should be held here, so that the people of Orkney might meet their prince, clearly understand the duties and privileges of his position, and welcome him. And so it shall be on Sunday at the cathedral. However, I already hold the power to mint coins and make laws. Likewise do I hold the power of the pit and gallows. So try me further tonight only at your peril."

Michael watched Waldron carefully, knowing that his cousin was capable of moving swiftly and needed no weapon in his hand to be lethal. Clearly, he had not known about Henry's trip to Norway, and just as clearly, the news displeased him, but nonetheless he retained his unruffled demeanor. His two minions likewise seemed more relaxed than one might expect under the circumstances.

Waldron said, "What do you mean to do with us, Henry?"

"I do not want to cause a scandal by throwing you and our lord abbot into the dungeon, supposing his eminence the bishop even possesses one," Henry said. "However, your behavior does not incline me to trust your word that you will create no more trouble, even if you were to offer that word. Would you?"

"I don't think so, no."

"Exactly, so I will suppress my dislike of scandal sufficiently to confine all four of you to your separate chambers under strong guard. Yes, Michael?" he added, although Michael had not spoken.

"I think you are being too lenient, sir," Michael said. "You would do better to find a stronger, more reliable place of confinement. The abbot here has already defied orders of the High King of Scots and the Lord of the Isles that ought to have kept him confined to the Holy Isle."

"I warrant that neither the King nor MacDonald set his own guards to keep him there," Henry said. "I shall not make that error. Indeed, I believe I hear my lads coming now," he added as noise from the stairwell heralded new arrivals. "I took the precaution before following Hector Reaganach up here to have my captain of guards gather a few men and send them after me."

A short time later, ten of Henry's men led the four prisoners, their hands trussed behind them, back to the stairway. Since Henry and Hector followed, Michael decided that he could safely remain with Isobel, who had been watching the proceedings with interest but now regarded him somewhat warily.

Lady Adela, on the other hand, glowered at Hugo, who had likewise remained behind and chose that moment to say something to her. Raising her chin in much the same way that Isobel did when she was angry, Adela said, "You have no authority over me, sir, and I will thank you to remember that."

His voice low, Hugo spoke again. Michael's ears were particularly sharp, and although he could not hear every word, he thought his cousin was taking the lass to task for having left the hall with only an unknown gillie as escort. Glancing at Isobel, he wondered if she feared he would say something similar to her.

He grinned at her.

The slight, unexpected tension Isobel had felt evaporated, and she realized that she had been waiting to see if Michael would take her to task as Sir Hugo was so clearly doing with Adela. Just then, her sister whirled from Hugo and began to stomp angrily toward the stairway.

"Just one moment, my lady," Hugo commanded sternly.

Over her shoulder, Adela snapped. "We are not married, so you have no right to speak to me as if we were, sir. Indeed, I would not marry you if you begged me!"

"Never fear, lass; I won't," he retorted. "I don't intend to marry for many years yet, for even the Bible says that a woman's heart is but 'snares and nets, and her hands as bands.' As for marrying a wasp-tongued shrew like yourself—"

Isobel watched in shock as her usually staid sister turned to the holy-water font, now beside her, snatched the water-filled glass liner from its stone bowl, and dashed its sanctified contents right into Sir Hugo's angry face.

As the outraged Hugo grabbed her by the arm, Michael

stepped hastily forward, took the glass liner from Adela, and put a hand on Hugo's shoulder.

Adela glared equally at both men, jerked her arm from Hugo's grasp, then turned on her heel and stormed toward the stairway.

Choking back bubbles of laughter, Isobel hurried after her.

Chapter 18

Let her go, Hugo," Michael said quietly when his cousin moved to follow. Understanding that he had not yet relinquished his battle fervor and thus had reacted only to knowing that Adela and Isobel had walked into danger, Michael added as he set the liner back in the holy-water font, "They did nothing wrong, and you know it. They thought they were obeying an order from the princess Margaret."

"I know, but that lass needs a strong hand," Hugo said. "I may have a word with Macleod, or with that aunt of hers. They should keep a closer eye on her."

"Macleod women are strong-minded," Michael said, smiling. "If you dislike that trait, I'd advise you to seek elsewhere to wed."

"Sakes, I don't want her," Hugo said. "I've too many things on my plate as it is. Moreover, we cannot just stand here. Those two are halfway to their chambers and will likely run into more mischief if we don't see to their safety."

Realizing there was no point to gain by trying to reassure him and not altogether certain he was wrong, Michael gestured for him to lead the way. His cousin's rapid pace told him that Hugo cared more than he was willing to admit about Lady Adela's safety, and he shook his head a little, wondering if his cousin's generally carefree nature was undergoing an unexpected change.

They were approaching the next landing when Henry stepped onto it from the quiet, narrow corridor they had searched before. Holding a finger to his lips, he gestured to them to follow him.

Isobel and Adela hurried to the bedchamber the latter shared with Lady Euphemia and, finding it empty, went inside. They had not spoken, because Adela was still angry and Isobel, suppressing her own amusement, had not wanted to stir her to say anything outrageous where others might overhear her.

As she shut the door, however, Isobel said, "What a thing to do, Adela!"

Adela whirled. "That man!" she exclaimed. "That arrogant, unfeeling, odious man! Someone ought to flay him."

"I'm sure that Waldron would oblige you, given the chance," Isobel said dryly, "but sakes, Adela, what has Sir Hugo ever done to you?"

"Done to me? Faith, he has done naught to me," Adela said, flinging her hands up. "He flirts with anyone wearing skirts, of course, so his smile means naught, nor his pretty words. Despite all that false charm, he could not even take a quarter hour to ride to Chalamine and collect your maid and belongings when he heard you had gone with Sir Michael, but he takes it upon himself to take *me* to task at every turn, to tell me that I ought to wear my hair free or

pinch my cheeks, or that I ought to have known a fake gillie
when I had no reason on this earth to think for a moment
that the horrid man was aught but what he said he was. And
then—"

"Peace," Isobel cried. "I can see that Sir Hugo has offended you, but to have thrown holy water in his face!
Adela, that is not like you at all."

"And what am I like, Isobel? Do you have any notion?
You, who took the first opportunity to leave Chalamine and
live instead with Cristina and Hector? Don't talk to me
about what I am like. You have spent all your time doing
just as you please, whilst I have spent mine tending
someone else's children and someone else's household. So
don't you dare presume to tell me what I am like."

"If that is what you think of me," Isobel said more tartly
than she had intended, "I fear that neither of us knows much
about the other."

Adela burst into tears.

"Oh, mercy," Isobel exclaimed, rushing to take her sister
in her arms. "Don't cry, love. What on earth has that
dreadful man done to you?"

Michael and Hugo followed Henry to a point near the
middle of the long corridor before he stopped and turned to
face them.

"My lads are seeing to that unholy pair," he said quietly.
"This corridor is not heavily occupied yet, as it contains the
rooms of certain of the bishop's minions who are of higher
rank than others and thus entitled to some degree of comfort. They have departed for the nonce, however, in order to
leave sufficient space to house everyone who will attend my

ceremony Sunday, so I think we can talk undisturbed for a few minutes, and it seemed wiser to speak here than to make it plain to others that we are conferring."

"Why are we conferring, Henry?" Michael asked.

"Because we need a plan," Henry said. "You and Hugo have apparently stirred up more than we knew if that precious pair was willing to molest two noblewomen to find what they seek. We all know that Waldron is not particularly nice in his ways when he is angry, so we must decide what to do next."

"I need to get to Roslin as quickly as possible," Michael said. "Perhaps I should leave at once."

"Nay," Henry said. "You do not want to make a song about it, lest you draw more interest than necessary. Moreover, I think Hugo should go with you, and if you both depart before the ceremony, it will just cause more talk. Our mother, for example, will be annoyed."

"Aye, she would be," Michael agreed. "But if you keep Waldron and the abbot locked up—"

Henry smiled ruefully. "You know I cannot do that," he said. "Part of my agreement with the Norse King is not to stir trouble with the King of Scots or the Lord of the Isles, and much as their graces dislike the Green Abbot, I warrant they will not take kindly to my arresting men who are not my subjects and keeping them locked up without even giving them fair hearing. Would you like to engage in a battle of words with that pair over who is at fault and why?"

Realizing that Waldron would invoke God and the Pope in such an exchange, might not even hesitate to accuse Henry and himself of stealing from the Holy Kirk, Michael shook his head. "Nay," he said. "I would not."

"Nor I," Hugo said. "Art sure you cannot simply stow them somewhere?"

"There is no dungeon here," Henry said. "Nor can I simply load them into a galley and take them to Caithness with me when I leave here. My own men are loyal, but others are here already, and more will arrive tomorrow. Many of them will know the Green Abbot if they do not know Waldron, and many fear the abbot's power, as you know. It would be better, I think, to allow them to attend the ceremony and depart afterward as if naught of any awkwardness had occurred."

Michael nodded, seeing his point. "Then mayhap they should see us departing as well, but for Caithness rather than Roslin."

"Why Caithness, and how would they know?" Hugo asked.

"We would tell them, of course," Michael said. To Henry, he added, "You have invited some of your guests to visit you at Castle St. Clair, have you not?"

"I have, of course," Henry said. "The bishop wants his palace back, and it is not far out of anyone's way to journey from here to St. Clair Bay. By the bye," he added on a more petulant note, "I have decided that I want no more to do with the French branch of the family. It is plain to me now that Waldron's early training is what led us all to this point, so I am going to return to the spelling our grandfather preferred. Henceforward St. Clair shall be spelled as Scotsmen pronounce it."

"I thought you preferred to avoid our mother's displeasure," Michael said.

"Aye, well, it won't happen overnight, nor do I intend to make a song about it. I warrant she'll have time to get used to it before she realizes what I have done. But what course did you have in mind for my guests at the castle, Michael?"

"I'm just thinking that if you were to invite Princess

Margaret and the others from the Isle of Mull and Ardtornish to visit you there, everyone would assume that Isobel and I were with them. We, on the other hand, could leave before they do."

"You must attend my ceremony. Everyone would notice if you did not."

"Aye, but we could leave directly afterward. Dusk is already growing darker, and you could explain a single galley departing by saying you've sent to warn the household at St. Clair to expect more guests. And, if you put the Green Abbot and Waldron off the island early in the morning so they can see your departing guests only from a distance, Hugo and Lady Adela can take our places with the group from Mull. You know yourself how often people mistake Hugo and me for each other, and Lady Adela can easily be mistaken for Isobel."

"Aye, that might work," Hugo said. "At least, it might if you can persuade that temperamental lass to be seen in my company again."

Henry grimaced. "Have you offended Lady Adela, Hugo? If so, ingratiate yourself again. Waldron must not suspect that Michael goes to Roslin. If there is aught to find there, Michael must be the one to find it and make all safe. We may not know what we guard, but we do know that our primary duty is to guard it well."

Hugo groaned but Michael nodded, suppressing a smile. He recognized, if Hugo did not, that Henry's amusement matched his own.

Adela was still weeping.

"Sir Hugo is clearly just as dreadful as you say he is, and

Cristina and I were beasts to leave you with all the responsibility at Chalamine," Isobel said gently. "But if you will not tell me what Hugo did, can you not at least say something?"

She had hoped that, by placing the blame at Hugo's door and her own, she might at least calm Adela, and was gratified when her sister's tears ceased at last.

But Adela said, "It is not your fault, Isobel. I don't know what made me say that. I would have welcomed neither your advice nor the behavior of which you were capable then. I was the eldest at home after Cristina and Mariota left, so it was my duty to assume responsibility for the household. Recall that Maura and Kate were still home, too, and all three of us are older than you are. Moreover, if you will forgive my saying so, Sidony and Sorcha were much easier for us to look after without you there to tempt them into mischief. Not," she added with a reminiscent gleam, "that Sorcha has ever needed encouragement in that regard."

"She does have a mischievous nature," Isobel agreed.

"Mischievous! That scamp would try the patience of God himself. I think I told you that her behavior is the reason Father refused to let her come here."

"You didn't, but I am not surprised," Isobel said. "And, of course, Sidony did not come because Sorcha could not."

"Aye, but—" Adela broke off at the sound of footsteps approaching the door. "Do *not* tell Aunt Euphemia about the holy water, Isobel. Pray, do not!"

"I won't," Isobel said, but she immediately deduced that the person outside was not Lady Euphemia when a firm fist rapped sharply on the door.

Raising a hand to silence Adela, she swiftly raised her skirts, drew her dirk from its sheath, and moved quietly toward the door. Before she reached it, however, the rap came again. "Isobel, are you in there?"

"It's Michael," she said to Adela, slipping the dirk back into its sheath and reaching for the latch.

"If Hugo is with him, don't let him in."

Fortunately, since Isobel was not sure she could keep Hugo out if he chose to enter, or that Michael would intervene to stop him, Michael stood there alone.

"I thought I'd find you here," he said, making no attempt to enter. "You've done well tonight, sweetheart, but come to bed now. We've much to discuss."

"I don't want to leave Adela alone," Isobel said.

"I've sent a lad to fetch Lady Euphemia," Michael said. "She'll be along straightaway, and in the meantime, Henry will wait out here to keep Adela safe."

"*Sir* Henry?"

"Aye, my lady," Henry said, stepping into view. "Had I known the pair of you would dash off as Michael tells me you did, I'd have left two of my lads to escort you. I don't blame you for being distressed, but I mean to make sure no one else annoys you whilst you are my guests, and lest you think I am not competent to guard Lady Adela until your aunt arrives—"

"I do not think that at all," Isobel hastily assured him. "Indeed, sir, I have been curious about something, and would like to ask you a question if I may."

"Certainly, madam. What is it?"

"You told me that you had once seen a map that would let you sail past the ends of the earth. Wherever did you see such a thing?"

"Why, my father showed it to me once when I was but a lad," Henry said.

"Truly? May I see it sometime?"

"Aye, sure, if we can lay hands on it," he said. "However, I own, I have not seen it from that day to this. I warrant it will reappear someday, though, and when it does, you shall be among the first to see it."

"Thank you, sir. In the meantime, I am sure that Adela could not be in more competent hands than yours."

To her astonishment, he turned bright red and bowed deeply to her as he said, "Why thank you, my lady. Did I tell you how glad I am that you have joined our family? I cannot doubt that your presence will much improve us."

Chuckling, she bade Adela goodnight and let Michael escort her to their bedchamber. They met Lady Euphemia on the way, but although she attempted to quiz them about what had happened, Isobel and Michael adroitly extricated themselves and hurried on their way.

"And to think," Isobel muttered as they approached their chamber door, "Adela believes that I have spent the past seven years doing just as I please, whilst she has been trapped managing my sisters and the household at Chalamine."

"Would you have wanted to trade places?" he asked, opening the door for her.

She grimaced. "You do know how to strike to the heart of the matter, sir. I would not, nor would I have had that option, as she herself reminded me. I was just thinking that families can too easily create a quagmire that one can step into without even knowing it exists."

"You may well accuse me of creating one for you now," he said, shutting the door. "Aye, and for the lady Adela, as well, because we have come up with a plan."

"As long as part of that plan is not to send me safely home with Hector and Cristina, or with my father, I want to hear it," she said, moving to poke up embers glowing on the hearth. "Fetch a couple of those sticks for me, will you?"

"Yes, my lady, at once, my lady," he said subserviently. When she looked up at him guiltily, he grinned.

"Impudent man," she said. "Would you have preferred that I send for a gillie to do it, or should I have asked you to tend the fire yourself?"

"I do have a fire for you to tend, sweetheart," he said, still grinning. "But first I think we should discuss our plan of action. Henry has put Waldron, the abbot, and the two louts who tried to help Waldron under lock and key, and he intends to keep them close held until after the ceremony, when he will put them into a boat and order them back to the Holy Isle."

"But Waldron will not want to go to the Holy Isle," she protested.

"Nay, he will not," he said, handing her the sticks she had requested.

"Nor do we know where the rest of his men are," she reminded him as she gently coaxed glowing embers to flame again. "We've seen only those two, and with all the people here for the ceremony, we'd never know which were his."

"Just so. That is why we mean to put them off our track by another means. You and I are going to Roslin, but Hugo and Adela—if she agrees—are going to make it look as if we go to Castle St. Clair instead."

She instantly saw his intent. "You expect Waldron, the abbot, or any other watchers to mistake them for us. But why would we be going to Caithness?"

"Because Henry is inviting a number of his guests to journey there with him on Monday. He will include as many of your family as will accept his invitation, and most folks will assume that we are amongst them. Are you finished fussing with that fire yet?" he demanded, holding out an imperious hand.

Letting him draw her to her feet, she said, "But won't they expect Hugo and Adela to be with us, too?"

"Aye, perhaps, but those to whom it matters most will be watching for me. Hugo will be dressed in my clothing, his ship will carry Adela, and it will fly my banner. I think the image will serve, as long as no one sees us depart earlier."

"But how will we get away without anyone seeing us?"

"I'm thinking we'll wear servants' garb, carry our own, and depart late Sunday night. Just in case anyone does see us, Henry can say that he is sending a boat ahead with servants to prepare those at St. Clair for more visitors. Unnecessary, of course. His people at St. Clair are always able to look after a horde of guests."

She thought for a long moment, then nodded. "I think it will work," she said. "But you know Waldron better than I do. Will he believe we are visiting Henry?"

He had become interested in her chaplet, the veil of which framed her face with soft ruffles. Finding the pins that held it in place, he began to remove them as he said, "I don't know what Waldron will think, but I believe the ruse will suffice to let us reach Roslin at least a few days ahead of him."

"Then you believe he will go there no matter what we do."

"I do. He believes we hold the secret, but since the most anyone seems to know is that the treasure likely came to the Isles in those ships, I think he has assumed until now that it still lies somewhere in the Isles and that we know where. However, it has to have occurred to him, despite his protests to the contrary, that I might have spoken the truth and knew nothing about it until he told me, himself. If he comes to believe that, he will know that by having confronted me, he has stirred my curiosity and will therefore want to watch me closely. Once he knows I have returned to Roslin, he may likewise deduce that the answer may lie at Roslin."

"I wonder why he hasn't searched there before now, if indeed he has not."

"He hasn't," Michael said confidently as he tossed her chaplet and veil aside and reached to remove the gold-lace net that still confined her hair. "I'm sure I have mentioned to you before how adamant our father was about keeping our private matters private. Even before I knew of the treasure, I took precautions to protect our privacy, and so does Henry, but we don't make a grand show of guarding Roslin. At the moment, it has only a minimal guard, but Waldron has never been alone there. Guests stay there only when I am at home, or Henry is, and although our people are discreet, guests never roam about without watchers to keep an eye on them. That was my father's way, and my grandfather's, and it has been my way and Henry's."

His words sent a shiver up Isobel's spine, but she understood the need for such precaution, however uncomfortable it made her feel. "Will they watch me like that?" she asked before she knew the question had stepped onto her tongue.

"Nay, lass," he said, tossing the gold net after chaplet and caul. "You are my wife, which makes you part of me and me part of you, and I am rapidly coming to trust you as I would trust myself. I am not saying," he added gently as he reached to undo the front lacing of her kirtle, "that nothing could ever change that, but at the moment, I cannot imagine what could."

The qualification annoyed her, but she decided her annoyance was unjust. Recalling that he had surprised her by not scolding her as Hugo had scolded Adela after the confrontation with Waldron and the abbot, she told herself that had she trusted him as she wanted him to trust her, she would have trusted him to accept that she'd had good reason to trust the gillie who had taken them there. Such reasoning made her head spin but reminded her, too, how complex trust could be.

The front of her kirtle popped open and Michael's warm hand slipped inside, instantly diverting her from her convoluted thoughts. "What are you doing?"

He grinned. "What do you think I'm doing? I'm getting ready for bed."

She glanced down at him. "Faith, sir, I believe you are ready now."

Needing no further encouragement, he had her kirtle and shift off her in a trice, picked her up without further ado, and took her to bed.

⟨∞⟩

The next day passed swiftly and without incident. If Isobel spent much of it trying to discern who among the increasing company might be allies of Waldron's, or which of them might wonder where the Green Abbot was, she was careful for once not to let her curiosity show. She spent much of her time at Michael's side, chatting with old friends and making new ones. But she took care not to neglect Adela or the rest of her family, even taking time to talk with Macleod.

"Ye make a fine lady for your husband, lass," he said with satisfaction. "I'm that proud o' ye. Now, if ye'll just find a man for our Adela, I'll be thanking ye."

"Who will manage Sorcha and Sidony if I do that, sir?"

"Bless me, but ye can find them husbands, too," he

retorted. Then, leaning nearer, he murmured, "In troth, lass, I'm thinking o' taking another wife, but I'm thinking she'll no want the burden o' looking after them lasses, so the sooner I see 'em off to live wi' husbands o' their own, the better satisfied I'll be."

Astonished that, after so many years, he was considering putting another woman in her mother's place, Isobel nevertheless promised to see what she could do for her sisters, and took leave of him soon afterward to rejoin Michael.

The following day's ceremony proved to be as lavish as Sir Henry had promised if rather more boring than Isobel had expected.

Kirkwall's cathedral teemed with the nobility of northern Scotland and the Isles, and included clan chiefs from as far away as Dumfries, Galloway, Knapdale, and Kintail, as well. The cathedral was neither particularly beautiful nor particularly large. The crowd of spectators filled it and spilled over to the grounds outside long before the ceremony began, but Henry had realized that it would, and began his procession nearly a quarter mile away.

The sun shone brightly in a clear azure sky, the breeze was light and not too chilly for comfort, and the pipers and other musicians played merrily as Henry and his entourage approached.

He had dressed splendidly in robes of silver, blue, and gray silk trimmed with miniver over a rich blue-velvet doublet and matching trunk hose, and he wore a simple round silver circlet on his head. He looked so much a prince of the realm that Isobel glanced at Michael, right behind him, to see if he had altered in a similar way. Reassuringly, he looked his usual calm self.

The members of Henry's entourage took seats that had been reserved for them on the front pews, and Michael joined Isobel in the second row, as Henry walked up to the altar and turned to face the assembly alone.

Trumpets sounded from both sides of the chamber, and then silence fell.

Henry opened his arms wide, looked up as if to seek guidance or offer thanks, and then looked at his audience and said in a firm, quiet voice that carried easily to the back walls of the chamber, "My lords, ladies, and people of Orkney, I, Henry of St. Clair, Jarl of Orkney, Lord of Roslin, do greet thee in the name of our Lord. On the second day of this month, in Maestrand, Norway, I took an oath in the presence of King Haakon, which I now repeat to you so that you may know what I have promised: Whereas the most serene prince in Christ, my beloved Lord Haakon, by the grace of God, King of the realms of Norway and Sweden, appointed us of his grace to rule over his lands and islands of Orkney, and raised us to the state of jarl over the foresaid lands and islands, we make known to all men both present and to come that we have rendered fealty to the same lord our King by the kiss of his hand and mouth, and rendered to him a true and due oath of fidelity to be observed so far as giving counsel and assistance to our said lord the King and his heirs and successors and to his kingdom of Norway. In the first place, therefore, we firmly oblige ourselves to serve our said lord and King over with the lands and islands of Orkney with one hundred good men or more, fully equipped in arms, for the convenience of our said lord and King, whensoever we shall have been sufficiently required . . ."

Isobel's attention strayed to a lady nearby whose head-dress stood so high that people behind her were craning to see Henry.

". . . we promise to defend the said lands with the men

which we shall be able to gather for this purpose not only from the said lands and islands but with the whole strength of our kin, friends, and servants. Likewise if it should happen . . ."

She glanced at Michael. So Henry expected him to help defend the Orkneys for the Norse King, did he? No wonder the King of Scots took a dim view of this princedom. That reminded her of something else, and she leaned closer to Michael.

"Why did he not call himself Prince of Orkney?" she whispered. "He called himself something like an earl instead."

"'Jarl,'" he said. "Jarl of Orkney is the highest rank in Norway except for that of its King. The highest rank in Scotland next to the King of Scots is that of prince. The difference is that in Norway, it's a bit of both."

She nodded but found the audience more interesting than Henry's speech, which went on and on until she was thoroughly bored. The people across the way, behind the lady with the tall headdress, seemed to be dozing. But at last it was over, and when Henry stopped speaking, the silence lingered long enough to make her wonder if everyone else had fallen asleep.

Then, suddenly, applause and cheering broke out, trumpets and pipes played wildly, and Henry and his entourage formed their recession and walked out much more briskly than they had entered. Michael joined them, taking Isobel's arm as he did, so that she felt as if she were actually part of the prince's entourage. The excitement proved contagious, and by the time they joined Henry outside and headed back to the bishop's palace, she was enjoying herself hugely.

The rest of the day provided more entertainment in the form of musicians, players, tumblers, jugglers, and their ilk.

Feasting and dancing lasted well into the night, but just as she realized that she was thoroughly exhausted, Michael took her arm again and leaned close to say, "It is time, sweetheart."

"Time for bed?" she asked, covering a yawn. "I'm nearly asleep on my feet."

He chuckled. "Don't fall asleep yet, lass. Our boat awaits us in the harbor, and we must still change our clothes."

Startled completely awake, she stared at him for a moment before her wits caught up with her. "Oh, mercy," she muttered, glancing around to see if anyone could have overheard him, only to realize that no one could have over the din.

"Don't look as if we're up to mischief," he warned her. "And don't go that way. We are not going to our room but to his eminence's kitchen. Hugo has our clothes outside and will have found someplace for us to change into them. Look as if you are stealing a few private moments with your husband," he added, kissing her soundly on the lips.

She responded instantly, putting her arms around him and kissing him back.

Ten minutes later, they were outside with Hugo, heading for a thicket that he had assured them was sufficiently sheltered for their purpose. And fifteen minutes after that, Hugo returned to the castle, and she and Michael walked with three other men to the harbor. Only when they reached the longboat drawn onto the beach did Isobel see that two women wearing hooded cloaks were already aboard.

When she hesitated, Michael chuckled and said, "Hugo's sense of humor will sink him one day. They are but men in skirts, lass, pretending to be female to augment the illusion he's created. Tell them I said to keep their hands to themselves."

One of the two, in servant's dress almost exactly like

Isobel's, moved to help her board. As she took the hand extended to her, she thought it unusually smooth for a man's but made no comment, certain the lad would not appreciate one.

Michael, swinging himself aboard behind her, said, "I'll be rowing for the present, lass, so just sit quietly there with your friend." To the other two in skirts, he said evenly, "I presume that someone has told you both that this lady is my wife."

"Aye, my lord, Sir Hugo said we was t' keep our hands to ourselves," one said gruffly, adding as a swift afterthought, "nobbut what we would anyway, sir."

"See that you do," Michael said.

So much for his confidence in her ability to take care of herself, Isobel thought, hiding a smile. Hugo's, too. She could as easily have worn men's clothes herself, as she had before. Hugo need not have made the two men wear skirts.

Not until they were some miles from the harbor did Michael leave his oar and return to assure himself that she was comfortable. She was dozing but woke when he said crisply to the two beside her, "You may both take an oar now. You need not think you can just idle away this whole journey."

"Do you really want us to row, Michael?" The voice was decidedly female, decidedly cool. "I think we would prefer to sleep. Hugo said he put blankets inside that locker. Pray fetch them out to us. Doubtless your bride would like one, too."

"Madam," Michael exclaimed. "What are you doing here? You must go back. Everyone will expect to see you tomorrow—aye, and as hostess at St. Clair."

His mother said in the same cool tone, "Do not stand prattling but do as I bid you. Jean is the proper hostess at St. Clair, and I cannot stand by and allow you to subject your new wife to this clandestine journey without a single suitable female to accompany her. And who, do you suppose, is more suited to the task than I am?"

That question being wholly unanswerable, Michael wisely held his tongue.

The journey east from Orkney and then south to the Firth of Forth proved tediously long but without incident, despite the presence of the countess and Fiona, her waiting woman. The countess remained cool but civil, and although Isobel did not warm to her, she could be civil, too. Michael kept horses stabled in the city of Edinburgh, so they encountered little delay and hurried on, although the day was already half over by the time they entered the harbor there.

The city fascinated Isobel, and it was as well that she rode a well-trained mount, because so delighted was she with everything she saw that she paid scant heed to its direction or guidance. They took only a dozen men with them, and the last ten miles passed swiftly. The countess and Fiona fell back a short distance with the men, and so Isobel passed the time by asking Michael question after question about Lothian and Roslin. He was describing a famous battle fought in Roslin Glen when they came upon the cart track leading down into the glen itself.

"The castle lies three miles yonder," he said. "We'll follow the river Esk for a time and then take a path up and out of the glen to its western rim."

"I thought you told me that the river runs right by the castle," she said, recalling his answer to an earlier question.

"Aye, it does, and curves around it on three sides, but the castle sits high above the water, as you'll soon see."

The glen was lushly green and eerie, almost as if it were

haunted, Isobel thought. Remembering the battle fought there, she asked him to tell her more about it. He did so, and by the time he reached the Scots' victory over an invading English army, they had begun their climb out of the glen, the others still well behind them.

The great round towers and square keep of Roslin Castle loomed ahead of them, less than half a mile away, turned golden in the setting sun.

"Why is it called Roslin?" she asked abruptly after moments of silence.

"Because of its location," he said. "Roslin means 'rock of the falls,' and there are two waterfalls that I'll show you tomorrow. Near the larger one, carved into a mossy rock wall, is an odd-looking head—not a bearded one, I'm sorry to say."

"Do you have any idea what to search for when we get to the castle?"

"I think so," he said. "I have been thinking about those bearded men in Henry's letter, as well as the underscored words and the many carvings at Roslin. I suspect we'll find that one particular likeness repeats itself many times. If that proves true, we need only find that likeness and follow where it leads."

The approach to the castle startled Isobel. She saw only too easily how it towered over the glen far below because, only a few feet from the castle wall, the ground fell away steeply to the river Esk, flowing swiftly in a sharp U around the high promontory on which the castle stood. The pathway they followed narrowed dramatically, becoming no more than a bridge over a deep ravine.

Riders approaching the castle could therefore proceed safely only if they did so in single file. For a good thirty feet, Isobel resisted looking down, because it was as if the world had fallen away from her on both sides, but she made no comment lest the countess think her a coward.

Inside the wall, servants flocked to the courtyard to welcome their master and the countess home, greet his bride warmly, and assure them all that supper would appear within the hour.

"Come, sweetheart," Michael said after dismissing their escort and leading her toward the huge keep in the southwest corner of the yard. Telling his mother in the entryway that they would see her at supper, he led Isobel away, adding quietly, "I'll show you where we'll sleep, lass, and give you time to tidy yourself."

"But don't you want to begin looking straightaway?"

"Not until after we eat," he said with a smile. "It is too late to do much exploring tonight in any event, and I don't want my mother hovering over us."

"You can show me the carvings at least."

"Aye, I'll show you some of them. You'll understand our dilemma better when you see how many there are."

"Your mother won't come down right away," she said, her curiosity growing by the minute. "If we change quickly, we can begin searching before we eat."

He laughed. "I can see that I'm going to have a hard time retaining my position as master of this castle, madam. Pray remember that I am."

She wrinkled her nose at him, but in the end, she had her way. The number and variety of the carvings he showed her did prove daunting, because although the countess retired after supper and they searched only a few rooms of the keep that night, the carvings were everywhere. Moreover, many depicted heads, and many of them were bearded. Occasionally they found two or three that looked alike, but in trying to follow them, discovered they led nowhere.

Isobel went to bed that night thinking they could search for a month without finding what they sought, but the next day she found Sir William's bearded men.

Taking advantage of the countess's decision to nap that afternoon, they had searched for a time without success. Wandering to the lower hall, feeling frustrated and depressed, Isobel had stopped near the huge fireplace and stood staring for some moments at a bearded face with a straight line for its nose, and cavernous eyes, before she realized she had seen one like it only moments before. Gathering her wits, she hurried back the way she had come and soon found the second one near a doorway. Passing through it, she found a third. Then, across the landing on the lintel of a second doorway, in a line of nearly similar heads, she found another.

Running to find Michael, she showed him what she had found, and together they discovered three more. But their search ended abruptly at the opposite end of the keep near a small chamber, apparently full of wine casks. No bearded face graced the framework of its door or any nearby wall.

Near a corner of the wine chamber, a colorful tapestry caught Isobel's eye, and thinking it an odd place to hang such a thing, she eased her way among the casks to have a closer look. A moment later, she exclaimed, "Michael, I think the head is woven into this tapestry! Fetch a candle and look for yourself."

He brought two, and she held them while he pulled the pegs at the bottom of the tapestry from the wall and lifted the heavy cloth to reveal a door. It opened easily onto a narrow, circular stairway.

Elated, Isobel slipped through, giving Michael one candle and holding the other to light her way. But elation faded quickly, for the stairway that had looked so promising led to a solid stone wall.

Chapter 19 _____

Disappointment surging through her, Isobel stared at the huge stone blocks, then turned back to Michael, who had stopped two steps above her.

"Perhaps we'll be able to move one of those stones," he suggested.

She shook her head, thinking that his father and grandfather must have been as eccentric as Henry or as mad as Mariota. Anyone could see that the large granite stones were as heavy and solid as they could be. The stairway led nowhere.

"It must go somewhere," he said, as if he had heard her thoughts. "The space below us here is a veritable warren of cells and dungeons, although Henry and I have thoroughly searched every one of them over the years. Still, let me see if one of the stones might be hollow inside."

Moving past her, he held his candle close to the bare wall, carefully examining it, then drew his dirk and methodically began tapping each stone with the handle.

After some minutes of watching him, Isobel turned with a sigh to go back up the stairs. As she shifted her candle, its light glowed stronger for a moment, lighting a section of the outer wall above the wide end of the lowest step. She knelt and looked closer, holding the candle near a figure carved into the stone.

"Michael, look at this," she said, scarcely daring to hope that it might actually mean something.

He moved to stand by her, resting a hand warmly on her shoulder. "It is just another carved head," he said. "Doesn't even have a beard. It looks more like the mossy one near the waterfall that I told you about. They call him the green man."

"Does this one look exactly like that one?"

"Aye, near enough," he said, knocking the dagger's hilt against the stone, and then trying to shift it. "This stone is solid. I don't think it can mean much."

"But it is the only thing here," she protested. "It must mean something. Moreover, it *is* the Green Man."

"Aye, well, the other one is green, too," he said. "But only because of the moss." When she did not reply, he shifted his candle up to look into her face. "What is it, lass? What are you thinking?"

"I tend to forget that you were not raised in the Highlands and Isles," she said. "The Green Man is the Celtic god of plants and vegetation. Since we're not in the Highlands now, it seems odd to find him here—odder still if he appears twice. If someone chose to honor a Celtic god in such a way here, he must have had reason."

Michael frowned. "But does it mean that we search here or at the falls?"

"Since the bearded heads led here, your father's message to Henry could mean we are supposed to look behind that stone for a key to the treasure's hiding place, but I'd like to see that other head before we attempt such a thing. Is it far?"

"Come, I'll show you."

They hurried upstairs and outside to a steep path leading into the lush glen—an apt location, Isobel thought, for the Celtic god of greenery. Soon trees on either side of them created a green canopy so thick that only occasional beams of sunlight penetrated it. Ferns, flowers, and dense shrubbery carpeted the woodland floor, obscuring their view. The cool air was redolent of herbal scents and damp earth. The trail zigzagged down until Isobel could hear rushing water, and soon afterward they came to the roiling, froth-filled river.

Michael strode along the path ahead of her, and when he came to an arched stone bridge spanning the river, he said, "We'll cross here. We'd get closer to the falls by following the track on this side, but the carving we seek lies yonder."

"Is there a path on that side, too?" Isobel asked.

"Aye, sure," he said. "I'll warrant fishermen have worn tracks along every bank of every burn and rivulet in Scotland." With a smile, he added, "Art afraid I'll get us lost, sweetheart?"

"Of course not, but I am not wearing stout shoes, and I don't relish the notion of clambering about on wet rocks near a waterfall," she said.

"We won't get that close to it," he said, holding back a branch for her. "The carving I want to show you is in the cliff face some yards from the water."

The path remained narrow, and with Michael again in the lead, they made their way up the river gorge without speaking. Except for the soft padding of their footsteps and the rushing sound of the water, the woods were silent.

Isobel realized that they were too silent. When a faint equine whicker sounded ahead of them, she said urgently, "Michael, wait!"

He had heard the sound, too, and had already stopped, but as she spoke, a vast, weighted net fell from the tree above him, ensnaring him in its web. Men erupted from the shrubbery and quickly overpowered him.

Isobel took two or three hasty steps toward them only to stop short when a hand of iron grabbed her upper arm from behind so abruptly that it nearly jerked her off her feet. A muscular arm clamped around her waist and the large, gloved hand that had caught her arm shifted to smack hard across her mouth, yanking her head back against a brawny chest as a harsh voice muttered in her ear, "How thoughtful of you to bring my cousin to me, lass. I'd expected to spend more time pondering how to entice him outside, but you've made that unnecessary. Nay now, do not bite me," he warned. "My gloves are thick enough to protect me, but biting is most unmannerly. If you try it again, I'll beat you until you screech."

Isobel ignored the threat, struggling as wildly as she could, kicking and biting until he cupped a hard palm over her mouth in such a way that her teeth could not gain purchase. Even then, she kicked and squirmed, but he tightened his hold around her waist until she could scarcely breathe.

"Ah, you're tiring," he said. "I think you need a lesson in conduct though, so we'll see if you learn quickly. I want to know how many people are in the castle."

"Waldron, damn you, let her go," Michael said, struggling against his captors but severely hampered by the netting. "What sort of villain makes war on women?"

"Not your sort, certainly," Waldron said. "Hand me his sword and any other weapons he might have, lads. Then wrap that netting around him and we'll carry him back to the castle to find out what he knows. Now, lass, tell me, how many?"

Isobel pressed her lips tightly together.

"Very well, then, I'll have my lads begin by cutting off his fingers and toes."

Shock surged through her. "You wouldn't dare!"

"You think not? Dom, take out your dagger," he commanded. "If she does not answer my question, begin with the little finger on his left hand."

"By heaven, you're a madman!" Isobel exclaimed as the ruddy-faced, barrel-chested man he'd called Dom drew a long dagger.

"How many?" Waldron asked again.

Michael had not spoken, but Isobel believed Waldron would do as he threatened. "I don't know exactly," she said, adding hastily when he looked toward his man again, "We brought sixty men with us from Kirkwall, but some stayed in Edinburgh to look after the ship, and Michael gave others leave to visit their families. I think a dozen came with us to the castle. There are the servants, too, a few guardsmen, a cook, the baker, and their minions. I can't think of any others."

"Where is Hugo?"

"He went with Hector Reaganach and the others to St. Clair."

"So he was the one pretending to be Michael. Who pretended to be you?"

She was silent, terrified that he would force her to name Adela.

"I can guess," he said. "They will both have to pay penance for that, I think. What about stable lads?"

"Oh, aye, there are several. I forgot."

"I wonder who else you forgot," he said. "Not that it will make much difference, but we'll unfurl him, lads. We cannot take him up trussed in that net if guards on the wall can see us. That pathway is treacherous enough without the added threat of a rain of arrows. But don't let him get free," he added sharply as he pushed Isobel toward another of his men, whom she recognized as Fin Wylie. "Don't let the lass slip away this time," Waldron warned him. "Not if you value your life."

"Nay, master, she'll go nowhere," the man promised, gripping Isobel around the waist nearly as tightly as Waldron had.

Remembering that Michael no longer had his weapons, Isobel watched as the others pulled the netting off, hoping he could still manage to regain his freedom, and determined to do what she could to aid him. As always, she had her dirk.

But Michael remained quiet as he said, "You do no honor to your family, cousin. I once admired your skills, your energy, and your clever brain. But I see now that you have only the instincts of an animal. Your brain serves no more to improve your character than would the brain of a badger or a wolf."

"Stand him up," Waldron said. "But hold him in place, and watch his legs and feet. He's no great warrior. Faith, I'd have bested him easily last time, had our Hugo not come to his aid, but even a rabbit will fight if a fox corners it."

Michael offered no resistance, standing to face Waldron, even thanking one man who picked up the hat he had been wearing from where it lay on the ground. Then, to Waldron, he said gently, "Is greed alone what drives you?"

"As I will say every time you ask me, I am bound by my word of honor to make restitution for a wrong your branch of our family committed years ago."

"By my faith, I do not know why you keep harping on that stupid tale."

"And I do not know how you dare speak of faith when you and your family have stolen from the Holy Kirk what rightfully belongs to it."

As he said the last words, Waldron's fist shot out, and although Michael clearly saw the blow coming, Waldron anticipated which way he would duck, for the blow struck the point of his jaw, and he slumped in his captor's hands.

"You vile, horrid man!" Isobel exclaimed angrily. "We have done naught to harm you or yours. You can have no cause to harm us."

He grabbed her arm again in his viselike grip, and Fin Wylie released her. Looking closely into her eyes, Waldron said, "If I did not know my cousin has better sense than to prattle his secrets to a woman, I'd question you harshly, lass. Still, he made a mistake in marrying you and another in letting me see that he cares what becomes of you. A man's courage is no greater than his willingness to sacrifice all he has. Only one who cares for naught and has naught to lose will fear naught."

"Michael is not so callous."

"True, and therefore he will soon tell me all he knows. You recall how you reacted when I threatened his fingers. Imagine how he will, when I threaten yours."

She gasped.

Laughing at her, he said, "Aye, sure, and it does astonish me that a fool like Henry and a weakling like Michael have kept their secrets as long as they have."

"Mayhap you should simply believe them when they say they do not know those secrets," she said. "I have found them both to be honest men."

"Have you, indeed?" He jerked her forward, saying, "Take him tenderly, lads. We'll leave the horses here. I don't want his men fearing us and rushing out to meet us on that damned path. As for you, my lady, you will behave decorously, or I'll slit his throat and yours before my men and I depart. Do you understand me?"

"Aye," she muttered, trying to imagine how she could put a rub in his way, if only to divert her thoughts from his apparent fascination with fingers.

She could think of no way to warn the castle and keep Michael safe at the same time, however. She could only be grateful that Waldron believed she could tell him nothing of importance. Trying to remember if she or Michael had said anything revealing that Waldron or one of his men might have overheard, she recalled the deep silence that had seemed too quiet for too long, and realized that they had not spoken at all for some time before the attack.

The journey back up to the castle seemed to take no time at all. As they crossed the narrow part of the pathway, Waldron leaned close to her, one arm tight around her shoulders, the other hand bruisingly gripping her wrist. She knew that to the men at the gate, and to anyone who might have watched their approach from the wall-walk above, he would look as if he were reassuring or consoling her.

As one of the guardsmen stepped in front of the gateway, Waldron murmured, "If they try to stop us, we will kill them, so be sure they understand that we are welcome. And do not imagine that they can succeed in overpowering my men, because you would be making a fatal error."

Believing him, Isobel forced a smile for the guardsman and said, "Sir Michael slipped on a wet rock and fell whilst he was showing me the glen, but by heaven's grace, his cousin's men came upon us and were able to help. We must get Sir Michael inside, however, so that he may rest and recover his senses."

"Then he is not . . ." The man hesitated. "Seeing him brought up like that gave us all a shock, my lady."

"We'll take him inside straightaway," Waldron said.

At a shout from the guard, the porter opened the main door. Frowning at seeing his master in such a state, the man said anxiously, "Shall I send for the herb woman, my lady?"

"No need," Waldron said. "Sir Michael merely took a knock on the head when he slipped in the glen. Is my aunt expecting us in the great hall?"

"Nay, sir, her ladyship be still enjoying her wee nap. Shall I send to tell her that ye ha' arrived?"

"Nay then, do not disturb her yet. We'll look after Sir Michael first."

As they passed into the entryway with Waldron's men herded behind them, Isobel heard the door shut, then noise of a scuffle. Looking back, she saw that Fin Wylie and another man had overpowered the porter. They bound and gagged him, then perched him on his own stool in his own alcove, no more than a widening of the entryway landing. No other men-at-arms were posted nearby.

Impulse tempted her to beg Waldron's men to treat the man gently, but she stifled it, certain from what she had seen of their master that such a request would stir him to do something horrid. As it was, they merely closed and barred the iron yett across the main door. Should anyone try to enter the castle now, he would find himself locked out.

The three men carrying Michael, two at his head and one at his feet, stood watching the others, and she saw Michael's eyes flutter open, then shut again. His lax expression did not change, so she could not tell if he was conscious or still comatose, but her relief at seeing him move was enormous.

Glancing at her, Waldron said, "He's no dead yet, lass, but you'd best hope he speaks quickly. I've little patience left."

She sighed, showing her frustration. "I do not know why you persist in believing he can tell you anything. He told me he does not know what you seek, let alone where it is. Surely, you cannot believe that either he or Prince Henry knows the whereabouts of any great treasure."

"Why not?"

"Well, surely, if they had a treasure, they would be extraordinarily weal—" She broke off, realizing her error too late.

"Exactly so," he said. "Extraordinarily wealthy. Do you ken naught of your new husband, lass? To be sure, he does not flaunt his wealth, but Henry certainly does. You saw for yourself the grand way he celebrated his new princedom."

"But you must know as well as I do that Prince Henry's wealth is inherited from his mother's family."

"They do expect everyone to believe that it's her money, but 'tis odd that my uncle never lived as well as Henry, or even as well as Michael does, come to that."

"Sir William believed in living simply," Isobel said. "But Prince Henry has a higher position to maintain. He is expected to do so in a grand style."

"Faugh, that tale simply covers his taking of a treasure that his supporters expected him to guard and that the Pope expects him to return to the Holy Kirk."

"I don't understand how anything he has could belong to the Kirk," Isobel said, hoping to keep him talking long enough for Michael to recover and defend himself. As the thought crossed her mind, she wondered what she could be thinking, since Waldron had at least ten men inside the castle now and heaven knew how many more outside. That the two of them alone could defend the castle, or themselves, for that matter, even if Michael did regain all his faculties, seemed impossible.

Waldron had not answered her. Instead, he gazed at her as if he were trying to peer into her mind to judge the truth of her words.

She gazed limpidly back at him and said, "Pray, sir, how *could* something in Henry's keeping belong to the Kirk?"

He shrugged. "I do not try to explain such things to females. 'Tis rare that they can understand any but the simplest political scheming."

"So it is a political scheme then, this treasure of yours?"

"Enough, lass. I weary of your prating. You merely seek to delay the lesson you have coming, or did you hope I'd forget?" With those ominous words, he turned to the man he had called Dom and said, "Take Sir Michael below. We'll make use of Roslin's dungeons, but leave two men at this door and take the others with you. And take devilish good care that you don't let him get away. I'm going to take the lass above and see how many men guard the ramparts. Send a pair of our lads up to assist me once you have him shackled below and have made sure we hold the castle. But tell them to await my command before they show themselves on the wall."

"Aye, master," Dom said. "Is it your wish that we give Sir Michael a taste of what awaits him before you return to deal with him yourself?"

"If he is obedient, just strip off his clothing and hang him, well spread, from the wall shackles," Waldron said. "Let him anticipate the kiss of the whip whilst he awaits me. If he gives trouble, you may punish him as you will, of course. Just take care that you do not render him unable to talk to me."

Dom's smile told Isobel that he looked forward to meting out punishment whether Michael disobeyed or not, and the thought chilled her. But Waldron gave her no more time to think about Michael.

"You may precede me, my lady," he said as politely as if he were an ordinary visitor.

Gazing up at him with an expression she hoped would pass for helpless innocence, she said, "What are you going to do to me?"

"That must depend on you," he said. "If you are cooperative and exert yourself to please me, you will doubtless enjoy my questioning. If you do not cooperate, I will teach you some methods the Holy Kirk employs. I warrant you have heard something of how they deal with heretics."

She did not try to suppress the shudder that shot through her, and saw by his reaction that he enjoyed her fear. With that knowledge threatening to undermine her confidence, she fought for calm as she said, "Do you deem me a heretic, sir?"

"I merely want answers," he said. "I'll get them any way I can."

His matter-of-fact tone, as if they enjoyed a casual conversation, frightened her more than any of his threats had. Her feet began to feel heavy and the steps of the spiral stairway more and more difficult to mount, as if each were higher than the last. She focused her thoughts on Michael instead, and what he faced.

When she hesitated at the next landing, Waldron gripped her elbow, pressing nerves there, and she cried out at the sudden, sharp pain.

"Just the first little lesson," he murmured.

"Has it occurred to you that if you kill me, or harm me

in any way, you will incur the wrath of the Macleans, the Macleods, and the Lord of the Isles?"

"I've no intention of killing you, lass. What a waste that would be! But whatever I do, their wrath means naught to me, nor are they at hand to aid you."

That last bit was certainly true, she mused unhappily, but she and Michael had escaped Waldron's clutches before, so perhaps they could do so again.

He stopped her when she reached for the latch of the door leading onto the wall-walk. "One moment, madam. I doubt that there can be more than two men on that walk, but should there be more, do not think you can play me any tricks. I'll defeat as many men as I must to gain what I seek."

Recalling the role she had chosen to play, she fluttered her lashes in the hope that it would make her look nervous or at least woefully feminine and complacent as she said, "I have no thought of flouting you, sir, not whilst you keep my husband confined below. You are far too strong and powerful."

"I think you like powerful men," he said. "Most women do, I've found."

She looked quickly down, hoping he had not seen her anger and would think her overcome, even shy.

"I am glad to see that you can show wisdom, lass," he said. "Open that door now, but mind you don't forget who stands behind you."

Nodding, she obeyed and stepped onto the walk. As she did, one of the lads she had met the previous day came around from the north side, smiling when he saw her. "My lady, be aught amiss? I saw them carrying the master up the hill."

"He fell and hit his head," she said. "But have no fear, for he is already much restored to his usual good health."

"'Tis glad I be t' hear that," the lad said. "Being alone up here as I be, I dared no go downstairs t' see if he were dead."

"Are those horsemen approaching yonder?" Waldron asked casually, pointing as he stepped around Isobel.

When the lad turned his head, he felled him with a single blow of his fist.

Isobel gasped. "Sakes, sir, do you hurt people just for the pleasure of hurting them? You could simply have sent him downstairs."

"I don't need to explain my actions to you, but had I sent him below, he might have met my lads and come to grief."

"Oh, then 'twas kindness," Isobel said, remembering the role she was trying to play and seemed so unsuited for. "I am sorry not to have realized as much."

Giving her a look, he said, "I'll just bar this door to be sure we're left alone up here to begin your lesson, but first I'll see if that lad was telling the truth."

She watched him maneuver the heavy bar, certain she could lift it by herself and hoping he would leave her alone long enough to escape him. But he grinned at her, and she knew that something in her expression had given her away.

"You'll come with me, my sweet. I have not enjoyed a woman in weeks, and I shall take great pleasure in enjoying my cousin's beautiful new wife."

Although she had suspected that he intended more than just to question her, or even to beat her, both of which he could easily have done by taking her down into the dungeon with Michael, she had not expected him to declare his intention so baldly and wished devoutly that he had not. Until that moment, except for one or two brief instances, she had been able to keep her fear at bay. Now, with the specific threat hanging between them, dread gripped her to her bones.

Her knees felt weak, and her hands trembled. Calling

upon advice Hector had given her years before, she bit her lower lip and forced herself to focus on pain.

Focus on your enemy, he had said. *Make a plan. Do not admit even the possibility of failure, for only if you truly believe you can succeed will you do so.*

Waldron clearly expected her to follow him now, since the wall-walk was too narrow for two to walk abreast. It was no more than a low parapet that in several places gave access to wooden hoardings, attached somehow to the stonework to protect archers and other defenders in times of siege or attack. She wondered how he thought he would find space enough there to ravish her.

As she followed him, she felt for her dirk in its usual place, but he kept glancing back, and she had a horrid feeling that even if she could find it in her to stab him in the back, he would look again just as she tried to draw it from its sheath.

Not since she had last faced him had she worn a dress that denied her access to it, and as he rounded the corner ahead of her, she jammed her hand through the slits. Snatching out the dirk, she concealed it in a fold of her skirt.

Her thoughts raced, seeking a plan, but he was so large, so skilled at fighting, that her only hope was that he would expect no resistance from her. In the cave, as far as she knew, he had never suspected that she had done anything but let Michael rescue her, and he still clearly believed as much, since he had just described her as a weak and helpless female.

That knowledge gave her an advantage, she knew. What she did not know was what she could do with it.

"No one else is here," he said, turning back with leering intent. "I fear our coupling will not be comfortable for you here, lass, but you have done naught to deserve comfort, have you? I'll test your obedience first, I think."

"How will you do that?" she asked, amazed by her sudden sense of calm.

"Come here to me, and I'll show you," he said.

"I want to know what you mean to do."

"First, to kiss you," he said almost amiably. "I want to taste my cousin's wife a little before I punish her. But if you give me further cause," he added in the same tone, "I'll just tip you over my knee and beat you until you scream for mercy, and then I'll beat you more."

She had been trying to judge exactly what he was wearing, and she decided that his leather doublet was the sort Borderers called a jack-of-plate. That meant she could not count on piercing it with her dirk and, by trying, might infuriate rather than incapacitate him. So she smiled and said, "I've no objection to kissing you, sir."

"I thought you would not," he said with a smirk. "I wonder if Michael knows what a flirtatious little bitch you are."

"He knows," she said with a sigh. "He does not approve."

He chuckled, reaching for her.

She allowed him to draw her close, offering no resistance, holding his gaze as he did, even fluttering her lashes, hoping to disarm him more by continuing to appear weak and helpless. She felt momentary fear that he knew her apparent compliance was a sham, but she ruthlessly suppressed it and widened her smile.

"Faith, but you're a bonny one," he said, grabbing her shoulders to peer into her face, as if he would memorize her features. "It will give me great pleasure to conquer you, and when you are mine, I'll teach you many ways of pleasing me."

He cupped her chin with one hand and tilted her face up, pulling her tight against him as he did. She let her body press against his, noting his readiness to claim her and the welcome fact that his jack did little to protect that part of him.

When his lips touched hers, she had all she could do not to stiffen or resist. Instead, she forced herself to respond, fervently hoping he would assume that she found him irresistible.

When he forced his tongue into her mouth, she nearly gagged but focused on the dirk in her hand, easing it from its concealing fold to one nearer the front of her skirt. Its point was down, and she knew no safe way to reposition it so that she could strike normally, but its handle was good, stout, leather-wrapped steel.

He raised his head, looking into her eyes. "I would have you show me true submission, lass. Unlace your bodice for me, and show me your breasts."

She licked her lips and said boldly, "I would prefer that you unlace me, sir."

A glint of pure lust lit his eyes, and he reached at once for her laces, jerking the tie loose and then grabbing the two sides of her bodice, one in each hand. As he wrenched it open, she clutched the dagger with both hands and jerked it up hard, driving its handle right into his bollocks, then ducking low, certain that he would fold forward to try to ease the sharp pain, as indeed he did.

When he did, she snapped her head up, striking the point of his chin hard enough to make her own teeth ring.

He staggered, and while he was off balance, she put her hands up and pushed as hard as she could, hoping to get enough distance between them to elude his grasp.

He lurched, hit the low parapet, and toppled over, twisting in a wild, desperate attempt to catch the rim, but his own weight and momentum carried him over.

He cried out once. Then she heard only the river.

Chapter 20

Michael's whole jaw ached, and the brief exploration he had managed when he regained consciousness revealed at least one loose tooth. He had come to his senses—or some of them, at least—to hear Isobel informing his cousin that he and Henry were honest men and knew nothing about any treasure.

It occurred to him that his fascinating, beautiful wife prevaricated with the dexterity of one well practiced in the art. He would take care to remember that skill in future, and to keep his wits about him.

Waldron's men had not been gentle with him, and he had had all he could do to keep feigning unconsciousness, especially when they nearly dropped him as they crossed the treacherously narrow bit of path just before the castle entrance. Knowing he needed as much time as possible to recover from the blow, and to be ready to grab whatever opportunity came his way, he had eased his eyes open just enough to look through his lashes, keeping his sore jaw slack and his body relaxed.

The lass surprised him. She had sounded perfectly calm,

although he knew she had to be terrified. She and Waldron had followed the men carrying him, and when Waldron grabbed her arm and jerked her forward as if she were not moving quickly enough to suit him, Michael had felt a muscle twitch in his cheek and other muscles in his body tense. Realizing his bearers would likely detect even such slight movements, he had allowed himself a weak moan and relaxed again, hoping they would see nothing much amiss.

At the castle entrance, he prayed that his own lads would make no trouble, because he knew the two at the gate would be no match against so many and Isobel might be hurt in a scuffle. But she dealt with them deftly, too, no doubt threatened into compliance, and moments later they were inside.

He heard the yett snap shut, and knew no one could get in. Then Waldron took Isobel up to the ramparts with threats of employing the Kirk's methods for heretics. His certainty of his cousin's most likely intention stirred a wish that he possessed the power to turn him instantly to stone, but since magical powers were mythical, he could do no more than any other mortal. Still, with Waldron on the ramparts, two of his men guarding the main entrance, and others searching the castle, Michael knew he'd have only the four to deal with below. Each was well armed, but that meant only that he would have weapons again, which was good, since Waldron had taken his.

Dom lingered at the entrance landing long enough to be sure Fin Wylie knew his men were to search the castle swiftly and without stirring rebellion among the servants. Then he ordered his own lot to carry their burden downstairs.

Michael's worry about Isobel's fate at Waldron's hands increased with each step, and he wished fervently that his bearers would go faster.

The men's footsteps echoed through the stairwell as they descended, grunting occasionally and complaining of his weight. He hoped Dom would stop them at the kitchen level, where someone might see them and raise an alarm. But they continued to the lowest level, where the only light came through high, barred vents, although they were still some ten feet above the river.

He retained his patience as they bore him into the largest cell, where it became clear that Waldron had not explained how the cells were arranged. Nor had he warned the men to provide themselves with torches, so the lack of light made it hard for Dom to find the wall shackles that his master had told him to use.

Brusquely, he ordered his three minions to set down their burden and help him locate them.

Michael waited only until they had turned away before rising swiftly and silently to his feet, grabbing the nearest man, and quickly throttling him. With no time for more humane treatment, he managed the deed before the others realized aught was amiss. As his victim slumped lifeless to the floor, Michael pulled the sword from the scabbard strapped across the man's back. The whisper of sound startled the others, and all three turned. Dom was first to draw his sword.

Michael knocked its blade up and thrust straight through the man's heart. The other two quickly fell, too, and leaving them, he hurried up the stairs.

The sound of voices from above stopped him midway up the flight between the kitchen level and the main entryway. Holding the sword, blade-down, against his leg, he pressed hard against the wall and listened carefully.

Isobel peered over the parapet but saw Waldron nowhere below. A dirt pathway made a tan ribbon at the base of the cliff, but his body was not sprawled there. To be sure, the river flowed on the other side of that path, and the path looked no more than four or five feet wide, but if he had fallen into the river, as fast and full and boiling as it was, surely he had drowned. And even if he were still alive, he would tumble along in the water for at least a few more minutes, and it would take even longer for him to crawl ashore and find a way back inside the castle.

Having thus reassured herself, she hurried to the stairway door with dirk in hand and found the young guardsman on the walk there, groggily trying to sit up.

"What's your name?" she demanded, helping him.

"Jeb Elliot, m'lady." He shook his head. "What happened?"

"Have you a sword, Jeb?"

"Nay, mistress, for what use would one be t' me up here?" he said, looking at her in bewilderment.

"But you must have weapons!"

"Aye, a bow and arrows by yonder hoarding, two axes hanging near them, a few spears at each tower, and me own dirk. Where be Lord Waldron?"

"Gone," she said curtly. "Hush now, Jeb, and get on your feet if you can. If not, just move back away from the door, because I want to open it."

"But why—?"

"Do as I bid you," she said sharply, slipping her dirk back into its sheath in order to have both hands free to deal with the heavy bar holding the door shut.

Remembering that the men Waldron had ordered to come upstairs might be waiting, she lifted it carefully, trying to imagine what she could say to them. Having decided to tell them he was on the far side of the walkway, dealing alone with two highly skilled swordsmen, she was almost disappointed to find the stairway empty.

"Follow me," she said to Jeb Elliot. "Keep your dirk near at hand but do not show it unless I tell you to."

"It's in me boot, but should I no stay here and keep guard on the wall?"

"We must help Sir Michael. Evil men have taken him to the dungeons. At least ten of them have entered the castle, so we cannot risk showing our weapons. We'll have a better chance if they think us unarmed."

He made no further protest but followed her silently.

Holding her skirt up with one hand, and lightly touching the wall with the other, she hurried down the stairs, slowing as she neared the hall landing.

Hearing only an intermittent murmur of masculine voices from the level below, and seeing no one in the hall, she took a deep breath and straightened her shoulders. Then, looking back at the lad long enough to command him to follow her but to stay silent no matter what should take place, she moved with careful dignity down the stairs.

Emerging on the entryway landing, she strode purposefully toward the alcove, making no attempt to muffle her steps. As she had hoped, one of the men Waldron had left there stuck his head out curiously.

"Your master requires your assistance above," she said. "Go to him at once."

"But he told us to stay here," the second man protested, emerging behind him. "Why should he now desire us to leave our post?"

"Sakes, do you think he confides in me?" Isobel

snapped. "I just obey his commands. Mayhap you, who know him better than I, believe you can disobey him with impunity. I dared not question him and can only tell you what he said."

"We'll go, my lady," the first man said, turning ashen. "'Tis only that it be most unlike the master t' send for us both after commanding us t' stay put."

She shrugged. "'Tis possible, I suppose, that I misunderstood him, for I vow the man makes me quake in my shoes. If you believe I am mistaken, then go and ask him what he wants. He stayed above to truss up the two guards he overpowered there, and threatened to kill them both if that lad on the stair yonder does not guard me well. I do not want to face your master again until I must."

As the two looked at each other, she held her breath and prayed that Jeb Elliot would not speak or allow his expression to reveal his astonishment at her lies.

After what seemed an age, the elder of the two said to the younger, "I dinna think his lordship will blame us an one of us goes t' make sure o' his order whilst the other stays at his post, but if her ladyship be mistaken, he'll blame us both if he didna mean for us both t' leave. I'll just go and ask him."

The younger guard grimaced and barely waited for his senior to vanish up the stairway before muttering, "Aye, *and* take credit for doubting a woman whilst making me look defiant if the master wanted us both straightaway."

"Then go with him," Isobel said as if his decision had naught to do with her. She had managed to turn casually and watch as the other dashed up the stairway, and saw to her relief that Jeb still stood there. Looking back at the remaining man, she saw that he was still trying to decide what to do.

His gaze shifted suspiciously to Jeb.

"Ye there," he said grimly. "Ha' ye weapons on ye?"

"Nay," Jeb replied, earnestly shaking his head. "I've only me bow and arrows above. I'm nae swordsman."

"Aye, well, ye seem too young t' trust wi' a sword, but come here t' me and let me see that ye ha' no dirk in yon flapping great boots o' yours."

Jeb glanced at Isobel, and she nodded, so he obeyed, grimacing.

"Stand wi' your face t' the wall," the guard ordered. "I dinna want t' look at ye, just to inspect your boots."

Isobel saw Jeb's lower lip tremble, but he obeyed again, clearly terrified to expose his back to an enemy. Hearing a sound above, and fearing the elder guard's return, she drew her dirk again and watched the younger one poke his hand into Jeb's boots, finding the dirk in the left one.

As he grabbed it, she put the point of her own dirk against the back of his neck, pressing hard enough to let him feel its prick. "Let go of that dirk now, and don't move unless you want me to slice off your head with this one," she said.

The man froze, then slowly eased his hand away from Jeb's dagger.

"Put your arms straight out from your sides," she said.

He obeyed, moving slowly.

"Move away from him," she told Jeb. "Don't bend to get your dirk," she added swiftly as he moved to do so. "Get well away from him before you do."

She still had her blade pressed into the man's neck so hard that a bead of blood oozed around its sharp point, but she was not certain what to do next. She knew Jeb was too nervous to be trustworthy and feared that the moment she stepped back, her captive would turn and confront her, perhaps even snatch the weapon from her hand. The wisest thing, she knew, was to kill him, but while it was one thing to kill a man attempting to attack her or mayhap one who had threatened her, it was quite another to kill one who had done naught but obey his master.

"Keep your arms out straight," she warned him. "I do not have much control over my temper just now, so you would be wise to do exactly as I say."

"Aye, my lady, I ken fine that I shouldna frighten a woman holding a dagger," he said, and his voice trembled enough to convince her that he meant it.

With a sense of relief, she took a step back, and as she did, a wraithlike shape sped past her, she heard a thud, and the man collapsed to the stone floor.

"That should keep him out of the way," Isabella said with satisfaction. "Never leave a villain standing, my dear, if you can render him senseless."

Isobel stared at the countess in shock, realizing the thud had been the result of the iron poker in her ladyship's hand making contact with the poor man's skull.

"Close your mouth, my dear, lest you swallow a fly."

Obeying, Isobel swallowed, but then her wits returned. "There is a second guard above, madam. We should remove this one before he returns."

"He will not return," Isabella said.

"Faith, did you knock him on the head, too?"

With a wistful smile, Isabella said, "Nay, for I was below him on the stairs, with no way to creep up behind him without his hearing me. However, my husband believed in preparing for any event, so he equipped the upper door with strong iron bolts on this side. I shot them both, so unless that man leaps from the wall and comes in through the main door, he won't trouble us. What have you done with Waldron?"

"How did you know he was here?"

"Our people are well trained to warn us of visitors, as you will learn. Now, where is he, if you please?"

Ruefully, remembering how fondly Isabella had greeted him at Kirkwall, Isobel said, "I'm afraid I pushed him off the wall into the river."

"Excellent, so he will not trouble us either. And Michael?"

"Below," Isobel said with a shudder as she imagined what they were probably doing to him. "Four of Waldron's men are with him, madam."

Isabella frowned. "Only four?"

"A number of others are searching the castle."

"I see, but only four are with Michael, you say?" When Isobel nodded, her ladyship said, "Then either Waldron trained those four even better than I thought, or he is a fool. Come quickly, my dear. Oh, just a moment," she added, turning to Jeb, who still stood gaping at her.

As well he might, Isobel thought. Doubtless she was gaping, herself.

"You there, Jeb Elliot," Isabella said. "I saw horsemen in the glen, and as far as I could tell, looking out from the one hall window that lets one see anything, our men still guard the gate and the upper track. Slip out now, and tell our lads to shut the gate and bar it. Then tell them to run up the Raven."

"Aye, my lady, straightaway," the lad said.

"The Raven is our battle standard, my dear," Isabella added as Jeb hurried to unbar the yett. "If those men below are Waldron's, it may frighten them off. If they are not his, mayhap they have been frightened off already. Now, shall I go first?"

"I'll go, madam." She could not bear the thought that Michael might have been badly hurt or even killed by now and that his mother might reach him first.

"I shall be right behind you with my poker, and you must keep your own weapon in hand," Isabella said. "Between us, we ought to startle those louts witless, but do not hesitate to employ whatever means you must to unman them."

Isobel did not answer, fixing her attention instead on what lay ahead as she listened for sounds of approach from below. She heard nothing, and nearly jumped out of her skin when a hand clapped over her mouth as she rounded a corner. Her dirk hand shot up, but another hand caught it in a hard grip.

"Unhand her, Michael," Isabella said coolly. "I find that I am becoming quite fond of this intrepid wife of yours."

"Madam!" Michael exclaimed. Taking his hand away from Isobel's mouth, he slipped that arm around her instead and gave her a hug. "What are you two doing down here? If you know—"

"Pray, keep your voice down," Isabella interjected. "Whoever remains below may yet prove difficult."

"They are all dead," he said. "Where is Waldron?"

"Apparently, your lady wife tumbled him off the ramparts," his mother said dryly. "Shall we go to the great hall and make ourselves more comfortable?"

"What about his other men?" Michael asked, shooting Isobel a look of amusement. "There were more of them searching the castle."

"Aye, but I sent word to the kitchens," Isabella said. "Doubtless someone thought to use the postern door to let some of our lads in to deal with them, because I have not seen anyone else. Shall we send for ale or wine, and ask someone?"

Isobel looked astonished, and Michael could understand why. His mother's attitude toward her had certainly changed.

The countess turned and went back up the stairs with her poker, and Michael hastily kissed Isobel and squeezed her hand before following.

"Oh, Michael, she locked one man outside on the ramparts, one of the two who trussed up the porter. She said there are bolts on this side of the door up there."

"Aye, there are," he said, chuckling. "How is our porter?"

Guiltily, she exclaimed, "Faith, he is still tied up! We just came to look for you. The other man who was watching him is lying on the floor near him, too, because your mother knocked him out with that poker she was carrying."

"In all that tumult, did she think to raise the Raven?" he asked.

"Aye, because she thought it might frighten away any of Waldron's men who might still be in the glen. I don't think it will, though," she added.

"Nor do I," he agreed, "but if Hugo has not arrived yet with enough men to deal with them, I'll have something to say to him that he will not want to hear."

"Hugo?"

"Aye, sure. You must have realized by now that I rarely go anywhere that he does not follow. He took Waldron's measure years ago. If Hugo was not close behind him soon after he left the north, I shall be much surprised."

"He is here," the countess said from the entryway. The main door stood open, the porter stood on his feet beside it, and Hugo stood at the gate, handing the reins of his horse to a gillie. Two of his men dismounted nearby.

Hugo strode to meet them with a grin on his face. "So you are all safe. I was confident, but I don't mind admitting I'm relieved. Where's that villain, Waldron?"

"I do wish everyone would stop talking about him," the countess said. "Does not anyone else want a cup of claret?"

"I do," Hugo said, hugging her.

"I thought you were all afraid of her," Isobel said in her headlong way.

Laughing, Michael said, "We are, sweetheart. Just wait until you stir her ire."

"Never mind that," Isabella said. "I warrant you are all more interested in whatever brought Waldron to Roslin, so you'd better attend to that. You can tell me all about it over supper later, if it is one of those things that you *can* tell me about."

Without bothering to deny their interest, they promised to return as quickly as they could to enjoy a cup of wine with her. When Isabella asked if there was anything she could do to make Isobel more comfortable in the meantime, Michael pulled Hugo aside to tell him briefly what had happened. "Are you sure the glen is clear of the enemy now?" he asked when he'd finished.

"Aye, for now," Hugo said. "We saw no sign of Waldron anywhere. Did Isobel truly push him off the ramparts?"

"So my mother told me," Michael said. "What I want to discover is exactly what that villain did to drive her to such a course, although I can guess."

"I can, too," Hugo said.

Isobel's conversation with Isabella having ended, she stepped in between them and said bluntly, "I have earned the right to take part in this conversation, have I not?"

"Aye, sweetheart, you have," Michael said. "We're returning to the glen. Fetch rope, candles, and tinderboxes, Hugo. I believe more than ever now that a cave or tunnel must be involved in this, and if one is, I don't want to get lost in it."

Having expected Michael to order her to remain safely behind with the countess, especially now that Hugo had arrived, Isobel was delighted that he had not. When Hugo returned with a long rope coiled over his shoulder, they hurried down to the glen, crossed the river, and were following the track she and Michael had taken when Waldron's men attacked them, before she thought about Waldron again.

"Michael, what if he didn't drown? What if he's waiting for us?"

Michael glanced at Hugo, and that gentleman said, "I have men posted throughout the glen. Even Waldron is not so skilled that he could get past all of them. Michael might succeed, but he is the only man I know who might, and I'm not certain even he could do it. Moreover, Waldron is one whose measure of courage depends on how many men he has with him, and if any still linger hereabouts, my lads will soon lay them by the heels. Since we have not yet seen or heard from Waldron, I warrant he's either dead or still riding the river Esk."

When Michael nodded agreement, Isobel relaxed, and soon they came to the waterfall he had described, and he pointed out the Green Man carved into the cliff nearby. As far as she could tell, it was exactly like the one in the hidden stairway.

"The pair of them must have meaning, but what can it be?" she muttered.

When the men just stood frowning at the image, she said, "What about the falls? Have you ever looked to see if there might be a hiding place behind them?"

"There is only a small recess," Michael said. "Hugo and I used to slither along a narrow ledge there, and under the falls, until his father put a stop to the practice. There was barely room for the two of us even then, as lads."

"Then mayhap the answer lies in the other direction," she said, turning away from the river and pushing into the woods to follow the base of the cliff.

Shrubbery clung to its face, making her progress difficult, but five minutes later, she saw what she had hoped to see. "Michael, there's a bearded man here!"

The two men came running, and shortly afterward, they discovered an odd drawing on a wide, squat boulder that looked like another bearded man. But although they searched in widening circles around the boulder, they found no more.

Returning to the boulder where they had begun their search, Michael leaned against a nearby tree and stared thoughtfully up at its branches.

Hugo sat on a fallen log and gave vent to a frustrated sigh.

Isobel returned to the boulder and stood looking down at it. It was about two-thirds her height and nearly the same width. "Can the two of you move it?" she asked.

The men looked at each other in the conferring way she saw so often, then got up as one and strode to wrestle with the great rock. Though it took some time, it moved more easily than either had expected, revealing a well-like hole beneath it.

Excited, Isobel said, "Something must be down there. Can we get down to see what's at the bottom? It looks large enough to accommodate even the two of you."

Both men agreed, but because they wanted to insure secrecy, it was two more hours before they had checked Hugo's sentries and their own gear, enlisted two more loyal St. Clair lads to help, and declared themselves ready to continue.

"I'm going first," Michael said firmly, looking at Isobel rather than Hugo. "Once I know what is down there, I'll decide who else goes."

They both nodded, and Isobel waited patiently, certain that Michael would find what they sought. Hugo lowered him on the rope, and soon she saw light flicker far down in the hole as Michael lit a candle with his tinderbox.

"Have them lower you both down," he said. "There's a tunnel, a big one."

"You go first, my lady," Hugo said with a grin. "Your husband would not appreciate my standing below whilst they lower you."

Eagerly, she let them ease loops of rope around her hips and under her arms as they had done with Michael, and moments later she was descending into the ground with a rapidity and lack of fear that amazed her. Michael caught her at the bottom and helped her free herself. "Show me," she said.

He yanked on the rope and as the men above pulled it up, he held the candle so she could see the tunnel.

"Why, it's enormous!"

"Aye, I'm glad we've plenty of candles and men who ken where we are."

Moments later, Hugo stood beside them, and Michael led the way into the tunnel. They had not gone far when they came upon four chests.

The three of them stood staring.

"I smell water," Hugo said.

"I, too," Michael said. "Let's go on a bit before we examine those chests."

Ten yards beyond them, the tunnel turned, and ten feet beyond that, they emerged into a large cavern with what appeared to be a medium-sized lake in its center. The path they had followed looked as if it continued around it.

"Shall we go farther?" Hugo said. "The air seems fresh enough down here."

"I remember this place," Michael said. "This is the cave I've dreamed about for so long. Someone must have brought me here when I was very young."

On the far side of the lake, they came to another tunnel. "These tunnels seem to be man-made," Michael said. "At least, they've been widened with tools."

"This one seems to lead back toward the castle," Isobel said. "Could it connect to that hidden stairway somehow, Michael?"

"I don't know how, lass. That stairway ends above the cellar level of the castle. Mayhap there is a connection there, but we've never found it."

"Perhaps it was never finished," Hugo said, peering into the darkness ahead.

"I want to see what's in those chests," Michael said. "I wonder why they lie so near the entrance and not farther in where they would be harder to find."

Neither of his companions had an answer, but when they opened the first chest, they found a letter on top.

"Have a care with that candle, lass," Michael warned as Isobel moved hers closer to give more light. "I don't want to burn it up before I read it."

"'Tis another from your father, and it addresses Sir Henry," she said.

"Aye, well, I'm going to read it anyway," Michael said.

She read it, too: *"Right worthy and trusted son,"* it began. *"The contents of this cavern have been entrusted to Clan Sinclair to keep safe for as long as such guardianship shall be deemed necessary by the Order of the Knights Templar of Scotland. In these four chests lie the rules you must follow in this regard, as well as other documents, relics, and valuables. None is to be sold or given away, since all within this cavern lies entrusted to our keeping; however, you will find within the rules some rights that accompany the trust, and one of those is to use your own judgment as to where their safekeeping may be best secured. Study all the contents of the cavern well, so that you may know what you hold here, and keep all safe. Commit thy work to God!"*

"He signs it 'William Sinclair of Roslin,'" Isobel said. "That could be either your father or grandfather, but it was your father who wrote it, was it not?"

"Aye, it is his hand," Michael said. He picked up a scroll of some sort that lay under the letter and spread it open on one of the chests. "Look at this," he said.

It was a map, but unlike any Isobel had ever seen, for it showed lands far to the west of Scotland and the Isles. "This must be the map that Henry saw," she said.

Michael rolled it up again. "I'm going to take this and the letter back with us, but we'll leave everything else, and put the rock back until I can get word to Henry to come here. He has the right to see it all as it is now, and to decide what we will do next. Now that we've found it, though, I fear it is no longer as safe as it was. Those two lads above know of the hole in the ground and now know that we disappeared for a time after finding it. I trust them, but we must do something to protect it better, and soon. However, I dare not make that decision without consulting Henry first."

"I agree," Hugo said. "Do you want me to return to St. Clair and fetch him?"

"Yes, as soon as we've finished here," Michael said. "Now, let's put everything else back as we found it and leave. Come away from that trunk, lass."

He held out his hand, and Isobel reluctantly put hers in it. It went completely against the grain for her to leave without discovering what else lay in the fascinating chests, let alone without exploring the rest of so intriguing a cavern, but she knew Michael was right, and she knew, too, that she could trust him to tell her, in time, as much about their discovery as he learned about it himself.

Hugo had scarcely glanced at the chests.

After Michael shut the lid of the one that had contained the letter and map, he looked the others over carefully.

Isobel watched him, and when she caught his eye, he said ruefully, "I don't remember such chests in my dream, but I always enter the cavern from the same direction. I was just wondering if whoever brought me here could have done so before the chests arrived from the Isles."

She had not thought about when or how the chests had got there, but the subject did not interest her as much as their contents did. It was nearly impossible to walk away from them, making her almost glad that Michael gave her no choice.

When they were all safely up out of the well-like hole, the men replaced the boulder and Michael ordered the two lads who had helped them to keep utterly silent about the incident and to see that the glen and castle remained well guarded.

"Do what you must to see that no one enters the glen or approaches the castle from this direction without keeping a close watch on them," he added.

"Aye, sir, we'll keep all safe."

Isobel sighed. Trust was difficult when curiosity stirred. She had a strong feeling that she would never learn all she wanted to know about the treasure.

Hugo was on his way back to St. Clair, armed guards surrounded the castle, and men continued to scour the glen and the banks of the river Esk without success for any sign of Waldron. Supper with the maddeningly uncurious countess was over, that lady had retired to her bedchamber, and Isobel went with Michael upstairs to their bedchamber, wishing she could speak her mind.

He had already put away the map and the letter from Sir William.

"What is it, lass?" he asked quietly as he shut the door. "You have been bursting to say something since we returned to the castle."

She shook her head. "It is just my old curiosity screaming at me, sir. I want to know what is down there. I want to see everything. Still, I know it is not my secret or responsibility but Sir Henry's—Prince Henry's, that is."

"Call him Henry," Michael said. "He is your brother now."

"Aye, well, that is what has been bothering me. I feel as if I am somehow proving myself untrustworthy by wanting to give way to that curiosity again."

To her surprise, he chuckled. "Faith, lass, if anyone has the right to be curious about what we found, you do. Do you think I am not bursting with the same curiosity? I promise you, if I did not know that God watches me, I'd be sorely tempted to sneak back there at the first opportunity and take every item out of those chests to examine thoroughly. The one chest we opened seemed to contain mostly documents, but I wager there must be gold, jewelry, and other valuable items as well. The Templars controlled much of the world's wealth, and a significant amount of what they held could be in those chests. I'd like to see what they contain, but we do not have that right. We do have a duty, though, to protect what we saw."

"So we cannot talk about it," Isobel said with a sigh.

"Only to each other, only when we know no one can overhear us, and even then, only rarely," he said. "Now, I want to ask you something."

She braced herself, knowing what he would ask and wishing she need not talk about it. "You want to know all that happened with Waldron," she said.

"I do," he said. "I'm guessing he had plans that you did not approve."

She smiled at his phrasing. "He made his intentions very plain to me. I had my dirk, and because he thought me only a weak, helpless woman, he believed as well that he had persuaded me to want what he wanted. I . . . I let him think that," she admitted, feeling obliged for some reason to explain that part to him.

"That was wise of you," he said, putting his arm around her and urging her nearer the bed. "What then?"

"He pulled me close and held me tightly enough that I could feel how full of lust he was," she said, grimacing at that distasteful memory. She hesitated, but Michael remained as patient as always, and at last, she said, "When I realized that his jack-of-plate would not protect him there, I put both hands around the dirk's hilt and rammed it into his bollocks as hard as I could."

He winced.

"What?" she demanded. "Do you think I was wrong to do that?"

Grinning wryly, he drew her close and kissed her forehead. "Nay, sweetheart, I was wincing, as any man would, at the nature of the pain you caused him, not disapproving of it. He deserved it if any man ever has. I thought after our first day together that you would be unlikely to surprise me much, ever again, but the extent of your ability to look after yourself, and others, too, astounds me. If the Order admitted females, I swear I would nominate you for membership in the Knights Templar."

Her frustration, and her discomfort with the topic of conversation, vanished, and she laughed, saying, "You would not!"

"I cannot, but I begin to think they made an error by leaving women out. Had it not been for you, after all," he added, his voice altering subtly, "not only would we never have met, but Waldron might well have succeeded in his quest, or worse."

"He could still do so," she pointed out. "If he still lives, he may return, and now that we do know where the treasure lies . . ."

"That is exactly why we must consult Henry before we do aught else. Only he has the right to move it to a place of greater safety if we can but determine where that may be. But in the meantime," he added, his intent now clear to the meanest intelligence, "I'm thinking that since we cannot explore the cavern or the chests, we might indulge ourselves in certain other forms of exploration."

"Are you, sir?" Her blood began racing at the thought.

But he paused. "Only if the memory of what Waldron tried to do has not put you off the notion," he said, pulling her close and looking into her eyes.

She looked back gravely. "I don't know whether to hope I killed him or did not kill him," she said. "But whatever happened on that wall-walk today has naught to do with how I feel about you, Michael. When I feared that those horrid men were torturing you again . . ." She stopped, unable to complete that thought.

"I know, sweetheart. I heard Waldron threaten you with methods the Kirk employs against heretics, and I nearly gave up any chance I had of besting those louts to leap up and try to throttle him. You cannot know how hard it was to keep still and let you go with him. I have come to love you, Isobel, more than I knew it was possible to love anyone, and I've never been so afraid in my life as I was then."

"But you did let me go," she said. "I'd like to believe it was because you trusted me to look after myself, but I know that was not the reason."

"No," he said. "I knew that was not the course most likely to aid us against him and his men. 'Twas more likely to sink us into disaster."

She nodded, leaning her head against his chest, and when he took her hand and held it gently, she moved it with her own to the tie of her laces. "Make love to me, Michael. I want to feel your arms around me and feel your body close to mine."

His lips claimed hers then, and she moaned softly when his tongue slipped into her mouth. Caressing her, his hands dealt with the laces, and then slowly and with great tenderness, he undressed her, pulled back the coverlet and quilt, and laid her gently on the bed. Stripping off his clothes, he slid in beside her and took her in his arms again, stroking her all over, caressing her until she wanted to purr like a contented kitten. But the more he continued, the more her body began to demand.

Heat rose in her until she could not stand it and pushed his hands away, shifting until she could lie on her side and do to him what he had been doing to her. To her astonishment, the passion she felt and saw reflected in him grew stronger as he responded to her touch, until at last, he surged up and rolled atop her, fitting his body easily to hers, knowing just how to stir her and himself to new heights. He took her there and they reached the peaks together, collapsing afterward in warm satisfaction, to curl close together and sigh in unison at the wonders of their love.

After a long, languorous moment, Michael said drowsily, "I have admitted my love for you, sweetheart, and I believe you love me, too, but I'm wondering if you will admit that you have changed your opinion of marriage. It is still 'forever and ever,' after all, and I don't mean to let you try to change that."

"It is just as well," she said. "Because forever is not nearly long enough."

Dear Reader,

I hope you have enjoyed *Prince of Danger.* The history of the Knights Templar and their missing treasure has fascinated historians and many others for centuries. When I discovered that Scotland was a likely refuge for the Templars who escaped the efforts of King Philip IV to seize the Templar treasury in Paris, and for the treasure itself, I began to look more closely into the Scottish history of that period and the century that followed.

The most likely route for the treasure ships, thanks to England's being between Scotland and France, was around the west coast of Ireland and through the Isles to the Scottish west coast. The most likely route from Ireland to Kintyre, where many believe they landed in late 1307, lies through the Sound of Isla (now Islay), which lies just north of Isla. And Finlaggan, the administrative headquarters for the Lords of the Isles, lies at the northern end of that isle. In 1307, Angus Og, father of MacDonald, first Lord of the Isles, lived at Finlaggan, and the chance that a fleet of ships passed along that northern coast without his knowledge seems unlikely.

Of course, it also seems highly unlikely that anyone offloaded treasure and carted it around the Isles, let alone all the way to Roslin Castle (or its later chapel) without many, many people knowing what was happening. I have, by the way, used the official British spelling for Roslin Glen and Roslin Castle throughout.

The Sir William St. Clair (or Sinclair) of Bruce's heart fame was not Sir Henry's father, as many have suggested. That Sir William St. Clair died in 1330 in Andalusia, with Sir James "the Good" Douglas and Robert Logan, while fighting the Moors during his attempt to carry the Bruce's heart to the Holy Land. His son, also Sir William, was Baron of Roslin from 1330 to 1358, when he died in a fall from his horse during the Lithuanian Crusade. It is that Sir William who married Isabella of Strathearn and Caithness. Henry was born in 1345.

Some question exists as to exactly when all the tunnels and cells at Roslin were dug. Many were created when William Sinclair, fourth Earl of Orkney, built his famous Rosslyn Chapel in the 16th century. Historians have debated his reason for hiring a host of miners five years before he began work on the chapel, and many reason logically that most of the tunnel work must have been done then, but there is no proof of that, and Roslin Castle was noted long before then for a proliferation of tunnels, cells, and dungeons, carved into the cliff on which it perched. Nearby Wallace's cave, named for William Wallace, who is believed to have taken refuge there, was also known long before then.

The source for Henry's speech in the cathedral is the text of his installation at Maestrand, Norway, as reproduced on the Rosslyn Templars website at www.rosslyntemplars.-org.uk/installation.htm.

If you are interested in learning more about the Templar treasure, I suggest the following sources: *Holy Blood, Holy Grail* by Michael Baigent and Richard Leigh (New York: Dell Books, 1982); *The Temple and the Lodge* by Michael Baigent and Richard Leigh (New York, 1989); *Pirates & the Lost Templar Fleet* by David H. Childress (Illinois: Adventures Unlimited Press, 2003); *The Stone Puzzle of Rosslyn Chapel* by Philip Coppens (The Netherlands: Frontier Publishing, 2004); *The Da Vinci Code Decoded* by Martin Lunn (New York: Disinformation Co, Ltd., 2004); and *The Lost Treasure of the Knights Templar* by Steven Sora (Vermont: Destiny Books, 1999).

It occurs to me that some of you may be skeptical about Isobel's memory in Chapter 17 of throwing Hector. You should know that the author, at five feet three inches and 125 pounds, did that very thing to her husband (six-four, 185) in our living room, the second year of our marriage. I swear, I meant only to give him an idea of what little I'd learned about self-defense, never dreaming it would work on someone so much larger, but his higher center of gravity did him in. I'd like to say he's behaved himself since, but he's looking over my shoulder and already laughing.

As always, I'd also like to thank my terrific agents, Aaron Priest and Lucy Childs, and my wonderful editor, Beth de Guzman. I couldn't do it without them!

If you enjoyed *Prince of Danger*, please look for *Lady's Choice,* the story of Sir Hugo Robison and Ladies Adela, Sorcha, and Sidony Macleod (Hugo's quite a guy), at your favorite bookstore in August 2006. In the meantime, *suas Alba!*

Sincerely,

Amanda Scott

http://home.att.net/~amandascott

About the Author

AMANDA SCOTT, best-selling author and winner of Romance Writers of America's RITA/Golden Medallion awards, *Romantic Times*'s Career Achievement Award for British Isle Historical, and *Romantic Times*'s Awards for Best Regency Author and Best Sensual Regency, began writing on a dare from her husband. She has sold every manuscript she has written. She sold her first novel, *The Fugitive Heiress*—written on a battered Smith-Corona—in 1980. Since then, she has sold many more, but since the second one, she has used a word processor. More than twenty-five of her books are set in the English Regency period (1810–1820); others are set in fifteenth-century England and sixteenth- and eighteenth-century Scotland. Three are contemporary romances.

Amanda is a fourth-generation Californian who was born and raised in Salinas and graduated with a Bachelor's Degree in history from Mills College in Oakland. She did graduate work at the University of North Carolina at Chapel Hill, specializing in British History, before obtaining her Master's in History from San Jose State University. She is a fellow of the Society of Antiquaries of Scotland. After graduate school, she taught for the Salinas City School District for three years before marrying her husband, who was then a captain in the Air Force. They lived in Honolulu for a year, then in Nebraska, where their son was born, for seven years. Amanda now lives with her husband in northern California.

MORE FROM AMANDA SCOTT,
"A TRUE MISTRESS OF
THE SCOTTISH ROMANCE"*

Turn the page
for a preview of
Lady's Choice

Available in mass market
Summer 2006.

*Romantic Times BOOKclub Magazine

Chapter 1 _____

Glenelg, the Scottish Highlands, April 14, 1380

Where is Sir Hugo?" nineteen-year-old Lady Sorcha Macleod demanded impatiently as she gazed down at the sparkling waters of the Sound of Sleat, the passageway that lay between the Isle of Skye and Glenelg.

Her younger sister, Lady Sidony, said calmly, "You cannot know that Sir Hugo ever received your message, Sorcha. The messenger has not returned, and even if Sir Hugo did receive it, you cannot know that he will come for her or that, if he does, he will arrive in a boat. He could as easily ride here from Lothian, through Glen Shiel, or from some other direction. He might even be in Caithness instead."

"Faith, Sidony, I don't care how the man arrives, just so he does," Sorcha said grimly. "But if he does not show his face soon, he will be too late."

"It is too bad that the Lord of the Isles had to die when he did," Sidony said with a sigh. "Adela ought to have been able to enjoy as fine and merry a wedding as everyone else has had, but this one will be dreadfully dull, I fear, and I still do not understand why Father agreed to hold the ceremony here instead of at Chalamine. The feast will be at the castle, after all, and everyone else was married there."

"Not everyone," Sorcha reminded her. "Isobel married at Duart Castle on the Isle of Mull, remember?"

"Yes, but Cristina, Maura, and Kate were all married at home, and I hope that you and I will be, too, if Father ever finds anyone who wants to marry us."

Sorcha shrugged. "I don't want someone Father chooses, but at least today the sun is shining, and the wee kirk of Glenelg is a pretty site. Lord Pompous felt strongly that Adela should marry him on the kirk porch here, since Father has no priest of his own at Chalamine. And Lord Pompous is to be her husband, after all, unless Sir Hugo arrives in time to put a stop to all this."

"I do not know why you are so sure that he would want to," Sidony said, pushing a stray strand of her fair hair out of her face. As children, the two girls had looked enough alike to be twins with their fine, silky soft, white-blond curls, but as years passed, although Sidony's waist-long hair retained its silky fineness and a soft wave, Sorcha's had darkened to amber gold and retained only its curls. To her frequent chagrin, living so near the sea, they tended to frizz in mist or rain.

Semiconsciously mirroring her sister's gesture, Sorcha tucked an errant curl under her coif as Sidony said, "Adela seems content enough with her wedding."

"Faugh," Sorcha retorted rudely, abandoning concern about her hair. "Adela would marry anyone who would have her if only to be rid of the responsibility of managing Father's household and us, especially now that he seems intent upon marrying the widow Lady Clendenin. But Hugo is the man who holds Adela's heart. I'm sure of it, and I am persuaded that he cares deeply for her, too."

"But they have met only twice," Sidony protested. "Once here in Glenelg and once at Orkney.

"Aye, well, it only takes once," Sorcha said with more confidence than one might expect from a young woman who had never met a man she wanted to marry, or had an offer.

"Do you think so?" Sidony asked doubtfully. "She said they quarreled the first time they met, and the second time, she emptied a basin of holy water over his head."

Sorcha had not taken her eyes off the Sound, and instead of replying, she exclaimed, "Three boats are coming!" Then, with mixed disappointment and concern, she added, "If I don't mistake that banner, Lord Pompous has arrived."

"You should not call him that," Sidony chided gently.

"Pooh," Sorcha said. "Ardelve is as pompous a man as I have ever met, and far too old for Adela. Why he must be nearly our father's age, though Adela is but four-and-twenty. Sir Hugo is of a much more appropriate age to marry her. She is sacrificing herself, just to get away from Chalamine."

"She is nearly *five*-and-twenty," Sidony said. "And Father said he had quite despaired of ever seeing her marry. In truth, you and I are old for wedding," she added with a sigh. "Not that I am sure I'd want to, even if anyone wanted me."

"Don't be a noddy," Sorcha said, affectionately patting her shoulder. "You are never sure about anything. Depend on it, if ever you do marry, it will be because Father commands you to do so. If you had to make up your own mind, your would-be bridegroom would likely die of old age, waiting to take you to wife."

"That *is* his lordship," Sidony said, too accustomed to her more decisive sister's scornful opinion of her habit of indecision to take offense. "Moreover, I can see the wedding party coming over the hill. Do you not think we had better hasten to meet them if we want Adela to carry this bouquet we gathered for her?"

"Aye, sure, and we've flowers for her chaplet, too, don't forget," Sorcha replied as they hurried to greet the small party of riders.

Lady Adela Macleod felt almost completely at peace as her wedding party approached the village. For the first time in too many years she was responsible for no one and nothing except to be in a certain place at a certain time and to say what the priest, a Macleod cousin of her father's from Lewis, told her to say.

The feeling was a heady one, and as she rode alongside her father, Macleod of Glenelg, toward the little hilltop kirk, the silence enveloping them was nearly as heady. But for a tiny tickle at the back of her mind, all was well.

The small group of smiling villagers and friends clustered near the kirk steps was quiet. Even her usually talkative aunt, Lady Euphemia Macleod, riding in her boxy, sheepskin-lined sidesaddle between two gillies mounted on ponies as placid as her own, remained unnaturally silent. At fifty, the whip-slim Lady Euphemia disliked riding and doubtless focused all her energy on keeping the boat-on-waves motion of her cumbersome saddle from tossing her to the ground.

The rest of the party consisted of Adela's father, her older sister Maura, Maura's husband and three children, and the few castle servants that had remained behind to prepare for the wedding feast. Other than the villagers, they were the only wedding guests, for the simple reason that, MacDonald of the Isles having died recently, nearly everyone else in the Highlands and Isles was preparing for the installation, in two days' time, of the second Lord of the Isles.

Adela, too, rode sideways but with nothing between her and her favorite bay gelding except a dark-blue velvet caparison to protect her skirts. One of her younger sisters, Kate, had embroidered the caparison with branches of Macleod of Glenelg's green juniper and sent it to her especially for the occasion.

Like all six of her sisters, Adela preferred to ride astride, but she had known better than to suggest doing such a thing in the splendid new sky-blue silk gown her father had given her for her wedding. Blue to keep her always true, he had said, citing from an ancient rhyme and having refused her favorite color due to his strong belief that to wear pink for her wedding would sink her good fortune.

She could see her two youngest sisters watching from the hillside near the kirk and realized how glad she was that they had gone on ahead. She had suggested that they gather flowers there for her bouquet and chaplet, because the grassy hillside always produced a plethora of bright wild-flowers, and because she wanted as little fuss as possible while she prepared for her wedding.

Her ever-superstitious father had disapproved of her not gathering her own flowers, a task he believed would bring her good luck, but once he had taken note of the day's brightness, his strictures had ended. However, he no sooner saw Sorcha and Sidony than he sighed and said, "I hope ye mean to make Ardelve a good wife, lass."

"I will, sir," Adela said. "I have always done my duty."

"Aye, 'tis true, but I'd feel that much better if ye'd done all ye could to bring good fortune upon yourself."

"It is a splendid day," Adela reminded him. Casting a swift, oblique glance his way, she added gently, "Yesterday was not as beautiful."

"Nay," he agreed. "It were cursed wi' a gey thick mist from dawn's light till nigh onto suppertime. 'Tis fortunate that when we arranged the settlements and all I succeeded in persuading Ardelve to put off your ceremony until today."

"Why do you believe Friday is such a bad day to wed, sir?" she asked. "Aunt Euphemia said many people believe it to be the best day of the week, because of being dedicated to Freya, the Norse goddess of love. She said the notion that Friday is unlucky arose only during this century."

"Aye, well, whatever our wise Euphemia may say, and however kind she were to journey here from Lochbuie for your wedding, everyone kens that when a Friday falls on the thirteenth o' the month, it brings gey bad luck," Macleod said firmly. "Sakes, lass, I'd no allow any o' me daughters to wed on such a bleak day!"

"But I do not think everyone does know that," Adela persisted quietly. "Ardelve did not, for one. At least . . ." She fell silent, deciding that she would be wiser not to repeat what Lord Ardelve had said.

"Aye, I ken fine that the man thought changing the day he'd decided on were a right foolish notion o' mine," Macleod said, unabashed. "Still, he agreed to it, and as ye see, the Almighty saw fit to bless the day I picked for ye wi' sunshine."

Adela nodded, and when Macleod fell silent, she made no attempt to continue the conversation. The only sounds until they reached the hillside where the kirk stood were soft thuds of the horses' hooves on the dirt path, cries of sea birds soaring overhead, and scattered twitters and chatters from nearby woodland.

Her sense of peace had not returned, however, and when she realized she was peering intently at each guest, she understood why. Sorcha had made it no secret that she expected Sir Hugo Robinson to arrive in time to put a stop to the wedding, and although Adela was certain that her younger sister was mistaken, she could not help wondering if he would, or how she would feel about it if he did.

Seeing no sign of that large, energetic, not to mention handsome, gentleman, she drew a long breath and released it. If she felt disappointment, she told herself it was only that he might have added some small measure of excitement to what was so far, despite the spring sunshine, rather a dull day.

As a gillie helped her dismount, Sorcha and Sidony came forward to arrange flowers in her chaplet, and to give her the bouquet they had gathered.

"These flowers are lovely," she said, smiling. "So bright and cheerful."

"Sorcha collected a basket of rose petals to strew along the path before you, too," Sidony said, hugging Adela before they took their places ahead of her and Macleod signed to his piper to begin.

Adela sighed deeply again, took another quick glance around the small group of onlookers, and placed her hand on her father's forearm when he offered it.

Reaching the far end of the loch, they crossed the narrow wooden bridge that spanned the river and rode along its opposite bank until they rounded a low hill and came into sight of the Chapel of St. Columba, its stone walls glowing in the sunlight. Sorcha and Sidony stood waiting to take their places ahead of the procession, one on either side of the path, each carrying a woven basket filled with rose petals.

Dismounting near the small stone bridge, where two monks in brown robes stood waiting near the entrance to the churchyard of Chapel of St. Columba, the wedding party gathered.

As the wedding party made its way solemnly up the path to the shallow porch of the kirk, Sorcha led the way and scattered her petals, wondering if the piper had mistaken Adela's wedding for MacDonald's funeral procession. The tune he had selected certainly seemed more appropriate for the solemn rite.

Behind the makeshift altar, the tall double doors stood shut and would not open to admit everyone for the nuptial Mass until the marriage rite was over. The priest, Wee Geordie Macleod of Lewis, stood sternly erect beside the altar with the bridegroom and chief groomsman to welcome the bride and her bride-maidens.

Calum Tolmie, Baron Ardelve, the bridegroom, was another of Macleod's cousins. He held a vast tract of land on the north shore of Loch Alsh, was wealthy and amiable, and thus, according to Macleod, an excellent match for Adela.

Sorcha disagreed, thinking Sir Hugo a far more suitable choice, although admittedly, she had never laid eyes on that gentleman. She still cursed her bad luck in having missed the trip to the Orkneys the previous year to see the Prince of Orkney installed, for it had been then that the more fortunate Adela and their sister Isobel, having each met Sir Hugo Robison briefly, had met him again and come to know him better, and both had mentioned him more than once since then. But Isobel was happily married to Sir Hugo's cousin, Sir Michael St. Clair (or Sinclair, as the family now spelled the name) of Roslin Castle in Lothian, so Sorcha had made up her mind that Adela should marry Sir Hugo.

Reaching the foot of the steps to the porch, Sorcha moved to the left and watched as Sidony moved to the right to make way for the bride and Macleod. He stopped on the lower of the two stone steps and let Adela proceed to the porch, where Ardelve took two steps forward to meet her in front of the altar.

Two low stools stood ready for the bridal couple to kneel

upon, and as they did, the priest stepped before them and spread his arms wide.

The piper fell silent. A gull screamed overhead as if in protest.

Instead of the blessing or prayer that Sorcha expected to hear, Wee Geordie said in tones that carried to everyone assembled there, "Afore I pray to Almighty God, begging Him to ha' the goodness to shine his face upon this couple and bless the union into which they be about to enter, I'm bound to ask if there be any amongst ye that ken just cause or impediment to prevent the aforesaid union from going forward. If ye do, speak now, or forever hold thy peace."

As silence closed in around the altar, Sorcha turned her head to look at the crowd. Others, likewise, looked around at their neighbors. Then, a low rumbling sounded in the distance—almost, Sorcha thought, as if God Himself had grown impatient and were muttering to the priest to get on with it.

The thought made her smile, but when she realized that heads were still turning, and all turning now in the same direction, she collected her wits and followed those looks. Joy stirred when she saw four horsemen riding at speed from the thick woods at the south end of the hilltop.

Mouths gaped, and neighbor looked at neighbor.

She looked at Adela, expecting to see her own joy reflected in her sister's expression, but although Adela, too, had heard the thundering hoofbeats and turned her head to look, she looked stunned.

Hearing more than one gasp from the small gathering, Sorcha smiled wider. Her neighbors and friends would talk of this day for years to come, she thought.

The riders were still coming at speed, too fast for safety.

Was their leader mad, or just drunk on the hope that he was not yet too late?

Villagers scattered as the riders bore down on the steps of the kirk. Sorcha moved aside, but she saw that Adela stayed where she was, her mouth open. Ardelve put his hands on his hips and glowered fiercely at the interruption, but he, too, showed no inclination to move. Clearly, he thought no more of the interruption than that some tardy wedding guests were making a scene.

Turning back to watch, Sorcha saw that all four riders were masked. A prickling of unease stirred as three of them reined in their horses near the villagers, making the animals rear, forcing folks back even farther. As they did that, the leader urged his horse right up to the steps.

Sorcha continued to smile, trying to catch the rider's eye, but he had eyes only for Adela, who stepped toward him as if she expected him to speak to her. Instead, he leaned near her, stretched out an arm, and as if she weighed no more than a feather pillow, swept her up and wheeled his horse away from the kirk.

Astonished at such a show of strength, Sorcha let her mouth fall open.

One or two people in the small crowd cheered, others looked stupefied, as the four horsemen rode off with their prize.

THE EDITOR'S DIARY

Dear Reader,

Ever meet a tall, dark and sexy stranger and see your destiny? Open those peepers a little bit wider. You won't want to miss a single word or a smoldering gaze from our two Warner Forever titles this November.

To Lady Isobel Macleod from **Amanda Scott's PRINCE OF DANGER**, marriage is a prison and husbands merely irritating encumbrances. Her domineering father and ferocious brother-in-law have proven as much to her. But when she comes upon Sir Michael St. Clair being savagely beaten by vicious strangers, she flies to the lone knight's defense, helps him escape, and flees with him into the rugged Highlands and beyond to Scotland's misty Isles. Alone under the stars with the man whose tenderness astonishes her, Isobel ponders her long-held prejudices. But as their relentless enemy pursues them, she faces a new danger—surrendering her freedom to this fearless yet gentle man . . . and linking her fate to the mysterious treasure that stirs mankind's greed and imagination to this very day. *Affaire de Coeur* raves "Amanda Scott is a master." This one is her best yet, so pick up a copy today.

Do you ever crave stability not passion? Kate Anderson from **Candy Halliday's MR. DESTINY** can relate. She's always wanted a stable marriage to a corporate attorney—no earth-shaking passion necessary. And she's finally found it. Never mind that their sex life consists of discussions in his therapist's office. But when a tall, dark and sexy patrol cop takes one look at her in Central Park and announces that he's her destiny, Kate just laughs. Officer Anthony Petrocelli's grandmother has always told him he would meet a beautiful blond with green eyes in Central Park when he was thirty-six and marry her. Now that he's met that stunning blond in the Park while thirty-six, he can't help but laugh. He wants to take Kate home to his family and disprove their silly prediction and Kate agrees. But after a little time with Anthony, sensible Kate can't help but wonder if stability is overrated. Maybe an unpredictable cop is just what she never knew she needed. RomanceReviewsMag.com raves Candy Halliday's last book was "fun . . . good reading and plenty of hot sex. What more can a woman ask for?"

To find out more about Warner Forever, these titles, and the authors, visit us at www.warnerforever.com.

With warmest wishes,

Karen Kosztolnyik

Karen Kosztolnyik, Senior Editor

P.S. With a dash of magic and spoonful of spice, next month's books will be twice as nice: Shari Anton weaves the enchanting and passionate tale of two headstrong lovers at cross purposes brought together by a spell fashioned centuries ago in MIDNIGHT MAGIC; and Kelley St. John delivers the steamy and hilarious story of a woman who creates alibis for a living and the sexy childhood friend she can't bear to come clean to in GOOD GIRLS DON'T.

*Want to know more about romances at
Warner Books and Warner Forever?
Get the scoop online!*

WARNER'S ROMANCE HOMEPAGE

Visit us at www.warnerforever.com for all the
latest news, reviews, and chapter excerpts!

NEW AND UPCOMING TITLES

Each month we feature our new titles
and reader favorites.

CONTESTS AND GIVEAWAYS

We give away galleys, autographed copies,
and all kinds of fun stuff.

AUTHOR INFO

You'll find bios, articles, and links to personal
Web sites for all your favorite authors—
and so much more!

THE BUZZ

Sign up for our monthly romance newsletter,
and be the first to read all about it!